The Diminishment of Joy

Kaybee Pearson

THE RURAL PUBLISHING COMPANY

First published by The Rural Publishing Company 2023

Print (Paperback): 978-1-923008-05-2
eBook: 978-1-923008-06-9

This is a work of fiction. Names, characters, places and incidents are products of the author's imagination or are used fictitiously. Any resemblance to actual events, locales, or persons, living or dead, is entirely coincidental.

Disclaimer: This is a work of fiction and is not intended to provide medical advice. Any advice whether medical or other provided by a character in this novel should not be taken as professional medical advice, diagnosis or treatment. Consult with your physician for the purposes of evaluation and treatment of medical conditions.

The author and publisher disclaim responsibility for any adverse consequences, which may result from the use of the fictional information contained herein.

Cover Design: The Rural Publishing Company
Layout and Typesetting: The Rural Publishing Company

The Rural Publishing Company
Email: hello@theruralpublishingcompany.com.au
Website: https://theruralpublishingcompany.com.au/

Dedication

To my dad whose generosity made my dream come true.

Story Riddle

If I were to ask you...

What is the one thing in all the world you could not live without, so important to you that if I threatened to take it away this would have an immediate and catastrophic impact on your future?

What would you say?

Think carefully.

I'll give you a clue:
The answer is the same for every single person on this planet.

The answer is, of course –
Your next breath.

Chapter One

In the summer first thing in the morning, Quamby Bluff Community Health Centre smelled of old heat and carpet dust, a familiar cosy sensation. Joy O'Connell keyed in a pin code to switch off the security alarm and walked down the main hallway turning on lights. As a courtesy, *not part of her job description*, she visited each office and community room flicking on air conditioners to make sure the staff began their day in cool comfort.

She was always the first to arrive, at eight thirty exactly. It would be another half hour before the doors opened and clients ambled into the centre. This was her favourite time at work when she had the place all to herself, to tidy up magazines in reception, cull out-of-date posters from the Notice Board, make a pot of plunger coffee and slowly contemplate her priorities for the day.

Last year she'd been fortunate enough to land this stress-free administrative assistant position at the centre, a job in her local village of Lower Teasel, five minutes from home. Maybe it lacked intellectual challenges she used to thrive on during her 'career days', but as she got older and less ambitious, this suited her just fine. It was busy enough to keep deathly boredom at bay on most days and she went home at night without work problems on her mind. Perfect. She pinched herself for good luck.

Her cupboard size office was packed with filing cabinets, shelves lined with arch-lever folders filled with pay records, pigeon holes for staff messages, and a key safe for government cars, as well as a personal computer, switchboard and cash register. After Joy took over the position, within a few months she'd re-organised all administrative systems for efficiency and auditing purposes in line with her decades of experience working in government jobs. Anything that came in or out of her admin space was now accounted for.

Joy opened her Outlook calendar and studied the day's activities. This Thursday would be a mad house until after lunch. At nine, the Roaring Forties art group was in the Common Room splashing paint on canvases with their raucous laughter echoing down the corridor, adding to the cacophony of the pre-school jazz ballet troupe dancing to the Unicorn Stomp in the Shamrock Room. And then around ten thirty the health department's visiting podiatrist would see elderly clients at fifteen-minute intervals. They'd be lined up in chairs along the hallway with their support workers in attendance assisting with walking frames. Joy kept the podiatrist's appointment diary including any cancellations and rescheduling. Nowadays, at her insistence, cash payments and government vouchers were put through the cash register for later reconciling with head office, instead of stashed in jam jars in a top desk drawer.

At eleven, a seniors' social group met in the Shamrock Room for a karaoke sing-a-long. Joy, a baby boomer, was always surprised to realise she knew most of the words to the White Cliffs of Dover and other songs from World War II. The fact she hummed the tunes for the rest of the day most annoyed her and made her laugh at the same time. She wondered when her generation of baby boomers retired and began attending senior sing-a-longs if they'd be stuck singing the White Cliffs of Dover or something more updated like Can't Get No Satisfaction in parody of Mick Jagger. Or maybe people wouldn't be singing in the future. That was depressing. Why did that pop into her head like some sort of premonition?

She knew most of the seniors by name. Occasionally, she'd be invited to one of their eightieth birthday parties, or sadly more frequently there'd be a funeral service to attend. One gentleman – a keen gardener – kept donating potted ferns and cacti to her office cubicle and although she didn't like cacti much, she didn't have the heart to say *no* to his thoughtfulness.

The last group of the day would be a lunchtime mixed-age pilates class in the Common Room. Class members were generally more subdued, in that *out of breath high* people get after exercising. They usually came and went without too much drama, needing top ups to their designer drink bottles, but not requiring assistance from staff, volunteers or carers to add to the crowd scene.

"Good morning, Joy. How are you feeling now?" Siobhan, the Centre's paediatric nurse interrupted Joy's concentration as she signed in for the day.

"Much better, thanks. Just a cold, easily cured using old Doris' recipe of hot lemon and brandy with a touch of tea tree oil."

Siobhan chuckled as she finished her signature with a flourish. "Brandy's my self-medication of choice too." She collected her bags and headed off.

Joy called after her, "Have a good day." Siobhan waved an acknowledgement maintaining the warmth of social connection.

To Joy, work was more about the people these days than achievement. She was happy to be seen as a receptionist and not someone with a postgraduate university degree. She deliberately kept her work history from the rest of her colleagues, not wanting to confuse her new role.

True, occasionally she still needed to be reminded to pull back from defending her steady stream of innovative ideas, aware that her manager, Jane, liked to maintain the status quo at the centre. These setbacks didn't upset Joy the way they used to in her past life. Nowadays she didn't need to change the world to make it a better place. She simply desired to see out the next ten years of her work life in a smooth, easy slide into retirement.

"Hellooo everybody!" A booming voice ricocheted through the centre, belonging to the one and only Poppy Bryant. She stopped at the reception counter to sign in. "Thank god, you're back," she screeched at Joy with a wide grin. "The toilets blocked on Monday and it took the temp all day to find the phone number for the plumber."

"I keep all that information in my Admin Manual," Joy replied, reaching across to a row of folders with large black lettered titles, pointing to one clearly marked Admin Manual.

Poppy raised her hands and nodded, dramatically miming *of course.* "I told Sue it had to be somewhere obvious. The silly girl kept insisting she'd looked. Not to worry; we worked it out in the end. Even if it was the hard way," she brayed. "Are you feeling better? We've got a busy day ahead; I hope you're up for it."

Not waiting for a reply, Poppy disappeared in the direction of the manager's office. Joy heard her strident voice shouting "gidday" and "how're ya goin", the vibrations bouncing off the walls as she passed other staff members in the corridor.

Joy winced. As much as she liked Poppy, her brash manner so early in the morning startled her sense of aesthetics.

Last week, Jane had gone off work for a hip replacement and would be taking at least two months leave. The staff team gave her a send-off with the usual fanfare: an afternoon tea, balloons and get well cards, and a basket of organic bath products.

As usual, Poppy had been promoted to act as temporary manager while Jane was away. This would be the longest period she'd been contracted for the position of manager. In the past, she'd only acted for a couple weeks at a time.

Joy saw this as good news. Everyone liked Poppy; she was a larger-than-life character – cheerful, boisterous, with a heart of gold. Whereas Jane was an excellent manager in terms of managing upwards to secure programs and budgets, she wasn't what Joy would call a *people person*.

Occasionally, it was a welcome relief to have Poppy in the job because she focused more on the human side of managing. She never forgot that most of the time she was one of them, a community nurse, and only acted as their temporary manager for a couple weeks at a stretch each year. Staff could sneak through long awaited approvals for ergonomic chairs or a cappuccino machine for the staff room on her watch. She always seemed happy to oblige.

Thinking about it, Joy could use a sun blind for her reception window. During certain times of the year, the afternoon sun angled straight into her eyes, blinding her when assisting people at reception. She'd asked Jane for one some time ago but never got approval. Maybe Poppy would be more reasonable about her request.

Satisfied at the day's schedule, Joy turned from her computer to her in-tray and began sorting the various bits of paper into two piles: to action and to file. Having taken two days sick leave at the start of the week and with Wednesday her usual day off, the filing stack was larger than usual.

An invoice stamped PAID in red caught her attention. *Oh no*. Amberlie had processed an invoice for an advertisement on an online website *Service Directory in Health Care* that was actually a scam. And Poppy had initialled it, approving the nine hundred dollar fee for payment. Joy only hoped she'd caught the mistake in time to undo it.

With righteous indignation, Joy marched to Poppy's office waving the invoice under her nose. "Amberlie processed this invoice, but it's a scam," she declared.

Poppy scanned the page, looking increasingly sheepish but unsure what Joy wanted her to do.

Joy persisted. "It's nine hundred dollars off the centre's budget. For nothing."

Defensively, Poppy asked, "Are you sure? It looks legitimate to me."

"Yeah, well that's the bluff. They set up a website, post telephone and fax numbers anyone can get out of the phone book, and then charge us an exorbitant amount of money for the privilege. Look up the site; you'll see what I mean." Joy leaned across the desk and began typing in the web address on the boss's personal computer. A plain, basic directory in black font, without graphics, filled the screen.

"See, how amateurish it looks," Joy insisted, oblivious to the bruising red flush spreading across and up Poppy's throat.

***

Poppy was mortified at her first major stuff up as acting manager. She wished Joy would stop going on and on about it. How was she supposed to know it wasn't the real deal. The truth was she'd just approved all the invoices Amberlie had put before her, trusting the girl knew what she was doing. She'd been so busy trying to get through the long To Do list Jane had left her in handover. She didn't have time to double check everything her admin did.

It wasn't her fault know-it-all Joy had taken sick leave. The more Joy went on about it, the more Poppy felt judged, the more she doubted her ability to do the job Jane entrusted her with for the next eight weeks. Her stress climbed to a flustered hot and red level.

"The blame rests with me," Poppy stated slowly, hoping this would shut Joy up. "I'll talk to finance at head office, see if they can recover the payment." She forced a laugh, saying, "What would we do without you?" but thinking if Joy had kept quiet nobody would have been the wiser.

"You can try, but I think it's probably too late," Joy said with a bluntness that sounded as if she wielded a gavel and had pronounced a criminal sentence. If this was her way of offering assistance, she was certainly unaware of how critical her words sounded.

Frowning, Poppy watched Joy flounce out of the office, hating that sanctimonious attitude, always going on about saving taxpayers' money. It was government money; it belonged to everyone. What difference did it make if a few dollars went missing now and then?

Joy could be so annoying at times. Amberlie would have sympathised with the mistake, not criticised. She understood how it felt being new to the job.

And anyway, how was Poppy to know about the unethical practices of internet scammers, if their office millennial didn't even know.

Poppy waited for Joy to be out of ear shot before placing a call to Finance. She put a hypothetical question to the accounts payable officer. He helpfully explained that this particular scam was well known to the department, and that once a payment was processed it would be impossible to reclaim it. She effusively thanked him and hung up.

The mistake was made, nothing could be done. Poppy decided to sit on this particular problem before making any drastic confessions. With any luck, the payment would be buried amongst all the other centre payments and go unnoticed perhaps for years. Provided Joy didn't decide to draw any more attention to it.

***

Joy rushed back to reception, hearing both telephone lines on the switchboard buzzing like demanding wasps. Murphy's Law – as soon as she left her desk, the lines would go mental. Puffing from the run down the corridor, she answered with a slightly breathless *Quamby Bluff Community Health, Joy speaking.*

"I want to speak to the manager," an angry voice demanded.

In her calm receptionist tone, Joy said, "I'm sorry, Mrs Bryant is on another phone call. Would you like to wait?"

"How long will she be?" The woman sounded impatient.

"I couldn't really say," Joy said soothingly. "Would you like to leave a message so she can return your call?"

"When would that be? I'd rather wait if she's not going to be too long." The woman's voice had raised to an annoyed pitch. Joy was wondering how she could be expected to foretell the future and predict how long Poppy would be on a call or return a message.

"Mrs Bryant is a talker. If you wait, it could be awhile." Joy gave a light laugh.

"How long do *you* think?" the woman yelled down the line.

"I really can't say how long my boss will be on a call." Joy began to see this conversation was going around in circles and was finding difficulty remaining reasonable. She longed to point out how ridiculous the caller was behaving by making a flippant retort but bit her tongue instead.

"Who's she talking to? Can't you interrupt!"

Joy pulled a silly face. Striving to sound patient, she said, "She's on her private line so I have no way of knowing who she's talking to or how long their conversation will last. If you'd like to leave a…"

"You're not very good at your job," the caller jeered. This insult tested Joy's tolerance, however, she chose not to react to the bait. Instead, she did the next best thing.

"Please hold while I answer another incoming call." By the time Joy answered that line the second caller had hung up. Returning to the first caller, she said chirpy and upbeat, "Sorry about that. Mrs Bryant is still engaged on the other call." She was rewarded with a string of screaming, abusive expletives and threats to get her sacked.

Quavering from stress but in her most professional voice, Joy said, "My job does not require putting up with abuse, so I am going to hang up now." She ended the call and directed all new calls to the answering machine.

Taking a deep breath, she decided a break was needed. A calming cup of tea in the garden with some fresh air would clear her head.

Dreamily sipping a well sweetened English Breakfast tea in the centre's rose garden was having the desired effect releasing Joy's annoyance at the previous phone caller – for all of five minutes before her hide-away was discovered by a panicked volunteer.

"We've run out of toilet paper," Daisy cried out, expecting Joy to fix the problem immediately.

Joy wanted to be left in peace for another few minutes. "Can it wait until tomorrow when the cleaners go around replacing the rolls?" She hated being delegated to the office troubleshooter all the time.

"The storeroom cupboard is empty." Daisy spoke slowly so Joy grasped the full implications of the problem.

Joy inwardly sighed. It wasn't fair she had to do Amberlie's job as well as her own. Uncharitably, Joy broke the first rule of office etiquette. She blamed her job-sharing partner. "It's Amberlie's job to order stores," she said rather grumpily.

"But she's not back until Wednesday." Daisy looked worried.

"There's probably an order on its way." This belated vote of confidence in Amberlie did nothing to ease Daisy's concerns. Seeing her head shaking, she added, "I'll check the orders book. In the meantime, ask Poppy for approval to get a few rolls at the IGA on the centre's account to tide us over."

Daisy smiled in relief. As she turned to go, Joy stopped her with a question. "How come all our toilet rolls have disappeared so quickly? Last week, I unpacked a new order. The cupboard was stacked full at that time."

Daisy shuffled her feet, looking uncomfortable. "I can't say."

Joy nodded with understanding. Staff, or volunteers, or maybe clients, were helping themselves to items from the storeroom. Seriously, *toilet paper*? Of all the things they could pilfer, why would anyone want thin, one-ply government issued toilet rolls? Unbelievable.

Tea break over, Joy returned to her office. After checking Amberlie's store order, she typed an email to Poppy reporting the pilfering. It was a routine matter. She couldn't imagine what could be done about it unless the department agreed to install security cameras throughout the building. She'd already talked to Jane about extra security measures and received the same bland, blank look she usually got for suggesting any continuous improvement idea that fell outside her job description. Poppy wouldn't have the delegation to approve an expensive security system while Jane was away. *Even if it would cost less than that scam advertisement she approved.*

Once again, nothing would be done about government resources going missing.

Suddenly, a bright idea popped into her head. Poppy didn't actually have the delegated authority to approve the scam invoice. Maybe this could be worked to their advantage, arguing her approval was not valid? She'd talk to Finance about this angle.

The rest of the morning passed quickly and uneventfully. Poppy didn't respond to her email about the pilfering but that didn't bother Joy. She'd done her job by passing on the problem to the boss. It was on record at least.

Joy's tummy growled, it was lunch time.

The centre's lunchroom reflected the department's attitude to breaks: utilitarian, do your business and get back to work. It's only redeeming feature was large picture windows looking out to the rose garden. The community nurses, Georgie and Louise, squeezed around the laminate table with open cartons of low-fat yoghurt and mega mugs of steaming coffee, sharing information about their clients, trying to relax but not quite letting go of their work stress.

Joy joined them, throwing a plastic takeaway of homemade stew in the microwave, pressing ninety seconds, and rummaging in the cupboard drawer for a spoon. Sitting down, she began to unwrap a large lunch roll filled with cheese and salad. She couldn't understand how people survived the day without a substantial meal at lunch time.

Chewing with concentration, Joy listened to their concerns about one particular client, an elderly man living on his own.

"Mary, his fortnightly cleaner, reported a rat's nest under his bed," Georgie said, screwing up her face with disgust.

"He's got grief issues, his wife died last year," Louise explained. "He began hoarding shortly after that."

"Apparently his place is filthy; Mary found maggots crawling through a pot of leftovers on the stove," Georgie said. "And his personal hygiene could be better."

"I'll see if we can arrange home care twice a week, get him showered at least." Louise's tone became decisive and business-like.

The microwave beeped. Joy jumped up to retrieve her hot lunch. She stirred the steaming beef and vegetable casserole, picturing maggot infested food and became nauseous. Staring at her meal, she pushed it to one side, not that hungry anymore. In the future, it would be a better idea to find another spot to eat lunch, maybe outside under the barbeque pergola. She didn't want to seem unfriendly, but she wasn't inured to gross stories while eating. Nothing seemed to disturb nurses' cast-iron stomachs.

"Hello, how's everybody?" the big voice of Poppy echoed off the walls of the small room. Her large form pushed into a chair next to Joy, her soft upper arms and spongy thighs pressing against Joy's. Uncomfortable and feeling the need for elbow room, Joy shifted her seat a few inches to the right. Poppy did not seem to notice. She began unpacking a lunch bag with a small can of baked beans, a banana, and a tuna salad wrap stamped with a *Waist Not* logo. She popped the tab on a can of Zero Coke and took a swig, smacking her lips.

"Did you hear what happened to Consuela, Mr. Gray's home carer?" Poppy set down her coke and smiled conspiratorially at Louise and Georgie. "He didn't answer the door when she knocked. He's diabetic and doesn't take his meds reliably. So, she let herself in." Poppy paused to draw out the suspense. "The old pervert was porking his Shitzu in the lounge room!"

Everyone around the table burst into laughter. Except Joy who shouted, "Eeuuw," wanting to throw up. For a start she loved dogs and hated people abusing them. And for another thing it was just wrong, on so many levels. "Can we report him to the RSPCA or something?" she croaked.

The nurses ignored her protests, continuing their uproarious bellows, smacking the table like drum rolls. Finally, settling down, Georgie looked up at Poppy. "So, how are you going to handle it?"

She let out a spontaneous guffaw, rolling her eyes. "It had to happen on my watch." Then more seriously, she said, "Consuela of course is on stress leave. I'll send her to a counsellor."

"Maybe Tara could talk to her," Joy suggested. Tara, the centre's social worker, had a down to earth approach to issues that would shock the average citizen. Last year when mothers within Quamby Bluff's community began angry protests about a child sexual predator volunteering at the primary school's after-hours pastoral care program, Tara stepped in to take control, directing their outrage to productive legal action. The police eventually gathered enough evidence to charge him and he went to prison. Joy respected Tara immensely.

"Consuela won't be able to attend Mr. Gray now," Georgie said matter of fact. "But he's frail and needs home care."

"I'll talk to Dave and see if he minds taking over from her." Poppy became serious, her manner less jovial and more managerial.

Still shocked, Joy couldn't believe any worker, male or female from the centre, should have to risk exposure to Mr. Gray's sick behaviour. "Didn't he break the law?" she demanded, giving Poppy a glare as she waited for confirmation. "I mean, regardless of his dementia and needing home care. Why do we have to do anything for people like him!"

Poppy frowned, not appreciating Joy's holier-than-thou reaction. The other two nurses nodded in understanding but remained silent.

"Sometimes we don't have a choice. We're their last chance at dignified independent living, and usually it's none of our business what they get up to in the privacy of their homes."

To Joy, her words sounded like a dressing down. Poppy must have interpreted her concerns as interfering. An admin staff member was not supposed to question or pass judgement on departmental procedures.

Unlike in past jobs she wasn't an equal at the table. Being put back in her box reminded Joy of the centre's unwritten rule – listen; do not offer opinions.

She decided to eat lunch somewhere else tomorrow.

***

At three o'clock, Poppy walked down the hall corridor dragging a child's wooden rocking horse. She stopped at the reception window and with a bellow announced, "I've had enough of you lot – I'm clocking off early and taking this home for my foster kid." She cackled in good humour. "The boy gets bored easily; this should keep him busy. Don't know what else to do with the little bugger." She cackled some more.

To Joy the rocking horse looked suspiciously like it had come from the paediatric nurse's waiting room. Cautious not to point the finger, she asked, "Is that one made by the Men's Shed? I'm not sure what they sell for?"

"Is it?" Poppy pretended innocence. "I'm going to borrow it for the weekend. See if Conan will use it."

"Sounds good," Joy said agreeably. "I've set up a Register for Items Borrowed from the centre. I'll get you to sign out the rocking horse so we know where it's gone." The ledger was inspired after a stack of white soup bowls never returned after the Quamby Bluff Shire council borrowed them along with a number of white plates, cups and saucers for a Christmas function. Without a record of exactly what had been borrowed, Joy could not argue for their return. Jane wrote them off to natural attrition.

She pushed a ledger across the reception window and handed Poppy a pen, pointing to where her signature was required.

"Of course, you have a register. Our *Hun* has a register for just about everything," she snorted, as she scrawled initials. "I was planning to bring it back Monday, if you feel the need to check up on the *manager*." Another loud guffaw, this time sounding fake to Joy. She clenched her jaw, feeling a tad deflated at Poppy's sarcasm. *Was 'hun' short for honey or a reference to The Huns?*

"It's just, my memory's never been the same after chemotherapy. If it's not written down, I'll forget." *In other words, it's not you, it's me.* Joy hoped Poppy bought the diplomacy. She knew her system was necessary, but obviously it would take some time for staff to appreciate it.

Chapter Two

After work, Joy needed to debrief from the day. Honor was always good for a cuppa and sensible advice, and she lived two minutes' drive away, around the corner from the centre in a two-story Georgian country house. Joy loved sitting in her sister's immaculately decorated family room, looking out French windows onto established formal gardens with weeping willows, pruned hedges outlining garden beds with wild cottage flowers amidst winding stone pathways, with parrots and magpies flitting through the mottled shade. She envied her sister's ability to create perfection with magical ease. Honor was the only person she knew with a happy marriage, two teenage children (a boy and a girl) that were no trouble, and a life that had gone exactly according to her and Colin's plan.

Joy's life never went according to plan. She needed to whinge about gross stories at lunch, missing toilet paper and the boss borrowing play equipment for personal use.

Honor answered the door and welcomed her with open arms. She often turned up on Honor's doorstep needing a chat. In the kitchen, her sister rattled around arranging an antique paisley patterned tea service on a tray with a pot of Twinings Lady Gray and a plate of vanilla tuiles, a precise low calorie choice, not wanting to ruin dinner by filling up on cake.

Dry mouthed, Joy gulped her tea, dabbing the corners of her mouth with an embroidered serviette. Not waiting for the niceties of a family catch-up, she launched into a long explanation of her work day stresses. Needing words of encouragement and support, instead her well-meaning sister gave her a wake-up call to the realities of village life.

"Joy, the centre is not going to turn in one of their own to the police for the sake of a few rolls of toilet paper disappearing. What message would that give to the community? No one would come to the centre after that." Honor laughed, making light of Joy's intense sense of right.

"But it's stealing government resources. That's just wrong. Security cameras would be a deterrent but Jane won't even consider my suggestion." Joy's shoulders slumped.

Honor gazed sympathetically. "They won't install security cameras because that implies their clients can't be trusted."

"But they can't! That's the truth," she insisted.

Honor shook her head, as if trying for patience. "Joy, I love you, but you have a way of getting on a high horse over issues that in the scheme of things don't matter so much. Try not to let things get to you. Just let it go. This is the secret to happiness."

"What? Turning a blind eye to what's wrong with the world!" Joy was indignant.

Honor sighed. "Only to the little things. Like that saying, *don't sweat the small stuff.*" She patted Joy's knee. "People in Lower Teasel like things the way they've always been. You'll get on better with everyone when you let go of this need to keep improving things all the time. Remember why you moved here in the first place? To semi-retire from the stresses of work. Just let it go. What you don't see, can't hurt."

Joy's eyes teared up, feeling Honor's care and concern but at the same time thinking her sister undervalued her passionate principles. Fair enough, Honor was being sensible, trying to help her adjust to village life. Sure, she'd be better off sticking to her job description, keeping her nose out of things that weren't her problem and not bringing work stresses home.

Unfortunately, she simply was not built that way.

The adjustment from a sophisticated city person to living in a rural farming community was proving to be a steeper learning curve than she'd anticipated when moving to Eden Isle a few years ago. As Honor often reminded her, raising chickens and growing vegetables was easy compared to fitting in with the locals and not ruffling the feathers of the village's *old guard*.

But surely it meant something to put in extra effort and prove indispensable at work? Wouldn't that eventually lead to acceptance within the community?

Not according to her sister.

Maybe Joy should listen to Honor. She was the model of keeping out of the spotlight, minding her own business, never rocking the boat. Miraculously, this worked for her.

Look at her beautiful home and perfect life. Nothing out of the ordinary ever happened to her family. Her life played out like it was charmed.

Joy wished her life could be so lucky – but this wasn't in her cards.

Take last year as an example. Honor and Colin were the only people she knew that could plan a holiday twenty years in advance, put money aside every pay day without fail and then go on their overseas trip exactly according to schedule. *Who does that?*

And as luck would have it, they returned home from the Holy Lands three weeks later safe and sound after having the best holiday of a lifetime.

Two weeks afterwards that same tour bus full of tourists got blown up by terrorists, killing several people. Honor and Colin had walked around in some charmed bubble of protection, oblivious to the inherent dangers of the situation, and it all worked out fine. Of course.

In contrast, Joy's last overseas trip was a spur of the moment decision to go on a Buddhist meditation retreat in Nepal. Six weeks into her relaxing holiday, Maoist terrorists threatened to kill everyone in the monastery where she was staying unless bribes were paid. In a state of abject terror, Joy booked the next flight home – which happened to be on 9/11, the day terrorists flew planes into New York's Twin Towers causing panic and disruption at airports around the globe. Even after landing safely in Sydney, luck was not on her side. She became stranded when her connecting flight home was cancelled due to Ansett Airlines going into liquidation on that same day. A total shemozzle.

In summary, when Joy went on a holy retreat, the war caught up with her! When Honor and Colin went to the Holy Lands, the war waited until they returned home, safe within the bounds of the boringly peaceful village of Lower Teasel.

Honor joked about Joy being a *trouble-magnet* attracting problems into her life. But how could she be blamed for these things?

Clearly, she had not inherited her sister's charmed life. At the same time, she often felt judged by Honor, as if when things went pear shaped it was due to some failing within Joy's character. She was too out there, too opinionated, never rolled over and played dead – or something. As if Honor's good fortune was due to her good character and her penchant for always choosing the right course, rather than blind dumb luck.

Honor's voice broke into Joy's self-pitying deliberations. "Let me top up your cup of tea. And please finish off the tuiles before Col gets home and does it for us. We're watching our calories and he's a sweet tooth."

Joy took this as a hint to veer the conversation into more mundane topics. "How's Kodi enjoying her job at the Shire Council?" she asked, allowing Honor to fill in space with a running commentary on the goings on of her children.

Admittedly, it was comforting listening to her sister's rambling digression into everyday family minutiae. Her nephew, Nate, was excelling at his studies in chemical engineering at the ANU. Kodi had been recently promoted to Property Development Officer at the local council.

"She submitted a short story in the *Women Writers on the Isle* competition and won first prize," Honor was saying.

Half listening, Joy caught the bit about "...taking a course in Creative Writing at Quamby Bluff Community College". Honor's children gave every reason for her sister to be proud. Naturally.

Temporarily for the next quarter hour, the diversion succeeded – immersed in family, she forgot about work. Maybe living in Lower Teasel was the charm that would finally end her search for peace and security.

Finishing her cup of tea, Joy hugged Honor and said goodbye. Walking down the well swept stone pathway to the car, her heart held onto a niggling sense of disappointment at unfinished business. She often left her sister's home like this, feeling reluctant to get to the bottom of a serious issue by having a deep and meaningful conversation, as if this upset a delicate law of equilibrium. She needed to remember with Honor, those topics so important to Joy should only be mentioned lightly in passing – or preferably not at all.

As much as she respected her sister's pragmatic position, Joy felt it lacked the more noble principles that formed a foundation for a meaningful life. Some issues were basic black and white. Such as right versus wrong. If people readily ignored minor crimes, didn't this give tacit permission to turn a blind eye to more critical ones? Where did one draw the line? she wondered.

Chapter Three

"There you are!" Poppy's voice boomed across the courtyard. "I've been looking for you everywhere."

Joy stopped chewing her chicken sandwich; a look of annoyance crossed her face. She was on her lunch break after all. Apparently, there was nowhere she could sit for a quiet moment without work finding her.

She swallowed, pointedly looked at her watch before saying defensively, "I've got ten more minutes before I have to go back."

Poppy strutted across trimmed lawns to the pergola, stopping in front of the lunch table. Her dark shape blocked the sun, casting Joy in shadows.

"Take twenty for all I care," Poppy generously replied. "It's Friday! I'm inviting us all to the pub after work. It's been a tough week. I'm shouting the drinks."

This was typical Poppy when acting as manager; she focused on the wellbeing of her team members. She understood the best way to de-stress after a difficult week was to allow staff to bond over a round of micro-brewery apple cider. Unlike Jane who simply knocked off early expecting Joy to handle any late afternoon crisis and lock-up afterwards.

Her enthusiasm was hard to resist, even if Joy did not touch alcohol *except for medicinal purposes* and could think of better things to do on a Friday than spend more time with work colleagues. After work functions were not her scene. They invariably ended up as a debriefing when all she wanted was to go home and forget about the job.

But she had just been given extra time for lunch, so how could she say no. And earlier, Poppy had signed off on the purchase requisition for a venetian blind in reception proclaiming it was obviously an OH&S issue. This was going to make her office much more comfortable.

She liked Poppy's easy going attitude. Her staff were more than subordinates; they were colleagues and friends.

How could she say no to drinks? "Sure, I'll be there. But I can't stay long." Reverting to her work persona she asked, "Do you want me to send out an invite to all staff?"

"No, I'll do that." Poppy reached across to place her hand on Joy's shoulder to give it a squeeze. "I'm just glad you can make it."

Joy waited for Poppy to turn and walk away before shaking the stiffness from her shoulders. She didn't want to appear rude but nowadays she froze when anyone made physical contact. This self-consciousness started happening after a mastectomy and breast reconstruction surgery five years ago.

Before this, she'd been more of a touchy-feely person like Poppy. A cancer scare and the failure of her body to remain healthy left a raw sense of fragility about life. The operation had cut nerves, leaving the right side of her abdomen lifeless and numb. Her fake breast felt alien.

She hated the casualness of unwanted touch and her inability to insist on this personal physical boundary with people. How did a person explain this painful shame to a coworker? She didn't have the courage to expose this vulnerability to someone so unaware as Poppy. Instead, she followed Honor's advice to *grin and bear it*.

Chapter Four

The Heritage Inn nestled among an old English style garden surrounded by ancient fir trees planted when military personnel settled Lower Teasel as a government outpost in its early colonial days. Antique white front pillars and wide steps fashioned from convict bricks welcomed customers, leading them through an old Huon pine doorway into a cosy den. An open fireplace displayed decorative logs and bunches of dried lavender; dim afternoon sun filtered through the lace net curtains, not enough to heat the pleasantly cool room but enough to preserve an old world ambience.

Joy arrived behind Georgie and Louise. They dropped into a deep cushioned settee positioned with other lounge chairs in a semi-circle in front of the stone hearth. Joy chose a high backed armchair upholstered in lime green velveteen. Tara rushed in and pulled up a piano stool, plonking down in a fluster. She immediately announced that Lachlan would not be coming; he had a kid to collect from day care. In unison, everyone moaned to demonstrate their disappointment.

Joy was not surprised at the news; Lachlan, the centre's Youth Worker, never attended activities outside of work, not even staff Christmas parties.

She envied his ability to escape these affairs and avoid peer censure at the same time. *I won't stay long*, she decided.

The Inn's owner, Martine, sauntered in carrying a large platter stacked with a variety of cheeses, crackers, chips, dips and fruit. Poppy followed close behind, waving her arms with a flourish.

With aplomb Martine placed the tray on the centre coffee table and set out serviettes and cutlery in front of each person.

"Dig in with my compliments," Poppy shouted.

"Yum." Tara grabbed a handful of grapes. "I won't need dinner tonight."

Joy speared a piece of camembert and squished it onto a pepper water cracker. "Thanks Poppy; this is awesome."

"*You* are awesome," Louise gushed. Around the table heads nodded.

Poppy waved a humble dismissal. "What drinks can I get you people?" she asked digging in her handbag. "My shout." She flashed a credit card at Martine.

"No, that's too much." Georgie spoke for the team. "Let me get the first round instead."

Joy fidgeted in her seat. She only wanted a soda water and didn't want to feel obligated to buy a round for the rest of them. Being part-time, she lived on a tight budget. She knew Tara drank spirits, and Louise liked that fancy German cider flavoured with winter spices. It all got too expensive. She wasn't planning to stay that long any way. "Um, I just want a soda. So, I'll get my own, if you don't mind."

Her voice was lost amongst the others ordering. Martine produced a small notebook from an apron pocket and began scribbling notes. "And what can I get you, darl?" she looked at Joy.

Defeated, Joy asked, "Do you have a sparkling mineral water? I'll have a bottle, no need for a straw, thanks." Martine nodded, took one last scan around the table, satisfied she'd taken everyone's order, and gracefully exited to the bar.

After the hungry horde had grabbed their first selection of delectable savouries, Tara launched a discussion about Mr. Gray's condition. She argued for a complete medical and psychological assessment. Consuela had been to see her for counselling and Tara was naturally concerned. The nurses contributed their own opinions about the next steps to take, with Poppy listening but staying unusually quiet. The conversation then moved on to other tricky clients, with ideas thrown around and suggestions passed on to Poppy for her final decision.

From Joy's point of view, as expected, the evening had become serious much too soon. She wondered if it was appropriate to be discussing clients' confidential case notes in a public space, even if they were the only ones in the room at the time. Despite names not being mentioned, most members of the community in Lower Teasel, if they were listening in, would recognise a client from even sparse details; this was a small rural town after all and everyone knew everyone's personal business. And they all gossiped. Out of the goodness of their hearts, of course.

Drinks arrived, circuit breaking the heaviness of the conversation. Poppy raised her glass. "Cheers." A clinking of glasses against other glasses and bottles followed. Then a pause as each person took a sip or swig from their beverage, luxuriating in that initial hit of alcohol to the brain.

"I propose a toast to us – a tough week and jobs well done." Poppy's booming voice cut into the quiet room. "My second week as acting manager and you haven't driven me crazy yet. I'll count that as a success." The nurses chuckled. Joy clapped. Tara smiled indulgently. The mood mellowed to a companionable team-like atmosphere.

Poppy leaped up unexpectedly. "I reckon what you all need is some stress relief." Without asking, she stood behind Tara and began to vigorously massage her shoulders. Tara stretched her neck back and forth, wriggled her shoulders, and appeared to relax into the rub. "How's that?" Poppy murmured. "Better now?" After a few minutes, Poppy moved on to Georgie, working her way around the team members.

Joy became increasingly more uncomfortable the closer it got to being her turn. Truthfully, she didn't want a massage from Poppy. The whole thing creeped her out, if she was honest. Poppy didn't seem to understand the need for boundaries concerning her personal space; she stood too close when in her office; she bumped into her passing in the corridor; squeezed her shoulder when complimenting. It probably didn't mean anything.

Although as the days went by, these incidents became more frequent and intrusive.

Clearly, Poppy enjoyed touching, probably the reason she became a nurse in the first place.

Joy wasn't sure how to say a simple *No thanks*, without offending Poppy's generosity. The others seemed to be enjoying her attention. With increasing apprehension, she sat like a stiff board watching Louise's turn come up. Joy was next.

"You can do it harder," Louise said to Poppy.

"You mean like this," Poppy laughed. Playing to the crowd, she theatrically pumped her shoulders in a vibrating motion, rolling her eyes in exaggerated ecstasy.

"Oh, yes baby, harder, harder," Louise crooned suggestively, sending titters of laughter around the table.

For Joy, this was the last straw. "I'm just going to the ladies," she said, jumping up. She wanted to madly dash to the safety of a locked cubicle but instead forced a dignified stride, holding her head high.

In the bathroom, she leaned on the sink with tears pooling in her eyes. Why was she making such a big deal about it? Why not just say no and have that accepted by the rest of the group without feeling like a spoilsport? Poppy had this way of imposing her will on people with her brash in-your-face insistence on caring.

Taking a deep breath to calm a racing heart, Joy had a self talk. *It's only for a couple months and Jane will be back. You can cope with Poppy's intrusiveness until then. It didn't mean anything.*

Dabbing mascara from the corners of her eyes, Joy checked her hair in the mirror and practised a friendly smile a few times until it didn't look too cheesy and fake. *Grin and bear it.*

She'd have words to Honor on the weekend about that piece of advice. It definitely needed updating.

Looking in the mirror, she imagined her grandson, Jaxon, receiving a motivational speech from his footie coach. *Be a team player.*

This new mantra didn't help either. Feelings of dread welled in the pit of her stomach as Joy walked back to the team with a toothy smile plastered across her face.

Poppy glanced over with a knowing look. "There you are!" she effused. "Just in time for your shoulder rub."

Joy froze, staring at her boss pushing the issue to its sore point. A fleeting thought crossed her mind at glimpsing that cunning analytical glance. *Did Poppy get pleasure from causing creepy discomfort?* Did anyone else feel this way?

"Yeah, well... I just realised... I forgot... one of my classes on furniture restoration is on tonight. It's on chalk painting. I have to go." Without waiting for a response, she rushed out of the den towards the exit. In the background, Poppy gave a snort of laughter and others groaned, registering their disappointment at Joy letting the side down by leaving early.

Chapter Five

End of week three on the job as Acting Manager, the centre this Friday afternoon relaxed into a client-free space of a normal office building. By two o'clock volunteers had shuffled satisfied clients into community cars and courtesy buses, leaving an empty silence in their wake. With sighs of relief, staff then proceeded to their offices to concentrate on government paperwork behind the quiet of closed doors.

Poppy sat at her desk, head down, shoulders slumped, scrolling Facebook messages on her iphone, trying to forget the disaster of her speech at the Excellence Award ceremony at morning tea. Jane should have known better than to delegate the job to her.

The Minister of Health had attended to once again present Quamby Bluff Community Health Centre with a plaque for being "A Centre of Excellence in Community Health Services." A yearly Australia Day event. Everyone knew Jane was the solid rock behind this success. It was Jane's award. Her self-effacing humility allowed her to take leave at this time.

Jane passed on the honour of accepting the accolades to Poppy on behalf of her dedicated team. Left without even a hint of dot points on what to say in a speech. *You'll be fine*, she'd assured. No pressure.

What had possessed Poppy to ad lib a joke about Jane having a hip replacement on the mainland as a vote of confidence in Eden Isle's health service? Most guests laughed, getting her twisted sense of humour. She was sure the minister had smiled politely, not taking offence. Joy was the only person who looked mortified at the gaff. As if in organising the event perfectly down to the last detail, with her project plan, checklists and nit-picking schedule of details, Joy could have done a better job at public speaking as well.

At times like this, Poppy marvelled at how she could hate Joy for her smug, effortless competence and at the same time depend on this same reliable proficiency.

Poppy felt judged for stuffing up the event from a simple attack of nerves. She didn't do well under pressure; everyone knew that. So what if a TV camera crew from The Meridian, a host of politicians, senior managers from the department, and other Quamby Bluff dignitaries witnessed her monumental stuff up attempting humour – her impromptu joke dying a humiliating death? This hadn't stopped them tucking into an extravagant morning tea spread afterwards.

The centre's volunteers had gone all out making iced petit fours, scones, pasties, savoury toast, egg and chive sandwich quarters, and other delectable village specialities. At the end of the day, this was what mattered more, surely. The fruit cake had been especially delicious. Both pieces. To hell with diets at times like this.

People understood public speaking was the worst sort of stress. Of course, Jane would have done a better job of it. But Joy shouldn't have made her feel deficient. She already carried enough doubts about whether she was up to the job of managing the centre over such a long period.

She excelled at hands-on nursing, and baulked at the thought of paperwork and bureaucratic projects that were more political than practical. Managing was not her area of expertise.

Jane had managed the centre since it transitioned from a rural hospital to a community health centre about fifteen years ago. She still ran it like a matron of a military hospital, efficient, organised, according to community expectations. No surprise the centre continually won awards for being the model of excellence in community health.

As she reviewed each detailed item on the handover 'To Do' list resting on top of a stack of files, her confidence faltered. Its façade of focused efficiency – work to complete and jobs checked off as done – mocked her growing sense of ineptitude. The instructions distorted in and out of focus as her heart pounded with anxiety. Each time her vision corrected the list appeared to have grown, ever increasingly and unreasonably longer.

Poppy felt the burden of expectations on her shoulders.

With recent government budget cuts, the department had contracted her over the period as part-time, six hours a day for four days a week. Jane obviously could manage her well-oiled centre part time, but Poppy, an acting manager on L-plates, found it impossible to do the job in the allotted time. She ended up taking work home or staying back on unpaid overtime. Pride would not allow a sensible confession to senior management that she wasn't coping with the workload. Naturally, her stress levels climbed higher each day on the job.

This afternoon, despite leaving a pile of work behind, she needed to depart by two-thirty; she couldn't stay back. When Lachlan stood in the doorway at two fifteen wanting guidance on writing up his monthly youth worker report due Monday, Poppy snapped at the hold up.

"Talk to the hand; sort out your own problems," she said in her dramatic, over-the-top voice. Seeing Lachlan's consternation, she laughed in a jolly way trying to soften her refusal. "I'm leaving on time today and nobody's going to stop me."

To emphasise her point, she started packing the laptop into its leather carry case, shoving files into side pockets. Lachlan shook his head and marched off without arguing. Guiltily she decided to talk to him Monday morning to smooth things over. It was important for the staff to like her. But she had to go, now.

Lachlan's interruption had cost her. As she locked the door to her office, a dark shape blocked her exit down the hallway. Helen, a nurse educator from head office, stood there, tall and officious with a polite smile.

"Poppy, hi?" Helen's sentences always ended on a high note, as if with a question mark. "I hope you're not heading out?"

Poppy's teeth clenched with frustration.

"Sorry, I should have called to say I was coming. But I'm never sure how long I'll be at each installation. Have you got a minute?"

It wasn't a question; it was a directive. Poppy understood head office priorities took precedence over an acting manager's personal life. She begrudgingly unlocked the door and ushered Helen in.

Helen deposited her briefcase onto the desk, pulled out the manager's chair, sat down and adjusted its ergonomic levers to better suit her height. She pushed aside pencil cases, message pads and Poppy's TO DO list, clearing space and making herself at home. Then she fiddled with the personal computer's on-off switch, waiting for it to boot up.

Not a good sign.

"You got the email?" Helen finally noticed Poppy's blank expression. "I'm here to install the department's updated training register."

Not sure if she should admit she didn't have a clue about it but unable to think up a credible excuse at short notice, Poppy mumbled, "I skim read something about it." Then to lighten her failure with a self-effacing joke she chuckled, "but it didn't stick in my Teflon memory."

Helen enthusiastically filled in the gaps. "At the last monthly managers meeting, it was agreed managers prepare up-to-date staff records of all mandatory training in accordance with relevant Awards and professional registration requirements. It's a priority. Each manager will report on progress completing their registers at the next meeting." This had been Helen's agenda item; clearly, the adrenalin high from her win was still running through her veins.

Poppy's eyes glazed over. Another project added to a growing TO DO list. She wasn't imagining it – every time an item got crossed off more tasks were added. It wasn't fair. This was Helen's bloody fault.

In her mind, Poppy worked through the extra work required to update the staff training register. She'd have to identify mandatory annual refresher courses for each health professional, preferred suppliers of training courses, fees, dates, backfilling of staff... it went on and on. Not difficult but time consuming. She began to detest Helen's enthusiasm.

Watching all the fiddling and fussing about, Poppy estimated it would be at least another hour before she could get away. Helen wasn't even sure about that. When asked how long this would take, she'd responded offhandedly in a whisper, "I don't really know?" which was a useless answer and did nothing to alleviate Poppy's growing resentment of the situation.

In the middle of all this, Helen's mobile phone buzzed. Distracted, Helen answered in an annoying squeaky voice, "Hello?" and proceeded to spend valuable time on a personal call discussing what she'd be cooking for dinner and debating about what items needed to be purchased from the shops...

Pressure stoked Poppy's impatience building into a pounding headache. She needed to get going. Before it was too late. Before she lost it with Helen, who of course was unaware she was causing distress.

When Helen's personal call finally ended, Poppy forced a belly laugh. "If you don't hurry up, I'll bloody strangle you!"

Helen, having resumed concentration on the screen uploading, didn't respond. Instead, she moved the mouse around and poked at a few keys, appearing to know what she was doing.

While on the job, Poppy expertly hid her true emotions behind a mask of forced humour and loud sarcasm. Ever vigilant, she usually never lost control in public. Only in private did she allow fits of temper to erupt in all their ugly and damaging manifestations, secure in knowing her family loved her and therefore forgave these temporary bouts of rage.

Poppy understood she fit the stereotype of a jolly old lady and this lulled others into instant likeability. She used this typecasting like a magic spell to be seen as benign, kindly, one of the team. Most likely the reason Jane felt comfortable using her to act in the job for an extended period. Poppy was non-threatening. Lightweight.

She grimaced at the irony. *Waist Not*'s diet didn't seem to be working so far and she'd been starving for a whole month. *Note to self: never start a diet as a New Year's resolution.* Her husband wasn't helping her resolve, with his complaints about why he had to diet with her. Out of sympathy she shared the bottles of red wine at dinner times that helped add some flavour to their packaged meals. Probably the reason she wasn't losing weight..

Poppy stared at the clock again, hoping to give Helen the message to hurry up. She was meant to collect her foster child, Conan, from the childcare centre no later than three thirty, at Gorse Plains, a good thirty minutes' drive away. To make it in time, she'd have to leave in ten minutes. And that wasn't going to happen.

Helen scratched her head, squinting at the instruction manual, re-arranged the placement of the laptop cables, pushed pens and papers around the desk, but so far, had not actually installed anything. Oblivious to Poppy's anxiety. In no hurry to get on with it.

She watched a dithery Helen who was obliviously unconcerned at being useless yet at the same time dominating her office space. Poppy shuffled on the spot, wanting to pace in frustration. The cramped quarters would not accommodate a building need to discharge her annoyance.

How was it right that *Helen* could be in a senior position at head office and be so slow? And not be bothered about it in the least?

She'd agreed to look after Conan for this week as an emergency placement, and not the usual fortnightly weekends. She was doing a favour to all concerned. It wasn't what she'd signed up for. The kid's mother had relapsed into another binge on ice and Conan was at risk. Poppy's heart went out to him. But the lad wasn't easy to manage; in the terrible threes with a mouth on him, instant tantrums at the least denial of a demand, with no appreciation for Poppy's charitable sacrifices.

Conan was a handful, without the added pressure of responsibilities as acting manager of the health centre. Why had she allowed Child Protection to talk her into taking on the burden of a foster kid at this time? She couldn't say 'no' that was her problem.

A memory of being Conan's age and her mother accusing her of selfishness flashed across Poppy's mind. She lived her life proving her mother wrong. Her mother remained stubbornly unconvinced. *I am worthy*, she repeated the words in her mind as an affirmation. A poker of stabbing pain inside her head accompanied this last thought. And a surge of hot anger washed away all rational thought.

Helen chose at this moment to mumble, "Hmm, that can't be right. I'll need to phone IT Support." Absently, she reached across the desk to the handset, knocking Poppy's jar of mixed lollies so they spilled into the wastepaper bin. "Oops," she giggled. "I hope you're on a diet."

Poppy watched her supply of comfort candy disappear into the rubbish and Helen's cavalier attitude with sudden hatred. *How useless was this woman!* She knew after the program was installed Helen would be credited with its success, and yet Poppy would be left with the bulk of the work, with all the responsibility for making it operational.

She suppressed a biting remark, aware a nurse educator from head office held superior status within the nursing hierarchy. But it was too late.

Helen became the object of her overwhelming anger that since childhood had festered and swelled, to be pushed down deep, only to unexpectedly vent out of control at the worst moments.

She imagined pushing Helen off her chair into the bin, pulling her away from the desk and out of her office, marching her out of the building's sliding glass doors with a good kick up her backside. *Just get the hell out of here*, she wanted to scream. Unreleased pressure built up, ready for an explosion. Suddenly she had to escape the claustrophobic confines of the office before actually acting out a fantasy of throttling Helen.

She recognised the signs of an escalating mood swing. Remembering her husband's advice to just walk away, she caught herself in time. "I'll be back in a minute!" she grunted, marching out of the room. All she had to do was walk down the corridor, past reception, through the sliding glass doors, outside for some fresh air.

She could do this without causing a scene.

Good, there was no one in the corridor blocking her escape.

***

Awareness came with a delicious sensation of pain. Wondering the source, Poppy found herself in the receptionist's office standing behind Joy seated at a desk. On route to escape Helen's cloying helpfulness and get some fresh air, she must have diverted to the receptionist's office wanting to let off some steam and release the tension building in her system. An obvious choice. Joy had always been a friendly, touchy-feely sort much the same as her. It was a subordinate's duty to accommodate a boss's moods.

Captive, captivating, Joy clutched the hands around her throat in an excruciating, vice-like grip that caused ripples of delight through Poppy's groin. Poppy was pulled roughly forward which pinned her torso to the hard back of the chair. Caught in the moment and excited by the pain, Poppy increased pressure around Joy's throat. Her sensitive bosom pressed into Joy's shoulders, providing an unexpected opportunity to push deeper rubbing up and down against the admin's tight shoulder muscles.

"Just relax. There, there, that's better," she crooned between honeyed shushes as if pacifying a fractious mount. She whispered in Joy's ear, saying she'd chosen her to strangle instead of Helen. It was an endearment, sharing this moment of physical communion.

Joy stiffened and jerked a shoulder as if fighting the caress. A playful gesture, not a serious rejection, Poppy understood. It was all the encouragement required. She tightened her grasp, enjoying the admin's struggles.

In a matter of a few minutes, shivers of bliss coursed through Poppy's loins, building into a mild orgasmic release. She came with a soft groan, her face buried in Joy's springy hair. A fragrance of coconut vanilla shampoo wafted through her nostrils with a calming sensuousness. All the stress caused by Helen dissipated from her body, in cascading tingles of renewed vitality. She sighed, relaxed and sated, adrift in the clouds of companionable pleasure, unaware of her surroundings except for the safe intimacy of the room.

Experimentally, she rubbed a cheek against the softness of Joy's face and tightened her grip around her partner's throat, magnanimously encouraging the forthcoming reciprocal reaction of gratification.

Frantically, Joy scratched and pried Poppy's strong hands apart and away from her neck, breaking the hold. Immediately releasing the strangling, ending the moment too soon.

Poppy shrugged, somewhat puzzled. It was Joy's loss. If the woman didn't wait for her own ecstatic moment, it was her loss, not Poppy's problem. She straightened and composed herself, ready to get back to work.

Joy, on the other hand, remained hunched over her desk stiff as a statue. Not happy or relaxed as should have been the case. In fact, after taking in a noisy gulp of air, she began to yell. "What the fffff... You frigging scared the shhhii... out of me!"

Poppy stood behind the chair and stared at the back of Joy's head; a pepper grey bob messed up into frizz. In good spirits and wanting to laugh at the sight, she was strangely disorientated at hearing disgust in the admin's tone of voice. This was not the reaction she expected.

"Go strangle Helen then!" Joy shouted as she swivelled sideways to look up with an expression of revulsion.

The receptionist's loathing ruined the wonder of the experience, the special friendship they had just shared. Confused, Poppy didn't know how to respond. Her blank look must have caused Joy to change tact.

Joy's face changed from disgust to a more neutral conciliatory expression. Her voice took on the cadence of a person pacifying a rabid dog. "It's alright. Helen can have that effect on people. I suspect everyone has wanted to strangle Helen at some time." She paused, looking wary and alert.

Not following the conversation, Poppy asked, "What?"

Joy stumbled on what to add, as if making it up on the spot. "I don't know what it is about her... she... has a way of annoying people; it's just her way, she's really quite nice, she doesn't mean to..." Joy babbled on for a few minutes before her speech trailed off, unable to come up with any more phrases that described Helen.

Poppy was bewildered by this rant. What was the woman going on about?

Joy searched her face, taking her measure and the danger she posed as if eyeballing a predatory lion in the circus ring. Carefully testing the water, she said, "I don't think you realised how strong your hands were squeezing my neck." It came out as an accusation. A damning judgement.

Poppy puzzled about why she had to explain any of it. A moment ago, she was positive Joy shared her proclivity for release by this method of neck hugging and had freely participated in the amusement. Why had the woman so quickly renounced what was an obvious moment between them? Poppy was finding difficulty processing this muddle and could not find the right words to express her surprise. Joy persisted in staring at her, wary and cautious.

Growing realisation and justification began to percolate into Poppy's consciousness. Clearly in her state of distress caused by Helen being so annoying, she'd misread the *Joy* situation. Confused, she wondered now if the woman's tightening grip and sexy wriggling had indicated something other than a building moment of bliss between them. She thought Joy's struggling had been signalling playful excitement.

It seemed Poppy had been terribly mistaken. *Gil will not be impressed. He'd warned her about this happening so many times. It wasn't her fault. She'd blanked out. He'd understand and forgive her, of course as usual.*

Wracking her brain from any memory of the last ten minutes, she recalled entering the receptionist's calm office expecting to gossip in her usual dramatic, unrestrained way, proclaiming with tongue-in-cheek self-pity how Helen was driving her crazy and should be throttled. Then she must have demonstrated her annoyance in a physical way. But it must have gotten out of hand when Joy responded to Poppy's teasing neck hugging in an encouraging way. That must have been it. Joy must have encouraged her to take things to the next level.

Now the woman was acting odd. As if she hadn't known what was going to happen. As if she were judging Poppy as some kind of freak.

But if Poppy had misread the situation and let things get out of hand, Joy must be to blame for her part in it. She'd always been friendly and smiley, which indicated she wanted a closer relationship than simply one at work. How was Poppy to know, when put to the test, the woman was fickle?

Smirking from this observation, Poppy resorted to her reflex response in awkward situations, a belly laugh accompanied by an ear-splitting attempt at playfulness. "Oh, sorry Hun! Did I give you a fright? You poor old thing. I guess I went a bit too far. Ha, Ha, Ha."

Joy remained stock still, watching Poppy, guarded and distrustful.

"I wanted to get away early this afternoon. But you know Helen, she fusses and fiddles about. Ha, Ha, Ha. I'd better keep an eye on her before she stuffs up Jane's computer." Poppy waited for Joy to smile in good humour. Instead, she received a frozen stare as if the receptionist waited for a feral cat to pounce. *I thought she liked massages. What's her problem?*

Poppy shrugged off Joy's weird behaviour and headed back to her office. Her husband was right when he advised she should just walk away when things got too much to cope with. The short break from Helen worked. She felt more composed and in control, as if the pressure inside her head had been released.

Poppy found Helen in her office packing up. She'd switched off the PC, snapped shut her briefcase and was attempting to re-position note pads, pencil cases and papers to their original spots on the desk. "All done," she chirped in a sing-song voice that signalled a happy ending to the training register installation. "I set up a shortcut to the register and left a memo indicating where to find the pathway to the online instruction manual." She patted the memo resting on the keyboard with pride.

"No worries." With her brightest faux smile, Poppy guided Helen towards the door with a hand on her shoulder. If she left now, there was time to collect Conan without Child Protection labelling her late and unreliable.

In a chatty mood, Helen stopped at the doorway. "A few managers have found the register difficult to populate. If you have any problems, just call me."

"Yes, yes. I'm sure it will be fine." Poppy's bulky form pushed towards the door.

Oblivious to the non-verbal cues, Helen continued to provide supportive advice. "I'm waiting on approval to establish a working group to provide extra training and iron out teething problems with the new system."

"Okay, jolly good," Poppy cut in, grabbing the door handle.

"An email will be sent out to you all by the end of next week with the details."

"Jolly good, excellent," Poppy repeated, this time pulling the door closed, moving Helen on. She walked her down the hallway and waved her on her way.

Lachlan stood at reception signing off his shift. Feeling a twinge of guilt about Joy, Poppy wandered over to ensure they were good with each other before she left for the day.

"I'm heading off now, too," she began, smiling brightly at her.

A flash of panic crossed Joy's face. She backed up her swivel chair a few feet from the doorway. She didn't return a smile.

Lachlan looked at them sensing the awkward dynamic. "Is everything cool here?"

A booming laugh erupted from Poppy. "Poor Joy, I scared her when I tried to give her a neck massage!"

Lachlan looked puzzled.

Joy defensively declared, "I don't think you realised how strong your hands were squeezing." A tone of desperation filtered through her words.

Poppy forced another uproarious laugh.

The deflection succeeded. Lachlan shrugged, not comprehending the real story. "Whatever. I don't want to know," he declared, tired after a long day and therefore lacking sufficient interest to delve deeper into whatever these women were on about.

With head down and rapid steps, Lachlan hurried to the exit. Poppy yelled after him, "Have a good one."

She grinned at Joy. "Well, that's me gone, too. Enjoy the weekend." She didn't wait for a response. She could see putting a humorous slant on the earlier incident hadn't repaired their relationship; it would require something a bit extra. She'd bring her some chocolates, or flowers, Monday to make it up to her. That usually worked with her daughters.

Chapter Six

For the past twenty minutes since Poppy left her office, Joy had functioned on auto pilot. No, in fact, she hadn't functioned at all. Someone observing her would have seen her sitting at her desk, arms hugged tightly to her chest, unmoving, staring at a computer screen but seeing nothing; in a numb state of nothingness.

Later, Joy would never be able to recall the period from then to now, this state of not functioning – except for sitting, breathing, relieved to be breathing. Only a sharp pain in her right shoulder from a tense muscle barely registered, her mind a blank.

The centre on this Friday afternoon was quiet and empty. Joy was alone in reception. So alone. No clients, volunteers or staff wandered through the hallways. The place echoed silence, a blank, numbing isolating silence. Like an injured pademelon, if she remained quiet and still, she'd be invisible.

When Lachlan stood at the reception counter signing out of the building, she performed the routine with a habitual, polite smile. Mute. She couldn't talk. She went through the motions, a receptionist ritual done on auto pilot. As if everything was normal – until Poppy stood in the doorway.

Her first conscious awareness was a terrifying sense of panic when Poppy returned and stood next to Lachlan. Joy wanted to flee from the malevolent, incomprehensible creature that suddenly appeared, arising from the dreaded shadows at the end of the corridor.

She could not make a move.

Poppy blocked her escape route, grinning and chatting to Lachlan as if nothing had happened. As if things were back to normal. As if Poppy was her usual *sane* self.

Joy suppressed an urge to leap out of the chair and fight her way out, to flee from the terrifying bulk filling in the doorway. Years of indoctrination into proper behaviour at work overrode an instinctual flight response to run. Instead, she jerked back her chair with an involuntary shove putting as much distance between them as her small office would allow. When the chair bumped against a filing cabinet and stopped with nowhere else to go, she froze.

Lachlan had asked if everything was alright. In response, Poppy had done her jolly Santa routine for his benefit. "Poor Hun, I gave her a fright," she boomed, sounding as if it had been amusing.

Like Joy's ex-husband.

Joy had the presence of mind to speak up in defence. *I don't think you realised how hard you were squeezing my throat.* It wasn't an accusation, more a plea for some kind of explanation that would make the cobwebbed muddle in her mind coalesce into something that made sense.

Twenty minutes ago, Poppy had walked into her office, and without saying a word, put both hands around her throat and began to strangle her. What the...? Joy hadn't done anything to annoy or anger her. It didn't make sense. At the same time, Poppy had whispered in her ear, *If I don't strangle you, I'll have to strangle Helen.* It didn't make sense.

Poppy had scared the life out of Joy. She'd had to pry the woman's hands away, all the time panicking, horrified that she wouldn't be able to breathe and would die. When Poppy gave up and didn't continue with the strangling, Joy remained frozen with shock. Relieved to be breathing. Aware the bulk of Poppy stood behind her, trapping her in a chair pushed up against the desk. Blocking an escape.

Poppy hadn't been laughing; she'd look bewildered as if she didn't know where she was or what she'd done. Confused at Joy's reaction. This had scared her more than anything. The woman was out of touch with reality and capable of anything. She'd had to talk her down for her own safety.

And yet, only a short time later, Poppy stood at reception laughing to Lachlan about it, expecting him to share in the humour of Joy's reaction. Laughing at her horror, adding to the confusion. Nothing made sense.

No admission of guilt and therefore no apology was forthcoming.

Lachlan looked puzzled, not understanding the dynamics of the situation. "Whatever. I don't want to know. I'm out of here."

Lachlan's failure to be outraged hurt Joy the most. He walked away without questioning Poppy or even checking to see whether Joy was really all right. She needed him to care at this one moment, incapable as she was of defending her person. That lack of attention to her predicament came as a point of despair.

Her role as a colleague had been relegated to the impersonal – within a boundary of work hours. Anxious to go to sports practice, he left her alone with Poppy. This was not a safe position, alone and unprotected with Poppy blocking the exit. The impact of this failure to come to her defence froze in her gut. No one was there for her. Work was not a safe place anymore.

Thankfully, Poppy made no attempt to continue with her sick humour, but instead left at the same time. Even so, the dread of her presence lingered.

Joy did not make a move to escape. Her body, like her mind, had ceased to function. Unable to register feeling anything other than a pounding heart. A blankness pervaded her thoughts, as if the strangling had choked more than air from her lungs; it had sucked the spirit out of her, too.

The wall clock ticked the hours. After five, the cleaner found Joy at her desk unmoving.

"Are you still here? Go home already. The weekend has started." With efficient movement, a vacuum cleaner was plugged into a socket. The hammering noise disturbed Joy from an enervating stupor.

"Sure. Of course. Home." She picked up a handbag from under the counter, ignored a dirty coffee mug and scattered papers, and did not bother to tidy the reception desk in her usual practice. Roused to leave, she couldn't get away fast enough.

Chapter Seven

Honor opened the door to her sister noting she was unusually late for a Friday after work. "Come in, you must be tired after a long week," she said in soothing tones. Keen to discuss a family issue that had recently come to light, she motioned Joy towards the family room where a warm pot of tea and lemon cake waited. Her sister obeyed with a shallow nod.

Honor watched Joy sink into the corner of the sofa, scrunching down in its overstuffed cushions, silent and still. Normally on a Friday afternoon Joy was all hyped up with energy wanting to debrief on all the incidents and upsets at the centre that had driven her to distraction, telling stories and laughing at how ridiculous people could be. Not now. She seemed rather listless. Maybe she was coming down with that virus going around Lower Teasel. On closer inspection, Joy's neck seemed flushed. Probably a fever coming on.

Honor poured tea into two cups, adding sugar and milk in exact measurements to suit each other's individual tastes. Joy accepted the cup and held it with a vague look, as if she wasn't quite with it. She was definitely coming down with something. Secretly Honor was relieved to have a quiet sister for once. It was refreshing to have the floor and be the one to start with a conversation she wanted for a change.

Honor sat on the edge of a chair opposite Joy, resting a cup of tea on her lap. "I was at the post office today – guess what Auntie Sheryl told me? Kodi was seen at the pub with Lachlan Chapman after netball practice on Thursday." Honor paused theatrically for the dire implications of this to sink in. "Apparently they were all lovey dovey, and didn't care who saw them." Her hands shook as she sipped tea.

Joy blinked, as if coming out of a trance. "They've started dating?" Everyone called the Post Mistress Auntie Sheryl but she wasn't actually a relative. She was, however, a busybody who blew gossip out of all proportion.

"That's what we all think," Honor said with a puckered face as if she'd snorted wasabi up her nose. "He's divorced and a single dad. What's Kodi thinking?"

"What's Lachlan thinking; she's only just turned twenty," Joy mumbled.

"Nowhere near mature enough to take on a ready-made family. Not to mention, Auntie Sheryl says Lachlan's ex-wife is a bit of a psycho." Honor paused realising how uncharitable that sounded. "I hope it's not gone too far. Col's got to talk sense into that girl." Honor went quiet, imagining Kodi's reaction, the stubborn, independent child that she was. It would not go down well.

Honor continued to vent about what she believed was an impending tragedy waiting to befall her family, needing sisterly support. Not used to such family disasters, she went on and on inventing worst-case scenarios, each one compiling on the other until it started to sound like a reality TV show. It would have been humorous, if not for her real distress.

Joy for once was the perfect listener, not interrupting to contradict any over-the-top narratives. She stayed unnaturally quiet, allowing Honor to spill out all her motherly concerns fully and completely. Gazing out picture windows to the garden beyond, daylight savings' sunbeams glittered through oak trees, shining on flower beds of crimson roses and shasta daisies. A picture-perfect scene of peace and tranquillity. Joy's heart constricted into a tight ball.

In truth, very little of what Honor was saying was getting through to Joy's conscious brain. Hearing someone else's problems served as a calming balm distracting but was not enough to dissipate the fugue gradually penetrating her mind. Aware enough to nod at appropriate times to indicate family solidarity, she lacked the energy to fully participate in the dramatics of the conversation. She sat and nodded, in a daze to which Honor was totally oblivious.

Taking a sip of cold tea, it caught in her throat causing her to choke. Her throat felt raw and swollen; maybe she was coming down with a sore throat.

"Are you okay?" Honor stopped momentarily.

Embarrassed at spluttering and coughing, Joy quickly mopped damp tea splotches from her blouse. "Sorry for being a klutz. It went down wrong."

"It will stain unless you wash it out as soon as you get home," Honor said automatically before returning to discussing Kodi's love life.

Joy waited until Honor's monologue ran its course.

Finally coming to an end, her sister's common sense prevailed. "Maybe it would be best to wait and not say anything. After all, it is Kodi's life. She is old enough to make her own decisions." Honor said this as if asking for Joy's opinion.

Suddenly too enervated to engage in further discussion, Joy deposited her teacup on a mosaic topped end table and stood up. With her last remaining presence of mind, she said what Honor expected her to say. "Whatever happens, you're her mum and you'll be there for her."

A look of relief crossed Honor's face. "You're right. Families must stick together."

"It will be alright, Honor. Trust the universe."

With a wan smile, Joy left Honor to ponder that comforting thought. Sitting in her car, she puzzled as to what possessed her to say such a trite aphorism.

Trust the universe?

The irony of the moment brought no sense of light relief. She couldn't compose a coherent thought to describe what Poppy had done only a few hours ago, yet here she was giving out sage advice to another as if she knew what she was talking about.

What stopped her and kept her silent about confessing she'd been strangled at work by her boss?

Of the two sisters, she was the one that always had a robust, controversial opinion about everything and anyone.

Except – not now. She'd sat there in front of Honor and hadn't been able to say a word about what had happened. She wanted to. Her sister would have sympathised. Normally the comfort would have been welcomed. So, what was going on?

Her brain had shut down; her body too, with a pervading feeling of numbness. It wasn't shame that kept her quiet. It was the inability to process an incomprehensible, random act of violence.

It wasn't until she was home, in the safety of home, standing in the kitchen looking through the fridge for some leftovers to heat up, that the panic set in. A heart racing so out of control it was bound to lead to a heart attack; a head spinning out of control with images of Poppy's hands around her throat, knowing she was going to die, helpless, powerless feelings of shock, horror, violation. Unable to make sense of what had happened. Spasms of nausea clenched her gut. She needed to cry, to scream, to purge – but couldn't do any of these things.

All she could do was curl up in a ball on the sofa and spiral down into hell.

Chapter Eight

Poppy's husband, Gil poked at the strip of carrot and lettuce leaves next to a saucer size quiche representing dinner. With a look of perplexity, he decided to fortify his empty stomach with a gulp of red wine. "Ah, that's good," he said grinning to placate his wife. Conan's plate of baked beans on toast looked more inviting. If the kid turned up his nose at it, then he might confiscate it for the sake of *not wasting food*.

Now was not the time to complain about this starvation diet she'd put them on. From her frown it was clear it had been a tough week at the centre. It was best for all concerned to keep her sweet.

In many aspects, his wife was the same fragile sweetheart he'd married all those years ago, needing reassurance and a strong shoulder.

He watched enviously as Conan tucked into the meal as if he'd not eaten in a week. Which was probably true given that his mother had gone on another ice binge leading to this emergency placement. The worst time for poor Poppy to be burdened with more responsibilities, but that was Poppy – couldn't say no to helping out, even if it was too much for her.

Later, he'd sneak an energy bar from a stash in a gym bag hidden in the boot of the BMW.

"Aren't you going to ask me about my day?" Poppy expelled a forced laugh. "Have I got some stories to tell."

Automatically Gil tensed at the recognisable display of tension. Quickly running through past conversations, he recalled something about an award ceremony happening. "Did you ace your public speech today?" he asked, desperate to engender a positive tone into the conversation.

"Ha. All the press and the politicians were there to witness my monumental stuff up. What a disaster! I tried to inject some humour into the proceedings – big mistake. Went down like a wet sheep in a dam."

"Sugar, I'm sure it wasn't as bad as all that," Gil soothed. "Not everyone gets your sense of fun."

"All I said was Jane was so confident about the Isle's health system that she had a hip replacement on the mainland."

Understanding the political inappropriateness of Poppy's joke, Gil's stomach fell. Knowing he couldn't say this, instead he burst forth in chuckles, slapping the table in raucous mirth. "Good one! That would have put a hot poker up their smug asses."

Conan, too little to understand the conversation, joined in the laughter with a mouth full of beans. Bits of chewed mush spat forth across the table. He wiped his mouth on a pyjama sleeve.

Poppy ignored the kid. "Nerves got to me. I blurted it out, without thinking. You should have seen Joy's face. It was priceless." Poppy started hysterical giggling. "All her careful organising and then I go and stuff it up!" Gil joined in the laughter hoping this would alleviate tension in the room.

"God I sometimes hate how easy everything is for her. You should see how much she eats for lunch." Poppy stabbed a knife into the quiche with a killing jab. "Like she could always do a better job given a chance," she grunted, continuing to stab at it until it resembled a mutilated carcass.

Gil nodded to indicate understanding, wary to say the wrong thing. Finishing off his glass of wine and pouring another, he let Poppy vent her frustrations about managing staff.

"Then at the end of the day, when I was packing up to go, Helen arrived out of the blue wanting to install a training package on Jane's computer. You know I had to get away early to collect Conan from daycare. She kept fiddling about, not sure how long it would take."

"That's the pits," Gil agreed.

"I got so mad I wanted to strangle her. But instead, I did what you told me. Just walk away. That's what I did. I walked out of the office to get fresh air."

"Good lass," Gil said.

"Well, actually no. Not so good." Poppy paused for effect. Gil took in a deep breath bracing for what was to come. "I found myself in Joy's office, standing behind her chair. Apparently, I upset her by giving her a spontaneous neck massage."

"You don't remember?" Gil asked. He knew all about her spontaneous neck massages.

"Not exactly," Poppy admitted. "Joy said something about strangling Helen instead of her." She waited for Gil's response, but he was speechless considering the implications of what she'd done.

Finally, in a contrite voice she said, "I may have crossed the line this time."

Gil wanted to remind Poppy that they'd had this talk before. Eventually these spontaneous stress releases were going to get her in serious trouble. His corporate managerial brain worked furiously, wondering how best to deal with this immediate problem. She'd been transferred from her last position due to a similar misunderstanding. Fortunately, the employer had agreed nothing had to go on record.

"Were there any other people around to see you do it? If not, then it's your word against hers. A manager against a subordinate."

"I may have accidentally mentioned something to Lachlan when we were checking out for the day."

"Shit, Poppy!"

"I felt terrible about it and apologised to Joy straight away. Then later when I saw her and Lachlan talking, I panicked and tried to lighten the situation by turning it into a joke."

"Hmmm, your outrageous sense of humour," Gil mused. "That's good. We can work with that." At one level, he understood his wife's dilemma. His position as Director, Business Strategy within a large construction firm had its moments. If he could have gotten away with strangling some of his staff, he probably would have as well.

He began to put together a strategy on how Poppy should handle the incident when she returned to work on Monday. It was important for her to control the narrative before Joy placed her own interpretation on the event. It was a neck massage. Poppy had to lead with this.

"First up, you need to give Jane a heads up and get her on side with your version of events. Plead stress from the workload she left you with; play on her sympathy. Then on Monday, you have to go in and convince Joy it was a misunderstanding. Can you do that?"

Poppy frowned, seeing Gil's concern and knowing she was in deep trouble this time. Joy was a stickler for the rules. She was going to be a problem. It was more important to convince Gil that all would be Okay. With a deep belly laugh, she said, "No worries, darling. Trust me. I can handle Joy – she's an amateur."

A bored Conan wiggled in the chair. "Can I have sweets now?" he whined, demanding attention.

The interruption was all Poppy needed to change the conversation to more practical matters. "How about tinned apricots and custard?" she asked. Pulling her bulky body from the dining table, she waddled into the kitchen. Setting three bowls on the benchtop, she decided they could all have dessert tonight. Occasionally rules were meant to be ignored.

Chapter Nine

Ten o'clock on Saturday Joy crawled out of bed, not having slept all night. She pulled on a cotton bathrobe over a t-shirt and pyjama bottoms, more for security than warmth. Her tired heart continued to pound relentlessly as it had for the last sixteen hours, as if running a Formula One trial on high octane.

To get to sleep last night, she'd tried deep breathing, hot brandy in milk, listening to music – nothing helped. A nightly habit of reading a novel to relax and guide stressful thoughts towards more pleasant narratives didn't work. She hadn't been able to concentrate; the words jumped and shimmered on the page out of focus, her mind spinning.

She hated this feeling, unable to control her racing heart. A scream of frustration – or was it terror? – stuck in her throat, unable to be expelled. Tears wouldn't come either. Weird because she usually cried easily, watching sad movies, reading sentimental poems, hearing tragic love songs, believing it was therapeutic to weep and wail on occasion to get it all out. Instead, a woozy numbness clouded her being, damming feelings, waiting until it was safe again to feel. Because feelings exposed a person, made one vulnerable. Feeling anything would blow her world apart.

This morning, thoughts like loose papers whirled around her mind with no place to catch and settle into sense making. Something terrible had happened to her. Poppy had strangled her. It didn't make sense. This couldn't happen at work; there were rules, policies, codes of conduct to protect her. A manager couldn't behave like that. But Poppy had...

Maybe it was somehow her fault? She should have been more assertive about personal space with Poppy. It was creepy the way Poppy stood too close, wanting to give massages... Maybe she'd given off the wrong signals, leading Poppy to believe it was ok to touch her. A wave of nausea overwhelmed Joy.

Not bothering to shower and dress, she paced from the lounge room to the kitchen in bare feet, shivering despite bright rays of sun streaming through the French windows warming the wool pile carpet. The Federation cottage was surrounded by birch and oak trees and remained pleasantly cool even in the heat of summer.

A soothing cup of tea would fix things.

On second thought, with a throat so raw, she wouldn't be able to swallow. Her stomach would throw it up.

She paced back to the lounge room, hugging her chest. Her jack hammer heart hurt so much she feared having a heart attack. Restless with no place to go, she wanted to run, escape, hide, do something to feel normal. All she wanted was for the gut clenching, disembodied terror to subside, dissipate, stop. And no matter what she tried, it wouldn't – it was in control.

Joy lay on the sofa clutching a soft blanket. Pulling it over her head, she created the closest she could manage to a dark, protective cave.

A knock on the back door startled Joy out of a zombie-like stupor. The cheerful hello of Gemma in the background unlocking the latch and letting herself in, set her mind at ease.

"Mum, are you alright?" Gemma called out. "Auntie Honor thought you were coming down with the flu?"

Gemma was bending over her, patting her back.

Joy flinched. She loved her daughter, but suddenly being touched caused her already rigid shoulder muscles to tense even more in a knee-jerk rejection of intimacy. "Something happened at work yesterday." Joy pushed up from the sofa and sat with the blanket covering her knees.

"What?" Gemma asked, taking in her mother's dishevelled attire.

Joy was lost for words. How did a person say the incomprehensible?

"Tell me," Gemma ordered, ready as usual to come to her mum's defence.

Staring quizzically at Gemma, she began to describe what happened in a flat, unemotional tone. "I was sitting at my desk, lost in concentration reading emails, and totally without any warning Poppy put her hands around my throat and told me she's strangling me instead of Helen. I thought she was going to kill me." Once she started telling the story, she couldn't stop. All the details came spilling out in a rush.

Gemma stood rooted to the spot, not saying a word until Joy finished. Then she shouted. "Wha-a-t the...? Why didn't you tell me earlier? Oh My God. This is serious, Mum. You were assaulted! You have to report it to the police."

Joy shook her head. "She's my boss. I don't want to get her in trouble."

"That doesn't matter! I'll report her if you don't." Gemma pushed the collar of Joy's robe away from her neck and began an inspection. "You've got red marks from where Poppy's hands bruised your neck," she stated with concern. "You need to see a doctor." Reaching into a jean pocket, she extracted a vial of emergency flower essence. "Open wide," she instructed, sounding like she was talking to Jaxon. Cold drops of homoeopathic alcohol were shaken under Joy's tongue.

Joy gulped from the sting. "She was so out of it I don't think she realised what she was doing or how hard she was squeezing."

"Oh Mum, I'm so sorry. You must have been so scared."

"I feel quite sick about it even now," Joy confessed. "I'm so tired, I didn't sleep at all last night. My heart was racing out of control." Staring out of the French windows to the wild garden beyond, she tried to recall what the protocols were for reporting injuries at work. "I should write up an incident report and send it to Occupational Health & Safety as soon as possible. But I can't think straight."

"Put in a grievance report," Gemma advised. "See how the department handles the incident. Decide later whether to report it to the police."

"Thinking about it, I'd better prepare Jane."

"This is bound to blow up."

"I feel bad bothering her at home on a weekend when she's recovering from a hip replacement."

"She'd want to know. It reflects badly on the centre, and they've just received an award for excellence. Not good."

"The department will have to stand down Poppy pending an investigation. She's clearly too stressed to continue acting as manager. They may want to bring Jane back early from leave. What a mess."

"I'll get your phone." Gemma walked over to a brocade handbag dumped at the entrance way and rummaged through it until she found Joy's mobile phone. "Make the call now, Mum, before you get too tired."

Punching in the speed dial code for Jane's home number, Joy's hand trembled from each unanswered ringtone. Finally, she heard Jane's brisk *hello.*

"Joy, I heard what happened. Poor Poppy – she must have been under such a lot of stress," Jane said.

Joy was taken aback by her manager's first words. Not sympathy for her but sympathy for Poppy, the strangler. She'd phoned prepared to spill out the story, but Poppy had got in first.

Joy remained speechless staring at the phone, unable to fully process the implications. Did Jane expect her to accept stress as an explanation for Poppy's bizarre behaviour?

Picking up on Joy's ultra-sensitivity, Jane added, "I'm sorry this was so upsetting." Too late to redeem herself in Joy's heart.

Still feeling the need for understanding, she tried to explain. "Poppy put her hands around my--"

Jane interrupted. "I know, a spontaneous neck massage."

"--coming from behind--"

"I know. Poppy gave me all the facts."

"There was no warning. I wasn't expecting--"

"I know." Jane cut in with a brusque tone. "Look if you need to take a couple days off, that's fine. No need to see a doctor for a medical certificate."

This was another disconnect that didn't make sense, throwing Joy off balance. Of course, she needed to get a medical certificate if she had days off due to an OH&S incident. It was workers compensation. She knew that much. Didn't Jane have a responsibility to explain the correct procedures to her?

"I need to put in an incident report, and I was hoping to go to the office tomorrow to write it up on the work computer? I can email it directly to the Occupational Health Officer as soon as possible."

Silence on the end of the line indicated Jane was thinking about it. "Sure. Okay." Her tone was all managerial lacking the softness of compassion. "I know Poppy is really upset. She didn't expect your reaction. Give her a chance to apologise before compounding it further." It sounded like a directive Joy was obliged to accept.

Joy ended the call with a growing sense of disorientation. Jane seemed so calm and collected, not worried in the least. As if it was just another day at the office.

Gemma gently pried the phone from her hand and guided her to a chair at the shabby chic kitchen table where a pot of English Breakfast tea brewed. "How did that go?" she asked, pouring nature's steaming miracle of succour into handmade pottery mugs and passing one across.

"Not like I expected," Joy answered in a daze. "I got permission to go to the office on Sunday." She cradled the mug and went thoughtful, her heart racing with anxiety. "Jane wants me to meet with Poppy."

"I'll come with you, Mum. You don't have to face her alone." Gemma's fierce support bolstered Joy's determination to face Poppy and set firm boundaries for the future.

"It's okay, Gem. I have to do it, no matter what."

Gemma studied her, as if deciding this was the truth. Slowly, she nodded. "Have you eaten today?" she asked, changing the subject. "Let me make you scrambled eggs. You'll feel better with something in your tummy."

Her daughter's motherly solicitude made Joy smile and feel normal again, even if for a short moment.

Chapter Ten

On Monday morning, Joy keyed in the security code at the centre at eight thirty a.m. sharp, dreading the meeting with Poppy. Not bothering to open up individual offices, turn on lights or her colleagues' air conditioners, she raced directly to her office cubicle and closed the door. The personal computer screen blinked on as soon as the mouse was pushed aside to make room for her brocade bag. She'd forgotten to turn it off yesterday after spending two hours composing a report for OH&S about "the incident". It had been a struggle to write objectively and put the event in an order that made sense while sick memories of being strangled kept drawing up raw emotions, making her feel like spewing. The report was emailed to OH&S and copied to senior management in the form of a grievance. She kept a hard copy, expecting some fall out despite Jane playing down its significance.

A favourite mug in a Persian pattern with a gold leaf rim, dirty with dried black dregs of coffee grounds left from Friday, taunted her fastidious nature. It could sit there forever, for all she cared. There was no way she could walk down the hallway to the kitchen to wash it without feeling exposed and vulnerable. Her whole body was shaking from nerves.

The plan was to stay long enough to say her piece to Poppy and then leave. The receptionist at Lower Teasel's Surgery had kindly fit her in to see Dr Vitkay as an emergency appointment in the afternoon.

The first staffer to wander in was Siobhan. After the usual pleasantries and signing in, the nurse walked off to her clinic. On the spur of the moment, possessed by an obsessive need to confide in a colleague, and edgy waiting for Poppy to arrive, Joy followed and cornered her in the children's play area.

"I need to tell you something terrible that happened on Friday," Joy said, her voice cracking from stress.

In a rush to get the clinic organised before patients began arriving, Siobhan faced Joy with a look of bare tolerance.

With self-centred anguish, Joy ignored Siobhan's press for time and poured out the whole distressing story, further humiliating herself by sobbing throughout the telling.

Siobhan reacted with shock. "That's sick!" she exclaimed, spontaneously reaching out to offer a hug.

Joy flinched and retreated a couple steps. However, this show of empathy gave some comfort and enabled Joy to pull together her fracturing emotions.

A pink handkerchief was dug from a jean pocket and used to wipe tears from the corners of her eyes. "I have to talk to Poppy about it. That's departmental policy. I needed a bit of support first." She blew her nose before stuffing the soggy cloth back.

Siobhan shifted feet on the spot and glanced around the room. "I'm sorry, but I have a lot to get done before the clinic opens. I won't be able to come with you."

"Oh, God no. I don't expect that. This is something I need to do on my own," Joy said with a decisive nod as if convincing Siobhan.

She walked back in the direction of her office, wracked with nervous tension but determined to get it over and done.

She ran into Poppy in the foyer.

"There's our Hun! I'm so sorry!" Poppy's booming voice sounded jolly and contrite at the same time. Mortified that Poppy wanted to do the *apology* conversation so publicly, Joy came to a dead stop.

Poppy kicked herself for forgetting to buy a bunch of flowers on the way to the centre, as Gil had suggested. In a last-minute act of desperation, she'd picked a purple petunia from the flower bed next to the car park. Thrusting it forward at Joy with fake aplomb aiming for a good ol' buddy attitude, she had to admit it looked wilted and pitiful – and clearly did not impress its intended target who just stood in the middle of the foyer with disgust written all over her face.

"I need to speak with you in private," Joy demanded.

The upstart wanted to play it formal and official, rather than as friends making up after a misunderstanding. Poppy's demeanour changed from bravado to calculating. "Come to my office," she said coldly.

Tossing the petunia in a waste basket, Poppy sauntered to the manager's office and took a seat in the swivel armchair. Posing relaxed, she waited like a good negotiator for Joy to open the discussion.

Joy closed the office door and remained standing. Looking down at Poppy, she waited for an apology or at least an explanation. When it was not forthcoming, she broke down in tears.

"I haven't slept all weekend. I didn't want to come to work today after what happened on Friday. I'm not coping."

In a measured tone, Poppy said, "I told my husband I may have overstepped the mark this time."

"Why me? Did you think it was part of my job description to be your personal stress ball?" Her voice came out tight, each word thrown like a stone.

Poppy waited to respond, eyeballing Joy, noting the flushed face, trembling hands. Clearly upset but trying to control her emotions.

Her first instinct was to crush the woman with a scathing denial, dismissing her interpretation of the event as an over-the-top reaction to a trivial misunderstanding. Make her feel small and foolish. Poppy was the boss with all the power in the situation. But Gil's advice to use Joy's natural tendency towards empathy was worth a try first. He usually reads people better than her.

"It wasn't about *you*. It could have been anybody. I was under a lot of stress with the award ceremony, Helen arriving when I needed to leave early, the TO DO list Jane left me getting longer every day; and then I took on extra work at home with this foster kid needing an emergency placement and that caused extra pressure at home. It's been fairly tough for me and I admit to not coping temporarily. My husband says my sense of humour can be outrageous at times, especially when under stress."

Joy nodded, seemingly appeased. Poppy smiled inwardly. The strategy was working.

Or maybe not.

"Do you think what you did was some kind of joke? It wasn't at all funny to me." Joy stared at her, accusingly.

Poppy was over it. Gil's managerial trick using empathy against her wasn't working. She shook her head warily, studying Joy, wondering where this was heading.

Flustered, Joy babbled on. "I don't talk about it but I've been a witness to domestic violence in the past. One of the reasons I moved to Eden Isle was to move to a safer, more peaceful life nearer family. When you came from behind and started strangling me, you caught me unawares. I was scared for my life. It felt like an assault. You probably didn't mean it to feel that way, but it did."

The audacity of being lectured at tested her patience. So much for Gil's plan. Looking away she fiddled with a pen on the desktop, casually twirling it around in circles. Knowing Joy, the woman wasn't going to let this go easily. She was going to be a problem.

Poppy affected a look of care and concern to encourage Joy to continue spilling her guts. All the time her mind worked at the next tactical move. It would be no good if Joy went blabbing to senior management. Down the track she'd cut her off at the pass. She grinned, amused at the cowboy analogy. An image of tightening a lasso around Joy's neck and choking the *feeling sorry for herself* spew from the whinger's mouth gave her momentary pleasure.

"You should know, I've spoken to Jane and put in a grievance along with an OH&S report," Joy was saying, almost sounding apologetic.

A grievance – the stuck-up bitch always on about rules and proper procedures. She was going to get her in trouble over this.

"You do what you have to do to follow procedure," Poppy said, acting the part of a composed and understanding manager. "Report it as an assault if you feel you need to." This last statement was a gamble. She needed to gauge the risk Joy posed. Did she intend to escalate the issue from an internal investigation to a legal matter?

Joy frowned. "I can't say right now what I'll do, but I don't want to get you in trouble. That's not my desire. We've worked well together before this happened. All I want is for your agreement to never touch me again – not in a bad way and not in a good way – ever again."

"Of course, Joy. I'll respect your personal boundaries from now on. No more spontaneous neck rubs. Got it." Poppy sensed a watershed had been reached in their conversation. She shifted in the chair preparing to stand up. "If you need to see the department's employee assistance counsellor, you have my permission to do so during work hours."

A look of relief crossed Joy's face. "Thanks, I will. I've got a GP appointment this afternoon, so I'll go now and take the rest of the day off as sick leave."

Poppy extracted her body from the chair and followed Joy out of the manager's office and down the corridor. She waited while Joy collected her handbag from reception and then marched alongside her as an escort out of the building. She expected Joy would see this move as supportive and caring, whereas it was a calculated tactic. She was pleased to note the curious looks from volunteers and staff, reminiscent of a previous administrative assistant being escorted out of the centre a couple years ago accused of stealing money from the jam jars.

Returning to her office, Poppy had an urgent call to make to senior management to fill them in on important background information – before Joy's emails were read.

Chapter Eleven

A vase of roses rested on the mantle of the fireplace in the old Victorian residence now converted to counselling chambers. At least an attempt with interior design had been made to set up the Employee Assistance Counsellors waiting room to convey a welcoming tone. The fact it hadn't succeeded was probably Joy's fault given her state of mind.

It had taken over a week to secure a crisis appointment, way too much time to ruminate. Irrational thoughts escalated and combined with erratic emotions spiralling into a black hole of heart pain. She was helpless to bring them under control. The world spun fearful and unsafe. She desperately needed to return to her old self, someone she recognised as calm and reasonable.

She hoped after a few sessions of therapy she'd be able to get her head straight about what happened and begin to work through it.

The only other occasion she'd felt this out of sorts was years ago when she went into shock after discovering her second husband's gambling addiction had left her deeply in debt. When first married and captivated by romantic lust, she'd trusted Pete with joint credit cards, joint bank accounts, and a joint mortgage. Unfortunately, it hadn't taken long for disillusionment to nullify the spell she'd fallen under. An empty bank account and maxed out credit cards will do that. If Pete had opened up and told the truth about losing all their money and got treatment for his addiction, they may have made it through the crisis. It was the cover-up that was the ultimate relationship killer. When the truth came out, he mistakenly believed she loved him enough to forgive the betrayal.

It only took one counselling session to realise she didn't.

It took many more to come to terms with the failure of another marriage and to let go of all the promises and dreams attached to it.

After the divorce, she vowed never again to mix romance and financial independence. The truth was at her age, after a mastectomy, arthritic knees, and a general decline in attractiveness, she'd probably never have another opportunity to put this resolve to the test.

It helped of course having a secure job that paid well in being able to recover from the set-back caused by her ex. From that day onwards, work became more than part of her identity. It came to represent a cradle of personal safety and financial security in a world not always safe for a woman.

Joy shook off bad memories and took a seat at the far end of the narrow room next to the magazines. She wasn't here to discuss the past. She needed to make sense of a more recent betrayal.

It was a relief to be here despite nervous exhaustion from a heart that would not stop pounding. The meds prescribed by Dr Vitkay couldn't be taken if *driving or using heavy machinery* according to the packet instructions. As much as they helped calm her, Joy followed directions meticulously and declined to take a tablet before driving to the appointment.

The dunny brown sofa cushions were too soft, the seat too hard; the background mood music was on the wrong radio station – and what was it about clinic waiting rooms where the magazines were as old as the building? Joy rifled through them to check. They were obscure ones she'd never heard of: Recreational Fishing, Horse Owners Quarterly. Also, it didn't help the ambience that a teenage girl wearing sunglasses hunched in a corner chair, a tissue held to a snivelling nose, scrolling up and down on a mobile phone.

Joy reached over and turned off the radio. The noise frazzled her nerves. The girl continued to scroll and ignored the intervention. Joy was grateful.

The counsellor was running late. Each passing minute intensified her nervous tension. Taking deep slow breaths, she attempted to relax muscles in her fingers that were clenched into fists. A drink of water would have been good but the bottle she'd meant to pack was at home on the kitchen bench. Currently her brain was mush, unable to plan ahead or remember much of anything.

"Joy, come this way," a soft voice from the doorway announced. Joy looked up to see a young woman with frizzy blonde hair tied back in a bright red head band. The counsellor was dressed in a baggy beige smock with black leggings and Doc Martins. Her demeanour radiated instant likeability.

They walked down a hallway to the counselling room with its wood floorboards creaking in harmony with her knees.

"I'm Bev. How are you?" Discreet eye contact indicated professional scrutiny had begun.

Joy didn't know where to begin to answer the question, especially in a public corridor. Wasn't *how she was* the whole reason for this hour-long counselling session? It was impossible to sum up her confusion, distress, incomprehensible anxiety in a few trite words. She managed to mumble *been better* for the sake of politeness.

They entered a spacious area with tall windows curtained in dark green velvet. The room was dim with natural light, and cool without the need for air conditioning. Joy thought it must have been a sitting room when it was a residence in the old days. It was furnished with functionality in mind: a couple of upholstered chairs opposite each other at one end, and a desk with a laptop, filing cabinets at the other end. A mobile phone on the desk pinged, announcing an incoming call. Only one exit.

A coffee table between the chairs had a box of tissues and a glass of water on hand. That was a relief.

After taking a seat, Joy took a few sips of water to hydrate a cottonmouth, waiting to see if Bev would answer the phone or devote all sixty minutes of their session to their conversation alone. This would be a good indicator of how their professional relationship would unfold.

Bev lifted a manila file from the table and studied it briefly before asking, "What can I do for you today?"

For Joy this question was as good as permission granted for the whole sorry story to gush forth. As much as Joy hated recalling the strangling incident, some obsession caused her to go over and over the details as if by doing so they'd begin to make sense. She needed to know what had possessed Poppy to do what she'd done.

The mobile phone pinged again, distracting Joy and causing her to pause. "Ignore that," Bev said. "I signed up to Facebook the other day. I'm involved in a group protesting the logging of old growth forests. It keeps letting me know when a message comes in." She waved for her to continue.

Joy forged on with an intense monologue. Toward the end she had an insight. "It was like my ex-partner, Pete. Towards the end of our marriage, he punched a hole in the wall during a fight and said afterwards that it should have been my head," Joy explained. "The next day he viewed the damage and laughed. I'll never forget him saying *look at that, did I really do that! I can't fucking remember!* Turning it into some kind of joke." She paused for a wave of nausea to surface and crash on the shoreline of her fragile equilibrium.

"Just like Poppy," Bev clarified.

"As if she expected me to laugh about it with her," Joy said, tears dripping down her cheeks. "Poppy never apologised either." Her ex dismissed the ruined wall, the same as he ignored the hole punched in her ruined heart. "It was just the once, but I left because of the unpredictability of the gambling situation. His lies felt like a betrayal of my trust. I guess I valued security more than my love for him. I never wanted to live in a state of not knowing what he'd do next."

"And now the fear has returned because of Poppy's behaviour which you didn't see coming."

"Exactly. I don't understand why she did it. Why me? I was sitting at my desk minding my own business; I'd done nothing to annoy her." Joy pulled several tissues from the box and blew her runny nose. "I reported the incident but now I feel awful getting her in trouble. I feel sad that our relationship has changed, where I can't trust her now."

"You need to focus on your needs now, not Poppy's feelings. Reporting it was the right thing to do."

"But why did she do it? It doesn't make sense."

"I'm not able to diagnose Poppy without personally seeing her and I can't – professionally that would be a conflict of interest. But from what you've said, it's likely she disassociated at the time and probably doesn't remember exactly what she did."

Joy dabbed her eyes miserably. "She was my boss. I liked her. Now she'll lose her job over this. But, I mean, who does that to their subordinate? It's totally nuts. She must have been temporarily crazy at the time. This scares the hell out of me."

"How has the department handled the incident so far?" Bev asked.

"I couldn't bring myself to go back to the office to get the forms to fill out for workers compensation, so I sent my daughter Gemma. Amberlie, the other office admin, gave her a hard time and kept saying come back tomorrow. When Gemma returned the third time and was given the run-around again, she put her foot down and demanded the forms."

"It's your right as an employee. They are supposed to provide the forms within two business days," Bev told her. "Otherwise you can lose pay, even with a medical certificate."

"I think it's because Amberlie's new to the job and doesn't know what she's doing. Anyway, she got aggressive with Gemma, told her not to raise her voice – Gemma hadn't, that was just Amberlie's excuse--"

"Were you able to put in a claim on time?" Bev interrupted, steering Joy to get to the point.

"The insurer has accepted my claim. My GP gave me two weeks off work. I'm waiting to hear back from the department on the grievance I submitted at the same time as the OH&S report."

Bev shook her head. "It's rare for a stress claim to be accepted by the insurer so quickly. Most of my clients are forced to go through a drawn-out legal fight to get their entitlements. In fact, your case is the first I've heard of where a claim was granted without any reservations."

Bev sounded as if she was surprised Joy achieved a difficult milestone so soon. Did this make her lucky or special or something? An employee getting a stress reaction after her boss's surprise strangled her would be a no-brainer for an insurer's approval process surely. Joy looked up, puzzled. "I just want them to keep Poppy away from me."

"The department doesn't have a history of taking these incidents seriously, I have to warn you. Another client of mine is off on stress leave after being traumatised by a male nurse exposing himself to her while on night shift. She refuses to return unless the department gives assurances he'll be transferred. Her managers have laughed it off, joking she's lucky to receive flirtations from a younger man. The union is liaising on her behalf, but it's been months and no progress has been made."

Joy was shocked. "But that's sexual assault; he could have raped her."

Bev glanced out the windows as if gaining composure. Clearly there was no love lost between the counsellor and her employer. "The department denied her workers comp arguing she's overreacted and there must be something in her history that's the real problem." She turned to Joy. "You must be careful what you say about your ex-partner from now on. It could be used against you in a workers compensation case being labelled a pre-existing trauma."

Joy stared wide-eyed in disbelief. Surely a manager strangling a subordinate had to be taken seriously by the department. "I left Pete ten years ago and I'm well and truly over the guy. Since then, I've been a hard-working employee and held high level positions over the course of a long career." Didn't that prove she recovered quickly and wasn't suffering any lasting trauma from that brief moment in her life? "In truth, my job was the saving grace, allowing me to get on with living. It kept me busy and not dwelling on Pete, my biggest mistake."

After Pete, Joy had followed guidance from self-help books to take control of her future. After paying off joint debts, she used her strategic skills to create a savings regime that aimed for a comfortable retirement. With only ten years left of work, she refused to consider retiring in poverty like so many women of her generation. A plan for financial security was mapped out, ticked off and operating smoothly.

"From a psychological perspective, previous traumas never go away. They lie dormant until a door is opened through another trauma." Bev pronounced this with an air of wisdom.

Joy's heart sank. "I wrote something in the incident report about having witnessed domestic violence in my past." She kicked herself. "I was in fact thinking about my daughter and her ex-partner's relationship, not Pete." Why hadn't she gotten around to signing on with the union? In every other job, she'd been a member.

"I won't write anything in my notes," Bev reassured. "The counselling experience will teach you how to reframe your thoughts to desensitise to past trauma. Without the expertise of a qualified psychologist, what can happen is that the more you remember an unpleasant experience and talk about it, the more you also freshly recreate it in your memory, in effect re-traumatising yourself time and time again. Good news is that the brain is pliable and capable of transforming old beliefs through Cognitive Behaviour Therapy – CBT. We'll work together to help you re-write the scripts from past traumas to lessen their negative impacts on your present. How does that sound?"

Joy breathed a sigh of relief. "That sounds wonderful."

With a flick of a wrist, Bev checked an antique watch peppered with shiny jet jewels. "We've gone over time," she said, switching from an empathetic persona to a business one. "My initial assessment confirms Dr Vitkay's. You have a post-traumatic stress reaction from the incident at work. I suggest we meet weekly for the next month to check on how you're coping." Bev handed across a Department of Health brochure titled *Understanding Trauma Reaction* along with a typed sheet on *Releasing Emotions*.

Joy shoved them into her handbag and pulled out a pocket diary to write down dates and times for future sessions. Getting up from the chair, her body felt stiff and achy. She walked from the room hunched like an old lady needing a walking stick.

Back at the car, the inside was boiling hot from being parked in the sun. She turned on the air conditioning, switched the fan to high and waited in the driver's seat unable to drive until the woozy gauze cleared in her head. The tight fit behind the steering wheel felt confined and claustrophobic. She'd talked too much. Not accustomed to over-sharing private feelings with anyone other than family, this self-indulgence sat in her gut similar to undigested take away fried chicken – part guilty pleasure, part nauseous mistake.

Faintly dissatisfied, the session hadn't been as helpful as needed. Bev had focused on understanding Joy's responses to the incident and that was okay. More importantly, what she hadn't addressed was the elephant in the room – Poppy's bizarre behaviour.

What was wrong with Poppy? This was what Joy needed to know in order to work out what decisions to make about her future. If she returned to work, what could she expect? How safe would it be? What did the department need to do in order to protect her? These were all questions requiring answers before she could ever contemplate returning to her job.

The car interior began to cool enough for the steering wheel to be touched without burning a hand. Suddenly, Joy had an urgent need to get away as fast as possible. But where to go? The cottage seemed empty and lonely. She didn't want to burden Gemma with problems. Honor would be at home but could she handle her sister's well-meant platitudes at this time?

The worst concern, more mundane, was not knowing what to do with herself during the yawning gap of two weeks off work on sick leave. The meds made her dopey and unmotivated; not feeling normal. She was not used to being idle and unproductive, lying on the sofa watching soap operas on the TV.

Bereft, she tried to shake off the dread accompanying the black hole of uncertainty. It was an unfamiliar experience to be so muddled in thinking she was unable to plot a course ahead even for the next couple hours. Her forte, and sense of pride, was in making order out of chaos through planning and establishing procedures, checklists and numbered steps to achieve goals. Not knowing what next step to take over the next couple hours, let alone the next couple weeks, was disorienting and left her feeling helpless.

Restless and needing some form of escape from the peculiar emotions playing havoc with her sanity, and being in town already, she forced a decision. She would take advantage of Plover Point's shopping mall, grab some lunch and get in some retail therapy. This was what she'd normally do in times of stress.

After dragging her feet around the shops for a couple hours, Joy regretted the idea retail therapy would relax her. Instead, she felt tired, faint and sick to her stomach. Not being able to make a decision about the smallest purchase, she hadn't bought a thing. At first, she decided the woozy cotton wool sensation in her head was due to lack of food. But after stopping for a salad sandwich and a strong cup of coffee, her anxiety grew worse. The notion of driving through rush hour caused immediate panic. How was she going to concentrate with a head full of fog? She obsessed so much about this, she almost called Gemma to pick her up and take her home. But pride in being independent won the day.

Making it home with only one minor error in judgement – that gained a finger from an irate driver – Joy collapsed on the sofa and curled up in a foetal position.

At six thirty, Gemma and Jaxon checked in to see how the counselling session went. "Mum, are you okay? You look white." She felt her forehead, noting it was clammy. Jaxon stood in the background keeping his distance, unsure about his granny.

"My stomach's cramping. I shouldn't have eaten when I was in town."

"I'm worried about you. I think you should stay with me and Jaxon tonight, just to be on the safe side."

"It's anxiety, Gem. There's nothing to do but ride it out until it dissipates in its own good time."

"This can't go on. I'm going to put you on a natural therapy regime, starting with Hypericum. My clients have gotten good results from it. Stop taking those anti-depressant meds the GP prescribed. They're not doing you any good."

Joy was too exhausted to argue, especially when Gemma was in her natural therapist role. She trusted her daughter's expertise even though it conflicted with Dr Vitkay's. His meds made her tired and weepy. Maybe it was worth giving Gemma's prescription a try. She'd think about it – later.

As much as she loved Gemma and Jaxon, it was a relief when they finally left her alone. That night she crawled into bed at eight thirty and slept for twelve hours.

Chapter Twelve

Fiona Blackwell snapped shut the Occupational Health & Safety Committee's file containing a copy of her monthly report on the mid-north, the area of Eden Isle under her management as Community Health Coordinator for the department. The wall clock read five minutes to midday, but it ran slow, like most government operations. Most annoying. Taking one last gulp from a take-away cappuccino to brace her nerves, she gathered notes and a pen prepared to face her boss, Leland Gunn.

He'd called this high noon meeting to discuss Quamby Bluff Community Health Centre before they faced the Committee's questions this afternoon. She'd been foolish to hope he'd be too busy to read her report or miss the significant incident. No such luck. It stuck out like a puss-filled pimple at the tip of a nose ready to pop. She wondered if he'd buy her explanations and provide back up if the Chair decided to drill down into details. *The less said the better* was the motto she lived by.

She entered the sombre quiet of the Regional Manager's office and took a seat by a round coffee table at the back of the room, spreading out notes.

Leland scrawled a signature on some papers and slid the bundle into an out tray before joining her.

"Good to see you, Fiona," he said. His effusive charm did not fool Fiona. The man was a sharp political player with ambitions for the top job. "What can you tell me about Joy O'Connell's bizarre account at our star performing health centre?"

Fiona paused to steady her nerves. Not a good sign if Leland was leading with the *Centre of Excellence* agenda. This flagged the issue as red hot not only internally but also outside of the department into the larger government arena. She prayed the Minister of Health was not in the loop already. "I've spoken to the manager acting at the centre while Jane Manners is on sick leave. Poppy Bryant admitted to placing her hands around Joy's neck as a gesture of light relief. She often gives staff massages on the spur of the moment. Joy has totally over-reacted in this instance."

Leland nodded with an air of wisdom. "I see. Has she taken any days off work as a consequence?"

Fiona flicked through her notes and pulled out the original medical certificate and squinted at the scribbled writing. "Her GP diagnosed a stress reaction and gave her time off to rest at home. He also recommended counselling. Poppy sent her to our employee assistance counselling service. We expect her to return to work soon."

"I believe the insurer has approved Ms O'Connell's claim for workers compensation?"

Leland was shrewd. He already knew the facts and was testing her. With the insurer accepting a claim without question the stakes were raised higher, formalising it into a Worksafe matter. The unanswered question on the table was how she was going to manage perceptions, including answering the grievance Joy had lodged. "I understand her claim flags potential liability issues that I will need to manage," she answered, stating the obvious.

Leland looked satisfied. Getting down to practicalities, he said, "First, I want business as usual to continue at the centre. We don't want to give the impression that anything out of the ordinary occurred. Do many staff know what happened?" Leland's eyes drilled into Fiona's like lasers of judgement.

"Poppy confided to the centre's social worker during a counselling session. I believe she also said something in passing to a youth worker. I don't think Joy would have had time to say anything; she left work fairly quickly." Fiona's voice trailed off. It didn't look good.

"Second, it's crucial we keep a lid on this. We don't want staff gossiping and running down the centre. Make sure all staff and volunteers understand their obligations as government employees for confidentiality in what is above all a highly personal matter."

With dawning understanding, puzzle pieces started to fall into place. Fiona knew what Leland expected of her. "It may not be relevant, but you should know – Poppy said that on the day of the incident, she'd questioned Joy about toilet paper missing from the store's cupboard. Someone's been pilfering supplies and Poppy was trying to get to the bottom of it." When Leland laughed, Fiona blushed at the unintended pun. "She wasn't blaming Joy, at least not out right. But the implication is that Joy's over-the-top reaction later that afternoon could have been due to guilt."

Leland leaned back in the chair and gazed up at a framed original oil painting on the wall, as if studying it for inspiration. With its splotches of orange, smears of red and trails of black paint, to Fiona the canvas was so abstract it could represent anything from a scene of carnage to a madman's nightmare. Perfect for the occasion.

"We can't accuse her of anything at this time. Not while she's off on workers compensation. That would look like a set up." Leland rubbed his nose, thinking. "If she's a security risk, you'd better get her office keys back." As an afterthought he added, "And assign a return to work coordinator to keep a watch on her. We have to be seen to meet our obligations under the Act."

Fiona jotted notes to remember all the instructions.

"Out of curiosity, does Jane want Joy back?"

Fiona looked up, puzzled. "You mean given a choice between keeping Poppy on as Acting Manager and Joy being transferred out?"

Leland returned to gaze at the oil painting rather than answering, remaining neutral.

Fiona was unsure how to frame a response. She decided to tread carefully, anticipating what he wanted to hear.

"Apparently, Joy is not well liked by some of the staff and volunteers. Poppy was saying Joy got them off-side with her zealous campaign to receipt everything. They feel like she's treating them as cheats and criminals. It's my fault, I'm afraid. I arranged for Joy to transfer from head office to the centre with the imprimatur to improve the admin systems, but she got carried away, went over the top."

"Hmm," Leland said. "No love lost if she doesn't return to the centre then." It wasn't a question, more a summary spoken aloud. He moved to get up, signalling the meeting closed. "If there's nothing more..."

"One last thing," Fiona rushed to add. "I'm drafting a response to the grievance."

"Good. Run it past me before sending it out." As Fiona walked to the door, Leland contributed last pieces of advice. "In your letter, try to smooth out the situation so it doesn't escalate." Noticing Fiona's worried expression, he mused, "Mollify Joy's sense of wrong with... not quite regret or apology but... a reinterpretation of Poppy's behaviour that downplays its inappropriateness... make it seem... unacceptable but not intended to distress her."

Leland returned to sit at the executive desk. "Let's see if that will work," he said quietly as if speaking to himself.

Fiona entered her well organised office taking in the neat stacks of files in bamboo trays, bookshelves filled with colour coded policy folders in alphabetical order, and a leather diary opened to a current To Do list. Too late it occurred to her that Leland hadn't spelled out a strategy for the committee meeting in the afternoon. Her confidence faltered wondering how to reinterpret Poppy's crazy into harmless fun in such a way that committee members would buy the story. She suppressed a moment of guilt about Joy, whom she'd mentored and transferred into the position at Quamby Bluff Community Health Centre for the express purpose of establishing auditable administrative systems after the previous receptionist was implicated in regularly pocketing half of the centre's banking over a long period of time. Shafting the woman for the sake of bureaucratic expediency didn't feel good, but it was part of the job description.

Hopefully Leland would take the lead to assuage the committee members' concerns. She didn't want to be the fall guy if their fabricated narrative didn't pan out.

Chapter Thirteen

Gemma's pacing dug grooves in the family room carpet at her Aunt Honor's. At the same time, she waved a crumpled letter from the Department of Community Health in righteous fury.

Joy curled up on the sofa under the influence of an acute attack of anxiety, unable to respond to the ravings. After collecting the registered letter from the post office and deflecting Auntie Sheryl's nosey questions, she'd made it to her sister's place and then collapsed in a heap of emotional stress. The response to the grievance was not what she'd expected. She needed calming support and rational discussion. Gemma's hot-headed outrage was not helping the situation, even if it demonstrated an unwavering loyalty.

Honor was busy in the kitchen preparing a tray of tea and biscuits with the aim of smoothing troubled waters, staying out of sight until her niece's venting ran out of steam.

"*Regarding the alleged strangling...*" Gemma read from the one page letter with disgust "*...Mrs Bryant admitted to being under a lot of stress at the time concerning another employee and admitted she placed her hands around your neck albeit in a joking manner!*" Her shouting caused Joy to flinch. "How does a boss strangle a subordinate in a joking manner?" she asked with arms raised to the ceiling dramatically. "*We don't condone this type of behaviour from an employee of the State Service...*" she continued pacing, "*...and have reminded Mrs Bryant to re-read the department's policy on Respectful Behaviour in the Workplace... she promises to return as a future role model for the Centre's staff. Taking into consideration her exemplary employment record and her remorse, I have determined no further action into this matter is required...* You've got to be kidding me. That's their disciplinary action in response to what happened – she's going to be a frigging role model – I don't believe it."

Joy roused herself enough to sit upright. "It would be funny if it wasn't so lame," she said meekly. A strangling neck massage had now become one done in a joking manner. The employer's response to the incident was a slap in the face of the victim. They chose to put more weighting on Poppy's *opinion* on *why* she did it rather than the facts and evidence of *what* she did – placing more importance on forgiving Poppy's stress at the time rather than acknowledging the seriousness of Joy's traumatic reaction afterwards.

So much for thinking she'd get Poppy in trouble and that she could lose her job over it. Instead, they were treating it like an innocent misunderstanding. A manager temporarily loses her mind and takes out her stress on an unsuspecting admin assistant by strangling her, and the department dismisses the grievance as if it was a normal day at the office giving staff neck rubs. Joy's stomach clenched in pain. How could she return to work under these circumstances?

"So Mum, this is what you have to do next time your boss tries to strangle you: wave a copy of the Respectful Behaviour Policy in her face – or better yet, get it laminated and use it as a shield. That should hold off the nutter until she comes to her senses and magically transforms into a model citizen!" Gemma danced around the room in a theatrical display parodying a sword fight, using the letter to fend off imaginary thrusts.

Despite feeling gutted, Joy had to laugh.

Honor picked this moment to enter the family room carrying a tray of rattling teacups. "Do you think Poppy might have thought she was being funny and didn't mean to scare you? She and her husband Gil go to our church every Sunday with that little foster kid. They seem like such a nice family."

Both Gemma and Joy stared at Honor dumbstruck.

"I mean maybe give her the benefit of the doubt, that it was a stupid thing to do but she was stressed and didn't mean to...." Honor stopped after the dawning realisation that playing devil's advocate was not helping.

"Who does that? I mean nobody does that Auntie Honor. You don't assault someone and threaten to kill them as stress relief." Honor looked abashed.

"Homer Simpson has a lot to answer for," Joy said, trying to inject a lighter perspective before the situation blew up. Unintended, a flashback of Pete punching in a wall and laughing in her face gripped her stomach in a vice.

"Yeah, maybe it's funny in cartoons but not in real life," Gemma snorted in disgust, flinging onto a cushioned chair with dramatic flair. The letter scrunched in her hand. "The same as sticking your foot out to trip up someone isn't seen as humorous nowadays. It's not funny to deliberately hurt someone, and it's just wrong to laugh about it afterwards."

In a motherly gesture, Honor handed around teacups with a chocolate chip cookie the size of a twenty cent coin on each saucer. After saying her piece and Gemma jumping at her like a wildcat, she kept quiet.

"You want to know what the joke is? The policy states the department has *zero* tolerance for disrespectful behaviour. It sets out a list of increasingly severe sanctions from warnings on a personnel file to demotion and losing your job depending on how bad it is." Joy bit into a cookie and chewed vigorously, allowing the irony to sink in. "It doesn't even mention physical violence. It only talks about disrespect in the context of verbal abuse and bullying."

"I guess having to read the tedious policy in full was considered the ultimate punishment for a disrespectful manager," Honor commented drolly trying to redeem herself, before sipping tea.

Gemma laughed. "Gives new meaning to the word *zero*." Jumping from her chair, she commanded in a stage voice, "*We won't tolerate disrespect in our workplace, so ple-e-ease stop disrespecting one of our managers by complaining about being assaulted.*"

Joy signalled for her to sit down. "As if a manager is not expected to be familiar with departmental policies beforehand," she said with slumped shoulders. "How could they allow her to manage staff if she didn't know HR policies?"

"When we said zero tolerance what we meant by *zero* was – if a stressed-out manager accidentally strangles a subordinate before realising it's against the policy, then of course it's only fair to give them one more chance," Gemma mimicked with sarcasm.

"The problem for me is they've established a new precedent with this. If they won't penalise a manager's behaviour for strangling an employee, then where do they draw the line?" Joy asked.

"They've set an impossibly high bar," Honor agreed.

"What's left? Poppy would have to kill someone, I guess, before your department took an assault seriously," Gemma said with a concerned frown.

"But don't forget, if she hadn't read the zero-tolerance policy stating it was disrespectful to kill your subordinate at work, then the department would have to give her another chance to be a role model – taking into account her perfect employment record and the fact she apologised afterwards," Honor quipped.

Joy and Gemma laughed, even though her words were horrific and not actually funny.

The room went quiet as they considered the implications. Finally, Gemma spoke up.

"Mum, if you don't report it to the police already, I'm doing it for you."

Chapter Fourteen

How quickly a potentially romantic date with a burning hot guy combusted into a fire blackened landscape of disappointment, Kodi belatedly conceded. Grabbing a fist of free peanuts from a plastic bowl provided at the bar during happy hour at Draught Horse Pub, she chewed vigorously while preparing the next argumentative onslaught. Sitting on a bar stool next to her, Lachlan concentrated on nursing a schooner of frothy beer, looking shell shocked and chastened.

"So, you are telling me you can't remember anything that was said between you and Poppy that afternoon? Not even my Auntie Joy complaining about Poppy squeezing her throat too hard?"

"As I said before, it sounded like office banter. I was in a rush to collect Dora from childcare and I didn't take any notice of a thirty second exchange."

"But you have to try! Auntie Joy's reputation is being smeared and she's in no position to defend herself. Poppy has free rein to put whatever spin she wants on things, and no one can dispute it. My aunt is an innocent party in all this. You've got to speak up and help her case!"

Suppressing the sinking feeling that her excessive pushiness sounded a lot like his psycho ex-wife, Kodi inhaled the wrong way. A salty peanut skin caught in her throat causing a scratchy irritation that resulted in a spluttering cough that sprayed bits of chewed peanuts into the air. Her face turned a most unattractive shade of red. She gulped cherry cider and held up a hand to indicate she wasn't choking. This was turning out to be the worst date ever.

Lachlan shook his head, perplexed at her intense persistence. "Look, all I vaguely recall is Poppy joking about scaring Joy." Seeing Kodi's hopeful expression, he quickly added, "but I don't remember her exact words or any context."

"If you came forward with this information..." Kodi pleaded.

"It won't do any good. Trust me." Lachlan leaned forward for a make-up kiss. Kodi pulled back with a jerk. Making another attempt at peace, he said, "My dad advised your aunt to seek legal advice."

"He would say that," she scoffed.

"Dad says if they haven't already assisted Joy back to work as quickly as possible that means they most likely don't want her to return." He looked apologetic.

This insight was too much for Kodi to cope with. In one last ditch effort to convince Lachlan to stand up for what was right, she launched into more pleading. "Tara told mum that when counselling Poppy the woman was bewildered at what she'd done. But Poppy has turned it around by telling everyone it is bewildering as to why Joy left so suddenly! That's how rat cunning the woman is."

"Poppy is my boss. I have to work with her." He swigged beer, swallowed a belch, obviously content with his own reasons not to rock the boat.

Kodi remained unmoved at that selfish career decision. In fact, she wanted to punch the smug look off his face. "And Joy is only *the admin*," she said dripping with sarcasm. "They should have stood Poppy down. She's a danger to staff. The woman's batshit crazy."

"We're all a bit scared of her to be perfectly honest," Lachlan conceded. "No one wants to get on her wrong side."

"But you're still not going to do anything about it?" Kodi accused with a glare of disgust. If looks could laser beam sense into someone's brain…

At the back of her mind, where emotions were rational and calm, a part of Kodi understood all too well Lachlan's position. Eighteen months before, in her first job out of school working for Quamby Bluff Shire Council, she'd been in a similar position, afraid of her boss and afraid to expose the corruption happening under her nose. That experience left in its wake an important lesson: holding back vital information and not wanting to get in trouble with the boss caused all kinds of trouble for innocent people later on.

Unfortunately, it also left Kodi with a deep abiding righteousness about speaking truth to power. She was a lot like her Auntie Joy in this respect. Once she dug her heels in, she was fixed in position and would not be moved.

Holding her head high, she announced, "I'm sorry, Lachlan, but I can't forgive you if you stay silent when you could help my Aunt. It's just not right. Family is my priority."

Lachlan had tried to remain a good sport throughout Kodi's rambling lecture. She was young and immature, with the stereotypical temper of a redhead. He liked her and apart from this evening, they usually got on fine, for all of the four weeks they'd been seeing each other. But that didn't mean he had to take any more of her naïve criticisms. "Right. I'm done for the night." He thumped an empty beer glass on the bar and stood up ready to leave. "Do you need a lift home?" he asked, more abrasively than intended.

Kodi's face crumpled. "Not from you," she huffed with bravado.

"See you later then," he smirked, trying to lighten their parting. He was sure he felt Kodi's imaginary daggers pummelling into his back as he strutted out of the pub.

＊＊＊

Kodi's parents were having a quiet night in, drinking a glass of red in front of the TV. Lucky for his daughter, Col answered the phone. Honor would have asked too many questions before agreeing to collect Kodi from the Draught Horse.

As it was, Honor couldn't help expressing an opinion about her daughter's love life.

"What kind of man takes a young girl to the pub for a date?" she asked while Col grabbed his car keys from the hall table. She was looking for reasons not to like Lachlan.

"It's a place to have a quiet drink after netball practice," Col answered, injecting reason into the conversation. "Don't fuss, dear heart."

"He can't even be bothered giving her a lift home. That's not very considerate." Honor stood holding the door open, dithering about whether to accompany Col. "Maybe he's over the limit. That's why he didn't want her in the car. I don't want our daughter dating a young man with a drinking problem."

Col exhaled a gruff laugh. "If he's over the limit – which I doubt knowing his family and how respectable they are – then he's being responsible by not driving Kodi home."

Honor stopped to contemplate this perspective. "He does come from a good family. Lachlan's father is a lawyer in Plover Point and his mother is a physiotherapist." Col pecked a kiss on her cheek and moved past.

"Occupational therapist," he corrected.

"I'm coming with you," she decided. "I want to check things out for myself."

As Col pulled the door shut, she pondered, "What would have happened if we'd been away and not available to pick up Kodi?"

Col smiled, took a deep breath, and prayed for patience. "She'd most likely walk home, my dear. It's only two or three kilometres from the pub."

"You're deliberately missing my point," Honor complained as Col opened the passenger door of the Mazda sedan for her.

Kodi was waiting out front under a spotlight of the pub's wide veranda. Her feet were doing a shuffling dance as if she couldn't stand still and wanted to get away as soon as possible. The give-away clue to her mood was in how she crossed her arms and chewed a nail on her index finger. As a dad, even without Honor's motherly intuition, he could tell things had not ended well between Kodi and Lachlan on this occasion.

Col pulled the car into a parking space and beeped the horn gently. Kodi waved and ran over, jumping in the back seat. "Thanks," she said, buckling the seat belt.

After a few minutes of silence, Honor lost patience. "Okay, tell me why Lachlan couldn't be bothered taking you home?"

Col darted a frown at Honor. "We don't mind picking you up, honey, any time, from anywhere."

"I know, Dad. Thanks." Kodi looked out the window as they passed shops on the main street of Lower Teasel. She gathered her thoughts. "It was my fault. I guess we sort of had a fight. He would have taken me home, if I'd wanted him to – but I didn't."

"What happened?" Honor asked out of concern, and nosiness.

Kodi sighed dramatically. "I got stuck into Lachlan about Auntie Joy. He claims not to remember any of the conversation when he was signing off that afternoon. I was pushing him to put in a statement with management to help her credibility. But he won't do it for me."

Col glanced at the back seat and saw the dejection in Kodi's slumped shoulders. "Honey, you've got to realise Lachlan is a young man with a bright future. It's in his best interests not to get involved. Joy's incident is a sensitive one."

"I can't forgive him if he doesn't speak up. Auntie Joy is getting slandered by gossip. It's not fair." Joy's voice raised with passion.

"You are a lot like Joy," Honor commented philosophically. "Always wanting what's right, speaking out against injustice. But you'll learn, hopefully not the hard way, that you can't force people into doing what's right."

"Each to his own conscience," Col agreed.

"It's called WIFM – the *what's in it for me* principle." Honor twisted to smile encouragement at her daughter.

"Kodi, your young man would be best to keep out of it. There may be liability issues at some stage. Under the Act, all employees are responsible for safety in the workplace. If Lachlan knew Joy wasn't safe, he should have taken action then and there – not walk away and ignore it."

"Are you implying he's equally guilty?" Kodi demanded, surprised at a sudden protective regard towards Lachlan.

"No, honey. I'm just saying..." Col concentrated on the road and didn't say another word.

Honor was unusually quiet as well. Col was impressed with her restraint knowing she'd be itching to ask Kodi if they'd broken up. He was sure she was sitting there with fingers crossed.

Chapter Fifteen

A flushed Gemma escorted Constable Chugg to the door while Joy remained seated at the kitchen table feeling unsure about whether reporting the incident to the local police had been a good idea. Although the constable didn't know Poppy personally, he spoke in glowing terms about how important Quamby Bluff's Health Centre was to the community. He was all praise and compliments about Jane's hard work making it successful after the government almost closed it down fifteen years ago. *What would Lower Teasel do without it?* he'd asked rhetorically. *How long have you lived in Eden Isle?* he'd asked more pointedly. Joy was sure this was a deliberate attempt to make her reconsider pressing the issue and causing a stain on its perfect reputation.

He'd listened to her account with a faint hint of scepticism and refrained from asking in-depth questions. He didn't take down notes. Apparently, this first interview was only preliminary. He would need to interview Poppy and hear her version of the incident before deciding on how to proceed. It would come down to Joy's word against Poppy's.

Joy had to admit when she related the strangling to a dispassionate official, someone who didn't know her personally, it did make her sound like the crazy one. Who ever heard of a boss strangling an employee out of the blue – for no reason? The only redeeming feature to her version of events was that no one could possibly have the kind of imagination that would make up a story like this. It was too bizarre.

Gemma returned to the kitchen with a look of chagrin. "Sorry, mum. That didn't go like I expected. On TV the cops are all sympathetic and ready to jump in to defend the defenceless victim, raise the banner of justice and stick it to the bad guy."

"Yeah, well, no…" Joy cradled her head in her hands. Seeing her daughter's crestfallen face, she said, "I'm glad we did it. It was the right thing to do. It's only fair he needs to interview all the parties involved before taking further action. The centre's reputation is at stake. There could be some backlash from members in the community. I don't want to get Poppy in trouble. I just want to keep her away from me."

"What's the point of interviewing her if she's not obliged to answer his questions? That doesn't seem fair to me."

"It's all a mystery. I've never had to do something like this before. The whole issue about proving *intent* seemed to be a problem for the constable. How can someone strangle a person without knowing this would cause them harm? It seems like a no-brainer. But the law sees it differently than us average citizens. We'll just have to wait and see."

Relieved her mother was being philosophical and not holding the disastrous interview against her, Gemma brightened. "On a positive note, he did say there was always a first time for every criminal. He wasn't dismissing the matter completely."

"It did bother me when his first question was how the department handled it internally, as if that made a difference." Joy gazed out the window, caught up in thought and not really seeing the overgrown garden beyond. Fatigue wrapped around her shoulders like a life sapping cloak.

"He was gauging how seriously they were taking it. Which doesn't go well in my favour."

"Didn't the letter from Fiona Blackwell say don't hesitate to contact her if you have any further concerns?" Gemma looked crafty. "If it was me, I'd take up the offer and give her a serve... I mean why don't you highlight your concerns for the record?"

"If you think it might make a difference..." Joy was ambivalent. On one hand, she felt a need to point out the department's error in judgement in the matter. Afterall, they'd based their conclusions on an incident report and one interview with Poppy, whose career was on the line. Of course, she'd put the best possible spin on the incident.

No one bothered to interview Joy personally, *the victim*, to hear her version of events. She was after all the only other employee involved and present at the time of Poppy's crazy behaviour.

If they had bothered to speak to Joy, they would have seen Poppy's version of events simply did not make sense. No boss would come up from behind and surprise an employee with a neck massage – applying enough pressure to cut off breathing – in a joking manner. That was crazy thinking.

The proof was in the after effects of the assault on her nerves. Dr Vitkay's medical certificate supported this. The insurer in accepting the workers compensation claim supported this.

Management had stopped at the point where they heard the version they wanted to hear. The version that was the simplest and least controversial.

The question on her mind: was it worth protesting procedural unfairness, voicing concerns, and rocking the boat even more?

Joy had loved working at the centre. She wanted to get back to the job. She didn't want to be a troublemaker.

But if the department refused to label strangling as occupational violence and manage it accordingly, then she would never feel safe returning. It was in her nature to try to explain this for the sake of the truth. For the record.

But not today. Right now, she needed to lie down and take a nap.

Chapter Sixteen

The call to her old mentor, Fiona Blackwell, had been a mistake. It had taken a full week before Joy built up the courage to make the fateful phone call. That was not a bad thing. She'd practised her argument, composed her thoughts; taken a nap so she'd be refreshed before phoning. All good.

Where had it all gone pear shaped?

With a sinking feeling, Joy perched on the edge of the Oriental scarlet bedspread in her master bedroom flustered and perplexed as Fiona ended their conversation rather brusquely.

The conversation had started off quite professionally. She'd thanked Fiona for the expedient response to the grievance and for the opportunity to discuss concerns arising from the findings of the investigation. But as she related more and more of her side of the story, anxiety got the better of her. It felt as if her brain ceased to function. She lost words, lost her train of thought, lost the plot.

During the disjointed monologue, Fiona had retained the poise of a seasoned public servant: super rational with the right tone of sympathy, with an unwavering, unmovable hold on her initial position. *Your concerns are noted* was her standard reply to each and every point Joy managed to bumble.

Joy was no fool. Throughout a long career, she worked in the government for enough years to understand *noting her concerns* meant they would be filed away in a bottom drawer of a secure filing cabinet, never to see the light of day. *Thank you for calling.* So polite. So not caring. It was frustrating to realise suffering from trauma meant she was not at her best when being bested by the best.

With the benefit of hindsight, it would have been prudent to set out her concerns in a letter in a logical manner, rather than rabbit on randomly. Fiona's cold, unshakeable demeanour caused Joy's emotions to fizz and spurt like Jaxon agitating a soda bottle. How could she have been so stupid? She didn't know herself lately.

In the aftermath of the humiliation, the toughest bit was knowing she hadn't asked for nor sought Fiona's sympathy even if this was given insincerely and condescendingly. She'd implored Fiona to do something about keeping Poppy away from her at work. This plea went unacknowledged as if it was too big an ask. Fiona ignored the appeal, deflecting discussion to less mutually acceptable solutions.

At one point, Joy had been thrown into a panic when Fiona suggested a face-to-face meeting with Poppy. *This would facilitate your ability to move on and for things to return to normal*, Fiona had recommended. *It will give Poppy a chance to help you understand her point of view and to give another personal apology. She feels a lot of remorse at what happened.*

Joy's first befuddled thought was *when had the first apology happened?* She must have missed it. She couldn't recall any remorse on Poppy's part until a complaint was submitted to head office.

Fiona expected her to accept the invitation. It would be proper and correct to agree to an offered olive branch to resolve the matter.

Joy's agitated response was to ask if a support person such as Bev could attend as well because she couldn't face Poppy alone. Fiona had hesitated long enough for Joy to presume the cost benefit analysis wasn't working out in her favour. Bev's presence cost money. Budgets were tight. Joy was more a nuisance than a priority.

At the last minute, Joy recalled Bev had advised against a similar meeting to the one suggested by Fiona. She said it would be like putting a victim of domestic violence in the same room as the abuser in order to sympathise with his point of view. In the conversation with Fiona, Joy had pointed this out. Fiona had disagreed with the analogy.

Joy didn't want to appear recalcitrant. But she couldn't do it.

It was hard enough to leave the safety of her home most days. Being in the same room as the woman who strangled people and laughed about it afterwards was beyond frightening. It was life threatening.

The idea caused such overwhelming dread, she pictured running from the meeting screaming as if pursued by a gunman.

No. Reconciling with Poppy was impossible. She'd never be able to do it.

This was the first time Joy had acknowledged what lay deep in her heart: she was not prepared to forgive Poppy's actions. For her, zero tolerance was an actual visceral reality.

Rather than push, Fiona deflected the refusal by mentioning they'd received Bev's email. Joy was aware of it because Bev had discussed it before sending it. If Joy were to return to the centre, it must be with gradual baby steps in order to overcome aversion to the site of a traumatic experience. Knowing Bev had her back was reassuring. With her and Dr Vitkay's support, she was confident the department would not insist on a premature return.

Fiona accepted this with surprising equanimity as if anticipating it. The next step, she explained, would be for the department to appoint a return to work coordinator.

The number of people on the workers compensation team was starting to add up: Fiona as Area Coordinator, Joy's GP, Bev as her counsellor, and now a return to work coordinator. All supporting Joy through the transitional stage of her rehabilitation.

Joy welcomed this new support person assigned presumably to assess her safety needs before returning to the centre. In her head she'd begun compiling a list of all the things that would make her feel safe at work: a lock on her office door and a second *escape* exit from the room; no more handling of cash; CCTV security system. And most important of all, keeping Poppy away from her at all times.

Fiona had offered reassurance. Joy would not be forced to return until she felt ready.

The current medical certificate ran out again in three days. With some concessions for her safety, she was leaning towards being convinced a gradual return would be alright – with lots of care and support from the team.

This illusion was dashed when towards the end of their conversation Fiona requested the return of Joy's set of office keys. *As soon as possible.*

This hurt.

They were treating her as if she was a security risk. Did they really believe she'd enter the premises and sabotage the files or do something even worse? She was a traumatised employee, not a bitter and twisted one. As much as she wanted to defend her honest, decent character, there was never an opportunity to do so during their short conversation. All she could do was obediently agree to the area coordinator's orders, good employee that she was.

The implication was that they did not expect her to return to work any time soon. Giving back the office keys felt like a door closing in her face.

It became clear lines were being drawn. Those in the inner circle. Those on the outside.

She began to feel less like someone on temporary sick leave. And more like a pariah banished from the centre because she was no longer healthy and whole.

Perhaps Gemma could take back the keys on her behalf.

Curling up on the bed, she had one last thought before falling asleep: remember to tell Gemma about the key register she'd set up. Amberlie was supposed to record the return of the keys and provide a date stamped receipt to the employee. For security and audit purposes.

Chapter Seventeen

"Here you go. Thought you might need this for your art group today." Amberlie chucked a cardboard box from Isle Office Supplies onto a table in the Shamrock Room. "It was delivered a few minutes ago." Looking as if she'd done Honor a favour, she waited for a compliment.

Honor acknowledged the gesture with a quick nod, thinking the purchase requisition had been placed in Amberlie's in-tray two weeks ago and had taken its own sweet time to arrive – luckily just in time. She continued to pull tables out from the wall and arrange them in a U-shape in preparation for the arrival of Wednesday's dementia clients. The community bus delivering them was due in fifteen minutes.

Undeterred, Amberlie began helping by opening the box and rifling through the contents. Cellophane bags of geometric shaped jewels in Kelly green, bottles of glue and cardboard cutouts in three-leaf clover shapes were dumped into random piles. "Looks like you're going with a St Patrick's Day theme today. Cool."

"You're right." Honor grunted from the difficulty of lifting a chair off a high stack in the corner of the room. She carried it to its place under a table.

"Did you hear Joy spat the dummy and walked off the job?" Amberlie was in the mood for gossip, unaware of Honor's relation to her job-share partner. "No one is sure if she'll be coming back. Poppy can't work out what caused such a dramatic reaction."

Honor stopped in her tracks, giving all her attention to Amberlie. "Really? What else is Poppy saying?"

"It's all hush hush – a personnel matter that head office is dealing with. Staff are not meant to talk about it due to confidentiality." Amberlie leaned across a table to whisper, "But there's a rumour going around about a laptop from Siobhan's office that she noticed missing last week, coincidentally."

Honor was incensed at the implied accusation that her straight as an arrow sister had something to do with stealing a government issued laptop. "Well, it couldn't have been Joy because I know for a fact, she went off on sick leave a few weeks ago," she said cuttingly.

Amberlie missed the cue and continued in a conspiratorial vein. "One of the volunteers told me Joy was escorted from the building by Poppy. She apparently looked all red in the face and really unhappy. Like she'd been caught red-handed with fingers in the till. Poppy said they're making Joy return her set of keys. That's not usual for someone on sick leave." Amberlie was deriving a great deal of pleasure running down her rival. She continued in a superior tone. "Before my time, there was another admin assistant who did something similar. She was stood down pending an investigation."

Honor was caught in a dilemma, not knowing how to back her sister without divulging too many personal details without permission. "You realise Joy has gone off on worker's compensation?" she said, a low-key defence that didn't clarify as much as she wanted. She thought back to the last conversation with her sister. Poor Joy was waiting at home expecting her work colleagues to send flowers and a get well card believing they knew she was going to be away for a while.

"Whatever. All I know is we've been instructed to continue business as usual, pretending nothing has happened." Amberlie beamed. "I don't actually care what the reason is. Poppy has given me Joy's hours. The longer she's away the more money for me."

Their conversation came to an abrupt halt when Shamrock Room clients began to shuffle in holding on to the arms of their carers. The room filled with loud greetings and questions about where to sit and volunteers shouting directions as they led seniors to chairs.

On spotting Honor, one of the old chaps pulled away from his family carer to stand directly under her nose. "Why is there a police car parked out front?" he demanded. "I'm not in trouble, am I?"

Honor looked around the room for assistance. "Of course, you're not in trouble, Harold," she said in a soothing tone. "Come and sit down while we make you a cup of tea."

Upon hearing Harold's shouts about the police, Amberlie raced out of the room in the direction of the foyer. She returned a few minutes later, breathless with excitement. "A constable has gone in to see Poppy along with Fiona Blackwell, the Area Coordinator. See I told you something was going on."

***

The next day, Honor insisted that Joy meet for coffee at the Village Spice Café. Being a volunteer, she was sworn to confidentiality under the state government's code of conduct. And although it was not her nature to interfere in another's business usually, she felt duty bound to apprise her sister of the gossip making its way around Lower Teasel. How did Joy get into these situations? She sucked in trouble like a vacuum cleaner.

The café was a cross between an antique shop and a village tea shop, with weathered oak floorboards and bay windows with frilly lace curtains. Old fashioned cakes such as Hummingbird and Black Forest were displayed in glass topped cases on a shop counter that could have been left over from the time it was an apothecary. Although she wasn't going to indulge in anything more fattening than a chai latte with skim milk, Joy normally had no such restrictions on calorie intake. The conversation Honor planned required a lot of gooey chocolate and cream to make it palatable.

Joy wandered in wearing casual jeans and a long t-shirt, clean and neatly pressed. That defiant purple splash in her grey hair had faded to a pastel lavender, much more subtle and stylish. Noticing how Joy checked out the room assessing it for safety, Honor's heart constricted. How much her sister had changed over the past few weeks from a confident and strong woman to a nervous mess. She wanted to shake some sense into her. It wouldn't be that bad if only she pulled herself together and got back on the horse.

Smiling, Joy approached the table. "Your honour, would you mind if I took the seat against the wall?" she asked. "I can't sit with my back to the room."

Honor shuffled to another seat. There was a scraping of chairs being pulled across wood floors. The echoes reverberated within the empty cafe. "I thought we'd meet for morning tea before it got too noisy. I know you hate noise and crowds nowadays." She studied Joy for signs of agitation. She was willing to postpone this conversation if Joy was in a bad space.

"You are a godsend. I so needed to get out of the house and be part of the world again. I'm such a recluse. If there's no reason to leave the cottage, I hide out." Her hoarse laugh was followed by dry throat clearing. Lately, she seemed stricken with a permanent sore throat; maybe she was suffering from an allergy.

A young waiter in a black tank top, black jeans and black Sketchers hovered over them, pad and pen ready. "What can I get you?" he asked.

Immediately, Honor ordered a chai latte. Joy scanned the menu, ordered a cappuccino, and then craned her neck to look towards the cake counter. "What special sweets are on offer?" she asked.

Stifling a yawn – from a hard night before – the waiter rattled off a long list of delectable cakes and puddings. Joy ordered two hazelnut slices. "I got one for you, too," she said, much to Honor's annoyance. "Tell me, what's been happening at the centre? Does anybody miss me yet?"

"I miss you." She smiled kindly. More seriously, she said, "It's supposed to be business as usual. However, we had a visit from the police yesterday. I expect you know what that's all about. A senior manager from head office attended the interview with Poppy. Of course, it's all 'hush hush' which means gossip is flying all over the place. One of my dementia clients was convinced he was going to jail." She laughed.

Joy leaned forward, serious. "I didn't want to get Poppy in trouble. But the department refused to take any measures to protect me from the woman. I was left with no choice."

Honor tried to steer the conversation in the direction it needed to go for Joy to understand the significance. "Amberlie's been telling people it has something to do with you being off work. Staff haven't been told why you're not there, so their imaginations have run wild."

"That explains why no one's sent me a get well card," Joy said, dejectedly staring out the window. "They made such a fuss when Jane went off..."

Honor took pity. In an attempt to cheer her up, she said. "I wish you were there. Amberlie's been filling in for you. She's so slow placing my stationary orders. I didn't think they'd arrive in time for our St Patrick's Day activities."

Recovering composure, Joy shook her head in disbelief. "I remember, we ran out of toilet paper for the centre and I thought she'd forgotten to put in an order. But then it turned out someone had been pilfering the store cupboard." She leaned in to whisper, "I don't suppose they've caught the person?"

Honor hesitated. She was being too subtle. Joy was not picking up on the hints. She tried again.

"Siobhan's laptop went missing a week or so ago. There are all kinds of rumours and accusations going around." She gave Joy a pointed look.

Something changed in Joy's expression. "They don't think I...? No way! They think the police were there because... You've got to be joking. They know me. I'd never do anything like that."

Honor suppressed an instinctive urge to shush Joy as her voice rose to a crescendo. A quick glance around the quiet café was reassuring; the drama in the bay window was purposefully ignored by the handful of diners sipping coffee and reading copies of The Meridian newspaper.

Joy continued to wail in fury. "And I've been gone for weeks now." When the embarrassing scene subsided, Honor received a hurtful glare from Joy. "Is this what you wanted to talk to me about?" she accused.

"To warn you," Honor blurted. "I'm not sure what you want me to do, if I should say something or not?" She wanted to say how much she hated being put in the position of piggy in the middle, wondering whether to defend her sister or pretend it wasn't happening.

Normally, in these situations, she got on with the job by keeping her head down and avoiding office politics. It wasn't fair that Joy had put her in this situation, especially without any guidance on what to do.

The heavy oak door of the café swung open, diverting Joy's focus. Noticing the sudden blaze of intention in her sister's eyes, Honor jerked her head around.

"Siobhan," Honor whispered in horror. Alert to a potential scene about to unfold, she clamped her hand around Joy's arm to hold her in place.

"I'm going to explain," Joy said, struggling to be free.

Not noticing them at first, Siobhan marched to the counter with efficient purpose. She handed the barista a list of orders for take away coffees. Honor tightened her hold on Joy. Just her bad luck that Siobhan was on coffee duty this week for the community nurses at the centre.

A cappuccino machine began to grind beans and hiss steam, filling the room with that delicious, heady aroma familiar to all cafes. With bored impatience, Siobhan glanced around the room. Her eyes flicked to Honor and Joy. With blank indifference, not acknowledging who they were, she turned back to the counter and feigned intense interest in the jars of cookies lined up on the shelves behind.

Suddenly, Joy crumpled in the chair as if a get well balloon had popped and its hot air of defiance deflated out of her system. "She saw me."

"I know," Honor agreed.

"And she's not even going to say hi or ask how I am." Joy stated this with an air of finality. After a long pause, she asked, "Is it because of the police report? Is she blaming me?"

"Nurses stick together." Honor was disgusted with Siobhan's lack of courtesy. If only a dirty glare could bore holes in her stiff back to get through to a hard heart.

Siobhan shuffled on the spot, uncomfortable and impatient to get the coffees and go. A valiant effort was being made to pretend she hadn't seen them.

Joy slumped in the chair. "She was the one person at the centre I confided in after the strangling. Of all the people, she knows the full story."

The barista handed Siobhan the coffee order in a cardboard carry holder and tucked it in a small brown paper bag with complimentary cookies. He made some humorous remark and Siobhan joined in, all smiles and a happy face before picking up the holder. Balancing it rather awkwardly on an arm, she headed out the door with shoulders straight and a face so fixated on the exit she might as well have worn blinkers.

The give-away was right at the end when she couldn't help but glance their way. Joy was staring with a bewildered look. For the few seconds of involuntary contact with Siobhan, she gave a small shrug.

Which summed it all up, as far as Honor was concerned.

Not knowing what else to do, she said, "Joy, just let it go."

Chapter Eighteen

J oy agitated a dish cloth in the sink, staring out the window ruminating about the sorry state of her life. She'd been on leave for so many weeks, summer was over, and all the good weather had been wasted being a couch potato. When her medical certificate expired yet again, Joy panicked yet again at the possibility of being returned to the centre too soon, obsessively going over and over the reasons why this could not happen. Despite all the counselling sessions and medical appointments, aversion to the workplace was getting worse instead of better.

It was bad enough her employer had trivialised Poppy's behaviour. The trauma to her sense of rightness was compounded by a feeble attempt to discuss procedural concerns only to get stonewalled in the process. Her one basic occupational health and safety need was for that crazy woman to be kept away. Afterall, Poppy was only a temp and Joy was the permanent staff member at the centre. This decision was in Fiona's sphere of power and control, yet she refused to take any remedial action.

Joy was left fragile and agitated, consumed about why her side of the story was not being taken seriously. Her mind during the day – and at night in nightmares – wound in circles going over and over as many of the details she could remember of the incident. How anybody could entertain – for even one minute – a belief that Poppy put her hands around her throat for a surprise neck rub, squeezed with so much pressure she cut off her breathing and told her she was going to choke her to death and that this was done in *a joking manner*? Work colleagues were not even supposed to touch each other without permission. Poppy's behaviour was an insane thing to do to a person. Why didn't her employer think the same way?

Joy obsessively regurgitated this debate with Gemma whenever they caught up for coffee. Gemma became frustrated with her fixation and didn't help. *It must be the way you say it!* she'd cut in and talk over Joy's blabbering, no longer willing to listen to the same old stuff she'd heard a million times before. *Whenever I tell people what happened to you, they all express shock horror and agree Poppy must be crazy. I don't know why it's not the same for you?*

Gemma's exasperated temper hurt, like opening an oven door expecting the aroma of comfort cupcakes and instead getting blasted with a shock of hot steam in the face, singeing eyeballs.

To make matters worse, Gemma's question created a whole new set of ruminations. How was Joy's story so different from her daughter's version? Why wasn't she receiving the same empathy? Throughout her mainland career, she'd always been good at expressing opinions in a logical and rational way. She gained a reputation for winning arguments at management meetings.

"I state the facts. I expect they speak for themselves," she told Gemma, needing to justify.

"But you can be so unemotional when you tell your story, mum. When I tell people, I say outright that you were strangled by a madwoman and Poppy should be locked up. That's when people start to sympathise," Gemma had lectured.

Absently, Joy scrubbed a sandwich plate in the sink for the fourth time before rinsing it under a hot water tap and setting it to dry in a dish tray. Outside, the hydrangeas were turning from white to a pinkish green and the lemon balm was drying off. They'd need to be pruned before it got too wet. Turning attention to hot suds, she pulled up a coffee mug and vigorously cleaned it until it gleamed in the sunlight.

Joy doubted Gemma's advice. It was a work issue, not a personal one. Management saw weakness in emotional outbursts. In a competitive bureaucratic culture, weaklings did not receive sympathy. They were savaged without mercy.

The incident left her fragile as if stripped of armour. Her emotions were blocked up inside behind a wall of numbness. To express them was to expose a vulnerability to the outside world that left her unprotected and unsafe. Telling of the violation in full detail was too much of a risk. It was impossible to find the right words to defend this position to Gemma.

Instead, after her daughter left, Joy chose to self-medicate by watching the whole series of *24*. This was to become a daily routine starting from the time she crawled out of bed at ten thirty in the morning to the time she fell asleep on the couch late into the night. There was something about the hero shooting up the bad guys while continually being thwarted by the government bureaucracy, and ultimately vindicating his headstrong actions by winning in the end, that ironically provided temporary relief from symptoms of anxiety.

***

Waiting for Dr Vitkay at Lower Teasel's Surgery, Joy was joined by Michelle Jonas, the Return to Work Coordinator appointed by the department. Michelle was a young professional, immaculately presented in a tailored jacket over a soft dress, with high heeled sandals and a shoulder satchel that doubled as a briefcase.

Radiating sincerity and wafting Daisy perfume, Michelle introduced herself while shaking hands. Sitting on the edge of an adjoining hard plastic chair, she slid the satchel onto the floor in one smooth movement and turned willowy knees towards Joy. "The department has provided a briefing with the necessary details. There's no need to go over it again with me. I'm sure it would be upsetting to be reminded."

For one panicked second, Joy thought Michelle would pat her knee in sympathy. With relief that didn't eventuate.

"I'm very sorry to hear what happened to you," Michelle said in hushed and soothing tones. In one smooth movement, she twisted and unzipped her leather satchel. A Return To Work Plan was pulled out and handed across, ready for Joy's signature. "I'll give you time to read through it. It covers the last period of your medical certificate."

Not anticipating this development so soon, Joy scanned her first RTW Plan with a vague lack of focus. It looked like a pro forma printed straight off the computer. Not having any prior experience with workers compensation procedures and therefore not knowing what to expect, she was unable to draw a comparison as to its quality. Viewing it through the lens of anxiety and nerves made it difficult to concentrate on its contents.

Scanning the pages, she noticed two headings in bold type. Under the heading *Cause of Injury* Michelle had filled in the phrase *'neck stiffness'*. Under the heading *Nature of Injury* she'd repeated the wording with an added phrase 'and anxiety'.

This muddled with Joy's already fuzzy brain. The plan read as if she'd got a crook neck from Poppy's supposed neck massage, rather than mental trauma from strangling. It was the difference between writing a *bump* on the head rather than a *blow* to the head after being attacked. Words were so important.

Didn't Bev offer reassurance during their last counselling session that the department would consult with her to provide input into the RTW plan? Later on, she'd talk to Michelle about correcting the wording.

Joy glanced over at Michelle and received a reassuring smile. She appeared competent and caring.

"When you are ready, please sign the back page in the box next to your name." She was softly spoken with a soothing presence, well suited to the role of *hand holding* support.

Next to Michelle's impeccable work persona, Joy regretted wearing a t-shirt and track pants to the doctor's surgery. Looking as drab as she was feeling was not a good first impression conveying her dedication to the job.

As independent as Joy used to be, waiting for Dr Vitkay made her nervous as a kid about to receive a needle. If he didn't extend her sick leave, she didn't know what to do. As far as she knew, Poppy was still acting manager at the centre. The prospect of coming face to face with her at work triggered the onset of a panic attack.

Michelle's calming nature actually helped. Relieved she had an ally providing backup, Joy scrawled a spidery signature in the space provided and returned the form.

It didn't take much pleading to convince Dr Vitkay to agree to taking another period off work to recover. This time the diagnosis changed from a stress reaction caused by trauma to full blown Post Traumatic Stress Disorder. He wrote out another prescription for antidepressants and sleeping pills to see her through this acute crisis stage.

Joy was reluctant to continue on antidepressants especially since Gemma was so vehement about them. Her daughter had lectured *once you're on them for too long you never got off them.* Gemma insisted *Drugs make you numb and dumb, Mum.* She wanted to ask Dr Vitkay's opinion about Gemma's natural therapy regime but at the same time didn't trust in confiding to him. He was probably bound by some rules within the workers compensation system to follow standard protocols.

She was desperate to make the shaky, restless feelings of anxiety dissipate. If someone had offered illicit drugs, she would have popped them without a second thought if they promised relief. She so hated feeling this way. Maybe she would give herbal remedies a go.

Michelle joined the consultation for the last ten minutes, requesting Dr Vitkay's diagnosis and treatment advice. On the new medical certificate, he had ticked a large 'X' in the box next to *Totally Incapacitated for Work* alongside calendar dates indicating another two weeks' sick leave. Joy visibly relaxed knowing she was safe again. At the same time, with such a strong work ethic that had driven a long and successful career for so many years, she felt somewhat of an imposter taking more time off simply because she couldn't get her head right. She longed to get back to work. Home was safe but also socially isolating and mind numbingly boring.

Dr Vitkay was the medical expert in this matter. It wasn't her place to question his diagnosis. She must trust him. Another couple of weeks and she'd be her old self again.

Michelle took a few notes, acknowledged her approval, and filed a copy of Joy's new workers compensation medical certificate in the leather satchel. She asked the doctor to sign the RTW Plan but didn't leave him a copy, promising it would be posted later. Signatures were required from all parties on the department's workers compensation team first. It was quite a long list.

Michelle walked out of the surgery with Joy. "From now on I'll be the first channel of communication with your employer. If you have any concerns, put them through me, not Fiona. She's too busy. I'll liaise with members of the workers compensation team on your behalf." She offered to fax the medical certificate to the department's workers compensation payroll section.

Willingly, Joy agreed. At home, she was bereft of technology: no laptop or smartphone with internet; no fax machine. She'd always relied on the office computer system to send emails, do personal banking and look up information on the internet. The realisation struck her – she was out of the communication loop and totally dependent on Michelle and Bev to keep her informed. She trusted they'd do the right thing by her. That was their job after all.

As Joy neared her Baleno, Michelle chatted like an old friend. "Any plans for the weekend? My husband and I will be driving to Whalers Cove for a romantic weekend away."

"That sounds lovely," Joy said, trying to be polite. "But no, no plans except to lay on the couch watching DVDs, waiting for the meds to kick in. I babysat my grandson last weekend and got so exhausted I haven't recovered yet." She decided not to mention the incident where Jaxon accidentally broke one of her prized Carlton Ware creamers. This memory was a source of guilt and perplexing disbelief at how her anger had escalated out of control so fast. She didn't recognise that person she'd become.

Michelle laughed good naturedly. "I've heard lots of grandparents complain about that."

Her glib remark got under Joy's skin. The woman had just heard Dr Vitkay diagnose PTSD and so soon she was blaming Joy's fatigue on old age. Before the incident, she'd always had a lot of energy and loved babysitting Jaxon.

"Well, not me! That never used to happen before I was assaulted!" Joy said, defensive and feeling quarrelsome.

"Of course," Michelle drawled, looking concerned as if pacifying a fractious horse. "Take care. I'll see you at the next appointment."

Joy slunk into the driver's seat and locked the car door. She waited for Michelle to drive off before bursting into tears.

Chapter Nineteen

A hard knock on the front door roused Joy from the sofa. Reaching for the remote, she turned off the DVD playing the third series of 24. Three more knocks, louder and more aggressive, caused her to run to the master bedroom. Within the safety of the inner sanctum, she remembered Constable Chugg's message left on voicemail saying he was going to call around some time in the afternoon. Nervously, she checked her reflection in the dresser mirror and quickly finger combed the rat's nest of hair caused by sleeping in front of the TV. Smoothing out wrinkles in the oversized t-shirt she wore, she pulled it down to reach her knees over grey threadbare track pants. Taking a couple deep breaths, she braced for the first social interaction in days and padded down the hallway in bare feet to answer the door.

Chugg stood solid and commanding in full police uniform with shiny black, hard leather boots straddling the top two steps. One hand rested on a gun holstered on his hip and the other hung by his side holding a compendium. He looked to be in his late twenties with a permanent sneer of cynicism etched into his facial muscles. Joy beckoned him inside and took the lead to the kitchen table.

"Can I get you a drink?" she asked, remembering all the TV shows where the English cops sat around drinking cups of tea while asking probing questions with well-mannered civility.

Chugg shook his head and proceeded to remove his cap and place it with the compendium on the table. He remained standing while pulling out a notebook and pen from a shirt pocket. "Subsequent to our initial meeting, I've interviewed Mrs Poppy Bryant and her supervisor, Ms Fiona Blackwell and taken statements from them. Furthermore, after discussions with the Police Prosecutor, it has been decided to proceed with charging Mrs Bryant with common assault," he said referring to his notes.

At this news, Joy needed to sit down. "She confessed to strangling me?" she asked in amazement.

"When questioned about the incident, she admitted to placing her hands around your neck. However, she states this was done in a lighthearted manner. She expressed remorse for her actions and said that she hoped you would remain friends."

Joy snorted in disbelief. "Friends? She was my boss, not my friend."

Constable Chugg continued to explain. "The Police Prosecutor believes it may be difficult to prove intent in this case. It will be a line call, depending on the Magistrate's discretion. However, we are taking the matter of strangulation seriously. We require a statement from you, provided you agree for us to proceed with the charge of common assault."

It came down to this. Joy had to decide whether to proceed with taking Poppy to court. Lives would change irrevocably as a result. Poppy would not only lose her job because a public servant could not have a criminal conviction and continue to work in the state government; she would also lose her registration as a nurse. This would most likely force her into early retirement at the age of sixty-two years old.

The woman had attempted to strangle her. And it wasn't right. No matter how a person looked at it. She'd given Joy post-traumatic stress disorder as a result of her negligent behaviour. There was a principle at stake. Poppy needed to be held accountable for her actions. If the department had sanctioned her in any meaningful way, Joy would not be in this position, forced to make a decision. There was no other way to prevent Poppy from doing it again.

If her employer refused to protect her, the law would.

"I'd like you to proceed," Joy said gravely. Constable Chugg nodded with a sense of the inevitable. "I feel strongly that this is the right thing to do. I want people to know I don't take being abused at work lightly and won't let the perpetrator get away with it if I can help it." The more she said, the angrier she became. Anything less would be accepting the status of victim. She refused to be disempowered by the incident.

The department would have to take strangulation seriously after this.

Having made the decision, Joy experienced a sense of being more in control of her life again. "If I can use the OH&S incident report as my statement, I'll get a copy for you," she said, getting up from the table.

Joy returned and handed over three photocopied pages. Constable Chugg speed read through them, nodded approval, and attached a cover sheet. "Sign here and I'll forward your case file on to the Police Prosecutor." He scrolled through his notes and began to recite court procedures. "What happens from now on is that the Prosecutor prepares for an initial hearing in the Magistrates Court. With the long Easter break and other public holidays coming up, the court will have a backlog of cases pending. Your case will not be listed for several months, probably sometime in September."

Joy's heart began to race. "Do I need a lawyer? Will I have to go on the stand and give evidence at a trial?" The prospect made her feel faint.

"No. At the initial hearing, the Police Prosecutor will present our case and you will not be required to attend. The Magistrate will decide whether the matter should proceed to trial."

"Will she go to jail?" This outcome had only just occurred to Joy and horrified her a little. Her mind wandered into images of all the court trials she'd witnessed on TV crime programs, picturing being on the stand looking pitiful as she related her story, the jury gasping in shock and disgust at Poppy's behaviour as she gained their sympathy and succeeded in securing the judge's harshest verdict.

Joy half-listened to Constable Chugg's monotoned account of proceedings. "As it is a first offence, the Magistrate will take into consideration her character and history before passing sentence."

Rather than rejoicing at the imagined win, surprisingly these imaginings caused ambivalent emotions. On one side she felt relief that Poppy would be removed from harm's way making life safe again; on the other she pitied Poppy as the full weight of power wielded over another person's fate hit home.

However, a deeper underlying anger rose to the surface at what Poppy had done to her. She was satisfied with the decision to press on with the legal process.

Constable Chugg continued talking about police procedures for informing her of the outcome of the hearing and other details that did not stick in Joy's memory. He was shown out the door in a haze.

This state of mind was becoming quite usual for Joy. It tended to occur when too much information overwhelmed her capacity to cope.

Chapter Twenty

Poppy peered around the doorway of their ensuite, toothbrush in hand, waiting for Gil to finish reading the document on his laptop. He was taking his own sweet time about it. This was a good sign. His focused attention to detail was an attractive attribute. In the dim light of the bedroom, he looked sexy sitting in bed dressed in a black Star Wars t-shirt hugged tight against his flat stomach, the laptop resting on his taut thighs. Their diet was working for him at least. His tortoise shell reading glasses kept slipping as he frowned down at the screen. Adorable.

Impatient and needing reassurance, her question burst forth in a spray of mint bubbles. "Will it win the day?"

Lost in concentration, Gil mumbled *hmmm* and kept scrolling. After what seemed an interminable amount of time, he said in that droll voice used when teasing her, "For someone who claimed not to remember much of what happened, you've certainly written quite a statement."

Poppy swallowed toothpaste and licked her lips. "The lawyer suggested a good memory would assist with the credibility factor in court."

Gil smiled with fondness at his wife's silhouetted figure against the backdrop of the bathroom's fluro, dressed in a silky bathrobe that hugged her in all the right places as she waved a dripping toothbrush in the air with dramatic flair. "As I said before, it's going to be your word against hers, and you're her superior."

"Exactly. Admittedly, I made up a lot as I went along. But who's to say it's a lie, if I can't actually remember any of it." She turned to the sink to rinse and spit.

In the background she heard Gil say, "As stories go, it holds together. If I didn't know different, your version makes Joy seem rigid and controlling, prone to fantasy and exaggeration with hysterical outbursts when things didn't go her way. But as you emphasise, she was your friend and normally took jokes well. It's puzzling as to what caused such an overreaction that day. Brilliant, sweetheart."

Poppy came out of the bathroom with a gleaming white smile. "Nailed it. That is precisely the impression I was meant to make. Fiona and I talked it through at our prep meeting before we met with Constable Chugg. We agreed Joy should be seen as overreacting to a trivial misunderstanding."

"The woman doesn't stand a chance against you, darl."

"Who's to say Joy hasn't been equally as creative in her police statement?" Poppy climbed into bed and snuggled into her husband's shoulder. She knew Joy was too nice to reinterpret reality in a police statement. The fool would stick to rules and fairness. Honesty and predictability were not the best tools in a war chest if one played to win. Poppy had been in the game long enough to understand weasel words and narrative spin won the day.

Gil's vote of confidence in her police statement and the gleam of pride detected in his eyes, sparked a tender moment between them. After shutting the laptop and placing it on the bedside table, he gently pushed aside a wiry curl to kiss her cheek. This was all the encouragement required.

With a suggestive sigh, she rolled to the side to turn off a table lamp. The room darkened. Wriggling her silky cladded bum into his groin, she searched for the telltale signs of hardening. Not feeling it, she rolled over and grabbed his flaccid cock, squeezing and pulling at it with a rough pumping action. "Where's my meat?" she mocked. "I'm horny enough to shag the bedpost if you can't get it up." Straddling her heavy thighs across his torso, she grabbed a fistful of his hair, pulled his head back and lapped a slick tongue up the side of his neck, biting his earlobe and drawing blood.

"Fuck, that hurt," Gil shouted pushing her back. "Get off, bitch."

She slapped him across the face, grinning. He looked dazed as if seeing stars. Leaning over him, she held his hands above his shoulders and kneed her way up his body to position her pussy over his mouth. "Please me, boy."

Gil thrashed and kicked his legs, putting up a mock fight. "Go fuck yourself," he taunted turning his head away.

Sitting up, she slapped him harder. "Dog's follow commands, they don't issue them." Reaching across to the bedside table, she pulled across a leather collar with silver studs and began to fasten it around his neck. She watched his face register increasing fear as it was slowly tightened with gentle precision, one notch at a time, stopping at a notch too tight and waiting a long moment for his eyes to bulge and lips turn blue before loosening it, casually watching with disinterest.

"You are mine to use as I please," she intoned in caressing notes. "If you refuse…" She tightened the collar to demonstrate. This torturous ritual was repeated several times, with Gil kicking his legs helplessly. Working his hands free, he grabbed her bum and tried to pull her toward his mouth. With a jeer, she pulled back thwarting his efforts. "I decide, not you," she said, slapping his face, adding to the humiliation. Finally, the collar was fixed in a notch one short of cutting off his airway.

Bending backwards, she jerked the lead to pull his head up. He gagged and grabbed the collar trying to loosen it. "Lick me, dog," she ordered gruffly. She jerked the lead harder. Obediently, he stuck out his tongue, straining his neck but not quite reaching the target. "Useless cocksucker," she jeered. "And you call yourself a man."

Laughing she changed position to face his feet, pushing a flabby bum into his face smothering him, the weight of her thighs holding him immobile. "You're a shit sucking dog. No pussy for you." Leaning forward, she allowed him to catch a breath. The tip of her tongue sharply jabbed the knob of his erect, purple cock like a lizard dabbing leaking beads of liquor.

"Oh, baby. No. Too much," Gil groaned and squirmed, pushing against a butt cheek.

With brutal force she scraped teeth down his shaft. He grunted from the shock and searing pain.

Thrashing to get free, he hissed, "You fucking cunt." His cock softened from the shock.

Pushing her bum back in his face, she cut off complaints. She nuzzled into his groin, breathing hot damp breaths across his balls, whispering encouragement. "You want what I can give?" She rubbed his cock across her mouth tauntingly. Once again it engorged, bulged and twitched as if with a mind of its own.

Unable to withstand the onslaught, Gil lost control. Her experienced ministrations became too much. Writhing upwards with a heavy jerk, he dug his cock into the depths of her mouth. "Yes-e-s my love, my dearest. He's all yours."

Poppy expelled a groan of eagerness. She kept up a continuous stream of murmurs. "All mine, my beautiful boy, so big, so powerful." With expertise she licked and lathered, delicately bit and scraped until his moans almost reached a crescendo.

Suddenly she sat up and turned around. "This is boring. I'm doing all the work, you lazy shit. How long do you expect me to keep it up?"

"Fuck, I was about to come," Gil hissed breathlessly. She forcefully stopped his hand reaching down to finish the job.

"Selfish fucker, expecting to get all the pleasure. What about me? I get no satisfaction out of it."

He beseeched, "Let me do you. I can do you right now." He waggled his tongue and leered, desperately seeking her permission. "Give me a chance to prove myself."

In reply, she pulled the leash toward a sticky mouth smelling of cock. Plunging her swollen tongue between his lips, the collar cut off his airway. She stared into his soul, waited just long enough and applied just enough pressure to make his eyes bulge in pain and fear as asphyxiation took hold.

Overcome with excitement, she grabbed his fist, pushing her building orgasm into it. All the time rubbing her pussy against it, taunting, pulling the leash tighter.

A flash in his expression indicated the moment when terror transformed into his own head rush of ecstasy. "Not yet," she hissed. "I come first, you useless mongrel," she commanded. Too late.

His cock shuddered of its own volition and hot, white globs of gluey liquor spurted like a fountain onto his hairy thighs and across the sheets.

Poppy tweaked his cock in anger. "Mother will have to change your sticky soiled sheets now. You're such a lot of work, grubby boy." He groaned in shame and made a feeble attempt to stroke between her thighs in consolation, but he couldn't evoke enough motivation. He slumped in disgrace, his energy spent.

"What's the punishment for disobeying the rules?" she growled, giving his body a rough push and unbuckling the collar with disgust. Throwing it in the top drawer, she reached inside and pulled out a hard leather strap.

With vicious intensity, she flailed the strap across his cheek, missing his eye by a centimetre. A red welt puffed up along his cheekbone.

Cursing, Gil grabbed the strap out of her hand as she raised it for another strike and used it to slap her flabby bum with several stinging wallops. After each strike, she cried out, "More, more!" goading him on. "Ye-e-es, that's better than your limp dick," she mocked between gasps.

Provoked, he seized her throat with a meaty hand and teasingly caressed it. "I know what my bitch likes," he crooned, increasing the pressure around her throat.

"Filthy pervert," she croaked, grabbing his hand and trying to pull it free. Gil squeezed harder, cutting off further curses. A slow smile crept across his face as Poppy's face turned purple and torment clouded her face. He counted the seconds...nine, ten, eleven...She batted at his hand pathetically.

"Come for me, bitch," he whispered cruelly. She thrashed and fought ineffectually. "That's it," he crooned. "Your pussy loves it, baby." Suddenly, her body became rigid and waves of shuddering ecstasy turned her into jelly. Her eyes rolled back in her head and she collapsed on top of him. "Fuck," she moaned.

Gil sniggered and pushed her over, rolling with her. "At your service, Madam," he bragged. "Who's on top now?"

Chapter Twenty One

A scream fitting to a banshee added to the general cacophony at Burger Magic in Plover Point food court. Joy was amazed at how it managed to pierce the industrial strength safety glass separating the children's playground from the dining area. Although the ear shattering shriek caused her to jerk with surprise, when she managed to regain composure, she assumed it came from a kid's exuberant joy rather than from a murder taking place. From the sound, it could have been either – if context was taken out of the equation.

Burger Magic was the venue of choice for primary school children's parties. This April lunchtime, one of Jaxon's school mates was celebrating a ninth birthday and Gemma had insisted Joy accompany them, saying *mum, you need to get out of the house.*

It was true Joy had become more and more reclusive of late, suffering anxiety at the thought of leaving the safety of the home cave to venture out in public. It was frustrating trying to describe what PTSD felt like to someone who had never experienced it.

Honor tried to be helpful and tactfully implied it was mind over matter. Don't think about it if it upsets you. Think different thoughts and you will begin to feel better. That worked for her as a philosophy.

If only it was as simple as that for Joy.

Bev used CBT – Cognitive Behaviour Therapy – as her choice therapeutic intervention. She counselled that thoughts lead to feelings that lead to emotions. Not that dissimilar to Honor's New Age philosophy. The difference being Bev encouraged Joy to go over and over memories of the incident as if repetition would eventually lessen the impact or re-write it with a different ending. Joy believed CBT was having the opposite effect. She was willing to concede Honor's advice to ignore her thoughts altogether was smarter even if at times impossible.

From Joy's experience, they both had it the wrong way around. The amorphous, generalised feeling came first, then the thought was overlaid onto it as she tried to confine it with a label. Emotions were the way to release the feelings, transmute them back into energy to dissipate into the ether. It was the emotional release she was having difficulty with. There was a blockage in the system, similar to a plug on a volcanic vent. Sooner or later it was going to blow because her control mechanisms had become faulty after getting PTSD.

How could she put words on PTSD as an affliction? It was a restless grief building up in her body – a pressure of sadness, or fragility, or vulnerability. A worry of not being able to cope with too much stimuli. A lack of emotional strength – for any emotions, even good ones like happiness, excitement, passion. She hadn't felt joy for a long time. Or love. The intensity of these feelings scared her. She worried that deep emotions would send her spiralling out of control over the edge of a black hole. She couldn't cope with too much life happening around her.

Maintaining predictability, stasis, the boring mundane helped sustain a fragile equilibrium.

She didn't recognise the reclusive woman she'd become who could only manage to leave the house twice a week. Before the Strangling – *BTS* as Gemma referred to it – she'd been out every night of the week to some class or group meeting: furniture restoration, felting classes, Buddhist meditation.

Now it was once to Woolies and once to the GP or the counsellor. More activities than that would send her collapsing from exhaustion, as if she only had enough reserves for two outings and it would take another five days to build them back up.

She hated the fact her life had come to a halt. Before this, she believed in having a vision for the future, setting goals, and rewarding performance achievements. Moving forward. Motivated. On the go. This was the Joy she knew and loved – the woman before the strangling incident.

Sometimes, she refused to listen to her instincts. She wanted to dig up this deadened Joy from the grave of trauma and force life back in. When Gemma implored, *she needed to get out*, Joy said *yes* to this family outing to Burger Magic against all better judgement.

Being a long time fan of junk food, especially Burger Magic's double bacon, double beef with extra mozzarella cheese, made that decision easier.

Tucking into a juicy Double Magic burger as it dripped Magic barbeque sauce down her forearm, she now doubted that judgement call. Surrounded by families packed into tables, music blaring from wall-to-wall widescreen TVs, kids running between the playground and the toilets, pink milkshake spills dripping onto the tiled floors, cappuccino machines steaming milk, the aroma of ground Arabica beans mingling with the oily odours of fried onions, frying chips and grilling bacon, her five senses suffered an assault that was fast heading to overload.

Gemma noticed first. "Are you okay, mum? You look a bit pale."

Not wanting to be a spoilsport, Joy decided to tough it out. "Is it me or is it hot and stuffy in here?" she said cramming a half-eaten burger into its waxed cardboard carton and rummaging through wrappers and miscellaneous packaging scattered across the small chrome table. A clean serviette was uncovered. Relieved she waved it like a fan.

"You're not going to faint, are you?" Gemma's solicitude added to Joy's sense of claustrophobia. Too many people, all closing in on her. It was getting hard to breathe.

Jaxon chose this moment to run up to the table, flushed and sweaty, gushing with hyperactive enthusiasm. "Do you want a hug, granny?" He puffed sweet grape soda crush breath in her face.

Joy flinched unconsciously, desperate for more personal space to regain a sense of equilibrium amidst the scattering of her heightened awareness. A hug was the last thing she needed. She felt crowded enough.

Her grandson's eager face took on a crestfallen expression.

Along with increasing nausea, Joy added guilt to a growing list of symptoms. A balloon popped in the background momentarily scaring her and causing heart palpitations to race out of control. That was the deciding factor. "I need fresh air," she cried out, leaping from the table and fighting her way through the crowd towards an exit. Too shocked to move, Gemma and Jaxon watched her flee.

In a blind panic, Joy ran through the mall, down two levels of stairs, to Gemma's yellow Getz parked undercover in the shopping centre's parking lot. Gulping air, she leaned on the hood willing herself not to pass out. Oblivious to passing onlookers, she began to cry.

"Mum, it's all right." Gemma was there by her side handing across a cotton handkerchief. "Come on, you'll feel better sitting in the car."

Safe in the confines of the car, away from people and noise, with cool air from the air con washing across her hot face, Joy slowly began to breathe normally. "I'm so sorry," she began.

"It's okay, we understand. There's nothing to worry about, we'll head home."

"But Jaxon's party..."

"He's had enough sugar to last the week. Don't worry about him." Gemma turned around to the back seat and gave Jaxon a look.

Getting the message, he said, "I don't mind, Granny. Angeli was being mean and popping everyone's balloons. I'm over it."

Miserably, Joy assented. Somewhat agitated, she fumbled through her handbag searching for a packet of Murelax. Swallowing the tiny white tablet with a gulp of water, she felt relief. By the time they got home safe and sound, the anxiety would be anaesthetised.

Ashamed, she looked forward to turning into a numb zombie.

Chapter Twenty Two

Leland motioned Fiona to the chrome office chair next to his desk indicating he wanted this meeting over and done with quickly and effectively. He didn't keep her waiting by reading an email or signing correspondence as his usual ploy to play the big boss. Instead, he launched into an *inform and direct* tone of voice. Fiona picked up on the clues; the matter at hand was politically sensitive and required handling in a specific way. Instinctively, she sat to attention.

"You may not know yet, but Joy O'Connell has reported the incident to the police. The woman is not going to let this go; she's determined to make a point. My government contacts have informed me the police intend to charge Mrs Bryant with common assault. I'm surprised at this decision. Didn't you assure me it was a trivial incident and an over reaction on the part of Ms O'Connell?"

Fiona thought back to the initial briefing she gave Leland trying to remember her exact words. She should have trusted her instincts. She suspected this was going to blow up in their faces. Leland's question was rhetorical; however, Fiona felt a need for some justification.

"Mrs Bryant met with Constable Chugg to provide a statement in defence of Joy O'Connell's allegations a couple weeks ago. I was in attendance as a show of support. At that time, Chugg was not convinced there was a case to answer. He said it was a line call. He was taking it to the Police Prosecutor for an opinion."

"I needed to be kept informed."

"As we hadn't heard anything, I believed the matter didn't have legs."

Leland gave her one of his notorious looks that could freeze a boiled mug at twenty paces. Fiona had no response in the face of such monumental stuff up.

"I'll need to get our government lawyers onto it ASAP, see what they advise before we take any action that could jeopardise the department's position regarding liability."

"Do you want me to stand down Poppy pending the court outcome?" Fiona asked. Given the circumstances, all she could do was move forward with decisiveness.

"God, no," Leland shouted emphatically, his control cracking. "We've asked Jane Manners to extend her recovery time by taking long service leave. I want us to keep Mrs Bryant on at the centre to make a point we believe in her and stand behind her. She's done nothing wrong. You know the drill, extend Bryant's contract and find Jane a special project at head office to keep her occupied upon her return. Jane will understand we're protecting her, keeping her out of the legal dramas until it's all sorted so there's no stain on her reputation. She won't be a problem at least."

Fiona nodded. This task was easy enough, but she was not entirely convinced it was the best move on the part of the department. Hesitant to argue with Leland, nonetheless she had to put forward reservations.

"I believe on Joy's current medical certificate the GP has reviewed his diagnosis and changed it to a more serious and longer lasting medical condition – Post Traumatic Stress Disorder. This is not looking good for us as her employer as it may mean potentially a more permanent injury."

"And if Ms O'Connell is true to form, a civil case for negligence and/or a payout for whole person impairment," Leland interrupted, his eyes spitting black sparks of outrage. "Let me think." Staring past Fiona, he meditated on a favourite oil painting on the far wall for a few long drawn out minutes.

"I want you to have words with Ms O'Connell's GP, put pressure on him to allow her to return to work on part time duties, even one hour a week suggested by the counsellor would suit our cause. It will look better when the case comes up if she's back and we can argue no harm has been done. This continual *Totally Incapacitated For Work* crap isn't helping." Leland observed the sceptical look on Fiona's face. "This shouldn't be too hard to do; the GP works for us – he's part of the Health Department after all. With a last name *Vitkay* he's most likely from one of those Eastern European countries on a temporary work visa. I'll put money on the table, he's no stranger to this sort of behind the scenes dealing."

Fiona looked questioningly at Leland. "Behind the scenes deal? Such as...?"

"At this time, just allude to something. I'm going to have to inform the Minister at some stage. He may be able to pull some strings with his Liberal Party colleagues in Canberra to fast track citizenship or whatever." Leland was lost in thought and appeared to have dismissed Fiona from his mind without further ado.

"Hmm, whatever," she mumbled, making the point that his vague instructions weren't actually helpful. She wasn't comfortable testing Dr Vitkay's medical ethics against his political expediency. It seemed ironic that he probably wanted to immigrate to this country to escape the very type of interference she was now being asked to employ. Sensing delicacy was required under the circumstances, she opted for the *saying less is best* policy. "If that's all, I'll get onto it." Leland grunted some kind of acknowledgement having moved on to reading emails.

Fiona exited the office. Sometimes she hated her job.

Chapter Twenty Three

"What is it with you and op shops? This is the third one we've visited in the last half hour." Kodi moaned at her cousin. "We're in Plover Point. I want to check out the boutiques and jewellery shops."

"This won't take a minute." Gemma pushed open the glass door of the Salvos and marched in, a woman on a mission. A musty mix of dust, old leather and mothballs distinct to all second hand stores tickled her nose. Ignoring shelves of worn shoes and racks of pre-loved dresses, she made her way to the back where trinkets, dish sets and kitchen miscellanea were stacked in random piles on pine shelving.

"What are you looking for exactly," Kodi asked. "Maybe I can be useful."

Gemma glanced up and down the shelves, half listening to Kodi. "Found it," she announced triumphantly. She picked up a pale green creamer moulded with stylised cabbage leaves and painted with indistinct fruits. Giving it a thorough inspection for chips and cracks she said, "This will do. It's not Carlton Ware but I think Mum will like it anyway."

Kodi peered at it, unconvinced. "It's cute," she said for the sake of saying something.

"Mum collects small jugs and creamers. It's her thing. I'm replacing one that Jaxon broke a couple weekends ago."

"Oh, now I get it."

More talkative now that she'd completed the main shopping task of the day, Gemma confided the story behind the broken pot. "Mum reacted rather badly. I've never seen her that upset, especially over a four-dollar creamer she found at a market. Jaxon kept saying it was an accident and that seemed to set her off. Her state escalated from mild annoyance to a screaming out-of-control crazy woman. Totally lost the plot."

"That must have scared poor Jaxon," Kodi said.

"He was terrified. I had to intervene." Gemma paused, imagining the scene where she'd had to get tough with her mum. "I feel bad because I had to shout at Mum to stop. I was saying *what's got into you?* And Mum looked at me with this horribly guilty expression and then started to cry. She told me later it was as if she was standing outside her body watching her emotions escalate into a conflagration and she was helpless to stop it."

"Weird. Auntie Joy is usually so calm and self-controlled," Kodi said. "How's Jaxon after all that?"

"You know, for a little kid, he handled it well. He loves his granny and when I explained that she's not herself lately due to getting PTSD from work, he was okay about it. He felt bad about breaking the pot and he promised to be more careful in the future."

"This is your way of mending bridges, I assume? Replacing the broken creamer with a similar one." Kodi nodded wisely.

"Something like that. I'll get Jaxon to give it to Mum. It'll come out of his pocket money." Gemma stared at nothing in particular for a moment. "I won't let her babysit for a while."

Kodi nodded before realising what was coming next.

"I hope you're up for it?"

Gemma glanced at her cousin way too casually, pretending this hadn't been set up. She knew what Kodi was thinking from the startled look on her face. She wasn't good with kids. Honor had moaned to mum about it. *How could she date a guy with a two-year-old when she's never had to change a nappy before?* Honor had complained.

To cajole her into it, Gemma smiled encouragement. "Jaxon's a cool kid. He's nine so he pretty much does his own thing."

"Sure, glad to help out, just say the word." Kodi winced. "Jaxon won't know what hit him." Seeing Gemma's sudden frown, she quickly amended that. "I mean, we'll have so much fun it will be a whirlwind. I didn't mean I'd actually hit him. Geez."

"Good. I may need you in a couple weeks. There's a meeting of the Eden Isle branch of the Natural Therapists Association. I missed the last one so I'd like to go if possible."

"No worries," Kodi said, shaking her head.

Satisfied another issue was sorted and out of the way, Gemma headed in the direction of a cash register. "I'm starting mum on Hypericum. The meds her GP prescribed are useless."

"Auntie Joy is lucky to have you as a daughter."

"Too right." Gemma smiled. "About time she got something back for all the money she spent on my medicinal herb courses."

A portly volunteer with a big smile on her face greeted them at the counter. While Gemma rummaged through her handbag in search of gold coins, Kodi chatted to the volunteer. "I'm starving. Where's the best place to grab some lunch in Plover Point? We don't get to town often."

Overly helpful, the volunteer proceeded with a ten-minute discussion of the pros and cons of all the various eating venues around the CBD. By the time the two of them got away, they were confused by too many choices.

"How about the food court?" Gemma suggested.

"Sounds good to me." Kodi was happy to agree to any place that had food ready to go. "Afterwards, promise we'll check out a few designer shops."

"But we haven't been to the Golden Opportunity Shop yet," Gemma said straight faced. Her droll humour was rewarded with a feigned punch to the shoulder by Kodi pretending to be outraged.

More seriously, Gemma said, "Actually, I'd rather hear about this new boyfriend of yours. Are you two getting serious? I want to hear all the gossip."

Chapter Twenty Four

Kodi sniffed disdainfully at the musty banana yoghurt smell emanating from the baby car seat in the back of Lachlan's old ute. Her runners crunched on a year's supply of junk mail, empty juice poppers, and torn envelopes thrown carelessly on the floor. She wondered what else would be uncovered if she did some digging. *Don't go there,* she winced. Why he hadn't bothered to clean up the mess was a mystery. All it would take was one garbage bag. Her dad washed and vacuumed the family sedan every weekend as a ritual to masculine duties. Lachlan's shine was starting to tarnish. Reality was fast overtaking romantic illusions. This made it all the easier to do what she set out to do.

She'd agreed to his offer to drop her home after netball practice making a point that she had plans for the night. He'd appeared disappointed when no further explanation was forthcoming, but clearly, he wanted to make up for their last fight seven days ago and didn't push his luck. They'd texted a bit during the week but not as enthusiastically as usual.

She wanted to see the look on his face when she rubbed in the latest news.

On the short drive, Lachlan mostly talked about the game and how certain players could improve their tactics. Kodi gave him the cold shoulder treatment, staring out the side window and making unintelligible noises now and then to acknowledge she was vaguely listening. When he pulled up to the curb next to her house, he switched off the engine and turned expectantly to give her a kiss. *Men could be so clueless sometimes.*

"I thought you should know that Auntie Joy went to the police and they've charged her boss with common assault," she announced, puffing up haughty and superior. With arms crossed, she waited for *the look* that would be vindication and repentance rolled into one.

"Wow, good on her," Lachlan said.

Not the reaction Kodi had anticipated. She rubbed in the point further.

"Seeing as her employer wouldn't protect her, she had to go outside to the *law*. Now her side of the story – the Truth – will be heard." Glaring at Lachlan to ensure he felt her ire, she added, "And something will be done about that psycho woman at last."

Lachlan looked lost in thought. "If the police actually laid charges that's a good sign. It means they believe they can get a conviction." He smiled. "Your Aunt stands a chance."

Kodi pulled back, offended. "A chance? The police agreed Poppy assaulted her."

"Dad always says the legal system is not as straightforward as you may think. First of all, the police won't even bother to lay charges if they're not confident in getting a conviction, even when they know a crime has been committed."

"That can't be right," Kodi protested. "It sounds as if they treat crime like a game of point scoring, the more convictions the higher their performance rating. If they can't get a score, they don't bother." This did not sound like her notion of the police as good guys, the modern equivalent of knights in shining armour, the protectors and defenders of civil society.

"No, it's more about not wasting the court's time. There are backlogs and it costs money, and the judges get pissed off if the police put forward cases that don't have enough hard facts for a conviction."

Kodi sat back processing this new take on the legal system. It wasn't as black and white as she'd initially thought. Truth and justice, fairness and individual rights, were moral concepts without tangible substance. The system relied on proof, hard facts and evidence. What happened when justice depended on a boss's word against an admin assistant's word. "In the end, it all boils down to money and economics," she said with a sigh.

"It's frustrating for the police knowing some people get away with crimes. But cheer up, they must have enough evidence to charge Poppy. That's a good start." Lachlan's wry smile was full of sympathy.

Not a sexy moment but it did stir pings of warmth and friendship in Kodi's heart. Enough to give her second thoughts about breaking up with him even if that had been her plan. Maybe he deserved a second chance. She'd think about it.

"Thanks, Lachlan." As she got out of the car, he pulled her gym bag from the back seat and handed it across. There was something masculine and appealing about the way the muscles in his upper arm became defined in that stretch. In a rash moment, she forgot her grudge. With a bright smile to offset a stern voice, she said, "I'll tell you what a real crime is – your ute is like a tip! If you want to take me home in the future, you'd better clean up all that rubbish."

Grabbing her bag, satisfied at the look of surprise on Lachlan's face, she flounced up the path to the front door. Before disappearing inside, she turned and blew a flirtatious kiss in his direction.

Chapter Twenty Five

Babysitting Jaxon for a few hours while Gemma went to her meeting was not going to be as bad as she'd expected.

This evening Kodi had intended to be put off kids for life in the hope this would make it easier to break off with Lachlan.

Ever efficient, Gemma had fed Jaxon dinner and he'd had a bath before Kodi arrived. He was all cute and cuddly, dressed in Spiderman pyjamas, dewy skinned with damp curls smelling clean and herbal from shampoo. Overall, he was rather subdued having been given last minute instructions to behave. Not knowing what this meant exactly, he was wary of Kodi.

All that was required was to keep the lad entertained until bedtime. This was going to be fun.

After waving goodbye to his mum, Jaxon looked expectantly at Kodi. Having come prepared, she pulled out a pack of playing cards. "Have you played Snap before?"

They sat cross legged on the floor in Gemma's family room facing each other, each with a determined look of a warrior about to do battle. After shuffling, Kodi split the pack in two and handed across a pile to Jaxon. "Ready?" she taunted before slapping a card on the carpet. He followed with his own slapped card. The war had begun. When two cards matched up, the first to call out SNAP and claim the pile won that round. And then it began again. Until one player's cards were all won by the opponent.

Although new to the game, Jaxon threw everything into it. Kodi started off unwilling to give the kid any slack, being rather competitive. After twenty minutes in she'd decided it was better to ease off and let Jaxon win a few more hands so he could have more fun. Rushed, chaotic, yelps of success and groans of loss, mixed with lots of cheating and laughter followed.

Slapping and shouting SNAP as hard and loud as he could, proved to be a winning combination. He was totally pumped by eight o'clock bedtime. The top of Kodi's hand smarted from being slapped a bit too enthusiastically. Comparing each card stack, Kodi announced that Jaxon had the biggest pile so he was declared the winner. He celebrated by dancing around the room in a jerky, arm waving jig. She credited this particular dance routine to a popular video going around YouTube.

Kodi felt spent but in a satisfied way. She congratulated herself on being good with kids. Babysitting wasn't that big a deal after all. Perhaps she should give Lachlan a second chance instead of writing him off.

If the evening had ended then and there, before she tucked Jaxon into bed, she would have left with a sense of success rather than misgivings. Jaxon reserved his naughtiness for bedtime. He wasn't sleepy. He wanted a bedtime story. Kodi looked around his room and pulled out a couple of hardcover books from the bookshelf. Grimm's Fairy Tales. Eden Isle's Historic Ghost Stories. Quarrelsome, he shook his head at each one.

Frustrated, Kodi blew up exasperated. "What do you want?"

Sitting up against the headboard with a sheet scrunched across his feet, he thought about this. Stalling for time, he hugged a brown cushion shaped like an Emoji pooh to his chest. "How do you get PTSD?"

Wondering where this came from out of the blue, she took a punt. "You mean like what happened to your Granny?"

"Mum says she has PTSD and that's why she's not herself anymore. How can you not be yourself anymore?"

"I don't know, Jack-a-roo. Go to sleep." She heaved his legs down the bed so he lay prone with his head resting on the pillow, and pulled the ends of the sheet to his chin, tucking in the ends to wrap him tight like a mummy.

Wriggling free, he rested on one elbow. "Mum says not to upset Granny. I have to be really careful around her. But Granny looks the same. Will I catch PTSD from her and not be myself anymore too? I don't want to be anyone else."

Hearing his plaintive whimper, Kodi was caught in a dilemma not knowing how to explain that PTSD wasn't contagious. How could she say it was about Auntie Joy getting strangled by her boss?

She searched her brain for inspiration. Maybe she could make up a story. Term 1 of creative writing had just started but was totally fun. She'd give it a go.

"How about I tell you a bedtime story if you promise to go to sleep afterwards?"

"Will it be about monsters? I like stories about dragons and magic and monsters."

"Maybe, but I don't want you to get scared. Do vampires give you the creeps?"

Jaxon snorted with disgust. "I'm not a baby. I'm nine years old. I can handle it."

"Don't say I didn't warn you," she joked. "Let me see, where shall I start..."

In a spooky voice, she began.

Once upon a time, not that long ago, there lived an old crone in a cottage at the end of the road who understood the hidden mysteries. She was ancient, her complexion a map of wrinkles. The locals called her Gran J and they thought she was crazy.

Hearsay within the community foretold of foolish youths seeking Gran J's insight. It is said, if you studied her face for too long, it would speak without words directly to your vulnerable heart – exposing dangerous truths better left unspoken. Students of magical lore would do well to heed their community's counsel – to go prepared or leave well enough alone.

And so it came about that two brothers dared their youngest brother – let's call him Jason, like Jason and the Argonauts – to knock on the door of the crazy crone on the eve of the Day of the Dead to see if she'd answer a question. At the peak of the full moon, he was to ask her "do vampires exist?"

Being the youngest brother, Jason obediently allowed them to dress him in a cape and paint his face a deathly white and his lips blood red, mimicking a vampire on a journey to the underworld. However, before they pushed him out their front door, egging him on with jeers of loser and meow, he remembered his mother's advice to never arrive as a guest empty handed. He secretly filled his pockets with several Cadbury's Marvellous Creation bars before leaving.

Now Jason was not particularly brave. It was simply that nothing bad had ever happened to him up until this day. He strolled to Gran J's cottage on this moonlit night with an innocent excitement, sticking to the path and avoiding shadows only to avoid tripping up, not because he was scared. Every now and then to stay in character, he flourished his cape in sweeping vampire winged movements, imagining he looked menacing.

As you'd expect walking alone in the middle of the night, an ancient gravelly voice from the shadows of darkness startled Jason out of his reverie.

"Vampires and other evil creatures live among us." An old hag with a hooked nose covered in warts emerged from the blackness to stand in the

middle of the road, blocking the way. Jason halted, frozen, as if caught in a spell.

Kodi paused to check Jaxon's level of interest. "With me so far?"

"More," he said.

The infamous Gran J studied Jason as if he were a specimen in a petri dish. Several long minutes passed with the slowness of molasses. Jason's knees wobbled. Then with a decisive nod, she motioned him to follow. She shuffled along the path, leaning on a carved hawthorn cane for support. Her shoulder length bleached white hair reflected the moon light with a bristled static, as if attracting some unseen universal energy.

She led him to a run-down cottage, opened a squeaking screen door and disappeared inside.

"Sleepy yet?" Kodi asked, knowing full well Jaxon was wide awake.

"More," he said.

Jason entered into a dim room. He saw Gran J sitting at a round table lit with a circle of tea light candles. He joined her at the table and politely placed one of his chocolate bars in front of her as an offering. She nodded, placing a hand over the bar, and then stared past him as if seeing into another dimension.

"Do you believe in the existence of evil, young man?"

Jason had no immediate answer, so instead he nervously laughed with bravado.

"I never used to at your age," she said matter-of-factly. Tea lights sputtered, before their flames re-ignited, casting snaking shadows across her lined face. "Since you've taken the trouble to come all this way on this hallowed evening, let me tell you a story about the time a vampire caught me unawares," she intoned in a story teller's voice. "This is a tale a young man should heed, or disregard at his peril."

"It was a day like any other day, ten years ago today when I was a young woman in my prime. I sat at my desk at work staring at a computer, lost in my own world of thoughts. I was actually rather sleepy, because my office was warm and stuffy, being mid-afternoon; there wasn't much activity going on at the centre. Most clients had gone home. The staff buried themselves under mounds of paperwork behind closed doors. All was quiet, boring, an extremely ordinary day."

"It's these ordinary days you have to be extra cautious about."

"You see, I'd been lulled into a false sense of security and therefore wasn't paying attention. A foul creature crept up behind my chair. It trapped me against the desk. Then it whispered in my ear almost like a caress, inviting my cooperation. If I don't strangle you, I'll have to strangle another."

"I felt its hands squeezing my throat. I froze like a possum mesmerised by an SUV's high beams, unable to move. Taken by surprise, I didn't comprehend I was being attacked until it was too late."

"Being strangled at work, in the middle of a quiet afternoon, was inconceivable."

"This is what vampires do to their victims: they catch you unawares, behaving in such a confusing manner the situation doesn't make sense, and in this way, they upend your world, thereby binding you in a trance. Before you can figure out what's going on, they zap the spirit of goodness straight out of your blood, leaving you in a zombie-like state of nothingness."

Kodi's eyes narrowed as she watched Jaxon's reaction. "You okay? Not too scared?"

"Zombies are awesome," he said.

This appeased Kodi. Storytellers appreciate an audience paying rapt attention.

"Most people mistakenly believe a vampire bites its victim's neck and sucks out their actual blood. But that is an antiquated idea. In truth, it attacks the

neck because this is where the blood in your arteries and veins carries your life energy, pulsing back and forth between your heart and mind."

Kodi slapped the end table, rattling Jaxon's glass of water and causing him to flinch.

"No, it's not blood a vampire wants – it wants your heart song. Strangulation is the easiest way for vampires to extract light and joy from your body, by squeezing out your song."

"You're making this stuff up as a trick on Halloween," Jason accused Gran J.

Such sweet innocent flesh, a perfect target for evil, thought Gran J. To survive in this world, he needed to be told the truth. *"Beasts of darkness can only exist by sucking life from other beings; they can't create this energy for themselves. So, you see, when I was attacked by this evil creature, in a matter of seconds it didn't only choke the air from my throat; it sucked out my heart song."*

After a theatrical hiatus, Kodi added, *"...and fed on it."*

"What's a heart song?" Jaxon asked Kodi, confused. "I like music, but I've never heard of people having a song of their own."

Kodi replied in character.

"Your song is the warm resonance in your heart, what we call joy. Every innocent child is born with the seed of a unique signature melody. It grows and blooms throughout your existence, creating a fully-fledged song when you become an adult. "

Jason frowned, perplexed.

Kodi raised steepled fingers to her lips. In Gran J's voice she said,

"When we are inspired to sing our hearts out like song birds at dawn, and happily want to give all our love and joy back into the world in a choir of radiant light, these are our heart songs."

"Kodi, I think you've gone off track. I want to know more about vampires." Jaxon yawned.

"Are you sure? I could save the rest for later?"

Suppressing another yawn, he said, "More, please."

"Gran J dabbed tears from the corners of her eyes with a grubby rag. Then she blew snot into it. She felt compelled to explain more about vampires and the evil they inflict."

"I was devastated after the attack, left like a limp rag, all empty and bereft. The vampire laughed cruelly and cast a wicked hex, perverting reality to suit its purpose. My world turned from multi-colours to monochrome. The spell turned strangulation into a joke, thereby protecting its malevolent nature."

"The vampire's spell gained momentum across the centre. Under the power of its sorcery, I lost the potency of my words. I spoke and tried to tell my version of events, but not one of my work colleagues believed me."

"The vampire's spell warped my voice, my story twisted into something unremarkable, trivialised into simply another day at the office where colleagues played practical jokes on one another. I was told it was nothing to be concerned about, that I should get over it already and stop making a drama about it."

"Rather than seen as a victim of evil abuse, I transmogrified into a spoilsport; a whinger; not one of the team."

"As if strangulation could ever be funny," Jaxon said wisely. "It would be so scary."

"You can tell how powerful this vampire's enthrallment was on those around the centre," Kodi agreed. "Shall I continue?" She pulled the sheet up to Jaxon's ears. He snuggled in.

"What happened to Gran J?" Hearing about spells and evil enthrallment piqued his interest again.

"Well, no one believed in vampires. They still don't. So only Gran J knew the truth. The damage was done of course. She was banished from her community to live out of sight in isolation. For many years she existed in a grey vortex, a state between living and nothingness, circling around and around the details of the attack, unable to make sense of what had happened to her, lost without a heart song."

Cautiously Jaxon asked, "What happened to the vampire? Did it hang around?"

"The vampire continued to haunt the centre, unimpeded," Kodi replied. "It's still there, I believe."

"What does it look like?" Jaxon sat up in bed. "Is it like a black shadow in the shape of a giant bat?"

"Now that is as good a description as I've ever heard." Kodi tried not to laugh, imagining the apt description of Poppy.

"I hope it stays at the centre and doesn't haunt Granny's cottage."

Concerned she may have frightened him after all, she quickly switched into recovery mode. "I am certain vampires stick faithfully to their territory and don't travel anywhere else."

"I want to go to sleep now."

"Oh, okay." Kodi had a lot more to say. "We can finish it another day. Jason has to complete his mission and receive magical gifts." She tucked him in and kissed his curly head. "Good night, sleep tight."

"Don't feed the bed bugs vegemite," he whispered and then fell fast asleep.

Chapter Twenty Six

Joy glanced at the clock on the wall and then at the dot points on her prepared list of talking points. She always came prepared when seeing Bev. Forty minutes left in today's session. Bev was explaining the emotional toll taken on members of the Save The Isle Forests protest group to which she belonged. Apparently, a few of them had developed PTSD as a result of being manhandled and arrested by overzealous police. Joy assumed there was a link between their PTSD and hers.

At least this subject was preferable to the usual interrogation of Joy's family history and deep delving into past dramas that Bev insisted on during most sessions. It was odd because Bev had initially warned about discussing any previous issues, advising these would be held against her workers compensation case. So why did she keep returning to discussions about this side of her life? Even if she'd given reassurances that family issues wouldn't be recorded in file notes, it was worrying.

Personally, Joy didn't feel family history had any bearing on her getting PTSD. Bev wasted time redirecting counselling sessions down irrelevant rabbit holes, and this was not helpful. It was obvious why Joy was sitting here week in week out – she'd been strangled at work and reacted rather badly to this. Simple. Why couldn't this be acknowledged and accepted, rather than searching for other excuses and explanations hidden deep in her psyche? It didn't make sense.

The world wasn't safe now; this was her reality. Her life had been upended by Poppy for reasons she couldn't fathom. It wasn't helpful spending time trying to convince Joy that her psychological state was damaged long ago and if she only changed her thoughts, her world would magically become safe again and she'd return to 'normal'. Surely it was Poppy's crazy state of mind that required close scrutiny; it was her behaviour that was wrong and dangerous, causing Joy's PTSD – not some incident from Joy's past. Yet, Poppy was ignored; her family history was not examined or taken into account; she was allowed to return to her life as *normal*. In all these counselling sessions, the elephant in the room never mentioned was Poppy, the strangler – her influence was left out of the equation as if of no consequence.

As if it was only Joy's head that needed to be fixed, changed, re-programmed. This was not helpful.

What Joy needed from these sessions was not to get her head right. She needed the counsellor to step into her shoes, acknowledge and accept her version of the incident, what it was like living in this upended PTSD world, and then move on to discussing practical measures to help Joy adjust to *not being herself*. Not try to change her back. It was too late for that.

Instead, take the pressure off getting better within a prescribed return to work timeframe. Give her permission to be this new self; a Joy who lacked motivation, felt anxious about leaving the house, watched DVDs all day long like a couch potato, had trouble controlling anger. And then, work with that reality by offering practical suggestions on how to gradually move from being a couch potato to being mildly productive as a human being.

Not set a long To Do list like Joy used to have. But maybe help her to adjust to achieving one small thing each day.

At the moment, it seemed Bev had given up not just on changing Joy's thought processes, but on the counselling process altogether.

Joy was anxious to move on from Bev's logging rainforest monologue to a topic more personally relevant. They only had one hour and Bev was such a talker. If she didn't watch the time, sessions went overtime. Their conversations were the only moments of social contact in her small world lately. One hour a fortnight to talk to another human being about worries and irritations.

Desperate as she was to be seen and heard in order to feel normal, her only other outing for the week – to the supermarket – didn't really count as human contact.

Joy's attention drifted from Bev. It was difficult to concentrate during long conversations and her mind switched off. Instead, she pictured herself at the checkout at Woolies.

Chatting about the weather to the check-out chick at Woolies was not real heart to heart interaction. In fact, she hated the fake *how are you today?* question checkout operators were forced to ask as part of a corporate customer service procedure. It felt emotionally intrusive particularly on days when she felt like shit and was compelled to respond, and her response had to be a big, fat lie: *I'm fine* – when she wasn't. In reality, no check out chick wanted to know the details of how she actually was. This was depressing.

To revive her flagging spirits after an outing to the supermarket a few weeks ago, Joy started to compile a list of more creative responses to the *how are you today* question: *About the same; You wouldn't believe me if I told you; I'm waiting for my GP's diagnosis.* She added to the list every now and then. However, the next few times she stood at the Woolies' checkout her brain blanked out at the question, experiencing too much anxiety to remember to be clever.

Last week the question changed to *what are your plans for the rest of the day*. This made it easier. She would say *putting groceries away* – the truth of her sad existence. That would elicit a nod of acknowledgement without the expectation of continuing a pointless conversation neither party cared about.

Joy forced attention back to the room.

Bev's story was in full swing and began to enter into conspiracy theories about government interference in citizens' rights to free speech. All well and good, and in Joy's better days this would have been interesting and worth focusing attention on. But not today when she was needy and wanted their session to be all about her. There were more important things to discuss.

Impatient, Joy cut in.

"My grandson Jaxon broke something of mine the other day and my temper escalated out of control. I couldn't stop myself. I totally lost the plot and it was awful." Bev was momentarily befuddled at the interruption to her train of thought but recovered with professional aplomb.

"This is a common symptom of PTSD. Did you read the notes I gave you on *Releasing Emotions?*"

"It wasn't really about a four-dollar creamer," Joy remarked, not wanting to be subjected to an artificial therapeutic formula but instead needing Bev's understanding. "Although it was a favourite, I collect Carlton Ware. The trigger was Jaxon's insistence it was an accident. As if I shouldn't have gotten upset because he didn't break it on purpose."

"Is this similar to how you feel about what Poppy has done? That if she didn't mean to scare you, this absolved her of responsibility for the harm she caused?"

Joy thought about this insight. "I think so. I'm still broken as to whether she intended this to happen or not." She looked past Bev into space. "I've got this image in my head of a gift shop selling ceramic vases. A customer accidentally knocks one off the shelf and it falls to the floor and shatters. The shop owner rushes over and says *don't worry, we have insurance for breakages*. The customer walks away not having to pay for the damage. The vase gets glued back together, but it has lost its value. The customer returns and is welcomed with open arms by the unctuous shop owner."

Bev nodded. "Is this how it feels to be traumatised, like humpty dumpty being glued back together again?"

Joy began to tick off points using her fingers. "Like the shop owner, my employer is not out of pocket because of workers comp insurance. The customer, Poppy, gets off without having to account for the damage caused – walks away retaining her inherent value as an employee; she's welcomed back without consequence, seen not only as loyal but labelled a role model. The only one to suffer is me, the poor vase that sat on a shelf minding its own business..."

"Until a careless accident shattered your mental health," Bev completed the sentiment. "And we are here now trying to put you back together again but you feel you won't ever be quite the same."

"Yeah. I kept screaming at him *"I don't care if you didn't intend for this to happen – the creamer is still broken whether it was an accident or not. I do not have a creamer now."* He was too little to understand. I knew this but I couldn't stop yelling. It was awful. Never in my life has this happened where I literally could not stop my temper. All over a four dollar creamer I found at Lower Teasel market." She shook her head in bafflement. "Gemma had to intervene in the end. I don't recognise this person I've become."

"Jaxon breaking your creamer and claiming it was an accident was symbolic of all those injustices." Bev jotted down notes. "Good. This is good insight. We can work with this. I can reassure you, our goal in counselling is to facilitate your trauma recovery so you feel like your old self again. It may take some time but it is achievable."

Joy looked hopeful. She wanted to believe Bev.

She didn't like this person she'd become.

Chapter Twenty Seven

Gemma made a point of lunching at the Village Spice Café in Lower Teasel on a regular basis. About a year ago the chef had started experimenting with locally grown micro-greens, edible flowers, and bespoke salad dressings such as raspberry vinaigrette, dishing up a lunchtime special salad every Tuesday. They were the best ever and she drooled at the prospect of another unique dining experience.

On this occasion, she was flush with money. Last week her diary had been fully booked with natural therapy clients plus Jaxon's father finally remembered to deposit a well needed child support payment. It only equated to the price of a packet of cigarettes and came on a random basis, but it was nonetheless gratefully received whenever it arrived.

Swinging a homemade felt handbag across her shoulder, Gemma entered through the heavy oak door of the old building and looked around for Honor. Naturally her aunt was early. She'd claimed a round table covered with a homey tablecloth in a bay window overlooking Quamby Bluff, a well sought-after position during the lunch crush.

Catching her eye, she waved a greeting. Honor looked relaxed and perfectly dressed for the scene in a navy striped lightweight wool pullover accessorised with a red silk scarf tossed casually across her shoulders. Her white hair was glossed back in a thick plait. Gemma unconsciously pushed back her ginger mane, making a mental note to book a trim at the hairdresser for herself and Jaxon before the start of next school term.

The fashion gene had skipped her mother line. Her dress sense may not be as poor as op shop chic but it was definitely single mum's Best and Less. Under a khaki army jacket, she wore jeans, a soft flowing cotton blouse and faux leather ankle boots. Not as elegant as Honor's, but clean and tidy at least. Gemma decided long ago that nail polish and makeup were not a necessity on a tight budget, convinced being a natural redhead with freckles was her *look*.

She criss-crossed through crowded tables with animated conversations going on. A waiter carrying a tray glided past, leaving a heady aroma of ground bourbon-infused coffee beans, spicy Indian curry and pungent basil. She contemplated going off script and ordering pesto pasta or maybe the curry instead of a salad. Why worry about calories all the time?

Honor would most likely order soup. She watched her weight constantly and always discouraged Gemma from ordering dessert, implying a meagre appetite equated to femininity. As if a few kilos made any difference as to whether a single, working mum had any choice about a paucity of romance. Jaxon was too demanding of attention and there were not enough hours in the day to fit another male into her world. Even if she could ever trust another man after Jaxon's father.

Gemma loved her aunt and enjoyed their regular catch ups. Their lunches were more fun now than with mum. *Before The Strangling* – or BTS as she referred to it – her mum had lived life to the full, and that included indulging in good conversation and sensory culinary experiences. These past few months, it was hard to get her out of the house, let alone to a noisy café.

She wished mum could have a conversation about a new recipe, or a good book, or a nuno felting project with her these days. She missed the ordinary, normal conversations they had BTS. All mum talked about, obsessively, was the work incident and how it was being handled by her employer, and nothing much else. As much as she loved her mum, the intensity of a broken record stuck on repeat was becoming hard to listen to.

She was determined to be her BTS mother's daughter today and ordered dessert. Quickly hugging Honor, Gemma sat down and pulled out a tiny vial from a jacket pocket. It contained a blend of bush flower essences and local honey. "This is for you when you start to overly worry about Kodi. I'd like you to try it. You never know, it might help."

Honor stared at the bottle as if a skull and crossbones were blazoned its front. Maybe her auntie was a sceptic about natural medicines, but Gemma never lost an opportunity to turn her into a true believer. "There's wandering jew for letting go of clinging; honeysuckle for providing wisdom in the background, sort of like providing a safety net rather than a safety harness, to allow a child to become more independent before they leave home."

Honor looked stricken. "She's not leaving home, is she? What have you heard?"

"Nothing Auntie. Relax. A couple drops under your tongue three times a day. In a couple days, you'll be a new person," she instructed.

Honor undid the stopper and sniffed at the contents. "Or a lush after sipping brandy all day."

Gemma failed to pick up on the droll humour. "Sorry, I should have used water as the carrier. But it keeps better in a spirit-base."

Honor patted her hand. "Under the tongue?" Obediently, she tipped her head back and squeezed a stopper full of liquid into her mouth and swallowed. "Phew, that's strong."

Satisfied, Gemma changed the subject by grabbing menus and handing one to Honor. "What looks good?" she asked, studying it as if it hadn't been memorised many lunchtimes ago.

After a waiter took their orders, Gemma turned to Honor. "Mum told me you're worried about Lachlan being a single father."

Honor blushed. "I was having a good old whinge the other day. Joy shouldn't have taken it to heart. Even if I don't think Lachlan is good for Kodi, she's too headstrong to listen to anything I have to say about it. I only want what's best for her."

Gemma squeezed her hand. "She'll work it out eventually. She's sensible most of the time, even if a bit immature. There's nothing wrong with a mistake now and then, as long as we come out stronger, if not wiser."

"I know I can be controlling at times." She dabbed tears from her eyes and then laughed. "But you're starting to sound like me with a platitude like that."

"No way," Gemma lightheartedly gibed. "I'm my mother's daughter. What do you call mum? *A trouble magnet*, that's me, too. I'm a single mum at twenty-nine with an ex who was an abusive stalker and forgets to send child support more often than not."

The coffees arrived and for a few minutes their attention was on measuring sugar into their cups and sipping on cappuccino foam.

Finally, Gemma started where they left off. "Mum says Lachlan's okay but she's not sure Kodi is ready to take on parental responsibilities. Babysitting Jaxon the other night was a test, I guess."

Honor leaned forward. "How did that go? Kodi said they played cards and she made up a bedtime story to get him to sleep. She bragged about being awesome with kids after all."

"Hmm, I must talk to her about that story." Gemma winced. "Jaxon mentioned something about vampires."

"She's studying creative writing, although children's fiction isn't taught until third term." Honor sounded apologetic. "Apparently, Jaxon wanted to know how Joy got PTSD so Kodi thought it would be easier putting it in a story. It was her first practice run."

"I get that. Her intentions were good." Gemma stared out the window at dark clouds blanketing Quamby Bluff in shadows. "You probably heard. I can't have mum babysit until she's better. She's so emotionally volatile at the moment I can't trust her with Jaxon. I'll need to depend on Kodi to babysit again."

"I'm sure that won't be a problem." Honor sighed. "Joy worries me, too."

"Maybe babysitting but minus the vampire stories. Jaxon has been acting weird the last few nights. It may not be related. But suddenly he won't cross the hallway from the family room to his bedroom without turning on all the lights."

Honor laughed. "Kids and their imaginations. Kodi used to insist on a night light in her room because of the boogey man under the bed. I'm not sure if she's grown out of it to this day."

"Jaxon better grow out of this obsession soon or my electricity bill will go through the roof with the hall light kept on all night."

"Despite all the trouble kids cost us, I know you wouldn't trade Jaxon for anything."

"Same with Kodi despite her current boogey man," Gemma countered, referring to Lachlan.

They were having a good chuckle when their orders arrived. Miso broth with shiitake mushrooms and soba noodles for Honor. The Chef's Salad for Gemma: smoked chicken with pecans, sun dried tomatoes, snow peas, baby spinach and nasturtium flowers, crunchy garlic croutons, with a generous serve of creamy blue cheese dressing on the side. Tucking in to the delicious meal, Gemma decided the calories in a salad were low enough to justify a sticky date pudding with cream for dessert.

Chapter Twenty Eight

"Joy! Joy!"

Joy heard her name being shouted and debated whether to look around or hide behind the stack of groceries sticking up from the shopping trolley. Too late, the decision was made for her. A woman she recognised as a volunteer from the centre parked a trolley across the aisle blocking an escape.

"I thought it was you. How are you anyway? We haven't seen you around at the centre for ages." A breathless Daisy gave her an encouraging smile. "No one I've spoken to could tell me where you'd gone."

Joy was dumbfounded at Daisy's friendliness and the fact the volunteers didn't know why she was off work. "I've been on workers compensation for a couple months," she managed to say.

"Oh, no, what did you do?" she laughed.

For some reason, that triggered a sense of outrage in Joy. It wasn't as if she'd lifted a box and hurt her back or burned her finger on a boiling kettle. It was serious – she was strangled by her boss. "I didn't do anything. It was what was done to me that's the problem."

Daisy waited expectantly for her to fill in the blanks.

Joy obliged, with no holds barred. "While Jane was away getting a hip replacement, the manager filling in for her got stressed and decided to use me as her personal stress ball. She basically assaulted me."

Daisy looked shocked and sympathetic. "Poppy Bryant?" she asked knowingly. "I can understand her doing something like that. We're all wary around her. There's something creepy about her loud, over-the-top manner."

Interesting comment, Joy thought. "It sounds like Poppy is still acting as manager."

"Oh, yes," Daisy replied. "She went full time at the centre a month or so ago. Jane came back from long service leave and was transferred to a special project at head office."

Furious at this turn of events, Joy decided not to be discreet. "The police have charged her with common assault. It will go to court in September. I can't return to work until it's sorted."

Daisy nodded, taking in the information. "I'm sorry about what happened to you, but you are probably better off being away from that place. There's a lot of bad shit going on behind the scenes. I've put in a few complaints trying to alert higher management to what I've seen, but they never get back to me. Now, I've stopped reporting it."

Joy thought back to the pilfering of government supplies and assumed this was what Daisy was referring to.

But then Daisy said enigmatically, "One day one of our elderly clients is going to get terribly hurt, maybe even die, I'm afraid."

Before Joy could ask what this meant, Daisy was pushing her trolley away and waving goodbye. "Trust me, you don't want to know," she said conspiratorially. "You are better off out of it."

In her wake, Joy finished grocery shopping with mixed feelings. Daisy was the first person from the centre to treat her as a normal work colleague. And she had affirmed that Poppy was someone to be wary of. This vindication felt good. But hinting at some nefarious goings on behind the scenes at the centre was disturbing. In all the time Joy had worked there she'd never suspected anything so wrong it would endanger clients.

At the checkout, Joy unloaded two bags of barbeque chips, truffle goat cheese dip and a large block of rum and raisin chocolate before being asked *the question*.

"Got any plans for the weekend?"

If Joy had been in the mood for a conversation the pimply faced checkout operator's bored expression would have quashed any temptation. She continued unloading groceries. "You wouldn't believe it if I told you," she said with a wry smile.

The lad snorted and carried on scanning.

As she pushed the grocery trolley to her white Baleno and opened the boot, she wracked her brain for any memories of signs that could possibly implicate staff in wrongful activities. After loading the bags, she looked across to Quamby Bluff in the distance and ran a hand through her hair. Maybe she was too naïve and trusting, but she couldn't think of a single incident that pointed in that direction.

On the drive home, a sinister shiver ran up her spine with an accompanying thought. Maybe without realising it, with all her new administrative procedures, bookkeeping journals and audit trails, she was getting close to exposing some hidden corruption going on – and Poppy was given instructions to put a stop to her, one way or another. This would explain her bizarre behaviour and the department turning a blind eye, not following policy procedures, not encouraging her to return to work. It hadn't made sense up until now. But what if... something else was really going on?

The world turned on its head. It became inexplicable and unsafe in exponential ways. Joy did not know what to make of this new revelation. She sped up, wanting to be home in her safe cave away from too many unknowns as soon as possible.

Chapter Twenty Nine

Waiting in the doctors' surgery, Joy had a sense of déjà vu. How many times had she sat in this same hard chair over the past couple months?

Since the last medical certificate, another fortnight had passed with Joy impersonating a couch potato for most of it. Each day was Groundhog Day – the same mind-numbing sameness day in, day out. Pointlessness on repeat. She would awake in the mornings with dread, peering into a yawning abyss of bleakness, wondering how to fill in the hours ahead without first going mad.

At the same time, it was frustrating to be so listless. She could not get motivated to shower and dress most days, let alone vacuum or spring clean cobwebs from the cornices. All the materials for a nuno felting project planned for the Easter break remained stuck in a chest in a second bedroom, untouched. Out of sight. Out of mind.

Easter was next week.

Strange, but before the strangling she'd been excited about plans to take three weeks annual leave over Easter and just stay home. One of the Shamrock Room volunteers had asked if she was going away during the break and she'd replied rather arrogantly, *Why would she want to spend time at an interstate Bed and Breakfast when her Federation cottage was just like one?*

How things had changed. BTS, Joy loved relaxing at home. Especially when working full time and having an active social life, it felt like a luxury to be at home, not doing much of anything.

And when she was on leave, there was always a long TO DO list of all the neglected jobs wanting attention.

Time off used to go by so quickly with so many activities planned. For a working woman, being at home had been one of her greatest pleasures.

Now, she was bored and guilty at missing the opportunity to get things done during this forced period off work. PTSD seemed to sap life energy from her body, leaving a dry husk where a vibrant, lush woman once existed. Perhaps she wasn't broken so much as wilted.

Last session with Bev, she'd mentioned a longing for her cramped receptionist office. She missed a routine that forced her to get up, get going and achieve things. Despite the incident, a certain nostalgia lurked in her heart for her old office space, almost a home away from home feeling. She took pride in how it was set up with well thought out procedures and checklists, journals and filing systems, an achievement of organised efficiency just the way she wanted.

Although with Amberlie in the job full time over the last few months, the perfection of Joy's systems would most likely be messed up, given the cavalier attitude of the young, job share partner. Joy wondered how long it would take to bring the office back to normal after she returned. It was as daunting as it was disappointing.

And then there was Daisy's warning about bad stuff happening behind the scenes at the centre. Things that could injure senior clients. What was that all about? Her mind blanked out, unable to cope with a problem larger in scope than Poppy's presence.

As long as Poppy continued to work there, there was no way to set things right. She was the insurmountable elephant in the room. A pervasive, all encompassing, aversion towards Poppy blotted out any sunshiny wistfulness about the centre.

This was not going to change unless she succumbed to the department's pressure to forgive and forget what Poppy had done.

Despite all the counselling and GP appointments trying to convince her otherwise, her brain refused to budge on the issue of Poppy posing an ongoing threat to her life. It was the only thing that made sense in this whole return to work business.

All things considered, the dream of returning to the job morphed into a nightmare.

Joy's bum started to go numb from sitting on a moulded plastic chair in the doctors' surgery for so long. She wondered how long Dr Vitkay was going to be. The appointment was for ten thirty. A wall clock read five minutes to eleven. Where was Michelle? They were both running late. She checked her phone but there were no messages. This felt like a small betrayal. She'd begun to rely on Michelle's soothing presence before seeing the doctor. The smell of antiseptic turned her stomach. The waiting room was crowded with more patients, coughing and groaning in pain.

Looking up she saw the elegant figure of Michelle enter the room, calm and collected. With fluid movements, she sat next to Joy and leaned in to whisper. "I'm so sorry to be late. How are you?"

A simple enough question. Joy struggled to find the best answer. The socially expected one was *I'm fine,* except she wasn't. To tell the truth would be to expose her mental health issues to a waiting room full of locals. People who may not know her personally but would be interested enough in her condition to gossip about it to others. Lower Teasel gossip could be petty and mean. The risk of honesty in the wrong ears was too great.

And there was another side to this dilemma. Michelle appeared to be kind and caring. In another context, she probably was. But she worked on behalf of the department and her job as Rehabilitation Coordinator was paid by the insurer. If Joy automatically responded that she was *fine* would this be recorded in Michelle's notes and reported back?

It was in her best interests to reply to the seemingly innocent question with a particular truth: she was not fine. She wanted to be, but she wasn't yet. Michelle did not have any medical training or have an understanding about how Joy's life had been upended since PTSD. Where would she begin to explain how difficult life was for her every day? Michelle was at this appointment for a reason: to befriend and get the answer the insurer wanted to hear.

"About the same," Joy said. An answer that could mean anything and everything, and nothing.

Michelle nodded. "I've been waiting to talk with your worker's compensation officer at the health department but she's been difficult to pin down. I understand she's taken extended leave; they couldn't tell me when she'll return. I spoke to Hayden, the OH&S Officer filling in. I knew you'd want to know what progress has been made at the centre."

"Have they stood Poppy down pending the court case?" Joy asked expectantly.

"They had an OH&S audit and a CCTV security system has been recommended. I believe they've also put a lock on the receptionist's door as you suggested. This is all good news."

"But what about Poppy? I ran into a volunteer at Woolies and she hinted that Poppy was acting as manager to this day. Has Jane extended her sick leave?"

Michelle's doe eyes widened as if caught in a gun sight, hesitating long enough to give away obvious indecision on formulating a response. "I'm not sure of that," she mumbled. "The department is not obliged to take a position on Poppy's redeployment because she's on a temporary placement at the centre."

Joy screwed up her face in disbelief. "Are you telling me, they're saying it's a rostering issue and not a workers comp issue?"

Michelle hurriedly continued. "Apparently Poppy has stated she doesn't want to fill in as acting manager in the future. But as far as workers comp goes, *you* are the focus of our attention. Poppy is not our concern."

This left Joy suspicious. Michelle wasn't being completely up front. Did she think Joy was stupid?

Surely the department was required to keep her informed about Poppy's status at the centre along with all other OH&S issues for as long as the psycho persisted in hanging around like a resident ghost shadowing the corridors. Even after Jane returned as manager, they could roster Poppy to provide backup as a relief nurse at the centre. That was just as bad for Joy, particularly if security cameras were not installed quickly enough. A recommendation to install extra security was no guarantee it would happen, depending on other budget priorities.

"The department offered to try you one day a week on a trial basis. They've offered an office at the back of the building where you'll be alone and won't have to deal with clients." Michelle sounded positive and persuasive. "Alternatively, I could arrange a transfer for you to work at another health centre for the time being."

Joy wasn't convinced, even if this was the first encouraging sign the department wanted her to return. For some reason, being isolated in a back office without other people around seemed rather scary. Starting in another health centre in an unknown work environment with people that were strangers was even less appealing. It seemed obvious the department should understand this. She hated feeling put on the spot by Michelle, forced into a conversation about the pros and cons in a public arena.

Before discussing the full implications of each offer, Dr Vitkay called out her name. Perfect timing. She pushed out of the chair and straggled after him to the consulting room.

"How are you?" Dr Vitkay asked, referring to his notes.

It was the same question he'd been asking each visit for months. While he studied his file rather than look at her, Joy finally understood.

She used to think his question was about whether the time off work, the medications and the counselling sessions were working to make her better. After all, the medical model is based on curing illness and PTSD was a mental illness. Doctors looked after you to get you better, return you to normal. *How are you?* meant *how much have you improved since I last saw you?* as if a programmed timeline of recovery existed that she could be compared against.

But that couldn't be what he meant by the question. The pertinent question had to be *how have you been managing your symptoms?* Because at the end of the day, that was all she could do. She wasn't getting better in terms of returning to normal, she was just getting by.

And there was a limit as to how much she could manage. It was not as simple as mind over matter or positive thinking. It was a matter of changing her lifestyle in so many ways she didn't even know who she was any more. Sadly, it was the only way she could bear to be this new person PTSD forced upon her.

Joy sat stiff and weepy-vulnerable next to Dr Vitkay. Feeling pressured from the department and Michelle, she was not convinced her opinions were being taken into consideration. When held up against their perceived authority on the subject of what was better for her, she came out second best.

"About the same," she said, ashamed to admit she was no better. "I have good days and bad days, good weeks, bad weeks. But overall..." She had begun to notice that talking about her symptoms made her feel worse, as if she was reliving them all over again. This caused considerable distress. Because of this, she had started to develop an aversion to seeing the doctor. This would slowly creep up on her, beginning a couple days beforehand. It would dissipate a day or two after a consultation and then she would relax into feeling safe again until the next round of impending interventions.

What was the point of coming to these appointments every fortnight?

Ironically, Dr Vitkay insisted on keeping a close watch on her progress, and yet it was these consultations that set back her progress. A no-win situation. If left alone, safe at home, and not forced to think about returning to the centre, she reached a fragile equilibrium. Not quite normal as in being her old self, but at least for most of the time her anxiety lessened. It was only when out in public and interacting with other people that the PTSD symptoms flared up.

She wanted to get off the merry-go-round of medical and counselling appointments and be left in peace to work things out for herself. The workers compensation system wouldn't allow it.

Clutching a brocade handbag as if it was a teddy bear, she pulled out a pre-written list of symptoms from a side pocket and handed it across. It was humiliating to be in a situation each fortnight where she was forced to detail each and every symptom of mental illness to justify a new medical certificate. However, when at a doctor's mercy where at any time he might decide to send her back to work too soon, pride and self-respect were luxuries Joy could no longer afford.

By her way of thinking, an itemised account of symptoms would statistically validate what otherwise was a condition *all in her head*. Handing over a list of symptoms, instead of going over them ad nauseum, would make the consultation quicker and less painful.

Dr Vitkay speed read the list and added it to the medical notes. Over the last couple weeks since her last appointment, she'd suffered from one panic attack, continuous low-grade anxiety, feeling sick at the thought of leaving the house and insomnia. She regularly slept in until ten because she often woke up in the middle of the night from nightmares about Poppy and then couldn't fall back asleep until the morning. He studied a computer screen briefly and then turned his attention to her.

"How have you been?" he asked kindly.

"I feel worse than ever!" In an emotional gush, Joy poured out what was really bothering her – disappointment in the workers compensation process and how her employer was standing by Poppy despite the police charging her with assault. Through tears, she said this was a betrayal of trust; they'd failed to protect her and make her feel safe, and at the same time they were applying pressure for her to return to work as if nothing had happened.

Dr Vitkay appeared sympathetic, but then made an upsetting observation. "Every time you come to see me, Joy, you say the same things."

This caught her by surprise like a kick in the guts. She wasn't sure how to react. Was Dr Vitkay saying she was making it up? Or was he concerned she wasn't showing improvement? Maybe she was experiencing PTSD differently from other people?

With sudden insight, she realised no one had explained what exactly PTSD was after diagnosing her with it. Perhaps he was right – she was like a broken record with her mind going round and round, unresolved, coming back to the same spot, not better – just broken.

"I'm suffering anxiety right now. I feel faint and my heart is pounding out of control," Joy said defensively. The words came out as a croak because her throat constricted whenever she was stressed. He was her doctor, couldn't he tell?

As if reading her mind, he said, "I can't actually see your anxiety. I believe you are experiencing it but there are no outward visible signs for me to go on. You look perfectly normal to me. I have to believe your word."

This confounded Joy. She didn't feel normal, but no one else could tell by looking at her she was suffering from a trauma, not even a doctor. This was a revelation.

It reminded her of undergoing chemotherapy and losing all her hair five years ago. The doctor sent her to a workshop called "Look Good Feel Good" which showed how to apply makeup and wear a wig so she didn't look like she was dying. And it worked. When she went out in public people would gush in surprise *you look so good*. She didn't look like she had cancer so they felt better about that. She still had cancer and she still felt like shit, but she looked good.

This made her angry at Dr Vitkay. All he had to do was take her blood pressure or listen to her heart to tell it was racing out of control, if he didn't believe her. What happened to good old-fashioned medicine?

He looked concerned. "You need to try to get out more and socialise. Research has shown social isolation and inactivity can lead to depression."

"I get so tired. I can't seem to muster the energy for more than grocery shopping and workers comp appointments."

"You can order groceries online these days and get them delivered," he suggested.

Not that Joy had a computer or internet at home. And she actually liked grocery shopping at the local Woolies. As a weekly outing, it was familiar, quiet and felt safe and predictable. But instead of saying this, she gave a placating laugh. "Don't tell me that! I'll never leave the house."

He silently studied her as if weighing up the significance of the remark. Joy became worried he would send her back to work. She wasn't ready.

"Can I have more time off?" she asked with a tone of desperation. "I can't go back just yet." She wanted him to sign off the medical certificate before Michelle came in and discussed the department's proposed trial. "Could you issue a certificate for a longer period?"

Joy was becoming wary of Michelle's influence on the doctor' decisions. Purely based on intuition, she no longer whole heartedly trusted Michelle as a passive support person. More suspicious lately, she wondered if Michelle's role was a conduit for the department to apply pressure on her and Dr Vitkay to do their bidding.

"I'm going to give you five weeks off work over the Easter break. I'll be away for a while."

Joy smiled with relief. "I should be better by then."

"I want you to try to see friends, join a social group, or go for a walk every day. This will help as much as the antidepressants I've prescribed."

The relief Joy felt was short lived. Guilt set in as she debated whether to mention her daughter was a natural therapist and had taken her off prescription drugs and put her on herbal remedies. She wasn't sure if the law required her to follow doctor's orders to the letter, but it was probably better not to chance it. She'd keep quiet for now.

Doctor's orders – Get out and socialise. "My sister suggested I join a choir," she said to sound agreeable. Honor had urged her to join the church choir, saying singing was good for the soul and research had recently proven it to be therapeutic.

Maybe Joy wasn't the best singer but she loved to sing – in the shower, in the car on long drives, when ironing a pile of clothes. Honor's suggestion had seemed like a good one even if she wasn't particularly religious. Except since being choked, every time Joy tried to sing her throat closed up, all dry and tight, the notes flat and tuneless, resulting in a hacking cough and tears of sadness. Poppy had taken away her singing voice along with so much else. Another joy silenced.

She didn't explain this to the doctor. She'd taken up too much of his time already.

She didn't clarify this change in her voice to Honor, either. Instead, she'd declined Honor's offer saying she couldn't join a choir in the same church frequented by Poppy and her husband.

The other day, she'd made one lame attempt to explain to her sister the changes to her sense of self. It wasn't so much about losing the joy of singing as much as it was losing her voice altogether. Caught within workers comp, she was forced to do a lot of talking to doctors and counsellors. Ironically with all that talking, they asked the questions but never answered hers.

Their job was to extricate answers to fit a PTSD label and provide treatment with a predetermined formula. Each prescription the same no matter the person; a tick the box program, with no consideration of unique circumstances or the individual involved.

Honor countered saying doctors were required to follow standard treatment protocols. Why would they deviate from the rules?

Joy found it impossible to convey the sense of frustration with a rehabilitation process where self-appointed experts were allowed to poke, prod, and drill into her psyche and yet throughout this process, they managed to skillfully evade her own useful suggestions about what she really needed. They would not allow her to be an authority on her own self. Her voice was only heard in the context of the answers being sought.

The fact this treatment regime did not assist her recovery was not a flaw in the system. It was Joy's fault. She was recalcitrant. She lacked resilience. She was a lab rat in a case file. Joy lost her voice along with a sense of authority about self in this process.

It didn't help being stuck at home. Hidden from view. This, more than anything, rendered her voiceless and invisible to the outside world. Life had lost its colour and become monotone – black and white and grey. She didn't know who she was any more. Caught in a grey limbo, employed but not a worker.

Honor had argued to have faith in God's plan. "Your voice and verve would come back over time," she'd insisted. Her sister was naively positive like that.

A knock on the door interrupted Joy's thought process. Michelle joined the consultation. As per the usual routine, she handed a prepared RTW plan across for Dr Vitkay's signature and studied a copy of the new medical certificate.

Out of curiosity, Joy double checked the boxes on the plan labelled *Cause of Injury* and *Nature of Injury*. Nothing had changed from the first print out. 'Neck Stiffness' was still there despite the diagnosis of Post Traumatic Stress Disorder. Feeling headstrong, she pointed out the error.

Indifferently, Michelle mumbled, "The guidelines require the wording to come from the original workers compensation medical report."

"But it's incorrect," Joy argued. "Someone unfamiliar with my history would think I had soft tissue damage like whiplash. I want it on record that my injury was caused by my manager strangling me, and the nature of my injury is PTSD." She looked to Dr Vitkay for agreement. He watched Michelle.

"Sign this one today and I'll see about wordsmithing the phrasing with the department next plan." Michelle sounded impatient. Turning to Dr

Vitkay, she commented, "I see you've issued another certificate as 'Totally Incapacitated for Work'. Senior managers in the Department of Health have advised they want Joy to return to work on a trial basis for one day a week as soon as possible."

This seemed to cross some invisible line of authority with Dr Vitkay. His frown made it clear the decision was his alone. Michelle didn't press the point.

Joy breathed a sigh, releasing a buildup of dread at Michelle colluding in the department's interference. At least she could depend on her doctor to be on her side.

Dr Vitkay accompanied Joy and Michelle out of his consulting room and down the corridor to reception. Turning to Joy conversationally, he said, "You know Joy, I believe you are not getting better because you are experiencing what we would say in my old country is a crisis of the spirit. This is not so easy to treat with medicine."

If he meant this in a kind way, Joy in her fragile state with her woozy head and racing heart did not hear it that way. She thought he was saying her problem was not a real medical condition that he could treat and cure. It was something to do with lack of faith in religious beliefs and therefore a state of mind. Was this how her doctor saw PTSD? A mind over matter thing?

Hurt, she struggled to keep from bursting into tears. At reception, she smiled automatically and followed the rules, making an appointment to see Dr Vitkay five weeks hence.

On the way to the Baleno, hunched and holding all the hurt inside, her mind began spiralling uncontrollably around the issue of what Dr Vitkay meant by spiritual crisis. She began to doubt his understanding of PTSD as a real medical condition and therefore doubt his credibility as a GP.

Where was *spiritual crisis* listed in any medical texts?

How damaging would this be to the workers compensation case?

A burning intellectual anger replaced the devastating doubt caused by Dr Vitkay's medical betrayal.

Joy wanted to question Michelle. Paranoia stopped her, doubting whose side she was on.

Michelle walked her to the car oblivious to Joy's inner turmoil. Making conversation as if they were friends, she suggested Joy join a book club or a writing group. "Memoir and journaling are therapeutic, I've heard. And socialising is important in maintaining your mental health. It can't be good for you to isolate yourself from the rest of the world, Joy."

Joy wasn't in a mood to chit chat. Her mind was circling around PTSD, medical fact, and spiritual truths. "Maybe I'll start meditating again," she mumbled. "I used to belong to a Buddhist meditation group, but I dropped out when all this happened."

Michelle smiled encouragement. "Have a Happy Easter. I'll see you in May."

"Sure, you too," Joy said. She'd made up her mind to investigate PTSD and find out if it was a legitimate condition. Maybe Kodi would lend her a laptop. She'd download some research papers and make Dr Vitkay read them to prove a point. She wasn't faking, or a bludger. If he couldn't help her, she'd do it herself.

Chapter Thirty

An outdoor lamp cast a golden walkway of welcome. Joy traipsed up a stone path to the distinctive aubergine painted front door of Gemma's cottage. She grasped a chunky brass door knocker and gave it a couple solid thumps. The promise of an old fashion family roast dinner waited on the other side.

Her contribution to the get-together was meant to be a fruit pie; however, earlier in the day she'd burned the cherry filling on the stove while washing up dirty dishes. Mad at getting distracted, all remnants went into the bin, pie crust and all. A reminder she was unable to juggle even the simplest of multitasking these days. In frustration, she purchased a cheesecake and fresh raspberries at Woolies. Not homemade. Granny standards had dropped since… It would have to suffice. Gemma would be disappointed but Jaxon wasn't too fussy as long as dessert was sweet and creamy.

Rugged up against the winter cold in a hand knitted cable jumper and brightly coloured felt beanie, she jigged up and down on the verandah shivering. There would be a frost in the night. She must remember to leave before the fog set in and blanketed the country roads back to her place with ghostly shrouds of impenetrable mist.

She hadn't been over to their place for a couple months. This was partly due to anxiety about driving when it got dark. Dirt roads from Gemma's property on the outskirts of Lower Teasel were the worst. But the other main reason was that Gemma was only able to cope with her broken record PTSD monologues in small doses these days. It wasn't fair on her to place the burden of being a sounding board all the time. Joy relied on her daughter's common sense too much. She was determined to curb this tendency tonight and keep the conversation even and light.

An excited Jaxon greeted her at the door with a quick hug. He pulled her toward the family room and a warm wood fire. Gemma knocked about in the kitchen. Joy heard pounding like potatoes being mashed. The aroma of roast gravy smelled divine.

Jaxon took the opportunity to monopolise her attention. "Look, Granny, I had a monster accident on my bike. My elbows and knees got all banged up." He thrust an elbow covered with red and blue Spiderman plasters in her face. "There was blood everywhere," he said with pride.

Dutifully Joy inspected the plasters on his elbow and then moved on the next elbow and then the knees. "That looks pretty bad. Are you all right now?" she said, squinting with concern.

Jaxon shook his head. "I'll have to take a sickie from school tomorrow. I might get a fever." He affected a woebegone look similar to a hurt puppy.

From the kitchen, Joy heard Gemma's voice hollering. "No, you don't. You are injured, not sick kiddo."

Joy smiled. "Good try jack-a-roo."

To make a point, he limped around the room favouring his right foot to demonstrate the extent of the damage. "I need crutches like Angeli got when she broke a toe in soccer practice." His mournful acting was too much. Joy burst out laughing.

Gemma joined them in the family room wiping greasy hands on a dishcloth. "We may need to operate. Which leg needs to come off first?" she asked in a serious tone, winking at Joy.

Undeterred, Jaxon limped to the nearest chair and sat down with a bump. "A warm bath with Epsom salts before bed may help," Joy suggested with her best granny voice.

Jaxon looked across at his mum hopefully.

"We'll see," Gemma said without much sympathy. "How about setting the table so we can eat?"

Jaxon launched out of the chair and skipped to the kitchen to get cutlery forgetting to limp. A hungry tummy took precedence over a need for pampering.

Gemma piled roast lamb, minted peas, mashed potatoes and gravy on brightly glazed geometrically patterned plates. She passed the first to Jaxon and the next to Joy. "This looks amazing," Joy gushed. It was too much food but she didn't want to make a fuss. To start off a conversation, she said, "So my GP wants me to socialise more, join a group or exercise class. He thinks I'm suffering from a spiritual crisis rather than a medical condition."

Gemma cut into her meat, swished it in mint sauce and took a bite. She considered what Joy had said. "You've got PTSD, Mum. You can be sure of that, no matter what a rural GP says. But maybe he's got a good idea about joining a support group for PTSD sufferers."

"I thought the same, but for some reason there don't seem to be support groups for PTSD specifically. I don't want to go to a generic mental health group. Being traumatised and having your life upended is not the same thing."

"Yeah, okay." Gemma took another bite of dinner before continuing. "I get the impression you were upset about the spiritual crisis remark?" A frown from Joy confirmed her suspicions. "In my natural therapy studies, I've read about Dark Night of the Soul experiences. Do you think this could be what he's on about? It makes sense that experiencing a life-threatening event could trigger an awakening of kundalini energy."

"I have no idea." Joy shook her head. "I'm having enough trouble understanding what PTSD is. I spent yesterday afternoon at Quamby Community Online surfing the net searching for research papers that could explain it."

"How did that go?" Gemma asked cautiously. Joy understood she was wary of this becoming a heavy and emotionally laden conversation.

"I totally lost several hours of my life," Joy said lightly. "There's a lot of information, mostly about war veterans." Joy piled a fork with mashed potatoes and peas. "I prefer the blogs where people talk about their actual experiences. They make me see I'm not alone or so different from anyone else with PTSD." She paused, took a bite and swallowed wrong. Coughing and spluttering into a serviette, she croaked, "Sorry."

Pounding her mother's back, Gemma asked, "Are you alright? You do that a lot lately."

"Since being strangled," Joy agreed. Gemma frowned, silently concerned.

A scraping screech from Jaxon using a knife on an earthenware plate filled the silence around the table.

"Yum, that's good," he said. "Granny, can you pass the mint sauce?"

A sweet pungency of minty vinegar assailed the diners. "That's way too much," Gemma scolded. Jaxon giggled.

Despite an unspoken promise not to sound like a broken record, Joy continued with her obsession. "The meme I really liked said PTSD isn't about what is *wrong* with you – it's about *what happened* to you. I'm not sure if my workers comp team understands the distinction. They treat me as if I can talk myself out of it. This makes me feel judged instead of understood."

"I sometimes wonder if they are really trying to help you, mum, or if there's some other agenda going on," Gemma declared. "PTSD isn't the same as a mental illness such as depression; it's an injury that has an external cause. And someone else is to blame for it. At the very time you've needed empathy they pound you with a big stick of denial, redefining reality."

Joy grimaced at Gemma's bluntness. "It would have helped if they'd framed what happened as an injury to me instead of an illness. No one expected my knee to return to one hundred percent after my knee replacement surgery. No one blamed me for a slow recovery – or implied it was a mind over matter thing. I got a lot of sympathy and positive feedback when the best I could do was bend it seventy percent. It was understood I wouldn't be the same afterwards and would have to make allowances and change certain things in my lifestyle."

"Like you can't bend down to garden now," Jaxon said while chewing a mouthful of food.

Gemma nodded approval, including him in the discussion. "With granny's current medical treatment, it's implied that she'll return to her old self when she gets over being *sick*. They say her recovery is a matter of time and willpower. But we're not sure that's going to happen."

"She's not herself anymore, I know," Jaxon nodded wisely.

"Their assumption's not fair," Joy said looking at Gemma. "It puts unnecessary pressure on me. I'm beginning to think it would be more useful to have an occupational therapist rather than a counsellor." She gave a rueful smile. Gemma's eyes softened in sympathy.

Straightening in her chair, Joy's demeanour changed from meek to emphatic. "One researcher at Eden Isle University defined PTSD as a change to a person's brain where the fear remains even after all evidence to the contrary indicates the original threat no longer exists. But in my case, Poppy remains a real life danger that hasn't gone away. I'm not sure how that works?" She slumped again. "All the differing views get confusing."

"I wonder, if Poppy had been dismissed after strangling you and your employer had therefore made you feel safe would your trauma have become entrenched into PTSD?" Gemma asked.

Joy considered the implications and paled. "I believe that would have made all the difference," she said slowly. Her mind filled with a sad insight: the upheaval to her life probably had been preventable if the department had been more concerned about her wellbeing than about protecting the reputation of one of their managers. "It's too late now. According to my research, I'll have PTSD for the rest of my life. My symptoms may lessen but they can return at any time. I have to learn to live with it."

"Oh mum, I'm so sorry."

Joy shrugged, holding back tears. She focused on the cheerful dinner plate. She slowly cut into a piece of meat. Now that she understood the situation, there was no point going over what might have been.

Gemma picked up on her mood and quickly changed the subject. "Did you hear that Kodi babysat Jaxon for the first time? Auntie Honor thought it was a good idea to give her experience looking after kids." She rolled her eyes with mock drama.

"She was awesome. We played SNAP and I won, and then she made up a bedtime story about vampires." Jaxon beamed angelically.

"And you haven't been the same since," Gemma teased. Leaning elbows on the table, she stage-whispered to Joy, "He refuses to cross the hallway to the bedroom unless we turn on all the lights. It's costing me a fortune in electricity."

Jaxon looked sheepish. "There's a monster in the shadows."

Gemma expelled a loud sigh. "I keep telling you, there is no monster, sweetheart."

"Just because you can't see it, doesn't mean he's not real." Jaxon was adamant.

Something in the way he said this made Joy stop before agreeing with Gemma. A niggle at the back of her mind wouldn't let go.

After dessert, Joy and Jaxon helped clear the table while Gemma filled the kitchen sink with hot soapy water.

"Mum, why don't you tuck Jaxon into bed while I do the dishes?" she suggested with a knowing look in her eyes. "I'm sick of frog marching him across the hall yelling there's nothing to be afraid of with him wiggling and screaming in terror. I keep hoping that after doing this a dozen times or more he'll finally change his point of view and see I'm right."

A fleeting thought crossed the back of Joy's mind. *It's called exposure therapy.*

Gemma continued to vent. "I don't get it. Even if Kodi had told him a scary story, he watches scary DVDs all the time. He's never developed an aversion to the dark before," she lamented.

Joy decided to witness firsthand Jaxon's unreasonable reaction. Gemma expected some higher granny wisdom to what was going on, maybe even for granny to come up with a solution to the dilemma. The earlier tingling niggle in Joy's brain came back.

"Come on, Jack-a-roo. Go brush your teeth. You can tell me all about this monster lurking in the hallway while you're at it."

While Jaxon rinsed and spit, Joy lectured him about his stupid fear of the dark: *he wasn't a baby anymore, nine years old was too old for this nonsense, there was nothing to be afraid of in the four feet of dark hallway he had to cross to his bedroom, the house was safe and we were all nearby ready to protect him.*

Nonetheless, in the end, on the way to his bedroom she had to literally push him through the unlit passageway as he whimpered and struggled against her.

Joy sympathised with Gemma. This tedious process would have to continue every night until Jaxon got used to it. It was logical the more times he was exposed to the dark and realised nothing bad happened, he would begin to see their point of view – there was nothing frightening in that dark hallway.

However, even after Jaxon was pushed across the few feet of hallway into the safety of his bedroom with the overhead light turned on, he continued to tremble and whimper from the experience.

Feeling pressured at wanting to fix his irrational fear, Granny lost patience. In frustration she yelled, "Why are you afraid of the dark all of a sudden when you never used to be?" Unaware of making matters worse, her focus was on his fear, rather than on its source, as if by pointing out his imagination was faulty, the terror would magically go away.

Jaxon cowered from her wrathful presence and refused to speak – in his eyes Granny had become the monster. She stood determined and wasn't going anywhere until he changed his mind and saw things her way.

"I had a bad dream," he whined and began to cry big fat baby tears as if Granny was going to smack sense into him.

Granny rolled her eyes. "It was only a dream and dreams are not real," she stated without an ounce of sympathy, as if that sorted the problem.

Jaxon nodded his head but remained stubbornly terrified. The dream felt real. Her refusal to believe him made the rest of the world a scary place.

Expelling a drawn out huff, Granny dared him. "Tell me more about the dream. What made it scary?"

"There was a monster. And it kept saying *Kill Kill Kill.*"

Nodding, Granny softened her tone. "What did the monster look like?"

"I don't know," Jaxon cried. "It was sort of like... a dark blob."

"Did it have eyes?" Granny decided to drill down to the monster's specifications to establish what a dark blob living in the passageway's shadows looked like exactly.

"I don't know." He shook his head and whined. He didn't want to flesh out the scary monster's details, it was too disturbing.

Becoming more practical, Granny changed tact. "How about you draw a picture of the monster to show me." Jaxon perked up at this suggestion. It was something he could do; it put him in control.

He tottered across to a desk in the corner and pulled out a large pad of paper and coloured pencils from the top drawer. Soon he was immersed in concentration drawing his monster. After a few minutes, he showed Granny the picture, explaining all the fine details in a confident voice without even a hint of distress.

Granny saw that dismissing his fear, calling it stupid, had been the wrong approach.

Isn't the premise of all horror movies this very point: no one believes there is a ghost/psycho/monster in the house. All the other characters in the story dismiss the bumps in the night, talk each other out of their anxiety, and ignore their survival instincts. Their denial makes each of them complicit in compounding the victim's suffering as a result.

It was the monster that required scrutiny and a label.

Joy bent over Jaxon, studying the drawing. "So. This is the monster that lurks in the dark hallway scaring you when you try to walk through?" She wanted him to know she was on-side, empathising with his terror.

She no longer colluded in the monster's invisibility and subterfuge; she acknowledged its presence.

Jaxon nodded in relief, less anxious knowing Granny could see his monster for real and gave it legitimacy.

Granny understood what needed to be done. "Does it have a name?"

"I don't know." He puzzled over this.

"You can give it a name. What do you want to call it?"

He leaned over his drawing, grabbed a red pencil and wrote BICH MONSTER across the page, chuckling. It was the worst name he could think of.

Granny knew he felt more in control after naming his fear. Jaxon's fear was no longer amorphous and all-encompassing; he had confined it to a shape, cordoned it with a name. Jaxon's evil monster, his reality, had been defined, clarified and affirmed by another human being.

"You know now that the monster has a name, you can banish it," she stated with confidence. "All you need to do is throw a pinch of salt into the dark and shout BE GONE BICH MONSTER. It will disappear for good."

Jaxon's face lit up like a firecracker.

Granny encouraged him. "Why wait? I'll go get us some salt from the kitchen so you can do it now."

Granny returned and placed a spoonful of salt into his open palm. She opened the door to the dark passageway and motioned him forward. Trembling, he stepped forward into the shadow of the corridor, then quickly jumped back a step. Taking a deep breath, he threw salt into the shadows and stammered a rushed but word perfect "Go back – to your own home. Be gone BICH MONSTER!" Nervously he jumped backwards into the bedroom giggling.

Joy registered the look of relief on his face. A weight had been lifted off his small shoulders.

"There you see the monster is gone." Granny confirmed this out loud despite knowing in her heart reinforcement was not necessary.

Jaxon ran from his bedroom to the kitchen – without hesitation, without thinking – to tell his mum he'd cast out the monster with a pinch of salt. Not as easy as it sounded. With Granny's support, he'd drawn his fear, taken a good look at it, acknowledged its reality, and given it a label that defined its terrifying countenance. Only then could he manage his terror and successfully expel the monster shadowing the dark corridors of his mind.

A sobering thought passed through Joy's heart in a simple but profound epiphany: all Jaxon needed to banish his fear was *empathy* from the people trying to help him. Putting themselves in his shoes, giving him permission to feel it like it was. Giving legitimacy to his experience. With compassion, not judgement.

Not re-defining the situation, trivialising it or trying to talk him out of feeling afraid.

Chapter Thirty One

J oy opened the door to the Baleno. The winter sun was more direct at the seaside despite June being milder at Plover Point than at Lower Teasel. She stood for a few minutes for the rays to soak their warmth into tight shoulders and bank the heat in an oversize felted jumper she wore. Stale air smelling of baked vinyl escaped from the car's interior, replaced by fresh, salty sea breeze. Another counselling session with Bev was over and she was left wondering what was the point? A waste of a morning even if she didn't have anything better to do.

Getting into the car and driving off, she manoeuvred through city traffic before turning onto the highway. She drove home from Plover Point on autopilot, immune to the long stretches of highway meandering through native forests, broken by logged hillsides next to an occasional farm paddock dotted with cattle and sheep.

She decided Bev had given up exploring family issues. And Bev must be bored with discussing her state of mind ad nauseum, going around in circles and coming back to the same place. Gemma said it was called *Compassion fatigue*, where psychologists after trying to help PTSD sufferers eventually give up, having expended all their techniques without achieving the expected psychological milestones.

CBT and Exposure Therapy had been useless. The more Joy talked about the incident, the more ingrained it became. And the more distressing, compounded by her employer's attitude. She must be disappointing to her counsellor by failing to improve. Was there some innate stubbornness within her that refused to recover despite everyone's good intentions? She had come to a sad conclusion – counselling was not working.

Workers compensation processes required Joy's compliance. She must attend monthly counselling sessions until she recovered sufficiently to return to work. Ironically, the psycho who strangled her was not required to attend counselling, much less undergo a psychiatric assessment. The crazy stressed out manager was allowed to continue as if nothing had happened – as if she was normal.

It's all about me, Joy thought with some irony, *when it should be all about her*.

They'd spent the session discussing goal setting, a subject Joy knew all too well, having taught managers about business planning in a previous career as a management consultant on the mainland. It felt like sucking eggs to listen to Bev's tutorial, unaware as she was of Joy's work history. But Bev was so intensely committed to the exercise, she appeared almost hyperactive. Even if Joy had cared enough to get a word in, she wasn't sure if Bev's monologue would have afforded an opportunity.

At least, the session was practical steps to get her back to work, rather than delving deep into her mental state.

Joy felt too disheartened to enlighten the well-meaning counsellor about the pointlessness of setting goals. In her real world, the most she could do in setting a forward goal was to decide in the morning whether to put a load of laundry in the washing machine. If she could muster the motivation to achieve one bit of housework in a day before plonking on the sofa to watch another series on DVD, that was an achievement. Testament to how much money she spent on self-medicating through couch potato bingeing, the loyalty program she signed up with Isle DVD kept sending ten dollar vouchers every other month.

Forget long term plans like what she wanted to achieve by next month.

What was the point of planning anything until her court case was over? She reminded Bev that it wasn't coming up until September according to Constable Chugg. The court case was going to cause an enormous amount of stress, having to sit in court and give evidence on the stand.

Bev had looked abashed but persevered with the activity, ignoring Joy's opinion on the matter.

The Baleno bumped and lurched as it hit a patch of potholes in the road. The shire council promised every year to upgrade the highway this side of Stubblefield Junction and every year it had some perfectly rational excuse as to why it had to carryover the job to the next budget. For the next ten kilometres, Joy's attention was diverted to concentrating on steering to avoid the worst of the traps.

Past Willow Brook, the highway smoothed out to a newly resurfaced section with overtaking lanes for tourists speeding through the lush countryside in a hurry to arrive at some guidebook destination. These days Joy could never muster enough energy to rush. The Baleno glided along with cruise control set at a comfortable ten kilometres below the speed limit, allowing land cruisers and utility trucks to pass with ease. Once again, Joy's mind spiralled around the counselling session trying to pinpoint what was so unsettling about it.

Thinking about it – it was strange actually – why didn't Bev ever ask about her work history? Why was the focus always on her personal life? Especially when the whole reason for being at these sessions was work-related: what happened to her at work; and then, what needed to happen to get her back to work.

And another thing Joy wondered: why did Bev ignore her questions about Poppy? If anyone's mental health needed to be analysed to death, surely it was Poppy's. It was Poppy's state of mind that was the black unknown in Joy's mind, causing all the terror. What possessed the woman to strangle her?

If Bev, a highly qualified psychologist, could explain to Joy what motivated Poppy, maybe, just maybe this would be all Joy needed to work through the trauma. It was the *not knowing* that was causing her distress.

And yet, Bev would not go there, no matter how many times Joy asked and prodded for answers. This was strange.

For some reason in this session, Bev had decided rather suddenly that Joy needed to return to work as soon as possible. In her professional opinion, the longer she stayed off work, the harder it would be to get back. So, they'd spent the session stepping through the goals required to do this.

Credit to Bev's skills in influencing, she almost convinced Joy to return even if Poppy remained as manager. They'd drawn up a list of requirements and a timeline, and Joy was almost mesmerised into signing on the dotted line. She came to her senses in time, however, much to Bev's annoyance. She left promising to think about it.

In fact, this promise actually meant putting the idea to Gemma for her opinion when they met for lunch. Her daughter knew her better than she knew herself these days. Gemma wouldn't allow Joy to be talked into anything before knowing she was ready. When it came to questioning authority, Gemma's bullshit detector operated on high alert. Joy needed her smart judgement because she couldn't trust her own these days.

After all, she'd liked and trusted Poppy and never suspected any hint of underlying crazy in her personality. How bad was that?

A sign indicating the turnoff to Lower Teasel in five hundred metres caught Joy's attention. Checking the time on the dashboard, she relaxed seeing it was twelve thirty and Gemma was expecting to meet at one o'clock at Lower Teasel's Museum café. Being early was not so bad. She would order a cappuccino and read the newspaper and collect her thoughts after the disappointing session with Bev.

***

Lower Teasel's Museum café was a refurbished tram car with stalls and bench seats. Not the most comfortable setting but private at least. Gemma liked coming there because the food was cheap with generous serves. She tried to meet her mum after each monthly counselling session to check up on how it went.

She arrived to see her mum staring out the window. There wasn't much to see but a cement courtyard with scientific-type displays, weatherproof and childproof, designed to be cranked, bashed and climbed on experimentally all in the name of education. On the table, the Meridian newspaper was spread open to a middle page. A half-drunk mug of cappuccino coffee left next to it.

Gemma slid into the bench seat across from her mother, dumping her bag under the table. "Hi, Mum, how's it going?" she asked. "Have you ordered lunch yet?"

With preternatural calm, Joy pushed the paper across and pointed to a short item in a middle column. She returned to gazing out the window.

With a flare of panic, Gemma grabbed the paper and held it up to her nose to read. Shortly after, she began to emit stunted noises of disbelief, shock, and then anger.

"What the...?" she loudly exhaled, thrusting the paper onto the table and staring at Joy. "Assault charge thrown out of court! I thought Chugg told you it wouldn't be heard until September!"

Joy turned dead eyes to Gemma. "No one advised me it was coming up sooner. I wasn't even there to defend myself." She paused, a grimace of pain flickered and died. "Bev must have known before our session and she never said a word. How could she do that?"

"How could a judge agree that your boss strangled you as a practical joke! What kind of idiotic decision is that! It was occupational violence, clear and simple. He must have been got to, mum."

Joy smirked. "Poppy pleaded guilty to assaulting me. But her lawyer defended this by arguing we were sharing a joke and it went wrong. And she's *really* upset about it."

"It's crazy, mum. Just because she laughed about scaring you twenty minutes afterwards doesn't make it funny." Gemma was livid. "Who in their right mind *shares* strangling as a joke?"

"Apparently a Magistrate accepted it," Joy said with a blank face set in stone.

Gemma became concerned at her cold demeanour. She expected her mother to fall to pieces at any moment. Re-reading the court reporter's article, she stabbed at sentences. "The Police Prosecutor got so many facts wrong." With building disbelief, she read out, *The complainant took some time off work...Mrs Bryant applied a small amount of pressure.* "How in the blazes would he know how much pressure she applied!" Her mum shook her head in mild wonderment. "He should have said she left bruises around your neck! And that you've been off work for five months totally incapacitated. He couldn't be bothered checking the facts beforehand. He made it sound as if you are back at work and all is fine and dandy. Wasn't he supposed to be on your side?"

"I wasn't allowed to have my own lawyer," Joy murmured.

Gemma continued to stab the article and loudly paraphrase sentences from it. "The Police Prosecutor says, you were such good work colleagues, you gave each other shoulder massages! Nice one – if you let someone give your shoulders a rub then, hey, it must be permission to go to the next level and strangle them of course! Not. What a jerk!"

For the first time, Joy became animated. "I never let her give me shoulder massages. He must be quoting from Poppy's statement. She lied about that."

"I know, mum. And it's creepy. She makes it sound like you were *very* close friends. EUUW."

Joy paled. "Chugg told me the Police Prosecutor was half-hearted about the case. I guess, when it came down to it, he supported Poppy's statement over mine." Her voice trailed off.

"He was got to, mum. That's the only explanation. I mean look." She pointed to the article again and read out, *Mrs Bryant's lawyer handed Magistrate Smith a character reference from Eden Isle's Community Health Department in his plea in mitigation. In it, the department spoke of Mrs Bryant's impeccable character and unblemished work history.*

Joy nodded with understanding. "No judge is going to disagree with the state government." There was a long silence.

"Where was my character reference from the department?" Joy whispered. "They should have remained impartial at the very least."

"Better yet, they should have supported the victims of assault in their workplace. It's an abuse of power, mum."

Gemma could have wept for her mother at the enormity of the betrayal, from her employer and from the legal system. Attempting to inject something positive, she patted her mother's arm and said, "At least the article names and shames Poppy. It mentions the centre, but it doesn't mention you by name."

She was rewarded with a wan smile. "It was her first offence, so that was why he decided not to convict her or even make a record of it." Joy turned to the window to contemplate a sky rapidly becoming overcast with churning grey clouds. "In the last paragraph it says Magistrate Smith admitted that technically Poppy did assault me, even if he accepted, she was sharing a practical joke." Her breath misted the clear glass.

Gemma frowned in concentration. "That's rather a contradiction, wouldn't you say?"

"We'll see how the department interprets it." Joy sighed.

"You know how, mum. They'll see it as a get out of jail free card."

Joy shivered. Her blood chilled to ice like a beef carcass strung up in a butcher's cold room. "I'm not hungry so I'm just going to go home."

"Sure. Are you okay to drive?" Gemma studied her mother's face for signs of a meltdown. She saw a cold calm enveloping Joy, and mistook this for coping.

"It's not far to go."

"Drive safe. I'll check in on you later."

Chapter Thirty Two

As soon as Honor received the phone message from Gemma about what had happened, she finished craft work with the Shamrock Room's Wednesday group and rushed over to see Joy.

When Joy ignored the frantic knocks on the front door, Honor went around the back and used the key hidden under a flower pot to unlock the door to the kitchen. "Hello? Joy, it's me," she said in a loud but hopefully soothing tone. Making her way to the lounge room, she found her sister curled up like a foetus in a mound of soft blankets on the sofa.

"I heard what happened. Gemma texted me. I came right over." She sat on the end of the sofa, pushing aside Joy's fork-knifed legs. "I can't believe it."

Joy stirred long enough to pull a blanket over her head. "I want to cry, why can't I cry," she moaned. "My mind is spinning and I can't make it stop."

"Did you take your meds?"

"Two whole tablets. They should have knocked me out but my heart is revving like a stuck carburetor."

"Can I make you a cup of tea, Joyjoy?" Honor reverted to using her sister's childhood name in the face of a crisis.

"I'm not safe anywhere," Joy whispered. "My employer won't protect me from a cruel, crazy, stressed-out woman and the law won't either." A heart wrenching moan echoed through the room. Joy pulled the covers tighter to her chest.

Honor searched for words of comfort. "You're safe here. You're home. I'm here with you and you are safe." She patted Joy's leg.

"When a person hurts me, all she has to do is say it was a joke and everyone agrees. No one will protect me." She wailed. "If I'm the first victim, the court lets her off free as a bird. Without consequence." She began to hyperventilate. "She knows that! I'll bet she's having a good old laugh about it right now." She wailed some more. "No one cares that I got hurt."

"I care, Joyjoy."

Joy pushed up and grabbed Honor's hand. "The world's not safe. You've got to understand. People in positions of authority get away with threatening to kill a person and their behaviour is defended by those in power."

Unnerved by her sister's deteriorating mental state, Honor could only offer comforting clichés. "I've got your back. You're not to worry."

Joy twisted to fully face her sister. "Do you? That's what Bev and Michelle said, too. But they knew about the court report in the paper and didn't even bother to tell me."

"I'm sure that's not true." Honor automatically tried to inject positivity into her sister's doom and gloom mood.

"It is true. I phoned Michelle when I got home to tell her what happened, to say I wasn't coping and needed to see the doctor urgently. She told me she saw the article and decided it was better not to mention it until my next GP appointment. Didn't want to *upset* me." Joy was working up to a full-blown outrage. "I tried calling Bev but she didn't bother to pick up." She glared at Honor. "You must have seen it in the papers today. The centre gets the newspapers first thing every morning. Why didn't you tell me?"

Honor was dumbfounded by Joy turning the tables and going on the attack. Afterall, she'd come over expressly to comfort her sister and offer any support needed. It was obvious Joy was spiralling down into a very bad space, if she didn't even trust her own family.

In her most soothing voice, she said, "We didn't get the newspapers today. All the volunteers were complaining and asking where they were. In front of us, Poppy told Amberlie to phone up about it."

Joy sat up. Blankets tangled around her shoulders and feet. She stared into space. "That explains it. The department warned her. I'll bet she confiscated the papers before anyone could see the article." She rested her head in her hands.

"That makes sense. A big bouquet of flowers was delivered to Poppy at the office with one of those balloons saying *Congratulations*. We all wondered what the occasion was. She wouldn't tell us, but insisted they weren't from her husband and it wasn't an anniversary. She had this mysterious, smug smile on her face. Do you think the head office would be so gauche?"

Honor watched her sister crumple. A resolve hardened in her mind. The health department had a lot to answer for, starting with why they put their weight behind the joking strangler instead of her honest and hardworking sister.

"I'm going to write to your senior managers. No, I'm going to write to the Minister. The way this has been handled from the start is just not good enough. Someone has to be answerable." Honor stood up and began pacing the room.

Joy stared at her as if seeing her for the first time. This was the sister usually telling her to let go of stuff. It was so unlike Honor to take a stand, let alone rock the boat. "I'll help you write it." She collapsed onto the sofa and curled in a ball again. "Just let me get through this horrible anxiety first," she weakly murmured.

"Righto. I'll even let you sign it so I don't get in trouble at the centre."

Her sister's bravado was only a temporary glitch in a lifetime of common sense and playing safe.

Chapter Thirty Three

Gemma marched into the Village Spice Café on a mission. Her brave, stalwart mother was falling apart before her eyes and she felt helpless. There was only so much that St John's Wort and Emergency Flower Essence could do for her mum. Gemma had even started taking these remedies herself lately being so upset. She needed to talk to someone who would understand.

Her cousin's beacon of red hair shone like an emergency light in the crowded room. Kodi had beat her to the table and was studying the menu. A waiter was hovering about to take her order. A forty-five-minute lunch break didn't give them a lot of time.

With a huge sigh, Gemma dropped her handbag under the table and plonked into a chair. The waiter looked at her expectantly, pen poised over a pad. "Just a chai latte," she said. He nodded and with a flourish, strutted off. "I don't have an appetite lately," she explained to Kodi.

Kodi laughed. "Nothing stops me eating." Then she frowned. "How's Auntie Joy doing?"

"Not good. I'm really worried. She's spiralling down into a big black abyss, worse than when she was first strangled. For the first time since this all happened, I'm worried she might not pull out of it. I've been shoving prescription sedatives down her throat despite my professional and philosophical aversion to them!"

"It's tough, reading that the Magistrate decided it was a practical joke that went wrong. What a bonehead."

"Mum believes the government applied pressure. Her employer is the health department. Who's going to argue with them?"

"Your mum never stood a chance. Lachlan told me – his dad told him – confidentially of course, that Magistrate Smith has a reputation." She leaned forward on her elbows. With a stage whisper, she said, "There was a client of Mr Chapman's locked in a custody dispute. She applied to the court for an injunction against a violent ex-husband to keep him away from their children. Apparently, the story was that he was cruel and sexually abusive when they were married. Guess what the Magistrate decided?"

Gemma raised her hands in question.

"The ex-husband wasn't a sadistic animal. It was just *rough foreplay.* Can you believe it? That's a modern take on rape in marriage. Not." Kodi grimaced in disgust. "Some judges should retire long before senility affects their brains."

"It was bad luck Mum's case was heard by him, I guess. Knowing this doesn't help of course."

"Lachlan says she could appeal."

"I can't imagine her being in any state to do that."

"That's what they count on," Kodi said wisely.

"I wish I knew what to do. Mum says Honor is helping her write a letter to the Minister. That's bound to cause a few ripples of unease through the department."

Kodi gave Gemma an evil smile. "I've been thinking about it. A letter can be filed away, labelled 'Top Secret', and no one but the higher ups get to see it. If we want to cause a wave rather than a few ripples, we should make it more public."

"Like writing a letter to the editor of The Meridian." Gemma picked up on Kodi's thinking quickly.

"Exactly. We could write something now and I could text it through straight away." Kodi grinned.

Gemma put her brain to work. "It has to be about how a strangulation joke could possibly go wrong," she suggested.

"It begs the question: what would it have looked like if it had gone right?" Kodi giggled.

Kodi and Gemma began scribbling phrases and putting them into sentences until finally they were satisfied with the result.

"Okay, are we ready to press the button?" Kodi said, grinning like a shark about to take a bite out of a surfer.

"Do it." Gemma commanded.

***

The next day, their prose showed up in The Meridian's Messages to The Editor column. It read:

In relation to the report on 7ᵗʰ June that assault charges were thrown out when a manager who strangled her subordinate explained her actions as "a joke gone wrong", I can sympathise with her remorse. The time-honoured strangling joke is one of the hardest comedy routines to perfect. Perhaps she just needs more practice.

Chapter Thirty Four

Midday Saturday, the log fire was blasting out heat. Joy shivered. She pulled blankets over her head, threw them off, changed around to the other side of the sofa, pulled the blankets back, sat up and rewound the DVD to a previous scene having lost track of the plot, laid down, couldn't concentrate, and frustrated, finally switched it off and turned on the news.

After the weather report, typical winter weather across Eden Isle with rain, wind, and cold, the top story of the day was a robbery at gunpoint at the Eden Isle Bank at Gorse Plains. No shots were fired but the robber got away with a bag of cash. Employees were traumatised and counselling had been organised by the bank. The branch was closed for the day. Joy turned off the telly, the last thing needed was hearing about other workers being traumatised by an incident at work.

It was no use. TV was not providing the usual mind-numbing relief for anxiety, even after adding one and a half tablets of Murelax to the mix of St John's Wort and chamomile tea.

It was impossible concentrating while her heart jackhammered, pumping feelings of violation, confusion, disbelief, betrayal into a dust storm of questions. Emotions coalesced into jumbled thoughts without a landing platform. Rules, societal norms, laws, shattered into puzzle pieces that no longer formed a coherent picture. Her belief systems – employment policies, legal processes, medical science – all protecting right from wrong no longer held up when put to the test. Where did this leave her?

Messed up.

Or as Gemma would say, *brain fucked*.

Nothing made sense. This was what horrified her. A world of known, comforting beliefs, upended, turned upside down and sideways, mushed into gobbledygook. She felt trapped in an insane system. This terrified her.

Her heart pounded its way up her throat and out her ears. Unable to slow it down – forget Honor's *thinking positive* platitude and Bev's *change your thinking* CBT techniques – she was spiralling down into a black hole, helpless to control it.

Joy got up, wrapped a shrug around her shoulders and paced the room in flannelette pyjamas and bed socks.

There was a soft knock on the door. Joy froze. Her mobile pinged, signalling an incoming text message. Reading a text message was the safer option.

From Kodi. It read *I'm @ front door.*

Joy was not in a good space and did not want to see anyone, not even a favourite niece. She opened the door just enough to tell her as much.

Kodi pushed past, not taking no for an answer. "I've got a workers comp hotline that may be useful," she said, taking assertive steps towards the kitchen. She threw a postcard onto the table. "I'm making us a cup of tea."

Obedient to her bossy ways, Joy pulled the shrug tight and sat down at the table. In the background, Kodi clinked tea cups against a creamer and clanked spoons onto saucers. A kettle heated with a gentle humming. "Where are your... don't worry, I found the cookies," she yelled.

Joy picked up the card. *Compo Assist Hotline – Are you on workers compensation? Do you have questions? Call us.* There was a one-eight hundred number.

A rattling tray was dumped in the middle of the table. "One job done. Now let me explain," Kodi said, all business and official. She plucked the card from Joy's hand, gave it a scan and then began to lecture. "The hotline was set up by the previous Labor government to assist employees on workers compensation. They recognised all the rules and procedures were hard to grasp for first timers like yourself."

Joy grimaced distrustfully.

Kodi reached across, grabbed an Oreo and crunched down. Chewing, she said through crunches, "It's meant to be unbiased advice, totally confidential and the best bit, they're on the side of the employee." Kodi smiled triumphantly. She poured tea from the pot into a cup, added a heaped spoonful of sugar, splashed milk in, and pushed it towards Joy. Then repeated the exercise taking a sip from her own cup. "Ahhh," she sighed with pleasure.

Robotically, Joy took a sip of tea.

Watching her, Kodi started to offer comforting words. "It will all work out for the b...God, I sound like mum." She stopped short and laughed. "That Magistrate was a jerk, Auntie Joy. How could a Magistrate rule that strangling an employee was done as a practical joke? How could he possibly agree in a normal, sane universe that Poppy was *sharing* a joke with you? It's delusional."

Joy showed the first signs of animation. Her face flushed. "I know. It's all a lie. How do you share something with someone who is only vaguely aware of your presence, doesn't engage or encourage you, doesn't know what you are about to do because they are at work, concentrating on a computer screen, and have never joked around with you before and don't expect this to happen and you don't give them any warning – and it's a psycho crazy thing to do in the first place! And afterwards, Poppy never laughed. Isn't that an important give away. She looked bewildered. She didn't laugh. Because it was not funny." The more she said, the more her voice raised in volume and pitch.

Kodi nodded. "No one in a normal world thinks strangling – threatening to kill someone – scaring the shit out of someone – is funny. Bosses don't do that to their admin assistants."

"The Judge didn't even bother to consider the context in my case." Joy slumped in the chair.

"It wasn't as if two young men were at the pub fooling around, rough housing, play acting a fight. You and Poppy were two mature women in a workplace. You were just doing a job. What was Poppy doing?" Kodi emphasised each point with vigorous finger jabs of hot pink glittering nails in the air.

"No matter how I churn the facts around in my head, it always comes out the same way. *Just plain nuts.*" Joy felt defeated.

"Did you see the news about the bank robbery at Gorse Plains?" Kodi asked, seeming to change the subject. "It got me to thinking. What's the difference between someone pointing a gun at your head or putting their hands around your throat? No magistrate is going to declare it's a joke to point a gun at a person."

"Bank tellers get an outpouring of sympathy and understanding when that happens. And yet getting held up is an occupational risk and could almost be predicted and prepared for," Joy said uncharitably. "No one is going to question what happened or try to make you see it from another perspective."

"Not like being assaulted unexpectedly by someone you trusted." Kodi understood what she meant and didn't judge her mean-spirited comment.

"And for a start, bank tellers have Perspex between them and the guy with the gun. So, there's some distance between them. A gun can miss its target. Not like being strangled, which is up close and personal."

"And I was all alone during the incident," Joy agreed.

"Yeah. You had no one else who had shared the trauma to debrief with afterwards," Kodi added sympathetically.

"My employer won't protect me from a psycho and the legal system won't protect me either. I'm on my own." She began to whimper into a serviette. "I feel so scared."

Kodi nodded in sympathy. "You're caught up in a workers compensation system designed for the sole purpose of returning people to work. Not protecting them from crazy bosses that assault their staff."

Joy's whimpers ramped into hyperventilating tears. Mercifully, Kodi allowed her to rant and wail. Joy felt trapped in a horrible system surrounded by a posse of health professionals she used to trust, believing they were there to support her recovery. Now suspiciously they looked like collaborators trying to head her off at the pass. They didn't care about her as a human being; she was only an employee. No matter what the circumstances, ultimately, she had to return to a dangerous place with a killer lurking in the shadows.

"No matter how loud I scream *Strangler*, no one in the system will come to my defence. To them, Poppy is just a joker – a good ol' Aussie larrikin. No one believes me," Joy cried.

"Auntie Joy, this is what I'm trying to tell you – you are not on your own. Compo Assist may be able to help." Kodi was a firm believer, as only young people can be.

Joy picked up the card again and turned it over in her hand, wondering. Would the Magistrate's decision affect the insurer's opinion regarding her entitlement to workers compensation? Would they allow her to remain at home recovering? Or, would they now cancel her claim and force her back to work? If it was deemed a joke and not assault?

What would she do for money if she refused to go back and they cut off her compo? Worse, what if she was forced back and Poppy strangled her again? The dilemma was too huge to comprehend.

Joy doubled up with spasms of stomach clenching apprehension. Who could she ask for advice? She'd have to trust someone.

"Okay, you've convinced me. I'll give these Compo Assist people a call. See if they are of any use."

Kodi beamed in triumph. "I told mum I knew how to help." Grabbing another Oreo, she crunched away in silent camaraderie.

***

Kodi didn't overstay her welcome and Joy was grateful for this. As enthusiastic as Kodi was about Compo Assist Hotline, she wanted to think about it a bit more before deciding to phone. Advice was one thing; being in a position to actually influence outcomes was another. Joy closed the front door with a restless urge to run away and escape, but there was nowhere to go. She marched down the hallway into the lounge room, pacing back and forth. Thinking. Thinking. Thinking.

Logic had to prevail. Joy stopped pacing and stood hunched over with hands on her thighs next to a tall bookshelf in the lounge room. It was stocked with management texts and reference books from her past life as a management consultant, representing parts of her identity she'd been reluctant to give up. In desperation seeking common sense, she pulled out The Australian Pocket Oxford Dictionary.

Joy dropped it on the kitchen table along with a pen and pad of paper. Wrapped in a soft shrug, she scrawled across the page in large letters *Definition of a Joke – Oxford Dictionary*.

Turning to the entry, it read: *Joke, thing said or done to incite laughter*. She wrote this down. Under joke, was the entry practical joke. It read *trick played on a person*. She wrote this down and then turned the pages to follow the word trail.

Trick – *crafty or fraudulent, esp. mean or base; trickery – deceitful conduct*

Crafty – *guileful, ingenuous*

Guile – *deceit, treachery*

Ingenuous – *clever at contriving*

Contrive – *devise, think out, plan ahead, manage*

Studying her scribbles, she decided strangling was not a joke because it did not incite laughter from either party.

However, what about a practical joke? In court, Poppy argued it was a practical joke that went wrong.

The dictionary defined practical joke as a trick devised to be mean; trickery is deceitful conduct, treachery.

In other words, *cruel*.

Joy turned to the entry: Cruel – *delighting in another's pain; painful, distressing*.

A picture started to form in Joy's brain.

Anger began to burn away the fugue of confusion and senselessness.

Poppy's conduct went wrong because it wasn't funny. No one laughed.

On the other hand, the true meaning of practical joke if one followed the word trail was:

deliberate cruelty designed to elicit laughter on the part of the perpetrator.

How could deliberate cruelty in the form of an assault be anything but a crime? If anything, the joke perpetrated on Joy was from a Magistrate who allowed Poppy to use a defence of "practical joke that went wrong" as an excuse to get off a charge of assault.

Inspired, she pulled out a couple well-used management texts from the bookshelf and opened them to pages with exercises and case studies. Digging up rusty skills buried deep but never forgotten, she began writing.

Chapter Thirty Five

Fiona knew something was wrong when she entered Leland Gunn's office and he was pacing the floor. He motioned her to sit around the coffee table in the corner.

"You'll be aware, Joy O'Connell's court hearing occurred earlier in the month. Magistrate Smith dismissed all charges without recording a conviction." Leland pulled up a chair, sat down roughly, and opened a file on the table.

"Yes," she said hesitantly. "That was the outcome we were expecting. I believe we specifically arranged for Magistrate Smith to preside. Given his particular leanings on particular issues." Her voice tapered off when she noted the savage look on Leland's face.

"That woman just does not give up." Leland pulled a thick letter from the file. Fiona noted the gold insignia indicating the Minister of Health's letterhead. "She's written to the Minister with a list of questions about how her matter has been handled by the department. He's asked us to please explain."

"I assume the Minister would have been apprised of the court report in The Meridian already?" Fiona asked, stalling for time to compose her thoughts.

"I already responded to that Ministerial," Leland barked. "It shouldn't have been a problem given the editor ran with the heading *Assault Charges Thrown Out* like we suggested. Even if Mrs Bryant pleaded guilty to assault, Smith put that to rest with his judgement."

"Hmm," Fiona nodded in acknowledgement. She plucked the letter out of Leland's clutch and began to read it.

Leland kept interrupting her concentration. "She wants to know why Mrs Bryant got a character reference from us and she didn't! She's arguing this indicates we supported the perpetrator of a crime, and took a position of one employee over another, a manager over a subordinate, deliberately interfering in a private legal matter." He slapped the table to grab Fiona's attention. "This does not look good for us," he emphasised each word one at a time. "Smith just couldn't stop himself adding at the end that it was technically assault but the letter from our department mitigated sentencing. The bastard must have had an attack of professional ethics at the last minute."

Fiona looked up, artfully forming a bland, neutral expression. There was no point in engaging in a counter argument when he was in this frame of mind.

"Who wrote that reference? I want to know," Leland demanded.

"I'll find out," Fiona muttered, trying to finish reading the letter. "Probably someone in Personnel."

Leland paused for a few minutes. "She complained that we should have advised her of the hearing date. Is that something we should have done? Ask Personnel, while you are at it."

Absently, Fiona nodded again. Finishing the letter, she grimaced at Leland. "Joy wants us to sanction Poppy in some way. Point of fact, Poppy did plead guilty to the charge. And Smith agreed it was common assault. She's arguing that if we don't take action, we are giving the wrong message to staff – that we support a manager enacting killing an employee provided she does it in a joking manner." Fiona paused, waiting for Leland to laugh at the ludicrous situation arising out of all this.

When it wasn't forthcoming, she shrugged. "If we don't discipline a manager for assaulting a subordinate, then at what point do we take action? She says we've set the bar so high, anyone in the department can get away with anything, possibly even murder, and this goes against all that OH&S laws and the state government's code of conduct represent."

Personally, Fiona agreed with Joy's sentiments even if stated rather dramatically. It was not politically expedient to state this aloud, particularly in the mood Leland was in. In these instances, it was always wise to leave the decision to the boss. "What do you want me to do?"

"I want you to draft the response to this Ministerial. Include a response to Joy O'Connell for his signature."

As a manager, Leland could be ruthless in delegating the tough jobs. What did Fiona expect? It was her task to wordsmith a suitably expedient explanation for the past five months of stuff ups, mostly instigated by Leland in the first place.

Before letting him off the hook, Fiona had a few points requiring clarification. "Joy is saying the hearing outcome has set back her recovery, behind the starting line in fact. If we're found negligent in exacerbating an initial condition..."

Leland interrupted. "I know, it could impact on her current claim or even lead to an additional one in the future." He considered this. "We've got to get her back to work asap and put this all behind us."

Fiona shook her head. "I don't think that's going to happen soon enough." Leland took a deep breath. "If she can't be convinced to return... What about hinting at an offer to package her out? She might be amenable to twenty thousand dollars and a work reference given the state of her mental health."

Fiona began to pack up the loose papers and tuck them into the file. Closing it, she refused to look at Leland. "I'll put out feelers with her counsellor and the return to work coordinator. It will probably be for the best," she murmured.

Leland smiled broadly for the first time in the meeting. "Good girl. I know I can depend on you."

Fiona exited the office with efficient strides, trying to decide if she wanted to throw up due to his sexist *good girl* comment or the fact that once again she was delegated to the role of Leland's hit man.

Chapter Thirty Six

"How are you?" Bev asked in her usual breezy manner as Joy walked down the corridor to her consulting rooms. It had taken a few weeks to secure this emergency appointment and that felt like Bev had let her down at her time of need.

Joy gave her a sideways glance, wondering if Bev truly wanted to know how she was. Because whether she wanted to or not, she was going to hear it.

A fresh glass of water and a box of tissues rested on the table between the two counselling chairs. A nice gesture. Bev sat down first and opened a file of notes. She pulled out a questionnaire similar to one Joy had taken in February around about their second or third session. It was a rating scale of levels of stress, depression and feelings of hopelessness.

"Let's check on your progress," Bev said.

Joy smirked at the timing of this evaluation. Was Bev concerned that the outcome from the court hearing had sent her over the edge? She hadn't given a care a few weeks ago.

Joy ticked all the boxes with efficient strokes of the pen, knowing all her levels would rate in the extreme range. She said as much, handing it back.

"The court case has set back my recovery. I feel worse than when I first saw you."

Bev tallied the scores and frowned. "Looks like we're back to square one."

"Being told strangulation is a joke will do that to a person," Joy said. "I need to debrief with you."

Bev crossed her legs, leaned forward and affected a caring expression. She waited for her to proceed.

"Over the course of obsessing ruminations that spiralled me down towards a dark place from which I was afraid I'd never return, I decided the only way to cope with the court's decision without going insane was to look at everything from a CBT perspective. Rather than remain all upset and emotional, circling around my negative scripts, I decided to take into account the perspective of others."

Bev nodded approvingly.

"This is my reasoning, starting from the beginning." Joy paused to take a deep breath. She referred to a list of dot points. "My boss strangled me from behind. I wasn't expecting it. My employer accepted her explanation. Apparently, she placed both hands around my throat as a surprise neck massage. My grievance was dismissed without my employer taking any disciplinary action." She looked up at Bev.

"When the police charged her with assault, my employer supported her in court. She was given a character reference to use in her defence. The department declared to a court of law that her character was *impeccable*." Joy locked eyes with Bev's. "According to the Oxford dictionary, that means *faultless*.

"My employer defended her character despite Poppy pleading guilty to assaulting me.

"Poppy's lawyer didn't even go with the neck massage explanation. He went straight for the argument that strangling me was a joke. A joke that apparently went terribly wrong.

"In effect, they characterised strangling as larrikin behaviour, nothing to be concerned about.

"The Magistrate accepted this argument. Poppy, my manager, attempted to share a joke with me by way of strangling." Joy paused for this to sink in.

"In her defence, Poppy asserted that we used to give each other shoulder rubs at work. By the way this was a lie, but the Magistrate accepted it because of her impeccable character.

"This implied consent on my part. Consent to violate my private, physical person. If I gave permission to a shoulder massage, I must have tacitly given consent for Poppy to take things to the next level of physical contact – strangling. This was apparently something we could both laugh about." Joy's voice cracked. She took a sip of water before continuing.

"Due to her faultless character he dismissed her guilty plea, all the charges, and didn't even record the proceedings. She was given a clean slate to continue on her merry way. Faultless and blameless.

"To summarise, my employer, the Department of Community Health – a state government department – and the legal system both upheld Poppy's behaviour. She did nothing wrong in strangling me. It was trivial and normal behaviour between *friends* in the workplace. Strangling a subordinate in the workplace was an inconsequential action that simply went wrong for some inexplicable reason." Joy finally stopped to take in a deep breath.

"According to the CBT experts, *events don't make us unhappy, only how we interpret them*. Where does this leave me?" Joy paused to check that Bev was following the logical argument to its conclusion. Bev remained still, observing and assessing her mood. "CBT is based on a premise that it isn't the event that is the problem so much as my beliefs and attitude towards it. Right?

"The above sequence of events supports this premise. It wasn't my boss who had the problem; it's not my employer's attitude towards violence in the workplace that's the problem; it's not the legal system that accepts humour as a legitimate excuse for a violent person to get off assault charges that is wrong. It's my attitude to strangling that's the problem – not the systems that are clearly screwed up to the point of insanity." Joy spoke in calm, even tones as if addressing a committee meeting.

"The obvious question that remains unanswered is *at what point did Poppy's strangling joke go wrong?*"

Bev shifted and re-crossed her legs, looking uncomfortable. Joy smirked. *How could she refute a logical argument based on the therapeutic treatment she'd been using for so many months?*

Joy continued to the next phase of her reasoning.

"There were no other people around at the time of the joke, except me, of course. I was the only other person involved in the joke, the only other person whose opinion should count, and I did not think it was funny."

Joy raised her palms in a mocking gesture. "So, this is what I've concluded.

"*I must be what went wrong.* I'm the only one not seeing it as a joke! I'm the one *wrong* in what went wrong. That's why I'm sitting here today and all the other days having counselling, needing to change my thinking and feelings about the incident. I'm the one needing to be fixed. Not Poppy with her impeccable character."

"I'm the one with the problem because I'm the only one in this workers compensation circus not seeing strangling as funny, trivial or normal. My beliefs are clearly faulty."

"I finally get why I need such a lot of help and no one will leave me alone to sort things out for myself. Because the point of the exercise is to be *normal* again. And *normal* requires normalising and trivialising strangling like all these other authorities have done, so I'm not so upset about it. And then I can return to work as if nothing's happened."

"Because according to my boss, my employer, and a court of law nothing did happen except an innocent joke."

She sat back in a defiant mood with arms crossed waiting for Bev's response.

Bev cleared her throat and glanced down at the file as if looking for inspiration. At last she asked, "So where does this leave you?"

"Isn't it obvious? I need to get a sense of humour!"

Bev winced. "I'm not sure…"

Joy handed across an A4 sheet of paper.

"You may not be aware but before I moved to Eden Isle, I worked for the Commonwealth government as a management consultant. I used to design and deliver management development workshops. I've designed a case study for the health department to use in training staff about humour in the workplace. I'd like to put it past you before I send it to the area coordinator."

Case Study – "A Joke Gone Wrong"

Exercise: Choose the scenario most likely to demonstrate a joke* between a manager and her subordinate. Discuss your reasons, referring to prompt questions below.

A worker is quietly sitting at her desk looking at a computer screen, when her manager comes up from behind and

- points a gun at the back of her head, saying "If I don't shoot you, I will have to shoot Helen".

- puts her hands around her throat and starts to choke her, saying "If I don't strangle you, I will have to strangle Helen".

- places a knife blade between her shoulders saying "If I don't stab you, I will have to stab Helen".

Note The Australian Pocket Oxford Dictionary definition of a joke: thing said or done to incite laughter

Prompt Questions

Given the humour in each situation, which scenario is more likely to engender the most mutual laughter between the manager and her subordinate?

Are there any possibilities that the joke could go wrong? And if so, could the manager possibly be expected to foresee this?

What support could the organisation offer the manager should her subordinate prove to be lacking in a sense of humour?

(Please refer to the Respectful Behaviour in the Workplace policy, and State Code of Conduct when preparing your responses.)

Joy watched Bev's face as she read it. It remained neutral. "Well?"

"I can see you've put a lot of thought into it," was all she said. She added the sheet to her file notes. Joy was disappointed but remained defiant.

Bev looked at her watch. The hour was up. "I'm not going to be able to make another appointment to see you, Joy. The state government has decided not to renew my contract to provide the employee assistance counselling program. I finish at the end of the week."

"This week? Can I see you privately?"

"I don't think that will be possible."

"I could get a referral from my GP?"

"The department's workers comp insurer would need to approve it." Bev looked sympathetic but also unhelpful. She began to gather papers and pack up their session.

"One last thing. I've heard hints that the department may be considering offering you a package. Start preparing yourself. It would probably be good to get a lawyer to ensure you know all your entitlements. It's usual for a first offer to be in the region of twenty thousand dollars."

The sudden departure of her counsellor without any prior warning hit Joy out of left field. The news the department was going to send her packing deflated her smug defiance. She wanted to continue working. Would they give her a choice?

Her mind raced through all the questions she wanted to discuss with Bev if there had been time. Retiring from the workplace when she could in theory continue working for another ten years sent a cold shiver of doom through her body. Even though she hadn't been at work these past months, nonetheless she was employed; her position at the centre was held for her return; the department deposited pay into her bank account every fortnight (even if it was substantially reduced due to being on workers comp) and her superannuation and long service leave kept accruing. When people asked what she did, fooled into believing she was not off work forever, it was truthful to say *I'm a public servant.*

Pushed into early retirement had not been on the agenda. When she considered the potential to earn a living for so much longer, a twenty thousand dollars package to retire didn't seem generous or even tempting. Surely, they had to believe she would eventually get better. Wasn't that what the process was all about these past six months?

A package was devastating news. Delivered at precisely the wrong time. She needed a trusted counsellor more than ever. How could Bev do this?

With a sinking heart, the enormity of the betrayal was suppressed with a polite niceness ingrained into women since childhood.

"Well then, I guess now is the time to wish you all the best in your new venture. I'll miss you."

"Thank you, Joy. Good luck," Bev replied, polite in return.

Joy pretended not to notice an undisguised look of relief on her counsellor's face.

Chapter Thirty Seven

Honor surreptitiously checked her daughter's mood, afraid to say the wrong thing and get snapped at. Kodi curled in a lounge chair and pretended to watch *The Simpsons* on TV, loudly sniffling into a tissue. For the past few months, it was unusual on a Thursday evening for the family to be together after Kodi's netball practice. She and Lachlan must have had another fight.

Col noticed Kodi's wretchedness and impatiently turned up the volume. When that didn't work, he turned off the program and spoke up. "What happened now? Has that dropkick given you grief?"

Kodi looked up in a daze. Her eyes slowly focused as if coming out of a spell cast by her own misery. A waterfall of cascading tears burst forth. "He's moving to Plover Point to be near Dora," she wailed. Yanking tissues from a box, she blew her nose. It sounded like a semi-trailer foghorn. "He's dumping me." Curling into a tighter ball, she stared at the blank TV screen with rapt concentration.

"Darling, maybe it's for the best. God has something better in store for you," Honor said in a soothing voice. Kodi glared at her like she was the mother from *Alien*.

Col looked puzzled. "Plover Point is not that far to drive," he said with cool logic.

Kodi gave a hopeful smile.

Quickly, Honor intervened. "I heard his position as youth worker at the centre hasn't been funded in the new budget. He won't be coaching Thursday night netball any longer, darling."

Kodi dried her eyes with a fresh tissue. "They told him his youth programs achieved better than expected results. His services were no longer required because his ideas worked," she said with disgust.

"He was fired?" Col asked.

"Dear, you don't get fired anymore; your contract doesn't get renewed," Honor explained.

"Same difference," he muttered under his breath.

"Lachlan said there's been a re-structuring of Allied Health in the department. He lost his position altogether and Tara will be transferred to head office. If clients want appointments, they'll have to travel to see her," Kodi said defensively.

"Has the lad got a new job yet?" Col asked, ever practical.

Kodi nodded miserably. "At a youth suicide prevention center. That's why he's moving to Plover Point. And Dora lives there with his ex, so he plans to see more of her."

"I guess, with starting a new job and settling into a new home, he's going to be busy for a while," Honor gently reminded her.

"No time for me," Kodi agreed.

The room went quiet. "I'll make us all cups of tea," Honor said.

"I'm making a banana split with ice cream and chocolate sauce. And whipped cream and nuts," Kodi said defiantly.

Honor knew when to let things slide. It was best not to intervene in indulgent, post romance comfort eating. She wasn't convinced Lachlan's defection would be permanent, unfortunately. Time would tell. It was interesting that the two positions lost from the centre in the restructure happened to coincide with two staff associated with knowing the truth behind Poppy assaulting Joy.

She decided to ask Col when they went to bed if he thought this was more than pure coincidence.

Chapter Thirty Eight

J oy waited at the counter to check in with the receptionist at Lower Teasels Doctors Surgery. She was such a regular visitor at the surgery Gayleen smiled as if seeing an old friend rather than a patient.

Joy sighed with resignation. Another workers compensation medical appointment. Apart from a continuing medical certificate, she needed a referral to a new counsellor desperately. Before making any life changing decisions, she had to work through the pros and cons as to whether to take a package and retire early or stay on workers comp. This was difficult. What used to come as naturally as dreaming was now an impossible task.

She was surprised to learn from Gayleen that Dr Vitkay had not returned yet and instead had extended his leave for several months. In the meantime, a different locum was taking his clients. Joy was assigned to Dr Sasha.

"When will Dr Vitkay be returning?" Joy asked anxiously. She'd lost Bev; she couldn't face losing another trusted support person.

Gayleen couldn't say. It was a personal matter.

Joy looked around the waiting area but did not see Michelle. Not that her presence was particularly needed. It was starting to feel more like being minded rather than supported. If someone asked what Michelle got paid to do in relation to her case, Joy would find it difficult to pinpoint.

Joy picked up a Woman's Weekly Christmas Special magazine left on an adjoining seat. It was dated December from two years ago. She flipped through the coloured photos of glittering tinsel, sparkling rose cocktails, and bespoke crafted table decorations. It took a lot of work putting the merry into Christmas. She loved the traditional baking and all the planning that went into a big family Christmas get together.

Or maybe she should qualify that to *use to love it*. BTS. Had Poppy taken this joy away as well? Time would tell.

Would she ever feel like her old self?

Unable to concentrate, her mind wandered on dark paths of scepticism.

What did a *Return to Work Coordinator* actually coordinate? For the best part of the year, Michelle attended each medical appointment with Joy, bringing along a printed, pro forma RTW plan that consisted solely of one statement: *Totally Incapacitated for Work*. Despite Joy's insistence to change the wording from 'neck stiffness' to 'strangling' as Cause of Injury and 'PTSD' as Nature of Injury, the Plan continued to be re-printed exactly the same as the original. So much for taking into account anything she had to say about her RTW plan.

Joy wouldn't let go of the issue around the wording of the RTW plan which diluted the original incident to something unremarkable. Over time, an insurer and medical practitioners could easily forget she was strangled by her manager.

After complaining more loudly, Michelle discussed changing the Nature of Injury to 'anxiety'; however, Joy pointed out that PTSD was more than anxiety. If anything, she joked, it should be listed as 'abject terror'. But seriously, PTSD was a cluster of specific symptoms and therefore a more correct term.

In fairness, Michelle did earn some of her salary in organising a team load of people to sign the plan. That must have taken a lot of coordination. And she faxed off each new medical certificate to the department's pay officer. But that was it.

Apart from occasionally questioning Dr Vitkay's assessment giving Joy more time off work, Michelle often dissuaded medical tests, such as the occasion when Joy asked to see an ENT specialist about a persistent hoarse throat that had arisen since the strangling. Michelle took on the role of spokesperson on behalf of the insurer, second guessing them. The excuse was always *the insurer wouldn't approve,* meaning Joy would be out-of-pocket if she pursued these extra medical interventions. *The insurer will pay for the original injury but not any medical conditions arising later from it,* Michelle explained as if that was reasonable on their part.

Usually, Dr Vitkay ignored the intrusion into his professional judgments. But Joy began to take note of them and question whose side Michelle was on.

Joy wondered how anyone on her so-called Workers Compensation Team earned their salaries. After all, they were the beneficiaries of her workplace injury. Their jobs existed because of people like her. It was her money that paid for their services, at least in part. A fifteen percent cut of her salary each pay day, funding them to sit in their offices advising her what to do and think but returned nothing very useful. It did not seem like value for money.

If anything, she was getting worse, not better for all their 'help'. Yet Joy was the one incessantly required to prove at the end of every medical appointment whether she deserved another certificate which would then allow her to receive a reduced pay as a consequence of an injury. Why didn't they have to justify their pays as well?

A waft of Daisy perfume announced Michelle's attendance. Joy closed the magazine and threw it on a pile with all the others. Maybe Michelle could earn her money.

"Do you know anything about the department wanting to package me out?" she asked moodily.

Michelle's doe brown eyes registered surprise and then compassion. "I've been trying to get answers; the department's Workers Compensation Officer has been on extended leave."

"And no one's replaced Hannah?" Joy asked, knowing the answer. Budget cuts and all.

"Each time I've tried to arrange a case management meeting so I can coordinate your Return To Work Plan with input from the team, Fiona Blackwell refuses to take my calls and refers me back to Hannah. Messages left on her voicemail have remained unanswered so far." There was a hint of frustration in Michelle's voice, unusual for her.

Joy nodded in understanding. It was a typical bureaucratic circular chase, and a potent reminder Joy was insignificant in the scheme of things.

"It's been suggested if you didn't want to return or transfer to another health centre, a placement to Records Management at the Royal Isle Hospital could be arranged."

Records Management? In a dingy basement, filing old records covered in dust mites. That would be a cruel come down, an absolute humiliating way to end a long, successful career. It was a deliberate insult.

Michelle must have seen the look on Joy's face because this line of enquiry was not pushed further, much to Joy's relief.

"Remind me to show you my CV sometime," Joy remarked with obvious sarcasm. Of course, Michelle was another on her workers comp team that had never asked about her work history, professional qualifications or valuable skills she had to offer an employer. Why was that?

Did they assume she'd always been an admin assistant? Someone trained to smile politely and do others bidding with compliant servitude. A voiceless vassal easily relegated to a dark corner of a basement, filing.

As a consolation prize, Michelle handed over a prepared RTW plan for her signature. Joy skim read it and noted it looked exactly like all the previous ones. And like all the previous ones, Michelle had ignored Joy's list of RTW requirements. Of course. No one cared about Joy's input into the plan. Why would her personal opinions about her own recovery count?

They all knew better.

Joy? A command given in a Russian accent brought her attention back to the waiting room. *Joy O'Connell?* Looking up, she saw a tiny woman with blunt cropped steel grey hair dressed in a military-styled beige suit standing in the archway that led to doctors consulting rooms.

Dr Sasha held out a manila file opened like a book and frowned with impatience. The waiting area was filled to capacity, and she was a busy doctor.

Joy smiled obsequiously and leapt out of the chair. Wasting no time with introductions, the doctor did an abrupt turn and strode down the hallway to Dr Vitkay's room.

Once seated, Joy decided Dr Sasha, like the previous locum filling in for Dr Vitkay, needed to be informed about the background to her current medical treatment. It was tedious but necessary so she didn't get the wrong idea about the *neck stiffness injury*. Before she could open her mouth to explain being strangled and getting PTSD, she was interrupted.

"I'm not here to write medical certificates," Dr Sasha stated followed by a string of heavily accented ramblings.

The lecture was difficult to follow but the bits Joy managed to put together sounded like a telling off.

"Why you not apply for jobs?" Dr Sasha demanded.

Was the doctor implying it was all Joy's fault being off work. Was she accusing her of being a malingerer?

The locum continued to lecture. After a few minutes, from what Joy could decipher, it became apparent the doctor had very different views on workers compensation.

"If you do not want to return to job, I send you to Centrelink," Dr Sasha scolded.

A slow understanding of Dr Sasha's intentions percolated up from Joy's heart towards her brain in a flush of heated concern.

"You go on dole," she commanded.

Heat was replaced by icy tendrils of shock seeping down Joy's body all the way to her toes. What was this foreign doctor saying? Clearly the woman didn't know anything about the Australian system of workers compensation nor an employer's responsibility towards an injured worker. Sending Joy onto the dole or back to work rather than re-issue a medical certificate, without any prior understanding of her condition or what it would mean to her mental health if confronted by Poppy again... against Dr Vitkay's medical assessment... how could she do that?

Joy had been a good employee and complied with all requirements imposed by the workers compensation system. She'd attended doctor's appointments, gone to counselling, filled prescriptions for antidepressants, even tried to contribute to her return to work plan. It wasn't her fault none of this had helped. It was like blaming the vase for not doing its job after being glued back together. Her value as an employee was diminished irreparably. Surely this was obvious to the doctor.

"I'm a broken vase," she stammered. "I'm trying to make the best of it but I'm not the same as I was."

Dr Sasha snorted. "You not want to work. You lazy woman."

She did not see a mentally injured patient with PTSD in front of her. All she saw was a slacker milking the system.

Later, at home when Joy's emotional reaction subsided and intellect kicked in, she'd understand within this particular narrative, she was powerless. It was Dr Sasha's authority that set the scene: the way a situation or person was to be viewed; what to pay attention to; what to ignore; what was allowed to be discussed and what was to be silenced.

Dr Sasha was the supreme interpreter of the rules and the setter of boundaries. After meeting for a short few minutes, she believed it was her right as a doctor to pass judgement, not simply about Joy's medical condition but also about her moral attitude.

In this scenario, Joy would not be seen or understood. The system's political agenda weighed in favour of an employer and their insurer. There was no point in arguing.

The new doctor didn't see an employee so broken by her employer she was terrified of returning to work. Dr Sasha refused to conceive an employer could be at fault. Instead, it had to be Joy's fault. The blame settled on her.

Pressuring Joy to return to work, blaming her for being unable to, was so unrealistic it amounted to craziness.

Joy's last shred of trust in the health system unravelled in an explosion of disempowerment and panic.

A scream of anguish erupted in the room. "You can't do that!" she yelled at the doctor. "You don't know me." Joy doubled over in nauseous agony. Rocking back and forth, she began to hyperventilate in full blown hysteria.

Dr Sasha glared without an ounce of compassion. "You go on dole. No complaints."

Joy leapt out of the chair and dashed out of the consulting room and down the corridor, weeping and wailing like a hurt animal. Her only thought was to run away to some place safe. Her escape caught Michelle's attention.

Michelle's look of surprise and concern brought Joy to an abrupt stop.

"You have to talk to her," Joy shouted in distress. Other people in the waiting area perked up with morbid curiosity and then looked away embarrassed at the scene unfolding. Joy was too far gone to care. "I can't go back," she wailed.

Michelle hurried over and guided a hyperventilating Joy back to Dr Sasha.

"She'll explain workers comp to you," Joy shouted accusingly at the doctor.

"Do not yell or you will leave," Dr Sasha ordered.

To Michelle's credit, she took on the role of mediator like a natural. In the background, Joy rocked back and forth weeping uncontrollably. After explaining the law and assuring the doctor that Joy's employer was on board with it all, Dr Sasha relented. A new medical certificate and a prescription for Murelax were issued under sufferance.

"Joy will need a referral to a new counsellor as well," Michelle reminded the doctor. Joy was in no shape to ask for anything. She was eternally grateful for Michelle rising to the occasion. From an undefined, airy fairy role as RTW Coordinator she transformed into a marshal on a white horse cracking a whip.

"Maybe I send her to see psychiatrist, see what he recommends," Dr Sasha threatened.

Joy beseeched Michelle with a single look.

With smooth aplomb, Michelle responded, "The insurer would have to approve Joy seeing a specialist."

Dr Sasha stared at Michelle for a long moment and then backed down. Joy's arrow of esteem for Michelle shot to hero status.

"I send her to Marcus here at surgery. He is new counsellor from Department of Health." Dr Sasha scratched instructions on a medical form, slid it and a prescription across the desk, and snapped the file shut. She pushed back her chair, impatient to see the next patient.

Joy snatched the paperwork and squashed it into the outer sleeve of her handbag.

On the way to the car, Joy hiccoughed and wept noisily into a handkerchief. Too distraught, she didn't care who saw and didn't care about small town gossip that would follow.

Seeking Michelle's continued role as hero, she whimpered, "I don't want to see that counsellor who works for the Department of Community Health. It's a conflict of interest! I want my own psychologist, someone I can talk to about anything, not just work-related stuff. Someone who sees me as a person and not just a case file."

Michelle's eyes crinkled with sympathy. "Joy, you don't have a choice. You must comply with the plan. If the doctor says you see Marcus, that's who you must see." She continued walking to her car, not wanting to engage in an emotional discussion that would lead nowhere.

It hadn't taken Michelle long to revert to her old role.

Joy had only one thought.

"I can never go back to that doctor," she boldly stated.

Michelle kept walking. "It's up to you. You risk your compo payments, so think about it before making a rash decision."

Chapter Thirty Nine

By the next day, Joy stopped hyperventilating enough to commit to calling the Compo Assist Hotline. In PJs, sitting at the kitchen table with a calming cup of chamomile tea and a dish of blackberries and yoghurt, she felt as traumatised as Peter Rabbit after an encounter with Mr Macgregor.

Morning shafts of sunlight filtered through the branches of a backyard oak, casting patterns from a few stubborn brown leaves refusing to give up clinging to an autumn long gone. Warming rays through a dusty windowpane reflected off the pale blue chalk paint table top and off one rounded side of a porcelain Carlton Ware teacup. Joy's red rimmed eyes, dry from crying, squinted from the brightness. Her racing heart calmed down a notch in appreciation of the beauty of her garden wilderness and the gentle peace afforded by Nature. For a short moment, man-made rules and procedures perpetuated by bureaucracies and corporations took on an insignificant artificiality.

This feeling didn't last.

The Compo Assist receptionist answered in crisp tones. Efficient but not hurried, she controlled the conversation to elicit contact details and a brief – emphasis on *brief* – description of the enquiry, before scheduling a telephone conference at two with Jim, one of their consultants. The call ended quickly with Joy expecting more and yet, having to wait.

Restless and anxious for help, she found an exercise book of Jaxon's left behind after his last visit. She set it on the table with a pen ready to itemise her thoughts in order of priority. With an obsessiveness that flared up all too quickly these days, she began to scribble all the issues needing clarification. Dot points filled half a page, an indication of how much she was in the dark about the whole process, even after all this time.

Reviewing her work, it seemed as if each member of her workers comp team held a piece of the puzzle but no one was explaining much of anything, including how they fit into the whole picture. This added a new meaning to the *divide and conquer* maxim. How was she to navigate through all the conditions and rules being imposed by a system, and retain some independence and empowerment within the decisions being made for her, if she couldn't understand how individual components fit together?

Jim called at four minutes past two pm according to her wall clock. She was ready with pen poised. His voice had a mature and cultured tone, slightly British. Joy assumed he was not born on Eden Isle where locals drawled with a pitchy strine that to her ears sounded whiney. He began by first introducing himself and explaining how the Compo Assist Hotline was established by the previous government as a means of helping employees understand their rights and entitlements under the law. This was reassuring to Joy.

These good feelings translated into pouring out her heart to Jim as soon as he asked the fateful *how may I help you* question. He turned out to be a very good listener.

In the end, although sympathetic, he tried to talk her out of seeking a new doctor's surgery explaining that the insurer would have to approve the change. They would become suspicious if she began shopping around. This would mean giving an explanation. It would not be in Joy's best interests to tell them one of her GPs diagnosed her as having a spiritual crisis and the next GP wanted to put her on the dole and this had brought on a hysterical panic attack. He also advised that there were not that many choices of doctors on Eden Isle and she would have trouble finding another GP that had a space available on the books.

Joy conceded to common sense. "Dr Vitkay wasn't so bad. I'm hoping he'll return soon." She decided this would be a new mantra of positivity for her.

"Is there anything else I can help you with?" Jim asked politely.

Not wasting an opportunity, Joy moved on to the next dot point. She explained that Michelle, her RTW Coordinator, was on a crusade to place her in another section of the health department on a one day a week trial. A noble gesture but ill-founded according to Dr Vitkay. Joy wanted to know her rights if she refused a placement, for example, to Records Management. She wanted to return to her old job when fully recovered. Would they keep it open for her?

"It's up to your GP to decide when you are ready to return to work and under what conditions. When he writes up your return to work plan, he'll set out the steps that need to be taken." Jim was very sure of this process.

It didn't match Joy's experience. "So far, Michelle has been the one writing up my RTW plan without input from anyone else. It's always 'Totally Incapacitated for Work' because I can't return if the manager who strangled me is there. She's tried to get a case management meeting with senior department managers to discuss my needs but they keep delaying."

Jim's tone changed from helpful to stern. "The legislation is clear; it must be your GP who writes the RTW Plan. He can of course take into consideration any recommendations put forward by your psychologist."

"Oh, great," Joy said. "I don't have one at the moment. My counsellor lost the government contract to provide counselling. That's another health professional I have to change to someone new."

There was a short pause while she heard Jim jotting notes. "Of course, if you are considered Totally Incapacitated for Work then there is no requirement for an RTW Plan."

"Then it's pointless for Michelle to keep preparing them," Joy confirmed, hoping Jim would deny it. His silence was an acknowledgement. "I wonder what her job really is then? My minder..." she muttered.

Reviewing her own notes, she began another line of questioning. "I've heard hints that the department may offer a package. Do I have to accept it? I always expected to return to my job as soon as I recovered. I want to work until retirement."

"Again, the law is clear. You can stay on workers compensation until fully recovered for up to nine years. Your employer is required to hold your substantive position open for at least twelve months."

Joy breathed a sigh of relief. "Nine years would take me to near retirement age. But it now seems they don't want me back."

Jim was honest. "You're probably correct in that assumption. It's usual practice for employers to get people off their books rather than maintaining all the administration costs associated with these matters, particularly for employees with a permanent disability."

"But I don't want a package. They're offering less than six months' salary which doesn't sound reasonable when compared to staying on workers compensation."

"They assume you'll get another job elsewhere. Or go on the dole. However, if you are unable to work due to your injury, you are entitled to an offer that includes a percentage of your salary over the next nine years or until you reach retirement age, whichever is sooner. It may also include a lump sum payment if you have a permanent injury and something towards ongoing medical costs, if necessary."

Joy began to feel more like a statistic than a valued employee who used to take pride in her job. "How will I know if the payment is fair and reasonable?" Joy asked. She wasn't as willing these days to trust the system when it came to being fair and reasonable.

"We always recommend you seek legal advice before accepting any payout figure. A lawyer can explain your entitlements and the process for achieving a reasonable settlement." Jim was matter-of-fact as if the decision was simple and straightforward. Not one that would change her identity forever – from a mature worker to a retiree, that is, an old aged pensioner.

Joy was devastated, facing the prospect of not being wanted by her employer and being forced out of the workforce at such an early age.

"Is there anything else?" Jim enquired, ready to wrap up the conversation.

"Not for now. Thank you for your advice," Joy said.

"Feel free to call the hotline with any further questions. I'll keep your file open."

His parting words left Joy wondering why he felt the need to keep her file open. As if Jim expected her initial enquiry left many more questions to come.

Chapter Forty

That night, Joy woke from a nightmare in a cold sweat. Throwing off the overheated quilt covers, she sat up and glanced at the digital clock on the bedside table. It read three am. She flicked on a light. Took a few deep breaths.

Memory of the dream hung in the room like the burnt smell from an incense amphora.

She'd been at a job interview and the panel had been nodding and smiling, clearly pleased with her work history and interview performance. It felt as if she would win the position. They liked her.

At the end of the interview the standard question came up: Do you have anything you'd like to ask the panel?

Joy wanted to know about their organisational culture. Was it important to have a good sense of humour in the workplace?

They all thought it was.

What was their attitude to practical jokes in the workplace?

The panel members conferred with each other. Their voices were indistinct.

The scene changed. The mood in the room changed.

Some compulsion had caused her to blurt out a confession. She'd reported her manager to the police for assault over a practical joke.

There were murmurs from the panel. She heard snippets. Not very sporting. Not a team player. Heads were shaking. Did they want someone so sensitive to practical jokes?

Joy became worried she'd talked them out of giving her the job. She dug a deeper hole by pleading.

She was getting help to become less sensitive and serious. A team of doctors and counsellors were working on her with therapies and medications. They were helping her become an impeccable character.

She began to dissipate into mist. An image of an enormous bat resembling Poppy, brash and lecherous, coalesced in her place. Its toothy Cheshire cat grin pierced her heart.

Joy disintegrated into a thousand puzzle pieces scattered across a black void. Disembodied words resonated in a heavy pressing silence. Faultless. Impeccable. Broken. Lost.

Joy had woken from the dream with a stomach clenched in agonising nausea.

Dreaming about Poppy was bad enough. The notion of turning into her made it a nightmare.

Once the apprehension lifted, Joy opened a journal, ready to scribe some pithy insights about life. Being awake in the early hours of the morning was not unusual. Often writing streams of consciousness ramblings eased her anxiety. Maybe the dream would reveal a key to recovery through some archetypal Jungian symbolism.

After a few minutes staring at a blank page, she realised it was a mistake to believe at three am life would start to make sense in the darkest time of night... when it hadn't in the light of day.

Turning off the light and pulling up the covers, she rolled onto her side.

Sleep refused to come.

She'd lost her ability to enjoy dreaming.

Chapter Forty One

Fiona shifted in the seat trying to get circulation moving in her legs. A full complement of Occupational Health and Safety Committee members showed for the monthly meeting. They were jammed elbow to elbow around the oval table in the small conference room, half asleep listening to Leland drone on about charts and statistics for the Mid Northern Area. His sonorous voice held the stage as he plodded along, slow and deliberate, carefully elucidating every fact and figure on every page of the report.

As boring as it was, Fiona admired a true master at work. This was Leland's tried and true strategy used to prevent probing questions and uncomfortable explanations concerning specific incidents.

Surreptitiously, she darted a look at her watch. The hour was nearly up. She'd kill for a double shot cappuccino about now. Her mind wandered to the diary open on her desk, filled with afternoon appointments. In the background, someone made a remark. Leland was saying "That's a procedural concern. I'll let Fiona answer that."

Caught out, she had no option but to own up. "Could you repeat the question, Derrick?" She stifled a groan knowing the administrative assistant from the Gorse Plains Community Health Centre took his role as a union representative on the committee very seriously. Whatever the issue, he would not be put off with reassuring platitudes.

Derrick cleared his throat self-importantly and sat up taller in his chair. "What progress has been made concerning rehabilitating Ms Joy O'Connell to return to work at Lower Teasel's health centre?"

Leland gave Fiona a smirk. The bastard was enjoying putting her on the spot. Stalling for time, Fiona made a point of rifling through her notes, as if she couldn't bring to mind the specifics of the case. Her mind worked frantically, seeking the most expedient response.

"You'll be aware Ms O'Connell's matter involves details of a personal and confidential nature. Therefore, I am restricted in what I may divulge to the committee. Suffice to say, it is progressing along the accustomed procedural pathway set out in departmental policies. There are no concerns to apprise the Committee at this time."

Leland lounged back in his chair nonchalantly. He nodded approvingly but to no one in particular.

Derrick, of course, wasn't satisfied with being fobbed off. "I heard she was going to be given a package?" he accused. Murmured grumbles travelled around the circle.

Fiona was momentarily astounded at how gossip spread no matter how careful one was at keeping things a secret. "Yes, well, you will be aware that personnel handles this side of the proceedings. It isn't a simple or rushed process taken lightly. There are many stages and steps set out in legislation before a payout can be considered, let alone offered."

Derrick leaned forward looking as if he was going to argue. Leland, as the Acting Chair, decided to intervene. "It is much too soon to be discussing an option at the extreme end of the spectrum. Be assured all attempts are being made to protect the department's exposure and vulnerabilities to prevent an employee gaining advantage from an incident of this nature." He spoke to the group to soften the rebuke.

Then he focused attention on Derrick. "Thank you for your concern, Derrick."

Quickly, Fiona added, "We will keep you all informed as appropriate in due course."

Leland cast a reassuring gaze around the table, eyeballing each person, ensuring their amenability in light of Derrick's brusque assertiveness. Content that no residual tension lingered, he closed the meeting.

"That covers our agenda for today. Thank you for your attendance. We'll reconvene next month."

Derrick leaped up, grabbed a notebook and was first out the door. As other members filed out in a more orderly fashion, Fiona slowly gathered papers into a folder. Leland signalled to wait. When the space cleared, he asked in a hushed voice, "I assume Joy O'Connell declined the offer?"

"I put out feelers but Personnel pulled me back. They're insisting we follow formal protocols."

"Which means...?" Leland asked.

Fiona loudly sighed making frustration obvious. "Psych assessments, formulas to calculate a payout figure, the Crown solicitor getting involved, possibly going to a tribunal. It won't be quick."

"I see." Leland studied the wall, thinking. A moment later he slapped the table decisively. "Keep up the pressure, my girl." He leapt up and was out the door before he could see Fiona's dirty look.

Under her breath she muttered, "Maybe she'll quit and move back to the mainland – make all our lives easier."

Chapter Forty Two

A timid knock on the manager's door alerted Poppy to stop scrolling on her mobile phone and appear busy. One of the support workers, Dave crossed his arms and shuffled his feet in the corridor waiting to be invited into the office. Poppy pulled across a stack of papers and grabbed a pen, then said "Come in," with a curt voice. Rather than acknowledge him, she concentrated on reading for a full minute.

"Well, what is it?" she asked, turning and digging in an elbow on the stack. A beefy man in his early forties dressed in a hoodie and track pants, with tattoos across his fingers, stood to attention in the doorway.

"Sorry to bother you." His face erupted in a blush. "I'm Harold Gray's carer."

"Yes, I know, Dave. What's happening?" Poppy demanded.

Dave cleared his throat. "It's just that his dementia is getting worse, like he forgets to feed his Shitzu and um," he paused. "He gets aggressively agitated if I refuse to... you know... well, the dog needs to stay outside..."

Poppy noticed his blush had turned fiery red. Put the man out of his misery, she decided. "I'm aware of Mr Gray's... personal proclivities. Normally, I'd advise that you are Harold's carer, not his dog's. He is entitled to nature's release the same as any other person in the privacy of his own home. How he goes about that is usually not our concern." She gave a short laugh, smiling at Dave, hoping he'd join in. When he stared at her stupefied, she pressed on in a more patronising tone. "However, if you are saying his belligerence is becoming more violent and posing a risk to you, then we will have to look into it."

Dave's shoulders relaxed. "Maybe his yearly assessment could be moved forward?"

"Leave it with me. I'll consider how best to address the issue. It may be time for old Harold to be moved to a facility." Poppy knew this would pull on Dave's heartstrings. Sentencing an elderly person to an aged care facility was the final step in a downhill trajectory to his expiry date.

As anticipated, a look of guilt flashed across Dave's face. "Maybe he's just been having a few bad weeks."

"Don't we all! Not to worry. I'll look into it. We'll get him sorted." Poppy scrawled a reminder on a sticky note and stuck it on the computer screen. "Leave it with me."

Dave slunk away, duty done. Poppy rubbed steepled hands picturing old Harold being denied a release of his mounting tension, Dave keeping the Shitzu outside for its protection, and Harold growing more and more angry about the situation. She'd definitely have to intervene in the situation. It was a perfect opportunity to get out of the office and back to hands-on nursing.

She'd been discussing how much she missed home nursing visits with Gil over dinner the other night. Ever practical, he'd replied, "You're the boss – you can do whatever you want."

He was right. There was no rule that said a manager couldn't conduct an emergency assessment of a client's needs.

***

Harold Gray's single bedroom unit adjoined a block of other small, fibro board units owned by Quamby Brook's Uniting Church. The cement pathway leading to his front door was cracked and patches of moss made it a potential tripping hazard. The plastic door mat was twisted so it didn't sit flat.

Poppy bent down and retrieved a house key barely hidden under the mat. She opened a cobwebbed fly screen and knocked on the hospital beige front door. Mr Gray didn't answer, as usual.

Letting herself in, she found Harold in a wheelchair in the lounge room staring at a talk show on the TV. It blared out in full volume. A musty unwashed dog smell hung in the air. The threadbare plaid robe he wore could use a wash along with the pyjamas. She'd have words to Dave to toss the smelly blanket crossing Harold's lap in the wash while he was at it.

"Mr Gray, it's your nurse. I'm here to give you a shot for your diabetes," she yelled into the room. Harold didn't respond, although his dentures clicked together as if he was chewing vigorously. A thin streak of spittle ran down his chin.

Poppy closed in and patted his shoulder. "Harold? How are we today?" He jerked as if awakened from a stupor. "It's Poppy, you remember me. I used to be your nurse." Bending down to eye level in front of the wheelchair, unaware her large breasts pushed against his knees, she gazed up at him with clinical concern. "Is there anything I can get you? A cup of tea?" Automatically, she adjusted the collar on his robe and smoothed out wrinkles from the blanket.

Harold's yellowed eyes took on a gleam of recognition. A skeletal claw grabbed Poppy's hand and pulled it to his lap. The thin blanket began to tent as a pole began to rise between his legs.

Poppy allowed him to push her palm around, surprised his frailty didn't extend to certain parts of his anatomy. All part of the assessment, she joked to herself. "Feeling strong today, Harold? You must have been a lady's man in your younger days." After a thorough exploration of his strength of purpose, she extricated her hand from his spiny fingers. "There, there Harold. I know what you want."

His manner turned aggressive. "Bitch, bitch, bitch," he muttered. "My lolly, bitch, bitch." A hand streaked out, catching Poppy by surprise and pulling it back to his hard on. A groan escaped as a red tongue darted in and out of his cracked lips. She laughed.

"Hold your horses. You want your lolly?" she teased, studying a pinched anger warping his features with lust. Rubbing her palm up and down the blanket, she cooed, "That's right, your lolly. You want your lolly." Unexpectedly, she jumped up and pulled away. "Calm down, Mr Gray," she said cruelly. Giving the enlarged member a friendly pat, she left to go to the kitchen.

Cupboard doors opened and closed with loud bangs. "Where do you keep them, Mr Gray?" she sing sang, taunting. In the background, Harold kept up a mumbling chant about bitch lollies. "Found them," she shouted, pocketing a handful of treats.

Poppy opened the kitchen door leading to a backyard courtyard. Peering outside, she whistled. "Doggie, here doggie." A mud splattered Shitzu with a matted coat peaked out from under a camellia bush. Crouching down, Poppy offered a cupped palm filled with dog treats. "Good girl. You want some? Yes. Here you are."

The little dog slunk to within ten feet of Poppy, stopped and gave a timid bark. "It's okay. Good girl." Poppy kept a continuous stream of soothing phrases.

Hungry, neglected, starved for affection as much as for food, the Shitzu succumbed to temptation. With a wagging tail, it ate out of her hand. The rasping pink tongue tickled. Poppy stroked its head and then grasped its collar. She hauled it by the scruff of its neck. It yelped and wiggled trying to get free. "Gotcha," she laughed, carrying it into the unit.

Walking toward the lounge room, she called out. "Harold, I have your Lolly."

He'd thrown off the blanket and opened his robe, exposing his flaccid member. "Ready to go, Harold?" Poppy asked with a smirk. "Don't jump the gun, when I've gone to all this trouble for you." Reaching into a pocket, a tube of KY jelly appeared. One handedly Poppy squeezed a glob onto his penis and massaged it with efficient strokes until it sprung to attention. Harold's claws latched on but she pulled away. He hit out, getting agitated. "Wait you old bugger," she chuckled.

The dog tucked under her arm squirmed and yelping pitifully. "Shh, my smelly little shag rug," she said.

Poppy shoved Lolly onto his lap. Harold fastened on to the bitch and positioned its body to accommodate his inclinations. "Bitch. Bitch. Lolly bitch," he muttered, tightening his hold on the matted pelt. The wheelchair began to rock back and forth while he pumped. Quickly, Poppy clicked on the brake. Fascinated, she stood and watched.

She looked at her watch. It was taking too long. She would soon be missed back at the office. "Let me help."

Standing at the back of the wheelchair, she began to massage his shoulders with strong, efficient strokes. "There we are. Nice and calm now," Poppy cooed. Her hands moved up Harold's wrinkled neck to his boney head, rubbing its spikes of white hair with firm professionalism.

Bored, her hands found their way down to his neck again and experimentally wrapped around in a gentle caress. Pushing into the back of his chair, she tightened her grasp. "There, there. How's that?" she hushed.

Harold began to struggle for breath, thrashing back and forth in the chair. Poppy became excited. "Filthy pervert," she whispered hot breaths into his ear. Lolly yelped and leapt off his seat, gave a good shake and ran out of the room.

Poppy felt the tension in Harold build to the point of release. She squeezed his neck harder, feeling hot and moist between her legs. She momentarily lost control, pressing into the back of the wheelchair in need of a hard handle, but never losing her grip on Harold's throat. She came with a stifled cry of delicious surprise, followed soon by Mr Gray.

And then it was over. His body slumped over, limp. "There we are, Harold. All better now," she sounded clinical as if completing an everyday nursing procedure on a patient. She straightened her uniform and finger combed her hair. Harold did not move or make a sound.

Going around to the front, Poppy poked his shoulder. His clammy face was grey. She pushed him upright and checked a blue vein on his neck for a pulse. "God, I'm not giving the bastard mouth to mouth," she muttered. A faint, weak pulse was detected much to Poppy's relief. The man was exhausted from ecstasy, not expired.

On the other hand, Poppy felt quite energised from a job well completed. It had done her good to get out of the office and into the field again, working with patients in a hands-on way. She observed Mr Gray to ensure he was breathing. Later on, he'd be grateful for her liberality.

Slapping Harold's face, she attempted to bring him back to consciousness. "Can I get you a glass of water, Harold?" she yelled in his face. He remained unresponsive.

Maybe Gil was right. These spontaneous neck massages were going to get her in trouble one day. Harold was too senile to say anything. And who would believe a pervert who fucks his Shitzu? She was safe.

A few more nursing duties were required. Mr Gray needed his shot of insulin and Poppy had to write up his medical notes. She tucked in his gummy penis, adjusted sticky pyjama bottoms, re-tied his robe, and threw the blanket across his knees. Before leaving, she remembered to coax Lolly outside with a dish of dog food.

Gently placing the TV remote in Harold's gnarled fingers, she whispered like a kind mother, "All done. I'll be back next week to give you more lolly, you filthy beast."

Satisfied all was in order, she saw herself out the front door.

Chapter Forty Three

"How did it go with the Compo Hotline?" Honor asked, setting a brisk pace around the Town Common alongside Joy. Other walkers in the group marched on with determination to complete the circuit and continue on with several more laps. "Kodi was so excited to be able to help. We've all been so worried about you."

The *in her face* concern made Joy feel inadequate as usual.

Honor's Kathmandu hiking boots crunched gravel on a wide path. It meandered alongside a wetlands brook lined with willow trees, bulrushes and poa grass. The morning was perfect for the five-kilometre circuit: clear skies, a gentle breeze. If they got lucky like last week, a platypus might poke its head up in a burst of bubbles and playfully duck in and out on the surface of the brook.

Two weeks ago after the shemozzle with the new locum, her well-meaning sister had decided Joy needed encouragement to exercise. True, she'd been a couch potato for months despite Dr Vitkay's pre-Easter prescription for housebound anxiety and depression. She'd meant to join a group or start exercising but couldn't muster the energy. It was now the end of winter, she'd put on weight and had no level of fitness to speak of.

Her sister was convinced a brisk morning walk was all her sister required to lift the fog of depression. She was a member of Lower Teasel's walking club, *The Johnnie Walkers*. She bragged that for the last five years due to a healthy constitution, she never suffered from any malady.

Except perhaps an overabundance of self-possessed meddling, Joy grumbled under her breath.

Now twice a week at eleven, she came knocking with a bright, determined smile and a bottle of Isle light sparkling mineral water, insisting on these forced marches. Joy had doubts but gave in to demonstrate she was at least trying. Even if that meant splashing cold water on her face and slapping on a trench coat over pyjamas before leaving the house in Ugg boots.

Fifteen minutes in, she was huffing and puffing. Like a cliched blonde joke, it was too much to walk and talk at the same time. Honor on the other hand easily kept a continuous stream of conversation going without seeming to take in a breath.

"I wasn't sure if Kodi's suggestion would help or complicate things for you," Honor said, sounding apologetic. "She can't help it; she has this driving need to make things right."

Who does that sound like? Joy suppressed a reflex to respond with sarcasm. Honor was trying her best to be supportive.

She stopped and doubled over trying to catch her breath. "It's all very confusing. Each person involved has a different point of view on who does what. Jim from the hotline said Dr Vitkay is the only one supposed to write up my return to work plan. But so far, he's had nothing to do with it and Michelle keeps printing off the pro forma and filling in the blanks. Jim said it was a pointless exercise anyway because as long as I'm totally incapacitated for work I can't return. I don't know what to believe."

Honor stopped ten paces ahead and turned around, realising Joy was taking a breather. "I can't believe a state government department would deviate from the guidelines. I mean, they wrote them after all."

"I know. That's what I mean. *I'm* expected to comply and if I make even a tiny mistake there's the threat my compensation will be stopped. And a new GP who's never seen me before and doesn't know my history can force me back to work before I'm ready and I'm not allowed a second opinion because that's considered *shopping around*. Yet, my employer seems to be able to write their own rules and flout the system and no one oversees them to ensure their obligations are met under the Act. It's totally one-sided."

"I'm not sure it's as bad as all that," Honor replied, sounding dubious. She resumed walking with smaller strides.

"That's how it seems to me." Joy scuffed along, slouched and defeated. "Kodi was telling me according to Lachlan's dad, the department shouldn't even be thinking about packaging me out for at least another eighteen months. But both Bev and Michelle have hinted that's what they want to do."

"You haven't actually received a formal offer, so I wouldn't believe Bev or Michelle right now." Honor tried to sound reassuring. "Would it be so bad to retire?"

Joy didn't know where to begin to answer that question. Honor hadn't been in paid employment since her kids were born – although Joy begrudgingly admitted volunteering counted as *work*. Her sister was a member of numerous social clubs and created mosaics as a vocation not a mere hobby. But being out of the paid workforce for her sister was an altogether different choice from the bleak PTSD, poverty-stricken prospect Joy was looking at.

"It's probably just a threat to panic me. I don't know who to trust anymore. The truth is no one on my workers compensation team is there for me. Their loyalties lie with the department." Joy took a sip from a water bottle and shoved on the cap.

"I guess that's to be expected. The health department employs them," Honor murmured, as usual not entertaining her sour mood. Joy felt chastened at her sister's implication. Of course, it was naïve expecting professional ethics would triumph over political expediency. What did she expect? Honor was the practical one in the family. Joy was the idealist.

Several Johnnie Walkers overtook them, waving as they passed. Honor picked up the pace. After a few minutes they were back in a compatible rhythm. "Speaking of Kodi, she and Lachlan have split up." Honor resumed their conversation on less controversial grounds.

"Oh, what happened?" Joy puffed and panted.

"His contract with Community Health was terminated so he's been forced to move to Plover Point with a new job."

"Kodi must be upset." Joy was cautious in offering sympathy. In Honor's eyes, Lachlan was not the ideal partner she pictured for her daughter's happy ever after.

"It might only be a temporary split. As Col says, it's not that far from Plover Point to Lower Teasel."

"True." Joy didn't want to engage in a long and pointless discussion of what may or may not happen. Her own miseries took up most emotional reserves.

"Kodi can do better," Honor contended as if debating the issue and reaching a conclusion all at the same time. Joy kept quiet and continued walking.

After a few minutes, Honor chuckled. "You'll like this. Auntie Sheryl was telling me a cousin of the Mayor had a wedding at the bowls club recently. The tables were done up with white dinner sets, clearly recognisable as government issued crockery." Honor crooked her eyebrows suggestively. "The club secretary denied it, of course."

"No way! I knew dishes were disappearing on a regular basis, but I couldn't prove it."

"Another community service provided generously by our state taxes, courtesy of the Quamby Bluff Community Health Centre," Honor mocked.

Joy smirked. It was just another petty crime going unreported and unchallenged, a symptom of the corruption of small-town officials with the power to get away with bending rules to win favour within the community.

Joy had been so naïve thinking the centre's money issues could be sorted by implementing good administrative practices. The problems went a lot deeper than that. No wonder Jane never took notice of all her good work.

Being proved right at this point felt more akin to failure than victory.

They completed the rest of the circuit in a companionable silence. The Johnnie Walkers had completed their circuits and moved on to the Village Spice Café for rewarding lattes and cinnamon muffins. The common was left deserted much to Joy's relief. This time of day, there were no other dog walkers or tourists hiking the track wanting to stop and chat. Talking to strangers usually set off her anxiety, and she tried to avoid these situations as much as possible.

They returned to her cottage. "Come in for a cuppa," Joy offered. At the top of the driveway, a weather worn post box bulged and overflowed with junk mail. It had been a few days since the mail had been collected. Joy pulled out a bunch of letters puckered and stained from dew. Brushing off cobwebs, she joked, "It's probably only bills."

Once inside, Joy tossed the mail on the kitchen table. She went to hang up her coat in the hallway and exchange it for an oversized cardigan.

"I'll put the kettle on," Honor offered, heading to the kitchen purposefully.

Joy returned to sit at the table and began to sort through envelopes. "There's one from the Minister," she shouted in the direction of the kitchen, over the humming of a kettle. "It will be his response to our letter." With fumbling fingers, she tore it open.

Honor appeared at her side, stretching to read over her shoulder.

The letter was short and to the point. After reading it, Joy and Honor didn't say a word for a long drawn out moment.

"I'll get our tea," Honor said eventually.

When she returned with a tea tray laden with a mound of lemon creme comfort cookies, Joy had re-read the letter several times. "It doesn't make sense," she muttered.

"Okay, let's analyse it." Honor attempted to inject rationality into the situation, not giving Joy a chance to over react. "It says he'll get back to you after receiving Bev's advice. He's not dismissing us altogether."

Joy glared with contempt at the letter. "Yes, he is. It's a typical letter from a politician *when you never intend to give a response.* Bev is not my treating psychologist anymore. She is therefore not ethically able to provide advice on my medical condition. They are basically waiting on advice that will never come."

Honor looked stricken, fully comprehending the cunning strategy deployed in the letter. Aiming for a positive view she said, "Maybe the Minister's office didn't know that."

"Of course, they did. Whoever wrote this letter must have known. If they mention Bev by name, then they had to know Bev's contract for the Employee Assistance Counselling program was not renewed this financial year." Joy clenched her teeth as she studied the letter with mounting anger. "And anyway, what has my current *medical condition* got to do with providing answers to me?"

Honor stared at the letter as if it would magically transform into Cinderella's golden slipper rather than the ashes of betrayal. In a hushed voice, she read slowly, "*In relation to the incident at Quamby Bluff Community Health Centre... given your current medical condition, I believe it prudent to consult with your treating psychologist... to seek guidance on how best to respond to your correspondence... I'll get back to you...* He makes it sound like you are too fragile to hear the truth right now."

"You mean too *mentally unstable*," Joy snorted. "I've been pathologised."

Honor stumbled to a seat next to Joy and pulled across a plate of cookies. She offered them to Joy and then without waiting for a response, grabbed one off the plate and took a large bite.

"A perfect circular argument," Joy said. "They cause my mental health issues and then turn it around to imply I'm too unstable to hear answers to my questions about why it happened! Nice one!" She reached over and placed a crisp lemon cookie on the tea saucer and shook her head in wonder, gulping English Breakfast tea, its warm sweetness soothing a throat dry as toast.

Delicately, Honor poked at the letter with a manicured fingernail. "He says he'll respond to our letter after receiving Bev's advice. But that's never going to happen, is it?" She looked crestfallen, as if trying to grapple with an incomprehensible realisation that the rules of fair play in her faithfully just world didn't hold true this time.

Things like this didn't happen to Honor.

Joy worried this disruption to her sister's safe, predictable view of life would reflect badly on her. Trouble magnet that she was. "Nothing seems to go in my favour at the moment," she smiled wryly.

Honor surprised her. "I'm so sorry, Joy."

She loved her sister more than ever in this moment. "Now you know what I'm up against. I'm not paranoid."

"I never said you were!" Honor sounded hurt. "You need a professional on your side, if you are ever going to recover from this trauma." Honor began to take the matter in hand once again, as if she believed Joy incapable. "I'm going to ask around and find a good, decent psychologist you can see on a private basis. I'll text you a name and number as soon as possible."

Joy was lost for a response, unable to decide between gratitude for her younger sister's solicitude and chagrin at her domineering bossiness. In the end, she gave in. It didn't hurt to be mothered once in a while.

Chapter Forty Four

With a lazy start to the weekend, Gil stood in the kitchen sipping instant black Moccona from an oversize handmade pottery mug. It was heavy and rough around the edges, and he had to be careful not to catch his lip on a particular spot that drew blood. Poppy had presented it last year as a surprise birthday present.

She rarely got him gifts. This rustic mug had been made by one of the seniors in art classes at the centre and held particular memories, she'd explained, insisting he must delegate his tacky Kmart mug to the bin. Dutifully, *old faithful*, practical if a bit chipped, was thrown out to please madam. Gil smiled fondly at the memory of his favourite, mustard coloured ceramic mug and its slogan *Fishermen come with longer poles*. That tacky mug had served him well for ten years.

He waited for the toast to pop up, watching Poppy through the window. His dedicated wife played out the back with the new foster kid. The eleven-year-old, Sherriff, ("Riff" was the name he went by) arrived yesterday, another emergency placement. He was the first older child Poppy had been allocated which made it a different sort of challenge. What would they do with him?

Gil couldn't understand why she kept saying yes to placements when still acting as manager at the centre. That job was enough stress in her life without adding to the pressure by volunteering. To top it off, being the flu season, Poppy had complained about staff shortages. She'd been forced to undertake a home visit of an elderly man with dementia who required a community nursing assessment. It was likely she'd have to continue seeing this patient on a weekly basis for some time, until the flu season passed. Another extra duty on top of her growing To Do list.

Secretly, Gill suspected Poppy enjoyed an excuse to return to hands-on nursing as a respite from the drudgery of management. However, to show his sympathy for his overworked and overly caring wife, Gil had put sausages on the grill for Friday's dinner and offered to take the kid fishing today. Last night, he'd shown Riff how to tie knots for lures and sinkers. Not being good at teaching, Riff became frustrated and obstreperous. Gil eventually gave up.

This morning Poppy had decided to teach him how to tie knots using a longer, thicker rope, *to make it easier for Riff to get the hang of it.*

Gil observed her demonstrating a magic rope trick, laying the ends of a one metre piece of cord on the picnic table, crossing her arms over each other and picking up one end in each hand. Then by uncrossing her arms and moving her hands apart, she let the cord slip over the wrists in such a way it created a loose overhand knot. A simple but effective trick to tie a knot without letting go of either end.

Riff looked engaged for the first time since he'd arrived. Taking up the challenge, he began to practise tying the impossible knot.

After a few successful tries, he looked bored.

Undaunted, Poppy pulled a toddler's rocking chair in the shape of a horse across the patio. It was left over from a previous foster child,

Conan. Memories of the little demon made Gil smile. He wondered what happened to the kid and if his mother ever got clean from ice.

From under the picnic table, Poppy produced a much longer rope. With quick hand work, she hitched the rope to the rocking chair's horizontal handrail, stood back a few feet and gave the rope a tug. Like magic the knot released. *Clever girl.*

The sound of a toaster expelling two pieces of dark toast distracted Gil. He caught a piece as it careened in the air. The other landed on the counter. He smeared butter and vegemite on each slice, cut them in halves, tossed them on a plate, stuffed one in his mouth, and then returned his attention to the drama outside.

Gil watched Poppy demonstrating the highwayman's hitch again. It was the one used in all those iconic Western movies. The cowboy rides down the dusty main street of a Wild West town, hitches his horse to a rail and struts into the saloon, gets into a brawl, and with guns blazing jumps back on his horse. Needing a fast getaway, he gives the hitched rope a tug. Impressively, it comes free. He kicks his spurs into the horse's flanks and rides off into the horizon.

Riff practised the hitch with intense concentration. After getting it right a couple times, he once again looked to Poppy for further entertainment. Smiling, she fashioned a lasso, tossed it expertly over the rocking horse's head, and tugged it tight. She then untied it and handed it over to Riff to practice. This was a more skilled endeavour. After giving the horse head a push to start it rocking back and forth, she sat down to watch Riff's clumsy throws.

Gil decided to join the fun by first bringing refreshments. Turning on the kettle, he searched the cupboard for a tea tray and decided a bread board would work just as well. A cup of artificially sweetened coffee for Poppy and a cola for Riff, with a couple granola bars, and he was set to go. As a second thought, he made another mug of coffee and threw on an extra granola bar to have outside with them.

Gingerly making his way down the back doorsteps to the patio, Gil saw the duo had moved on to a new Wild West game. This one involved their wrists tied into handcuffs with ropes that interlocked with each other. The trick was to separate themselves without cutting or untying the ropes, or removing the handcuffs.

Riff began twisting, tugging and grunting while Poppy laughed at his antics. It looked to be impossible. It soon became apparent he was becoming bothered, ensnared in a closely intimate way to Poppy's curvaceous body, accidentally bumping against her ample bosoms. The young kid blushed with embarrassment. Unable to get free.

There was a trick to getting untangled involving cooperation from both parties working together.

Gil knew she was drawing out the game. She would stay in control while he squirmed and became more and more panicked at being trapped. This was her way of teasing.

Gil was often the subject of this kind of outrageous humour from her. She could easily offer Riff the solution at any time but was enjoying his increasing helplessness.

With care, Gil placed the bread board tray onto the picnic table. Taking in the situation as an outside observer, Gil became uncomfortable with Poppy tormenting the kid. This was wrong of her, even if she thought she was being funny.

"Hey, you guys. How about stopping for a break? I've brought drinks and a snack for us."

A red-faced Riff stopped struggling. Poppy flashed Gil an annoyed look as if he'd interrupted a moment with the kid. With aplomb she tightened the ropes and pulled him into her chest like a lassoed steer. "Give up, cowboy?" she demanded in his face, close enough for a kiss – still in a play acting role.

"Get these off me," Riff swore.

To Gil, it sounded more like *get off me, bitch*. But that was an unexpected thought bubble that had popped up from his imagination. Poppy was cooperating by expertly disentangling the twisted ropes, not bothering to explain how the trick was done. She'd save that for another day.

In a few minutes, they were sitting at the picnic table as one happy family. Riff ripped into the granola bar with frenzied hunger.

Poppy pushed her bar across to Riff. "You earned it, sweet cakes," she said. The compliment was returned with a grunt.

Gil observed the dynamic between the two of them with affection. Typical Poppy. She was so generous and was lots of fun. Riff would soon be groomed into a pleasing young lad given Poppy's dedication and attention.

Chapter Forty Five

J oy ended the call with a sharp jab to the mobile. She'd left three messages on the psychologist's voice mail within the past ten days and waited for a return call. It had finally come through. But not with the answer needed.

She sat at the kitchen table gazing out rain splattered French windows to a spring garden bursting with lush shoots so green they gleamed neon. Her mood did not reflect verdant hope. Why couldn't just one thing go right for a change?

She hated to disappoint her sister. Honor had been excited to pass on Dr Fellowes' contact details. She'd spent such a lot of time asking around a vast network of contacts for the most highly recommended therapist on Eden Isle. His name got the most likes.

Honor had explained to Joy that he specialised in a method of cognitive behaviour therapy involving mindfulness meditation. It formed part of an exclusive, patented three-month program that promised effectiveness with Post Traumatic Stress Disorder. Not really understanding the theory, nonetheless her sister had been convinced the emphasis on Buddhism would resonate with Joy and his expertise would facilitate a speedy recovery. Honor had enthused *she'd have her normal sister back again*.

This may have been true. Joy was yet to be converted. However, Dr Fellowes was fully booked well into next year and therefore would not take on any new clients. Not even ones with top of the line health insurance or desperate ones such as Joy. For someone who specialised in Buddhist compassion and clear thinking, his *no* sounded rather abrupt and dispassionate.

He'd used the excuse he preferred to work with clients that had an early diagnosis. It had been nine months for Joy. The longer the PTSD, the more entrenched the symptoms and the harder to shift. He was currently trialling his program on police officers with PTSD with the aim of publishing research findings in a renowned psychiatric journal.

Joy gathered that Dr Fellowes reputation relied on success and he wasn't willing to put a case to the test if there was a risk of failure.

It probably had not been wise to complain about current treatments not helping in the least.

Was it possible she'd ruined her chances by giving away too many details upfront? The gamble to intrigue Dr Fellowes with a bizarre case of a joking strangulation proved inadequate to win his support. Mentioning workers compensation and that her employer was the Department of Community Health was probably not the smartest move either. No one working within the health system wanted to be seen challenging the department.

Putting a busy caseload aside, it was no wonder Fellowes was reluctant to take on her case.

Honor was soon to arrive for another walk around the common. How was Joy going to break the bad news to Honor? She'd set her mind on this course of therapy like a true believer.

Once again, here was proof that nothing went right for Joy.

She was left with no alternative but to see Marcus Harmond, the counsellor from the department – so generously referred by Dr Sasha. This was bound to be an exhilarating experience.

Honor arrived on time with an impossibly positive attitude and a brown paper package. A designer jogging outfit in black latex with criss cross cutouts in strategic places moulded to her slim build. She wore the latest Nike runners with white hair in a bouncy ponytail, oozing energy and giving a much younger impression than fifty years.

Impressed but a tad jealous, Joy stretched a worn hoodie down grey track pants feeling every year of her ageing bones and achy muscles.

The light drizzle outdoors hadn't dampened her youngest sister's motivation to exercise. Apparently, come rain or shine the Johnnie Walkers marched on.

Excitedly, Honor insisted Joy open the package before they headed out to the common. It was a book entitled *Reclaiming Sanity Through Mindfulness* written by none other than Dr Charles Fellowes. Seeing her sister's satisfied expression, Joy concentrated on reading the back cover while working on how to respond appropriately.

"By pure chance, I came across it while shopping in Plover Point yesterday. It talks about the philosophy behind his program. It will be perfect to read before you start counselling sessions with him," Honor enthused.

Joy placed the book on a shabby chic side table in the hallway. "Thanks, this is incredibly thoughtful of you. I'll look forward to reading it."

Honor's smile lit up the room. "I just want you to feel good and return to being even better than your old self," she said.

Joy huffed. "Even better than my old self? Now I know what you really feel about me."

"Oh, I didn't mean... you know what I mean," Honor spluttered, appalled at the gaff.

"There's just one thing..." Joy started to say, but then couldn't face disappointing Honor.

"You couldn't get an early appointment, could you?" Uncannily, Honor had read her mind. "I wondered about that. Anyone who's good is booked up to god knows when. I'm sorry about that. Dr Fellowes was the only therapist on Eden Isle I could find who worked with PTSD clients and came recommended."

"I have the new guy at the doctors' surgery to fall back on. You never know, he might turn out to be okay." Joy gave a rueful smile.

"No harm in giving him a go," Honor agreed. "For now, the best therapy for you is a good long walk and some fresh Spring air." With no further discussion and a bossy command, she pulled her sister out the door.

Chapter Forty Six

The atmosphere of a counselling room at the doctors' surgery was sterile, and not only due to a smell of disinfectant permeating the walls. It was all polished floor tiles and laminate cabinets, crowded counter tops with medical charts and cotton balls in glass jars, chrome chairs with vinyl seats – and chilly as if this was the first time it had been used all day.

Obediently, Joy sat to attention next to Marcus Harmond, the new counsellor appointed by the department to "fix" her. He fiddled and poked at a government issued laptop, logging on and trying to open a document, slow and relaxed. No hurry to start the session, typical of a true public servant. "I'll read the referral before we start," he mumbled to the screen. Pleasant enough.

First impressions of the middle-aged, rather homely man seated at the desk were under-whelming. His thinning grey hair, tweed tie, a brown cardigan and matching old man suit trousers did not inspire immediate confidence. Not that she cared. Her expectations were low to begin with.

"Right. Let's get started." He swivelled in the chair to face her. His washed-out blue eyes conveyed a world weariness. This was a man plodding along in a government job until retirement. Joy knew the type.

"Pleased to meet you, Joy. I'm Marcus. Dr Sasha has recommended I see you for eight counselling sessions in regard to a diagnosis of Post Traumatic Stress Disorder."

The mention of Dr Sasha brought back all kinds of unpleasant emotions in Joy's gut. Suddenly, she was not in the mood to be pleasant and compliant. "Before we start, I want to make something clear. These sessions will not work if your goal is to return me to work." She glared, assessing his reaction. Getting an insipid smirk, she battled on. "What I need is support in deciding if I should accept a package and retire from the workforce. Or, stay on workers comp and try not to let it drive me insane."

Unmoved, Marcus nodded as if expecting attitude. *What had Dr Sasha written in the referral?*

"Do you trust me, Joy?" he asked. "Our sessions will only work with complete faith in each other and the process."

Caught off guard, she wasn't sure how to respond. Honestly, she didn't trust anyone who was involved in the workers compensation case. She glared, lost for words.

Marcus smiled indulgently. "Let me reassure you, Joy. I will not send you back to work unless you specifically wish to return. I know what it's like having PTSD. I used to work as a paramedic but had to leave the work I loved after a particularly distressing call-out caused me to become traumatised."

He went on to describe how the trauma impacted on his life. At the time, it was considered unmanly to admit to his colleagues that he was not coping. "The mythos among paramedics was that we were supposed to be bulletproof," he said. Consequently, he suffered in silence for too long, causing his marriage to break up and eventually he had to completely change employment direction. He still missed saving lives and being a hero.

Hearing his story and its similarities to her own experience relaxed Joy into a false sense of security. Perhaps Marcus did understand what she'd been through.

"I've gone over all the CBT stuff with my last counsellor. I'm never going to change my mind about what happened. I don't care what anyone tries to do to convince me otherwise." She looked hopefully at Marcus seeking understanding.

"Why don't you tell me what you think happened. I'd like to hear your story," he said.

Despite hating to repeat and relive the experience once more, some compulsion drove her to pour over every minute detail even when it caused increasing anxiety. She set about describing the original incident, the series of betrayals from her employer, the legal system and the medical system, up to the present moment where she did not trust him because he was employed by the Department of Community Health and complicit in the workers compensation system. Finally, she ran out of breath, light headed and shaky.

"That's the intellectual side. How has all this made you feel?" Marcus asked.

His question stumped Joy. It was the first time a counsellor had drawn a distinction between her intellectual narrative and the emotional hurt underlying it. She wanted to cry, whether in relief at being seen or in shame at being exposed she wasn't sure.

"It's like I've lost my armour. I'm left without protection or filters. When out in public my senses are so open to the bombardment of noise, crowds, busyness – all this demanding cacophony of stimuli – it's exhausting.

"Everything has changed. Leaving my house to go out in the world seems scary. What used to feel familiar, comfortable, even safe, is now dangerous.

It's like I'm naked. I feel so open and exposed. My glasses are not rose coloured anymore."

Marcus cut in. "When you refer to losing your armour, feeling naked," he paused and licked his lips, "are you saying you feel you need to defend yourself but lack defences? As if you are under attack – even now?"

Joy suppressed a cringe. "No, I mean the rules have been upended. What's right? What's a crime? I don't believe in the system." She paused to consider.

"I liken it to a poster of random black dots I used when training project managers. I'd hold up the poster and ask the class to stare at it until they saw a picture in it. Predictably, at some point the blotches would morph into a cowboy riding a horse. Once you saw the cowboy it was very hard to unsee it.

"We have a need to see a pattern in the blotches of life to make sense of our random world," she explained with sincerity.

"With cowboys coming to the rescue?" Marcus laughed.

The interruption offended Joy. Not allowing her to finish meant he'd missed the point. Not to be put off, she continued. "It was a project manager's insider joke. A metaphor – we superimpose a template over life to give us a sense of safety and surety. Projects were like this chaos of black dots. If we overlaid them with a template of a project plan, then we felt a sense of stability and confidence that everything was under control. This template is like wearing a suit of armour. The reality was that projects were chaotic, no matter how much we're under an illusion that all the bits and pieces fit into a coherent picture."

"Surely it's possible to manage the so-called chaos and be in control," Marcus said, once again cutting into her train of thought, trying to control the direction of the conversation. Joy ignored the supercilious man.

"Well, with large projects there are so many other people involved this introduces elements of unpredictability, no matter how good a project manager you are. They had to factor this into the critical path timelines," Joy said impatiently.

"But what I'm trying to say is with PTSD, it's like the picture has shattered into black dots again and no matter how much I try to get the cowboy back, it eludes me. I know the cowboy is one fat illusion. The chaos of black dots is reality."

"You don't believe in cowboys anymore," Marcus summarised looking peeved. He'd said earlier he liked saving people.

Suppressing a sigh, Joy persisted with explaining the obvious. "Since my PTSD diagnosis, all these people have been trying really hard to make me see the picture again, because for them it exists. The illusion is comforting, but I don't believe them. I don't believe it. I know it never existed and will never exist again for me. The world is unpredictable, unsafe, and not under my control. I've lost my bearings, drowning in a sea of scattered pieces of a puzzle without the box's cover picture. My PTS *disorder* is that I am literally *disordered*." Her face screwed up at the irony. "I don't like this person I've become," she added as a conclusion.

Marcus leaned forward with concern. "I like you, Joy. What I see is a person who is intelligent, attractive, gentle and nice."

His effusiveness caught Joy by surprise. It was too soon in their clinical relationship for his opinion to be taken as an impersonal observation. Appalled that he was flirting rather than conducting this session in a professional objective manner, Joy was thrown off track.

Pretending to be unruffled, she turned the flirting around. "I don't want to be nice anymore. *Nice* got me strangled. Poppy knew I wouldn't punch her in the face in self-defence. I was too nice and that made it safe for her to use me as a personal stress ball." Joy shook her head. "I didn't even swear at her. Can you believe it? She was my boss, so I didn't swear even when I wanted to, I stopped myself."

"When faced with danger the normal responses are flight or fight. You were trapped in your chair unable to escape and suppressed your instinct to fight. In effect, your survival instinct was to freeze. This manifested in PTSD – a frozen emotion, lodged in your mind as a blockage. We need to remove that blockage."

Joy laughed humorlessly. "You mean I should start swearing at you, let it all out?" Tetchiness was deliberate, to prove she wasn't girlfriend material in case he had ideas.

"There are other techniques that are just as effective and less melodramatic," he said, countering her antagonism with professional aplomb. "It is possible for you to be your old self again."

Joy did not want to hear this yet again from yet another person in the health system. They were weasel words to get her back to work. "I'm beginning to realise I'll never return to 100% of how I used to be. I need your help accepting this, rather than being told it's possible to be normal again, if only I change my view of what happened or think positively, or magically learn how to be more resilient. All this counselling crap has added to my trauma and only helped to drive me more and more crazy."

Marcus nodded in sympathy. "I understand how disappointing it must be for you when your trauma feels more entrenched in your system rather than improving after all this time. I can see how your faith in various counselling therapies would be shaken."

For a moment, Joy felt understood and accepted.

The congenial moment didn't last.

"Actually, it is possible for you to erase the whole PTSD experience from your brain as if it never happened. I'm qualified in a technique called

EMDR – Eye Movement Desensitisation & Reprocessing. It has an 80% success rate treating PTSD. It helped me to recover so I can vouch for it."

Joy wondered why this therapy had never been mentioned up to now by any other practitioner. "What does it involve?"

"I put you in a relaxed state, ask you to recall memories of the incident, and move my finger back and forth across your field of vision replicating REM sleep. This taps into your unconscious brain and unblocks the emotional energy of the trauma, reprogramming its hold on you." Marcus's sincerity held the persuasiveness of a true devotee.

Joy was suspicious. "It sounds like hypnosis? Isn't that a pseudoscience?"

Marcus smiled encouragement. "It's a fairly new psychotherapeutic practice similar to hypnosis. It desensitises the triggers causing emotional distress to help a patient gain perspective about the traumatising incident. Basically, I can remove your PTSD symptoms in a matter of five to eight sessions. It will be as if the trauma never happened."

Success promised in such a short time when nothing else had worked for her was too good to be true. She wasn't sure if she felt angry at the previous interventions that promised so much and failed, or astonished at the audacity of Marcus sounding like some quack that could simply wave his hands in front of her face and magically exorcise her demons and make her normal again. She didn't believe any of it, much less trust a counsellor she'd just met.

Joy gleaned phrases such as reprogramming, erasing memories, and *new* therapy. More messing with her brain and the mind. She naturally resisted more of the same.

She'd learned from internet research about how trauma physically altered a person's brain. PTSD wasn't just a mental condition – it was a physical change in the part of the brain called the amygdala.

Added to this, the drugs her GP prescribed worked by affecting brain chemistry – which was why Gemma convinced her to stop taking them, concerned they'd permanently change her brain and create a dependency.

She'd been through nine months of CBT where Bev encouraged *re-writing the negative scripts* about the trauma of strangulation. Stubbornly, Joy would never accept it was a joke despite all the pressure applied for her to change her mind. Joy fought against CBT and what she saw as brainwashing.

Now another counsellor wanted to mess some more, this time with her unconscious brain. Make her forget the incident altogether. This was the last thing she needed.

She wasn't even sure at this point if she wanted the demons gone. More recently, she wanted help in accepting this new Joy. Let go and move on – a new, blank Self requiring re-creation. This was the support she'd come expecting and in fact had explained to Marcus at the start. He hadn't listened. No one in the workers compensation process listened to what she actually needed in order to heal.

Philosophically, rather than be *fixed*, Joy wanted to learn how to *flow* and *transform*.

His eagerness to practise EMDR possessed the same zealotry she detested in religious evangelists. She concluded Marcus was anxious to get in more practice of this black art to keep up his professional registration, but the population of Lower Teasel was too small. She'd become a patsy to experiment on. This realisation caused her to be sceptical and cautious.

"As I've told my previous psychologist, I don't want to forget what happened and I don't want to lose my hypervigilance. The world is not safe, and a heightened survival instinct is the best thing to come out of all this." She said, daring him to contradict.

"But it's your fear of being strangled that is keeping you from going back to work and living a normal life." He sounded sanctimonious. "Realistically, what are the chances of that ever happening again, Joy?" Suspecting Joy wasn't keen on EMDR, his explanation sounded more like pleading. The anticlimax was evident in his tone of voice.

Joy's temper flared. She didn't like this man. "What was the probability of it occurring *in the first place*?" she retorted, pausing long enough for Marcus to ponder the question before answering. "One hundred percent. It happened so that makes it one hundred percent probability." She sat back in the chair, jaws clenched.

Before he could argue, she persisted. "As I explained, I taught project planning. In a risk analysis, it's not only the probability of an event happening that is part of the equation. You also have to factor into the formula the consequence or impact if it happens. An event rated as an unlikely or rare probability can nonetheless occur – and the consequences of this can be catastrophic. Probability is an analytical and impersonal concept, a figment of someone's thought processes. Whereas the consequences of those imagined events should they occur are real and very personal," she lectured. "A smart project manager doesn't hope it won't ever happen. She puts in measures to prevent or mitigate against that possibility." Joy waited for this to sink into the man's dense skull.

"Even if you believe it unlikely that Poppy would strangle me ever again, I believe if this did happen the impact would be something I'd never recover from. It would be a catastrophic consequence to my mental health. What could possibly make me override my survival instincts and return under those circumstances? Who in their right mind would want to erase that memory as if it never happened, and open myself to such a risk?"

Marcus appeared sullen, clearly frustrated at her stubbornness and not impressed with this demonstration of her intelligence. *What a surprise her attractiveness rating was declining.* Joy didn't flinch. It was important he understood her position from the beginning.

"What I need from counselling is for you to help me understand Poppy. All this time, no one has been able to tell me why she did it. Without that, nothing makes sense."

Marcus shook his head. "The problem with trauma is that it may never make sense," he said as if passing on words of wisdom rather than being acrimonious. "The harder you struggle with this impasse, the longer it will take to recover. That's why I encourage you to consider EMDR therapy."

Joy refused to accept this. The fact he was pushing EMDR was getting annoying. "What's the point if I can't find meaning in what happened? It's not only about Poppy. I need to know why my employer accepted her version of events. The woman assaulted me. Isn't that bullying at the very least? Shouldn't she have received some disciplinary action? The policy was supposed to be zero tolerance." While she pontificated, Marcus moved his head slightly one way and then the other, forcing her to shift her gaze in order to catch his eyes.

Abruptly, Joy suspected he was surreptitiously testing EMDR on her without permission. Alarmed at this breach of ethics, she dropped her eyes.

Marcus noticed and stopped. "In the policy, bullying is defined as repeated behaviour," he corrected.

This deliberate pretentiousness prickled under her skin. Like poking an annoyed echidna, her attitude became spikey. "You are right. It happened only once, so according to the policy – and you – it wasn't technically bullying. Point of fact, strangling me was a crime. Common assault according to the police." She sat back with arms crossed. She was sick of people trivialising Poppy's behaviour.

Weren't counsellors supposed to empathise with their clients, not be contrary? She really didn't like this counsellor, and this was the first of eight sessions Dr Sasha was forcing her to attend.

Marcus noticed Joy glancing at the wall clock. Clearing his throat, he announced, "Our time is almost up, so let's stop here for today. Dr Sasha has recommended I see you fortnightly. Before our next session, I'd like you to consider EMDR therapy." He turned to the laptop and began keying in appointment times. A printout of the schedule was handed to Joy.

Her head was pounding as she made an escape out the door and down the long corridor through the surgery. Walking past reception, she gave a halfhearted wave to Gayleen. These sessions with Marcus were going to be a trial rather than helpful.

Honor's book on *Reclaiming Sanity Through Mindfulness* took on new significance. It was going to have to keep her sane over the next eight counselling sessions. Joy made the decision to begin reading it without delay.

Chapter Forty Seven

Joy loosened a silk scarf felted with bright ribbons, tassels and coloured strips of wool from around her sweaty neck and unbuttoned her salmon pink trench coat letting cool air in. She was warming up to these regular constitutionals. Without asking, Honor started a second lap around the common with a bracing stride. Other Johnnie Walkers marched a few metres ahead.

Joy grinned. She was keeping up with the group. After only a few weeks, her level of fitness had improved. Now she could talk and walk without puffing and panting.

"I started reading Dr Fellowes' book. It's going to be good for me." Joy wanted to assure her sister. "I'm going to need it to keep sane if my first session with the new counsellor is anything to go on."

"Dr Sasha lived up to her reputation of being a mean bitch?" Honor asked.

"Without a doubt. She's forcing me to see Marcus for eight sessions. The guy is pressuring me to try this experimental therapy that's like hypnosis. He says it can erase the trauma as if it never happened."

"Hypnosis is alright. One of the volunteers at the centre told us her husband tried it to stop smoking. Daisy said it took a few goes but eventually he gave up the smokes. It couldn't hurt to try. Why not give it a go?"

Joy sighed. "It's just another therapy messing with my mind, promising to cure me of my illness. This approach doesn't work. As I said to Gemma, I want them to treat PTSD as an injury rather than an illness. An injury I'll have for the rest of my life that I need to learn to live with. That's the help I need. Not promises about making it disappear with a few esoteric waves of their hands."

"No magic bullet for you. It has to be practical, logical and scientific – or nothing," Honor suggested good naturedly.

Joy scuffed a big toe on a small rock wedged in the gravelled path. She caught her balance and marched on with purpose, testing her sister's comment for its veracity. "You may be right. I researched EMDR on the internet. All the scientific papers were written by the psychologist who invented it. No surprise, every one of his studies showed remarkable results. But the blog sites were not so positive."

"Really?" Honor muttered concentrating on the scenery ahead.

"People said the treatment made their symptoms a lot worse. Like intense nightmares about the original trauma they couldn't turn off."

"Sounds horrible," Honor mumbled.

"Yeah, well. I'd rather follow Dr Fellowes advice from his book."

Honor paused and pointed toward the brook. Water cascaded over a pile of rocks strumming a trickling, fairy melody as it pooled in a pond. A glimmering brown shape of a platypus frolicked in a froth of bubbles near the bank.

They shared a moment in silent wonder. This was magic. It suddenly dived under and disappeared.

A gentle breeze wafted across the common teasing Joy's hair, carrying the fragrance of pond water and mushrooms, wet decayed leaves and a whisper of cow pats from the neighbouring dairy farm. They waited but the platypus didn't reappear.

A warm ray of sunshine broke free of a mass of grey rain clouds, shining directly onto Joy's wind chilled cheeks. She inhaled deeply and contentedly.

"Gemma calls it Eco-therapy," she sighed.

Honor stretched up to the sky, arching her back.

"Dr Fellowes believes connecting with nature is as effective as other therapies and medications for depression and anxiety," Joy explained. "He says we need to slow down and pay more attention to what is around us instead of being immersed in the chatter in our heads. Walking in the countryside, listening to music, singing, gardening are all healing activities that quiet our minds and return us to equilibrium."

Honor grinned. "See, I knew what I was doing, inviting you to come on walks with me."

"Yes, your honor," Joy joked. "He also says it's okay to rest and do nothing; it's not being lazy. That's also healing."

"I'm not sure about that. Too much time on your hands to sit around contemplating your navel makes a person a misery guts, I've always found."

Although not intended as a pointed remark, Honor's words stabbed a sensitive spot in Joy's heart. "I'd like to give his exercises a go. He says we need to sit quietly and observe our thinking because our thoughts are what reinforce the self as ego. It's our egos that keep us separate from nature and harmony."

Honor marched on, not paying as much attention as Joy wanted. With extra sincerity, she kept chattering, hoping to excite her sister's interest.

"Apparently, all my inner chatter takes a lot of energy sustaining my ego. This is why I'm tired all the time. If I can sit and witness my thoughts without identifying with them, my ego boundaries will soften and I'll feel less lonely and separate from the world. Fellowes promises this is the path to recovery."

Joy was keen to get started but felt the need for encouragement. She doubted remaining committed to any exercise without Honor pestering in the background. It had been difficult to sustain motivation for anything lately.

Honor began to walk at a leisurely stride, looking lost in thought.

Joy became slightly worried Honor wouldn't be supportive. Spouting Fellowes philosophy out loud did sound a bit like new age gobbledygook. "You bought the book," she reminded Honor. "It's the mindfulness bit of his CBT-mindfulness process," she added rather defensively.

Her sister frowned. "Is this something you should do on your own, Joy? There's a reason Fellowes sees clients personally. He monitors their practice."

"It's not that different from Buddhist meditation practice. Unlike meditation where you stop your thoughts, according to his technique, it's about watching your thoughts, being in the moment with no other aim. He talks about facing your demons and not being afraid, making peace with them instead."

Honor considered this. "Is it like Christian contemplation? Facing purgatory – your Dark Night of the Soul? The mystics say this is the path to enlightenment," she said solemnly.

"Enlightenment might be aiming a bit too high. I'd settle for inner peace, being in harmony with the world, maybe a good dose of equilibrium thrown in for good measure." Joy laughed with a sudden sense of the ridiculous. "Oh God. Don't tell me Dr Vitkay was right all along! The cure is a spiritual one after all."

"You said it, not me," Honor joined in light heartedly.

Nature chose this moment to blanket the common in icy sleet. Laughing, they picked up the pace and power-walked the rest of the way around the circuit. They arrived at Joy's cottage wet and bedraggled, shaking their coats like shaggy dogs.

Standing together in the hallway hanging up their coats on wall hooks, Honor looked sombre for a moment. Joy braced for the *caring sister* platitude coming. Instead, she was warmly surprised.

"Joy, the more I think about it the more I'm sure this mindfulness stuff is what you need to do. Go for it."

Joy's face lit up as radiant as a sunbeam. Her sister's blessing refreshed as if being doused in holy water. Pervading Joy with pure, clean wholesomeness. Maybe even a hint of happy, for the first time in months.

In fact, how normal used to feel.

Chapter Forty Eight

After having a cup of tea, Honor headed home. In the living room, Joy stoked the fire, threw on another log, and opened the grate to let in more air to the wood heater. Soon the cosy comfort of a bursting blaze radiated warmth throughout the room. She settled onto a lounge chair, propped a pillow behind her back and an Alpaca throw rug across the lap, and re-read Dr Fellowes first exercise on mindfulness.

On the kitchen counter, her mobile phone rested in its charger, blinking unnoticed. Joy forgot to take the phone on the walk around the common. She wasn't expecting any calls and had no particular reason to check the phone for incoming messages. Friends no longer called for chats since the broken record of PTSD had taken over other topics of conversation making her a bore.

The first exercise was simple enough. Sit for a few minutes, take a few deep breaths and begin to scan the body from head to toe, paying attention to inner sensations. Are there points of pain, tight muscles, tingling, places that are hot or cold? Afterwards, Joy was to write down what she could remember in a journal.

As much as Dr Fellows promised it would be relaxing, to Joy it wasn't. She was left feeling antsy and restless as if something impending was on the horizon, out of sight but soon to emerge. After dutifully scribbling impressions as per the instructions, she closed the journal and went in search of comfort food from the pantry. She made a mental note. In the future it might be better to do the practices on a full stomach.

While sitting at the kitchen table scoffing chilli corn chips dipped in guacamole, she first glimpsed a light blinking on her mobile. The intrusion into her safe, private space caused mild anxiety. Whoever it was, she didn't want to have to call them back. A debate went back and forth in her head as to whether to hear the message or leave it for another day.

It might be Gemma needing help.

This was the only reason to check the message.

Curious, the caller was Michelle. This was a first. Her voice sounded high pitched with stress. Joy had trouble hearing on digital devices; voices sounded patchy and words ran together garbling sentences. She listened to the short call twice but missed chunks of it.

Something about giving Joy a heads up about a letter coming from the department. An appointment with a doctor next week. Undoubtedly related to workers comp.

They hadn't given much notice. Was that why Michelle felt it important to talk to her?

Whatever. She'd check the post tomorrow, see if the letter arrived. Only then, after reading it – and if absolutely necessary – would she bother returning Michelle's call.

Chapter Forty Nine

The next morning, Joy woke at nine thirty, wrapped a fluffy cardigan around her shoulders, plodded to the kitchen like a zombie on auto-pilot and made a mug of double shot plunger coffee. Waiting for the caffeine to clear the fuzz from her brain, she rested her head on an elbow sprawled on the kitchen table and contemplated life.

Gazing out French windows, a wild garden overgrown with exuberant spring greenery overwhelmed her fragile sensibilities. She squinted, eyes watering. It was too bright, buoyant... and optimistic. Annoyingly so, as if a mythical Phoenix arose from the brown decaying ashes of a cold, dark winter sprouting promises of new life, burning bright with enthusiasm. She preferred the sleepiness of winter.

She debated whether to pick up the coffee mug and return to bed.

Instead, she pulled across Dr Fellowes' book and dutifully began to read the text associated with the next exercise on mindfulness. Another hour went by before Joy decided to have a shower and dress.

The clock read eleven thirty. The familiar whirring of the postman's scooter passing the cottage jogged Joy's memory. Michelle's message about a letter from the department. She'd better check the post box.

A letter had been delivered from the insurer on behalf of Eden Isle's State Department of Community Health. It read:

Dear Ms O'Connell

Re: Workers Compensation Claim #18-666

MEDICAL EXAMINATION

We refer to your claim for compensation and wish to advise that we have made an appointment for you to be examined by Dr Jason Evans, Psychiatrist on 3 October at 6.45 pm (that time is correct) at The Grand Chancellor, Plover Point – Room 131.

The purpose of this appointment is to obtain an opinion from an independent specialist concerning the nature of your condition and your progress towards recovery.

A travel reimbursement claim form is attached. We will meet any reasonable cost associated with you attending the appointment. Receipts must be provided.

Please advise this office if you are unable to attend the scheduled appointment or have any queries.

Yours faithfully,

Senior Claims Consultant

How weird the insurer made an appointment out of hours and in a hotel room rather than a consulting room at a clinic or hospital. Being mindful, she monitored her body sensations. There was a deep ache in her chest. She took in a deep breath determined to think about this logically.

It was impossible for her to attend an appointment as far away as Plover Point at night – to meet a doctor at a hotel. Someone she'd never met and didn't know. How creepy was that? Driving at night caused massive anxiety and she avoided it except for dire emergencies.

Nothing about this doctor's assessment felt safe. Instinctively, her heart began to pound like a drum heralding alarm and self-preservation.

Was it her imagination or was there a disturbing tone to the scheduling that left a lingering sense of sinister intent. They placed brackets on *that time is correct*. This was the giveaway. They must have known it would cause confusion and distress.

Don't go there. Conspiracy theories would not be helpful. She quickly deflected her thoughts from dwelling on the negatives.

Give them the benefit of doubt. The time must have been a clerical error, even if the letter specifically stated it wasn't a mistake.

She dialled Michelle's number confident reason and common sense would prevail once her fearful, fragile state was explained to all concerned parties. The insurer wasn't some dispassionate robot lacking human decency. Michelle would sort out the mess with the insurer.

Michelle answered in a fluster of effusive apologetic ramblings. It became apparent after listening for a few minutes Michelle had already talked to Hannah in an attempt to reschedule the appointment, without success. Dr Evans was a busy specialist from the mainland; he only visited Eden Isle one day a month and Joy was fortunate to secure an appointment with him at all. His diary was booked out and even if they rescheduled, it would be at the same time next month.

Suspicious and angry, Joy interrupted. "This is Dr Sasha's doing, isn't it?"

"No. No it wasn't. It came from the insurer. This would have been in motion long before your appointment with Dr Sasha," Michelle said. "Hannah explained it's the next step towards packaging you out of the service. They need to assess your PTSD and how much it has affected your functioning."

"You mean, prove I'll never work again," Joy rephrased with disgust.

This move by the department elevated Joy's workers compensation matter to a new level. Suddenly, forced retirement became an impending reality. "The department is getting serious about me now," Joy said. "It's happening faster than I expected." It wasn't a choice anymore. Decisions were being made for her.

"I'm sorry, Joy, but you have to attend otherwise you risk the insurer cutting off your payments." Despite any sympathy she may have felt for Joy's dilemma, Michelle's role was to enforce the hard, institutional line.

Joy's faith in Michelle and in the reasonableness of the system deflated in a whoosh of disempowerment. "Can my daughter come with me as a support person? I don't want to be alone in a hotel room with a strange man giving me a medical examination without someone there for security. Even if it doesn't involve me getting naked. I'm assuming Dr Evans will limit his examination to my mental health only. The letter wasn't exactly clear on that point." Joy's apprehension manifested as sarcasm.

Michelle was in a placating mood. "Let me assure you it will be limited to a psychiatric assessment, Joy. I'm sure it would be fine under the circumstances to take a support person if that would make you feel more comfortable."

"It would," Joy mumbled, feeling disgruntled.

"I'll keep trying with Hannah to change the appointment time. I'll get back to you as soon as I know something."

"Thanks." Joy ended the call on a hopeless note. The appointment was next week. Not enough time for Michelle to argue and debate with a government officer just doing her job.

Joy was left defiant in the face of an implacable situation she'd been dumped in. There must be something more she could do.

It wouldn't hurt to get a second opinion on the matter. Maybe Jim from the Compo Hotline could offer some support or advice. Dialling the hotline, she booked an urgent consultation with him that afternoon.

Joy tossed the phone onto the kitchen table. The conversation with Jim had gone no worse than expected. She'd cried and pleaded to no avail. Jim had listened but then seemed a bit stern. He advised she could ask the insurer to change the appointment. But at the end of the day, she would have to comply with their directives – or risk compo payments being cancelled. She didn't have a say in the situation.

Apparently, after hours appointments were fairly common practice within the industry. So much for a sinister conspiracy.

Jim also told her it would be unusual for a psychiatrist to allow a support person to be present during an assessment. He dismissed her concerns about safety being compromised alone in a room with a stranger, saying Dr Evans was highly reputable. *There was nothing to worry about.*

A man would say that, thought Joy, not buying it.

It was time to hire a lawyer. Jim had recommended this during their previous conversation and she'd procrastinated. Let someone else fight her battles. Someone more familiar with the system and the rules – who wouldn't let the insurer get away with funny business.

Chapter Fifty

Despite a sense of urgency, Joy put a DVD into the player and lay on the sofa in an enervating stupor. She half slept through most of the second disc of the fourth series of Nikita. It finished. The room was dark. It was almost dinner time. She'd have to get up and move to install disc number three...

Or just keep lounging without motivation.

The trouble was once the DVD stopped, with its distraction of martial arts fights, gun fire, and warehouses and people being blown up in a maelstrom of chaos and carnage, Joy's brain took over the maelstrom with uncanny resonance. Her head pounded in fevered sympathy. Her bones and muscles ached as if at the receiving end of a sound beating. The old heart jived to a heavy metal beat stuck on fast forward.

She hated the body defying the brain's commands to calm down.

And hated knowing the mindfulness exercises and walks with Honor over the past few weeks had begun to work and now... her equilibrium had been unbalanced by the very people claiming to get her *better*. It showed how precarious feeling normal had been.

She'd started to connect back to nature, let go of anxiety and apprehension. And now they'd brought it all back again – so easily. It felt like a deliberate and concerted effort to keep her off balance and mentally unstable to prove a point. She hated this paranoid Joy, suspicious, clueless and powerless.

She wasn't in control. All the rules, policies and directives worked against her and in their favour.

Oh, god. This is how it felt to be a victim. This was a new realisation. She'd never before defined herself by this term. Knowing yourself as a victim was strange and disconcerting.

It was all getting too complicated. Maybe she could give them a big *fuck it* and attend the appointment. Not give them the satisfaction of knowing they got to her. Maybe it would work, if she drove up during the day and booked a room overnight. Not at the Grand Chancellor obviously. That would be weird. Maybe if Gemma came with – in case...

She played this scenario over in her imagination. No matter how she looked at it, having a medical examination in a hotel room freaked her out.

Resigned, she pushed up into a sitting position and stared at the phone, reaching a decision. It was time to bring in the big guns to intervene on her behalf.

She'd get Kodi to ask Lachlan for his father's work number. Mr Chapman was someone she could trust as a lawyer.

Chapter Fifty One

Gemma stared at her mother lying prone on the lounge suite trying to read her mood. "This is bullshit! It's a set up, Mum. It has to be."

The last thing Joy needed right now was more conspiracies and drama added to the scenario. The facts were bad enough. She pulled an alpaca throw rug over her shoulders and huddled into the sofa cushions.

"It's designed to intimidate you," Gemma added, working herself into an emotional pitch. "They won't get away with it. I won't let them continue bullying you."

Joy sighed. "Whatever it is, I have to go to the appointment." Her flat tone signalled resignation. She wasn't in a frame of mind to argue.

"I'm coming with you then," Gemma stated emphatically. "I can drive you. Kodi can babysit Jaxon. We'll stay overnight in Plover Point like you suggested. We'll need to book a room as soon as possible. The appointment is in two days." Gemma was in organisation mode, full steam ahead, no stopping her.

Joy paled, feeling pressured into a decision and not convinced it was such a good idea having Gemma come with. She pictured her hot-headed daughter barging into the assessment ready to give Dr Evans a piece of her mind while Joy watched helplessly from the sidelines. It would only make matters worse, even if the idea was appealing in a wicked sort of way.

Gemma missed the nonverbal cues, continuing a one-sided conversation. "Kodi had a massive fight with Lachlan over it. That's why she asked me to be the bearer of bad news. She couldn't face disappointing you," she was saying.

Suddenly the turn in topic registered through the chatter going on in Joy's mind. She shot up to a sitting position. "It wasn't her fault, or Lachlan's for that matter. Make sure you tell her that. I don't want to be the reason they break up," she stressed. Going thoughtful, she added, "In hindsight, I can see it was foolish to think his father would represent me. Mr Chapman's a local and obviously doesn't want to get embroiled in a case going loggerheads with the state government."

"His excuse was a full caseload and workers comp wasn't his area of expertise. But she thinks the real reason was his dad's involvement in the Liberal Party. There are rumours he'll compete in the next election for one of the marginal seats." Gemma said this as a matter of fact but looked disgusted all the same. "It's tipped for next March."

That made sense. Joy nodded with world weariness. If Honor had been there, she'd remind her of the WIFM principle.

"In fairness, he passed on some advice free of charge. He reckoned you have every right to refuse an examination outside of working hours. It was unreasonable of the insurer to expect this. And these types of appointments must be held at a clinic or other proper place of business. He was livid, Kodi said, that they'd booked a hotel room. He recommended you phone the insurer and insist they change it. Tell them you've had legal advice about it." Gemma stood firm and defiant as if he'd confirmed what she already knew to be true.

"That was generous of him helping me out even though I'm not a client," Joy said.

Gemma nodded. A thoughtful expression crossed her face. "That's right. He also said, there shouldn't be a problem with you taking a support person along to the appointment. To use his words, *it was bloody minded to deny you a sense of safety and wellbeing during a psychiatric assessment.*"

"That's what I think as well," Joy said.

"So, it's settled. I'm coming with you," she said gleefully.

Joy stifled a groan. It was turning out a disaster no matter what happened.

Gemma continued to voice concerns about her cousin. "Of course, Lachlan's dad hasn't redeemed himself in Kodi's eyes. None of the free advice makes any difference to her. Family loyalty means everything, and the Chapman family has let her down. I'm betting this is the final straw for Lachlan. It's once too often." Gemma looked smug about it.

"I thought you liked Lachlan," Joy said.

Gemma shrugged. "He's alright. She could do better."

"That's what Honor keeps saying." Joy gave a wan smile. Nostalgia pierced her heart. For someone so young and vibrant, her daughter was too cynical about men. After suffering abuse at the hands of Jaxon's father no man would measure up to the high standards she'd set since.

"Before I forget, Chapman left the name and number of a law firm on the mainland that you should call. He said they specialise in compensation claims and don't charge if they don't win." Gemma dug around in a jean pocket and pulled out a crumpled business card. She passed it to her mum.

Joy noticed Gemma's hand shaking. An immediate flash of guilt pierced through her gut. The situation was hard on Gemma, Joy realised with sudden insight, even if for different reasons. Her earlier display of righteous anger was a brave front.

Anything to do with lawyers and fighting the system would be dredging up bad memories. Her vexatious ex-partner had dragged Gemma through the courts with the aim of destroying her. Her daughter had lost a home and life savings fighting to retain custody and protect Jaxon from a violent father. There had been a time when the guy turned stalker, purely to intimidate her.

The courts and lawyers claimed to be on the side of truth and justice, but in reality, for Gemma it worked in favour of the male with power and financial resources. Her daughter hadn't stood a chance. Fortunately, at the end of it all, Jaxon's dad didn't actually want custody. He simply wanted to break Gemma. Her brave and beautiful daughter was stronger than this: she left everything behind and moved to Eden Isle – to get away and start over.

Joy studied the card with a blank look, lost in thought.

Gemma snatched back the card. "Give it here. I'll phone for you."

At that moment, Joy's phone pinged with an incoming text message. It was from an automatic secretarial service confirming her appointment with Dr Evans at 6.45 pm on 3 October at the Grand Chancellor Hotel. At the end of the message, it said DO NOT REPLY.

Joy held the phone to show Gemma the message as a fait accompli.

Gemma was having none of that. "Right, that does it. I'm talking to the insurer, Mum. What's their number?"

Joy had reached a point where she didn't care what happened anymore. Obediently, she pushed up from the sofa and stumbled over to the entranceway where she'd dropped her handbag earlier. Extracting an envelope, she handed it to Gemma and then returned to the sofa to lie down. Pulling the throw rug up to her ears, she didn't want to listen to Gemma giving a serve to the Senior Claims Officer. Let her hot-headed daughter get it out of her system. She'd deal with the fall out later.

When Gemma ended the call, she addressed her mum. "Well, that went better than expected. Anton was quite understanding when I explained the circumstances. He must be new," she quipped. "He's going to try to reschedule with a different specialist. You're not to do anything until he gets back to you. He'll send a letter." Gemma studied her mum assessing how much was getting through. She spoke slowly and earnestly. "Apparently, it's the department that recommends the doctor, so he's going to liaise with Hannah. In terms of me going to the appointment with you, he said it depends on the specialist. Some are more cool about it than others."

Gemma sounded as if she'd sorted it all in one phone call. But Joy was more confused than ever.

She had a medical examination in two days. Or did she?

Which person was she to believe? Michelle, her RTW Coordinator? Jim from the Compo Assist Hotline? Mr Chapman, the lawyer? Or Anton, the insurer sorting it out with the department's workers compensation officer? Each one gave different advice.

Michelle said she'd talk to Hannah and get back but hadn't. She'd told Joy it was okay to take a support person along. She was very clear, Joy had to go to the appointment.

Jim from the Compo Hotline said she couldn't take anyone along. He too stressed, she had to go to the appointment.

Legal advice from Lachlan's father was: don't go to this appointment. On the other hand, he couldn't see a problem taking a support person along.

Now Gemma was telling her the insurer was going to try to reschedule with another doctor, so she wasn't to go to the original appointment. But this depended on whether her employer allowed them to change doctors. Michelle hadn't been able to persuade Hannah so far. Would it be any different for Anton? And by the way, it may or may not be okay to take Gemma for support – depending on the doctor.

And then there was that text message from Dr Evans' secretarial service confirming the appointment with a DO NOT REPLY note, meaning she had no way to contact him to cancel.

She had forty-eight hours to make a decision.

If the insurer's letter didn't arrive in time, should she go to the original appointment or trust Anton had rescheduled?

Considering this decision could potentially impact on whether her compensation money was cancelled, leaving her destitute, all the differing opinions on what she should do and couldn't do were stoking her anxiety and befuddling an already muddled head. The uncertainty and pressure were too much to cope with. She sensed a panic attack coming on.

When she pointed this out to Gemma, her daughter laughed at first. "The situation is ludicrous, mum."

Once Joy began to weep, the cynical humour died down. Gemma reverted to the role of a more helpful and practical daughter.

"Mum, you are not to worry. What we'll do is book the trip to Plover Point as a contingency. I'll insist on accompanying you to the examination no matter what anyone says." She sat next to her mum and placed an arm around her shoulders. "It will all work out. Trust me. All bases are covered."

Chapter Fifty Two

In the final hours before the evening appointment with Dr Evans, Gemma had it all arranged. The hotel room booked; the car filled with petrol; Kodi knocking off work early in order to babysit Jaxon; and a mince casserole in the fridge ready to heat in the microwave.

They were due to head off at four thirty, Gemma saying she wanted to arrive just in time for the examination, so Joy didn't have time to stress about it.

With trepidation, Joy was throwing an overnight bag onto the back seat of Gemma's Getz when the mobile pinged.

A short, to the point text message from Michelle read:

Dr E appt rescheduled 2 Nov 6.45 pm at Cameron Chambers

From M

She showed Gemma who snorted in disgust. "What the? They left that to the last minute to be sure you were properly stressed out of your mind, mum."

Joy was too relieved to react, except to collect her bag and return to the house. Gemma elected to continue on to Plover Point. "It's already paid for. There's no reason to waste the luxury of a babysitter and a hotel room with room service, Mum."

On the other hand, despite the last-minute reprieve, the stress from the past week had exhausted Joy. She chose to go home to leftovers and a hot bath before bed, leaving the mini holiday to Gemma to enjoy on her own.

Lying in the steamy herbal bath swishing bubbles into mounds, Joy's tense muscles relaxed, and she drifted into a soporific state of mindlessness letting go of all the distrust and feelings of loss of control. Passing thoughts about the kafuffle with the appointment wandered in and out of her consciousness.

It was intriguing as to why the department elected to sort out only half of the problem. They'd changed the venue to an accounting firm rather than a hotel which was better but not a total relief. The department rescheduled the appointment with Dr Evans for next month but then left it at the same time in the evening. At least she had a whole month to sort out that oversight.

It felt weird thinking about rocking up to a business for a private and personal medical assessment rather than a clinical setting. While swirling bubbles into shapes and patterns on her tummy, she pictured the scene: walking into the accountants reception area at quarter to seven, no receptionist to greet her. Asking a junior accountant where to go for a medical assessment; being looked at as a crazy woman. How mortifying having to explain the circumstances.

It was as if the department couldn't concede the point and unnecessarily made it a battle of wills. They had to save face by leaving it a draw, rather than grant Joy the win.

Not that she wanted to fight. She simply wanted them to understand how scared she was for her safety. This was the whole thing about PTSD and why it was so difficult to leave the sanctuary of her home. The world didn't feel safe anymore.

Why was this so hard to understand? Why wouldn't they approach the process with empathy and compassion?

Joy closed her eyes and sank deeper into the bath, allowing the fluid to cover her like the warmth of a womb.

Chapter Fifty Three

The next week turned out to be a busy one by Joy's standards.

For a start, the 'no fee, no win' lawyer returned her call and took down so many personal details about her life and work she half expected to be handing over her bank account and credit card numbers by the end of the phone conversation.

His name was John Emerson; however, Joy decided to refer to him as Doc Martin in her private thoughts. The Sydney lawyer was so abrupt, wanted precise answers to his precise questions, wouldn't tolerate any digression or elaboration, impatiently cut her off from even asking questions to clarify exactly what he wanted from her, made her feel stupid in the process – it felt like he was on a timer and once the buzzer went off he'd hang up. Just the facts mam. As impersonal and efficient as an assembly line. In fact, he sounded more stressed out than she did when suffering the worst effects of PTSD.

And this was the one person in the ever-increasing membership of her workers compensation team that was being paid to be on her side.

Her champion was not there for emotional support obviously. It was so *transactional* – cold, hard business. That was all. How depressing.

When asked what the nature of the injury was relating to a claim for compensation, Joy began a bitter spiel about being strangled by her boss, getting PTSD, and the court deciding to let the woman off. Mr Emerson interrupted with a curt explanation that first offences were generally dismissed without more than a fine even if the offender pleaded guilty. Joy countered with disgust at the Magistrate's practical joke judgement, to which an unsympathetic Doc Martin replied as if reading from a textbook. Under law there were two defences open to Mrs Bryant regarding intent to harm: one, mental illness and two, humour. Joy became upset at the implication that being strangled could in any way be humorous, only to be talked over by the lawyer lecturing that if intent to harm had been proven, her boss would have been up for a charge of attempted murder rather than common assault. Awed by this realisation, Joy reigned in her emotions.

At the end of the interrogation, asserting her right to speak, Joy forced Mr Emerson to listen to one pressing issue – the scheduling of the medical examination in the evening.

To her surprise, his voice softened when he said *I'll look into it,* before hanging up. The man was a confusing mystery.

Toward the end of the week, Jim from the Compo Assist Hotline phoned as a follow up about the after hours medical examination. He was interested to hear how it had turned out and if the insurer was amenable to the changes she required. Happily, Joy related the story of a last-minute reprieve and the rescheduling at a new venue. Unfortunately, they hadn't changed the time. It was still in the evening, she confessed.

Jim listened and took down notes. He explained each month the hotline submitted a report to the Workers Compensation Tribunal, mostly facts and statistics about their workload. Occasionally, they made mention of any troubling issues drawn to their attention that the tribunal should be made aware of for advice or action. Joy's case had inspired him to add a note in last month's report about insurers booking out of hours appointments at unsuitable venues.

"It caused a few ripples amongst the members of the tribunal. As a consequence, the tribunal has asked if they can interview you to hear your story. This will assist them in presenting a case for change," Jim said.

This caught Joy by surprise. "I see," she laughed, embarrassed at the prominence given to her dilemma. Although it was a big deal personally, she hadn't expected it to be that important to the authorities.

"I'm phoning to ask your permission. Can I give your name and contact details to the tribunal to allow one of them to phone you? They'd like a statement. How do you feel about this?" he asked.

"That should be alright," Joy said hesitantly, weary from all the fuss and bother and not sure if she had energy to further a cause these days. Important as it was. At least she'd been heard this time, and by a workers compensation tribunal no less. They didn't think she'd over-reacted or was crazy. They were treating the issue as if it was worthy of attention.

As if she was worthy of attention – not invisible. Someone out there did care. Maybe there was hope after all. Some good could come from this.

"Great," Jim said. "You should hear from them within a week."

***

Joy spent the next few days getting her thoughts in order and painstakingly writing up a statement...

And waiting for a phone call that never came.

Chapter Fifty Four

Joy entered the counselling room in a sullen mood, not wanting to be there. To top it off, true to character the first thing Marcus said was "You look beautiful today, Joy. I can see you've made an effort to wear a pretty top and cardigan. Are you feeling as good as you look?"

She did not feel remotely beautiful. She was broken, probably neurotic and pathetically vulnerable. It was too ironic to believe any man would find her attractive now, especially when no one had given her a second glance during all the years she'd been vibrant, interestingly engaged in life, and actually made the effort to look attractive. The outfit she was wearing was old and worn, not even the latest fashion.

Drawing attention to how she dressed seemed intrusive and inappropriate.

Was using flirtation some kind of psychological test? Appeal to her ego, trick her into responding encouragingly to his overtures to prove she wasn't reclusive and avoiding human intimacy as she'd claimed?

She felt a steaming lava of anger slivering below the thin skin of civility. One more sleazy comment and it would spurt through the cracks.

Ignoring him, she plonked into a chair and slouched unladylike. "I've been such a couch potato since PTSD, I've gained weight and gone up a dress size. So, I feel fat and frumpy."

"Since my divorce my girlfriends have been all different sizes, from size eight through to size twenty. I found them all beautiful in their own way. To me, a woman can be interesting for many reasons, not only physically attractive in a traditional sense." He smiled in a pleasant, counsellor-like way that Joy supposed was a try at empathy. "Did you know we're about the same age? I'm only three years younger than you."

Joy bit back a remark that he looked older. Instead, the *good little compliant* client flashed a smile.

"There's your smile. I've caught a glimpse of a sunny, happy side, the person you were before PTSD," he enthused. "I can tell you have such a lot of life in you. Together we can get this person back."

Joy flinched as his observation hit a sore point. The old Joy was gone for good. Never again would she be a beacon of light and walk this earth all shiny and lit up like a Christmas tree full of light and spirit, believing an armour of goodness made her immune to cruelty, menace and maliciousness. That innocence had been sucked out of her during the strangling incident. It was dangerous to be vibrant and alive. And it was gauche to remind her.

"I've been doing some research on the eye movement therapy you suggested," she retorted.

His eyes lit up. "What have you decided?"

"I don't think it's for me. My sister gave me a book on mindfulness, and I've been practising it along with Eco-therapy. I think it's helping me achieve equilibrium especially since going on walks in nature."

"Eco-therapy? That's a new one I haven't heard of before. Where's the research papers on that?" he asked with a twinkle in his eyes. "You realise EMDR could be used in conjunction with your other practices," he pushed, not willing to let go of his baby.

To Joy the case was closed; she ignored the comment. There wasn't time to debate the merits of different therapies; she was here for some actual counselling. "Just as I was starting to feel better, my workers comp crap kicked in again and threw me off balance. The insurer made an appointment after hours in a hotel room for a medical examination by a doctor I've never met, Dr Evans."

"Dr Evans? That's great news. You are very fortunate to get him. He's a highly renowned psychiatrist from the mainland and extremely busy." Marcus looked off into the distance with an awed expression.

This was not the reaction she anticipated. "But it was at night in a hotel room," she stressed.

"That would have been the only time he was available. As I said, he's extremely busy. You should be grateful he wants to see you at all." Marcus wasn't going to allow her to spoil his moment of hero worship. It was clear where his loyalties lay.

"I have enough trouble leaving home during the day. It's impossible for me to drive long distances at night. Safety is a key issue." Joy was struggling to make him understand.

"I hadn't considered that. Would you prefer having our counselling sessions from your home? I could arrange home visits if this was easier for you?" Sincerity oozed from the guy.

Did he look sly or was Joy imagining it? Marcus had deliberately missed the point she was making and managed to turn it into something sounding suggestive. Her stomach twisted in nausea. Even a passing thought of a romantic interest made her feel ill and vulnerable. Having a man in her home during a counselling session where she was leaving herself open and exposed to raw emotions was too terrible to contemplate.

"No, don't do that," she blurted. "It's good for me to have an excuse that forces me to leave the house during the day. Otherwise, I would be more reclusive than ever." She hoped he wouldn't push the issue, deciding in an instant to keep talking as a diversion. "Sometimes with PTSD I develop aversions to places where I've experienced unpleasant emotions. If this happened in my home, my last place of sanctuary would disappear.

"My anxiety levels rise the longer and farther I'm away from home. The risk to safety increases the longer I'm in the public domain."

"Hmm. Let's try some word association. If I say *public domain...*"

Immediately Joy rattled off a string of words. "Unsafe, no control over others, exposed, no protection, no personal space, danger of violence..."

"Fine. What about private domain?" Marcus asked, jotting notes.

"Safer, more control. Isolated. My sanctuary."

"I see," he said. "Tell me about your property as a sanctuary," he murmured, not looking up.

"I like my property. It's a few acres. When I moved from the mainland, I had this notion of being self-sufficient, growing vegetables and raising chickens," she enthused. "The garden's a bit wild since my PTSD but that's brought in bird life and echidnas which is--"

"--One of my dreams was to live off the land," Marcus interrupted with a meaningful gaze deep into her eyes. "How big is your house? Do you own your property outright?"

"Umm, yes," she answered nonplussed. "Prices were a lot cheaper five years ago. It's a small cottage, three bedrooms." Joy wondered in what direction the conversation was heading and how it had anything to do with counselling. More like being on a coffee date and they were getting to know each other. "It needs a lot of renovation."

"It sounds like it's a lot for you to look after on your own." Another long moment holding eye contact ensued. Joy had no idea what was expected of her, so she fidgeted in the hard seat and remained mute. "What would your property be worth in today's market?" Marcus asked casually.

Joy crossed her arms tightly to her chest. Boundaries were being crossed. Her financial position wasn't any of his business. "I wouldn't have a clue. There's no way I could consider moving. Packing up, looking for another place to live – it would be too much with PTSD."

"So, you haven't considered quitting the job, packing up and starting new somewhere else? Get away from the workers comp circus that you say drives you crazy? Move back to the mainland?"

"My family is here..." she paused, instantly becoming suspicious. The guy wasn't even subtle. He was another plant paid by the department to get a job done. This time it was suggesting not to fight. Just quit and move away.

Her best interests were not at the heart of this counselling session.

It was not a time for guileless honesty. It was time to act the part, pretend to go along with the role of compliant employee, and speak the lie in order to survive. She wasn't a fool.

She gave the politically correct answer. "No, as I've continually stated, I've always expected to return to my job at the centre which I loved. If it wasn't for Poppy, I would have."

Marcus raised his eyebrows with scepticism. "So, you do want to return at some point. That's not exactly what you implied at our first session." He'd set a different trap and she'd fallen in.

"What I said was that I didn't want to be pressured into returning unless I was ready. There hasn't exactly been cooperation on the part of my employer." It was her turn to hold eye contact, call his bluff. "If the department is determined to package me out of the service, then I have to do what is best for me. I have rights and entitlements, you know."

The frown he returned hit a trigger. Before Joy could be stopped, she went off expounding about the intimidation tactics used by the workers comp officials, including the short notice given for the psych assessment, the differing advice received from each party, hiring a lawyer to have someone on her side, the tribunal getting involved about the night time appointment... She pulled up short. It hadn't been her intention to mention her involvement with the tribunal.

"I'm not going to be bullied into just quitting," she finished with a determined look. "I'm allowed to stay on compensation payments until I retire."

Marcus smiled, pleased at getting a rise out of her and at the same time acknowledging her fight back. "You are an intriguing person, Joy. It's a pleasure getting to know you." His smile dazzled. "I hope after our counselling sessions are over, we will remain friends."

Like that was ever going to happen. He was a minion of the department and therefore the enemy.

Joy rocked in the seat, dazed. The hour must be almost up. She gazed at the wall clock. How did he expect her to respond?

Calling him out on the flirting would be awkward. BTS, she was much more assertive in these matters. Instead, she blushed with mortification at the blurred ethical line between a sincere counsellor and an over friendly, lonely guy.

As if proving he was a friend, Marcus offered advice regarding the psychiatric assessment process. "They can be brutal," he was saying. "Dr Evans will ask a lot of questions that have nothing to do with your PTSD diagnosis. He'll question your past relationships, previous accidents or illnesses that may prove pre-existing traumas. He's a master at getting people to open up and spill their guts."

The implication she was once again being set up for a fall caused Joy to become angry. "What has any of that got to do with establishing how much impact PTSD has had on my life? Isn't that supposed to be the point of the examination?"

"In theory, you are judged on seven categories." He rattled off a long list too quickly and Joy struggled to keep up. "Self-care, social and recreational activities, travel, social functioning including relationships, concentration and persistence, and employment capabilities. But it's really designed to demonstrate a prior level of impairment in these categories before you got PTSD," Marcus said helpfully.

His candour worked to fuel Joy's growing suspicions and distrust in the system. No wonder the department scheduled the examination at Plover Point, requiring her to travel a long distance at night. The first test – *travel* – was in place before the official appointment even started. *Sneaky.* And what about Marcus flirting? Was that all part of their scheme to discredit her symptoms? She grew pensive, mulling over the implications of what she was up against.

Marcus observed Joy's pensiveness with a pleased expression. Job done. Abruptly, he ended the session by standing, signalling they were finished for the day.

Chapter Fifty Five

A waiter at the museum's Tram Café placed two plates of hamburgers and chips on the table. Joy pulled a plate across and spurted tomato sauce over the chips. She'd met Gemma for lunch after her counselling session with Marcus, needing to debrief. Her daughter was in full lecture mode. Joy couldn't blame her. Marcus rubbed her up the wrong way as well.

Gemma stopped ranting long enough to salt the chips and take a bite of the burger. Between mouthfuls, she lectured. "I've heard of therapists like him. They take advantage of vulnerable women, befriend them, move in and then take control of their lives. Don't fall for it."

"That's not going to happen. I've got PTSD but that doesn't make me an idiot," Joy reassured her daughter. "The thought of intimacy…" she screwed up her face. It was slightly ego deflating to be told that Marcus was probably a scammer after her money, rather than actually interested in her romantically. Her head had already reached that conclusion, although there was a tiny glimmer of hope in her heart… she wasn't totally dead from the neck down.

"I know what you mean. The guy's a sleaze." Gemma nodded furiously. "It's totally unprofessional. In my natural therapy studies, it was drummed into us that therapists cannot be friends with clients, even after they stop being clients. It crosses too many ethical boundaries. We must keep a clinical distance to ensure trust and safety."

"He must know that and doesn't care," Joy agreed, biting into her burger.

"That's my point, mum. What's he up to? Is he setting you up for a fall, like some kind of spy for the department?" Her face was flushed with concern.

"All I know is that I'm forced to see him because that horrible GP wrote it on the medical certificate," Joy said, choosing a long french fry dripping with sauce. "Six more sessions."

"Don't tell him anything he could use against you in a personal way," Gemma beseeched.

Joy blanched. She'd already divulged a lot more than intended. It was too late to do anything about that except brace for the consequences.

"I told him about Jim making a report to the tribunal," she confessed.

Gemma looked stricken. "Oh, Mum. They'll trace it back to you now. You'll be labelled a troublemaker."

"Maybe not. I've been waiting on the call from the tribunal. I prepared a statement. Jim said it would be in a few days, but I haven't heard from them," Joy looked glum. "Maybe nothing will come of it."

"I'm sorry, Mum. There are no wins in these situations."

Joy's heart fell at her daughter's cynical view of the world. Gemma was too young to have lost faith in heroes protecting the codes of justice and moral principles.

It was wrong to drag Gemma down into her PTSD world which filtered out goodness and trust and left only black blotches of disillusionment and shattered expectations of betrayal. As a mother it was her duty to promote the fairytale ending, sustain the belief in "the cowboy" riding towards the horizon as the sun set.

"I'll be fine, don't stress. At my age you begin to realise, everything in life works out for the best – if you wait long enough to see the bigger picture."

Gemma looked appeased. "As Auntie Honor would say..."

"Trust the Universe," Joy completed the adage. She began to rummage through her handbag for Aspirin feeling a headache coming on.

Gemma noticed a packet of antidepressants amongst the clutter. "Mum, what's this? I thought you weren't taking those since I put you on Hypericum."

"Hmm? Oh," she laughed. "I'm not. It's my big secret. I fill the prescriptions each fortnight and claim the reimbursement from the insurer, but the meds go into a bag I hide in the cupboard. I have to be seen complying with orders."

"But you are taking St John's Wort, aren't you?"

"Of course. It works better than Prozac."

"And it doesn't have the side effects," Gemma added confidently.

Joy grinned. "It's kind of funny. Every time I have a setback and get emotional in the doctor's surgery, Dr Vitkay ups the dosage of the meds. When I calm down again, he believes it's the drugs working. I call it a reverse placebo effect." She pictured the scene in her mind. "Interesting, the prescription never goes back to a low dosage when I'm feeling better."

"That's what I've been telling you, mum. It's a one way street you can't get off once you start taking drugs."

Joy popped two Aspirins from the foil packaging. Swallowing them with a few sips of water, she leaned forward to whisper. "You should see the size of the bag with all the pills I haven't taken. It's extraordinary and scary to see how much would be in my system now."

Gemma laughed. "What are you going to do with them? Become a drug dealer when they finally package you out?"

It was such a ludicrous idea, they both broke into hysterical giggles.

"I have no idea," Joy stammered between laughs, tucking back into her burger with gusto.

Gemma's phone buzzed. Wiping greasy fingers on a serviette, she gingerly opened the case and pressed answer. Joy pretended not to listen, but from the cryptic conversation, it was Kodi wanting relationship advice. Whether it was about her mother or her boyfriend, that she couldn't tell.

Gemma ended the call saying, "I can't talk right now. I'll call you back tonight after work." Looking up at her mother with a shrug, she said, "Kodi," and left it at that.

After a few minutes of silence eating the last of their meals, her daughter's face lit up. "I've just thought of an idea for all those pills. What about giving them to Auntie Honor to create a mosaic to hang on your wall? It could be a statement about your PTSD experience."

Joy wasn't sure about the idea but admired her daughter's streak of defiance. "It would have to resemble something like *The Scream*," she joked.

Gemma took her seriously. "How cool would that be!"

***

When they finished lunch, Joy drove home in a thoughtful mood. She owed it to her daughter to persevere with the workers compensation process to make a point about keeping the faith. She would endure whatever the system threw at her in order to prove a little person without power or resources who was in the right would eventually win over the might of the powerful institution.

Maybe she was not strong and did not bounce back like she used to. However, she was driven by principles and that alone would be her sustenance in the fight ahead.

Chapter Fifty Six

Seniors from the Shamrock Room shuffled out a back exit of the centre toward the community bus parked in the driveway. Their support workers grasped elbows to steady them on the pathway made slippery from a light drizzle. A grey morning for mourning Mr Gray, Honor thought sadly. Their second passing in the last four months at the centre. Death being a fact of life, and the nature of her volunteer work with dementia clients, didn't make it any less sad.

These times inevitably left her in a melancholy mood. There was something tragic about the lack of nobility at the end of a dignified life. Mr Gray may have been a cantankerous, *old so and so* when he attended craft at the Shamrock Room on Wednesdays, but before Alzheimer's, he'd been a pillar of their church parish and a respected businessman in Lower Teasel. A large turnout for the service was expected.

Dressed in a tailored black suit fitting the occasion, Honor stood at the foot of the bus steps assisting the frail elderly to climb up at the same time doing a headcount. Amberlie, in dangly jewellery and a short dress patterned with stylised scotty dogs over red leggings, skipped up full of enthusiasm. "Do you have an extra seat?" she asked.

"Did you know Harold?" Honor was caught by surprise. The admin assistant rarely entered the Shamrock Room if clients were around, turning up her nose at the *old man smells*.

"Not really," Amberlie replied. "But I know the family. A distant cousin on my mum's side. Anything to get out of work for a couple hours. Poppy gave me permission. She's covering reception. Awesome boss," she said brightly, adding to seal the deal, "The Anglican Church does the best morning teas. Poppy said to bring back a plate for her."

Reluctantly Honor acquiesced. "You can sit at the front behind the driver, with me."

Last to get on, Honor stood in the aisle and scanned the passengers. All seemed to be in order. Harold's personal carer, Dave, stretched out long legs at the back bench seat looking troubled. The tattoos on his knuckles stood out as he squeezed and un-squeezed a closed fist on his lap.

She signalled the driver to drive, pushing aside Amberlie's handbag to sit. The motor groaned and vibrated before the bus lurched off, causing Honor to clutch at the metal bar behind the driver's seat. Next to the window, Amberlie giggled as if starting on an adventure. Honor wondered if she'd ever been to a drawn-out funeral service and if the cakes and sandwiches at the end would make up for the tedium.

"Poppy was his community nurse, you know," Amberlie was saying conversationally. "She'd been assessing Old Harold's mental health. He would have ended up in an old people's home. She said it's probably better this way."

Honor was a bit shocked at Amberlie's pragmatism about death. "Really?" was the best response she could come up with.

"Yeah. Apparently, his carer had reported noticing suspicious red bruising around Harold's neck. Poppy was checking it out. He died on her shift. When he had his heart attack, she tried to resuscitate him. Gross!"

Amberlie mimed spewing by pretending to stick a finger down her throat and gagging.

Honor was confused. "Red bruising? Does this mean the department will have to hold an investigation into his death?"

A guilty expression crossed Amberlie's face. "I don't think so. It's sort of hush hush. I can't say too much or I'll get in trouble. Poppy's writing up the report for the department. She told me Harold was displaying some strange behaviours due to his dementia." She screwed up her face in disgust. "Some of it involved his poor little doggie."

There were some things Honor did not need to know in detail. Avoiding the taboo subject, she digressed to a safer topic. "That's right. I remember Harold talking about his Shitzu. What's going to happen to Lolly? He loved that dog."

Amberlie stifled a giggle. Rather inappropriately, thought Honor. The young girl leaned in to whisper, "Poppy feels terrible but during the panic of trying to resuscitate Harold, Lolly escaped and ran onto the road and got flattened by a delivery van." She started to giggle but choked it in when she saw Honor's horrified frown. "Poor thing," she mumbled into a hand covering her mouth. "Actually, Poppy said it would have been put down anyway. The family wouldn't have wanted the shaggy beast."

Honor loved dogs. Some kind family would have adopted Lolly. In fact, it would have been perfect as a therapy dog for Joy to take on walks and cuddle on the couch when she watched TV. This set Honor off on a thought journey, visiting the RSPCA animal rescue home and picking out a puppy for Joy as a present. She wondered if Kodi would think the idea was a good one.

Amberlie chatted away oblivious to Honor's attention being elsewhere. "Dave's asked for a transfer to the health centre at Stubblefield. Poppy feels bad like he blames her. She tried mouth to mouth on the old bugger. Like that's heroic, isn't it? I guess he's taken Harold's demise pretty hard." Her tone implied complete incomprehension that anyone would be upset at old Harold's death.

The bus pulled up at the curb outside the reserved parking spot opposite the Anglican Church. Honor stood and grabbed the back of the seat to catch her balance. "Okay, folks, no need to rush. Let's take it slow and steady." She nodded to the support workers. They began to assist their charges out of their seats and down the aisle and off the bus.

Groups of people crowded the church grounds. A solemn procession of black limousines drove past and pulled into the carpark. Amberlie disappeared into the crowd while Honor was kept busy keeping her Shamrock Room clients together as they crossed the road and entered the church. It was going to be a long morning.

Chapter Fifty Seven

After three weeks, Joy had given up waiting for the tribunal to take her statement. This was probably for the best considering Gemma's warning about being labelled a troublemaker. Not that anyone so far had taken notice of anything she'd said throughout the entire workers compensation process. Except Doc Martin.

Last week, she did receive a phone call from John Emerson. She'd been lying on the sofa watching an episode of Nikita as an excuse for a nap. She answered half asleep but instantly recognised his officious courtroom voice advising he'd spoken to the insurer. They'd given assurances the psychiatric examination with Dr Evans would be rebooked at medical consulting rooms during office hours. In her relief to have someone on her side achieving results so fast, she was a bit too effusive in praise.

"It's my job," Mr Emerson replied curtly. "Now I need you to listen very carefully to what I am about to say. Do you have a pen and paper to hand?"

Joy scrambled to the kitchen counter and rummaged through a mess of loose To Do lists and torn envelopes with shopping items to buy at the next grocery shop before finally finding a clean scrap of paper. "Yes, ready," she said obediently, pen poised.

"When you see Dr Evans, you are to remember he is not your friend. Write that down in capital letters. His job is to erode the evidence. Answer questions honestly but with clinical objectivity. Do not elaborate. Write that down. Don't make his job easy."

Joy scribbled madly, trying to capture his exact words.

"Do you understand?" he asked, sounding like she was a distracted eight-year-old.

"Yes, like being on the witness stand," she offered.

"I only need a yes or no response. Remember: do not elaborate," he barked. "Just state the facts."

"Yes," she said, biting back an urge to add *Sir*.

"I'll be back in touch when I receive a copy of Dr Evans' assessment report to discuss options regarding our ongoing strategy. Good luck. I'm sure you'll do a great job."

The phone went dead abruptly. No niceties of a goodbye.

Joy stared at the phone bemused. He's getting results. That's what she's paying for. This was all that should matter.

He's from Sydney, she reminded herself. They're all stressed out of their minds, in such a rush to move on to the next job. She was the same working on the mainland. It was one of the reasons she moved to Eden Isle – to live with less stress in her life. Now that was ironic.

Chapter Fifty Eight

At eight thirty in the morning, the wall heater in the waiting area of the Plover Point Medical Specialists Chambers was blowing out hot air, overheating an empty room. The deep pile carpet cushioned noise creating a homey feel to the space. Joy was the first patient to arrive. Kids toys in poster paint colours cluttered one corner. A small round table with an antique desk lamp hosted a few classy magazines: Mademoiselle, Country Living, and Men's Quarterly – all in current date. The smell of freshly ground coffee wafted through from the receptionist's desk, turning Joy's empty stomach slightly nauseous. Maybe she should have had a bite to eat before the assessment. On a usual day, she'd still be in bed; taking breakfast nearer ten o'clock.

Sitting down on a generously upholstered chair, Joy rested her handbag and a plastic sleeve with notes on the adjoining seat. Taking slow, deep breaths she made an attempt to practise mindfulness. She was mindful of her heart pounding up her throat and in her ears. With shaking hands, she extracted her notes and scanned over them for reassurance.

Her *Doc Martin* lawyer would probably be mad at her; but after weighing up Marcus's advice together with his, she'd decided to provide Dr

Evans with a list of her symptoms and all the changes to her lifestyle that PTSD had forced upon her – the same updated list she gave to Dr Vitkay at each appointment, for the sake of consistency and more importantly so she didn't have to go over the same stuff again and again.

After making her wait another fifteen minutes, Dr Evans manifested like a spectre, quietly studying her. She was surprised at how young he appeared. But then at her age everyone seemed to be young. He was dressed in an expensive grey suit that matched his dove grey eyes and ash blonde hair. He had the lean and fit appearance of a regular jogger.

Her first reaction was a wish she'd made more of an effort to dress up instead of wearing what used to be her work uniform: a floral blouse, jeans and flat lace up shoes. Dated clothes and wear worn from too many washings. His eyes flicked up from her head down to her toes. The assessment had already begun before they reached the consulting room.

He smiled warmly as he took the lead down a carpeted hallway, its golden amber walls glowing softly from Art Nouveau style sconces. "How was the drive from Lower Teasel?" he asked conversationally.

Joy wasn't fooled into believing this was simply social chit chat. "I drove up yesterday and stayed overnight. I was worried about sleeping in and missing the appointment. These days it's hard for me to get going early."

Dr Evans took a seat in a high backed, leather and steel executive chair behind a massive mahogany desk. A sports bottle with a high energy drink logo rested in one corner confirming Joy's first impression. The desk was cleared of papers except for one pad and two pencils meticulously positioned square to the desk edge.

Joy sat opposite, directly facing the doctor. Noting there were no props for her comfort such as a glass of water or a box of tissues, she rummaged in her handbag and pulled out a cotton handkerchief and a bottle of mineral water.

Dr Evans began a speech about the purpose of the medical examination. In respect to a claim for compensation regarding permanent whole person impairment, he would be conducting an assessment of her psychological injury. He emphasised she was not his patient and therefore he was not bound by the same rules for a doctor patient relationship, including confidentiality. His role was not as a treating psychiatrist but as an expert bound by the Expert Witness Code of Conduct issued as a practice direction by the Chief Justice. A report of his findings would be sent to the insurer and her employer. Upon request, her GP and lawyer may be granted copies to peruse.

"Do you understand and agree to this procedure as explained?" he asked methodically.

Joy nodded with grim determination.

He looked deeply into her eyes. "Tell me about yourself," he asked with a dazzling smile, conveying sincerity and attentive interest.

The question was vague and all encompassing. *Just the facts*, Doc Martin had stressed. But there was no simple yes/no response as John Emerson had directed. Where should Joy start?

It seemed important, if this man was to judge her fairly, Dr Evans should know her as an individual person, who she was in her entirety. Not only as a victim of assault but also the full life she'd lead up to this point.

Against her lawyer's better judgement, she began her story at the very beginning: where she was born, what she studied at university, giving birth to her first and only child, her career in the Commonwealth government on the mainland, marrying twice, undergoing chemotherapy for breast cancer, moving to Eden Isle... Like a necklace of Indian wampum beads, she began to string together the markers of her life, events that were meaningful and had been instrumental in forming and changing her in so many ways.

Occasionally, he would nod and jot down some comment on a notepad. Joy wondered what she'd said that was noteworthy. She was in the dark as to what specifically he was searching for as he sifted through the intimate debris of her life. There was bound to be a lot within over fifty years of well lived life.

Aware her face flushed and her heart raced, and her voice was too animated, nonetheless he'd turned on a tap and she let it run unstoppable. Afterwards she couldn't remember exactly how long she talked or what she said, only that she'd fallen under Dr Evans' spell and bared her soul. Joy kicked herself digressing down memory lane and irrelevant paths. Every good story depended on what to leave in and what to leave out. In her case, it would also decide her future.

After letting her ramble for a time, he directed the monologue by asking, "What about your marriages? Why did you get divorced?"

Remembering too late to keep it brief, that what she didn't share, he couldn't possibly know, she gave an abridged version. "Archer, my first husband, Gemma's father, was American. He returned to the USA with work. When the time came to follow, I decided Australia was home. We kept in touch and remained friends. Husband number two..." Joy sighed dramatically, "I guess I fell out of love. He wanted to keep trying but my career was more of a priority. I wasn't motivated to work on the relationship." She sat back satisfied at telling the truth, in her own way.

Dr Evans continued to pursue the relationships agenda. "Any relatives diagnosed with mental illness, or instances of domestic violence in your marriages?"

"No." Joy looked him in the eyes. Keeping it simple.

Dr Evans looked puzzled. "But didn't you say in your grievance report to the department you had witnessed family violence?"

Joy's mouth gaped. He'd read her grievance report then. What other information had the department supplied that she believed was private and confidential?

"I was referring to my daughter's relationship with her ex-partner which was so wrong and upsetting to me. No one should suffer from violence in a relationship. I haven't experienced domestic violence personally." She paused and glared at Dr Evans to make a point. "Only occupational violence once – when Mrs Bryant assaulted me."

He didn't look satisfied at this response but didn't pursue it further.

"In your estimation, how long did the actual strangling take place?" he asked.

"As long as it took Mrs Bryant to whisper in my ear *'if I don't strangle you, I'll have to strangle Helen'.*" Joy counted on her fingers as each word was said. "Around ten seconds," she confirmed.

"Only ten seconds," he repeated, writing this down.

Joy gritted her teeth and pointedly looked at her wristwatch's second hand click down ten seconds. Dr Evans looked annoyed at the antics. "Time seems to slow when you're waiting for something to end," she quipped.

"In relation to the incident at work, what did you expect your employer to do?" he asked.

Now that was a loaded question. Joy took a deep breath and thought carefully about how to phrase the response to keep it brief. "To ensure the woman who threatened my life was kept away from me as an occupational health and safety imperative. To be impartial in the court case, not support Mrs Bryant to get off assault charges by supplying a good character reference."

Compulsively, she didn't stop at that but instead continued to rant about how the department had continued to betray her throughout the workers compensation process. "In the research I've been doing, it's called *moral betrayal*. They say PTSD resulting from moral betrayal is harder to recover from, as well." Joy sniffed into her handkerchief.

Dr Evans smirked. "Another name for it is *moral embitterment*."

The twist in meaning wasn't lost on Joy. Words were so important.

"Why did you believe your life was in danger?" Dr Evans probed.

This question angered Joy. He'd read the report. "When Mrs Bryant came up from behind and placed both her hands around my throat and squeezed tightly cutting off my breathing, she also had her face to my ear telling me she was strangling me. The definition of strangling is to *choke to death*. So, at the time she was saying, *I am strangling you,* she was saying to me *I am going to kill you.*"

What part of *choke to death* didn't he understand?

Taking in his neutral expression, she continued to over explain. "She said strangle and I believed her. I had to pry her hands from my throat. She didn't do that voluntarily. There was no prior warning she was going to do it. I was caught completely by surprise, trapped in my chair. And afterwards, despite everyone now trying to convince me she was joking, she wasn't laughing or acting like it was funny. She looked bewildered and out of it – like a crazy woman." The memory brought back the original terror. Tears pooled in the corners of her eyes. She dabbed at them with a pink handkerchief.

"It wasn't only me she wanted to strangle that day. Everyone forgets Helen was the original target. That's why Mrs Bryant is dangerous."

"Have you experienced other situations that felt traumatic or life threatening?" he asked.

She knew full well what he was referring to. "I had breast cancer five years ago. It was the main reason I moved to Eden Isle, to be closer to my family."

As Dr Evans scratched a note, Joy felt compelled to explain the difference in the two traumas that affected her life.

"With breast cancer it is true I was also confronted with my mortality. The experience was very different, however. The diagnosis was a shock and a surprise but it wasn't sudden. I had lots of sympathy and support – no one questioned the diagnosis, or trivialised its impact on me or my family. No one questioned my symptoms as if I was faking or over reacting. No one treated it like it was a joke! Decisions regarding my treatment were under my control. My medical team listened to me. There was general consensus about the medical protocols for treating it." She stopped to take a sip of mineral water.

With nervous tension threatening to erupt into tears, she resumed. "Being strangled was an immediate threat to my life – not something months or years away. It was happening up close and personal right then – it was a total shock, out of my control, unnatural, by an outside agent – I didn't know how to process what happened! To make matters worse, there's not a consensus about how to treat it. Despite PTSD being a medical diagnosis, it's not well understood and therefore I get less support. I feel I need to explain and justify myself all the time. People see it as a mental illness that's my fault, as if it's all in my head and I'm the one who needs to get my head right. Not that the treatment isn't working. This is what messes with my mind."

"Would you say your cancer is in remission?" Dr Evans cut in pointedly. She was being too wordy.

"Actually, I think I'm cured. It's been five years and at my last checkup I was given the all clear. It was a relief because I wasn't able to take Tamoxifen which was meant to give me a better chance of survival."

"Why couldn't you take Tamoxifen?"

She kicked herself for elaborating. Too late. Press on.

"It was weird, but when I took it, about half an hour later I'd start weeping inconsolably and couldn't stop. It was impossible to work and take the meds. After being off work with chemotherapy for four months, I had twenty-seven cents left in the bank. I had to go back to work."

"You must have been one of those hormonal women," Dr Evans commented, jotting down another note.

Joy pulled back, reminded this man was not on her side. "Well, if that had been the case, my *hormones* never affected my work life over a successful career that spanned decades."

She began to wonder what any of this conversation about past events had to do with PTSD and the WPI scale Marcus had talked about. Remembering the list in the plastic sleeve, she picked it up and slid it across the polished desk.

"I've compiled dot points to do with my PTSD symptoms along with some specific instances that support what I'm trying to say about the effects and impact it's had on my life. My CV is attached to demonstrate there are no gaps in my employment history – until I was strangled by my boss, I had a strong work ethic."

Dr Evans slid the sleeve under the notepad with a bemused look. "You're an interesting person, Joy."

Great, she thought. *Now I'm an interesting person, like when you return from a disastrous holiday, and you tell everyone it was memorable. Doc Martin is going to give me the longest lecture about following his instructions after this*, she sighed. Too late. The damage was done.

Dr Evans squared his notes and placed two pens on top of the pad aligned exactly at ninety degrees. "That's all I need for now," he said, officially ending what had turned out to be a two-hour interview.

He walked Joy out of the room and down the corridor. Her head was spinning and she felt like fainting from stress.

"What are your plans for the rest of the day? Will you do some shopping in Plover Point?" Dr Evans asked, sounding friendly and sociable, now that the interrogation was over.

Caught off guard, she answered honestly. "I'm finding there's too much traffic and noise. The busyness of town elevates my anxiety. All I have energy to do is find a quiet spot to have breakfast and calm down enough to drive home."

Luckily, that was a good answer. It would be added to his notes, unbeknownst to her.

The truth was, after leaving the Chambers, she ran to a nearby public toilet block and hid in a cubicle crying her eyes out from the stress of it all.

Chapter Fifty Nine

An evening in early December, Gemma's backyard glowed with the warmth of red-hot coals in a fire pit dug into a patchy area of lawn located between a green garden shed and the side of a galvanised garage. Fairy lights were strung around a gnarled trunk of an old birch tree, giving it a festive facelift.

Joy inspected a camp table set up near the back door, nodding approval. Bright paper lanterns lit up bamboo dishes filled with prawn chips, a tub of homemade smoked oyster dip (Joy's contribution), a slow cooker filled with hot miso soup flavoured with seaweed strips and shitake mushrooms, alongside a plastic tureen of cherry punch spiked with sake. Environmentally friendly cardboard plates, bowls and cutlery were piled on one corner. Gemma had done a good job. She was a champion offering to host this party at her place.

Seated in wobbly chairs around the fire circle, family members, a few friends and a couple neighbours of Col and Honor's were rugged up with jumpers and throw rugs wrapped around their shoulders, their hands reaching towards the fire as if toasting them like marshmallows. The summer weather on the Isle didn't heat up until after Christmas.

Kodi arrived late carrying a platter of sushi, flippantly announcing in a voice that carried across the garden, "I looked everywhere but couldn't find wild dolphin sashimi caught by Japanese research trawlers at the shops. I had to settle for commercially farmed salmon." Before placing her plate in the centre of the table, she dramatically sighed, making a point about what she saw as her parent's politically incorrect trip to Japan.

Seated next to an amused Col, Honor harrumphed.

Joy hoped Kodi's sarcasm shifted the angst out of her system and wouldn't put a damper on the family get-together. It was a farewell dinner party for her niece's parents, meant to be a celebration after all. How lucky could they be buying the winning ticket in a Rotary Club raffle which was an all-expenses paid holiday staying with a Rotary exchange family in Okinawa for a week.

Honor seemed to take it in her stride, as if it was no big deal.

Col, more excited, held a Japanese for Dummies' Guidebook to his nose, busily swatting up on tourist phrases in Japanese despite the dim light.

Honor rolled her eyes. "They'll speak English, dear," she insisted.

"Sayonara origami," he said in reply, making light of his wife's assurances.

Kodi settled onto a stool next to her parents. "What am I going to do while you're away," she grumbled, making a point about being abandoned without so much as a *by your leave*. It wasn't as if Lachlan was in the picture and would keep her company.

"You can cope with takeaway for a week, child of my heart," Honor said sweetly, as if that was Kodi's concern.

"I'm sure pizza won't be a hardship," one of her neighbours quipped.

Joy noticed Gemma's smirk at the exchange. Deliberately positioned away from the crowd, Joy stood over a Japanese Hibachi barbeque, patiently grilling dozens of skewers of chicken yakitori. It was the only

Japanese main course she could find in her recipe books. She crossed fingers assessing quantities. Served with white rice, it should be enough to fill the hungry horde. There didn't seem to be any desserts in the cuisine, so Gemma improvised with a trifle made with lychees instead of peaches.

In the background, a champagne cork popped followed by spontaneous laughter. Turning around, she saw Jaxon weaving between chairs around the fire pit handing out plastic flutes and Honor's friend from the Johnnie Walkers spilling foaming champagne into each. Shouts of *Bon voyage!* filled the night.

"Jack-a-roo, could you bring a glass of champagne to the cook?" Joy yelled across. Dutifully, Jaxon complied. She smiled gratefully. In return, she handed him a cup of cherry fizz minus the sake. He grabbed a handful of prawn chips, stuffing them in his mouth all at once.

"Try the oyster dip. It's my specialty," Joy coaxed.

"Nah, I'm good," he replied before scooting off into the shadows.

Suddenly, out of nowhere haunting music began to play, sounding vaguely Asian with harps and high pitched flutes creating a distinctly new age atmosphere. Now that was trying a bit too hard to set a Japanese mood, Joy mused, imagining it was Gemma's idea. Probably from the natural therapy clinic's collection of meditation CDs. No one else seemed to mind from the sound of all the joking laughter and cross conversations going on. The evening was turning out to be a success.

The crowd, after helping themselves to seconds from the buffet and becoming mellow from good company, full tummies and alcoholic punch, one by one began to gush their well wishes for a safe trip and make their excuses before heading home. Joy was secretly pleased the evening ended reasonably early.

Gemma declined her offer to help with the clean-up. "It all goes into a garbage bag, mum. No big deal," she insisted. "Anyway, Kodi is staying the night. Between her and Jaxon, we'll be fine."

For once, Joy didn't argue, not being a party animal like BTS. She became tired quickly and couldn't take too much fun and frivolity nowadays. Driving on country back roads at night caused too much anxiety and so, she'd come with Col and Honor in their Maxima. They'd drop her home. No trouble.

The back seat of the Maxima was comfy and the droning vibrations from the corrugated dirt road created an almost hypnotic calm that settled through Joy's limp body. Gazing out the window, scrubby tea tree bushes and wattles lined either side of the road, with an occasional white gum, its white bark reflecting the high beam of Col's car like a ghostly spectre arising out of the gloom. They drove for kilometres of sameness.

Born and bred a city person, Joy needed streetlamps and reassuring road signs to feel secure in her place in the world. The moonless, pitch-black night and repetitive landscape transformed the road from Gemma's into something unfamiliar and disorientating. A stark clarity of isolation and aloneness overwhelmed her sense of comfortable knowingness. She began to worry Col had missed the turnoff to the township of Lower Teasel, stirring up an irrational PTSD anxiety. This happened when she was tired.

Obsessing, she wondered what would happen if a kangaroo leapt in front of Col's car. She'd heard stories. One urban myth told of an unlucky traveller whose car hit a roo on an outback track. Its body flew through his windscreen still kicking, killing him in a final act of revenge.

A country road in the middle of the night was nowhere to be lost or broken down on the side of the road.

The Maxima bumped and slid along the dirt track at a safe but mesmerising pace, endless sameness. Joy wondered if they should turn back to Gemma's, stay for the night. Rounding a bend, suddenly Col braked and slowed right down. Through the windscreen, Joy saw a ball of grey fur on four legs running down the middle of the road.

"A possum," Honor exclaimed. "Don't run it over," she commanded, as if Col would do such a thing.

Sure enough, a possum scampered with determination, head down, tail up in defiance of the car coming towards it. Col kept braking and slowing down more and more, following the possum, waiting for it to veer off into the scrub.

"You'd think the headlights would have scared it off," Col huffed, getting impatient.

But no. The car crawled along at a snail's pace and the possum kept sprinting as fast as its little legs would carry it – right smack in the middle of the dirt track. After several minutes, they realised it had no intention of moving aside to let them pass despite being in the glare of the spotlight.

In the front passenger seat, Honor hissed, "Go on, get off," while making sweeping motions with her hands. As if that made a difference.

No. It asserted its entitlements, its equal worthiness, to belong on this road without interference or intimidation. The pint size demon forced Col to continually brake and slow ever more. Most annoying.

Obviously for the possum as well, because after a bothersome eternity, the critter finally decided enough was enough. One of them had to give in first in this game of chicken. It abruptly halted its mad dash.

And turned to face the car – head on. The possum rose up on its hind legs to its full height – about the size of an Aussie football – faced the Maxima with raised claws in a gesture of menace and hissed at them with all its fury.

"Game on," Col laughed as he brought the car to a stop.

"I don't believe it," Honor laughed, too. "Silly thing."

Here they were in a sedan exponentially larger in size and weight, an armoured machine indestructible in comparison, with the power to flatten the creature in seconds into an unrecognisable pulpy blip on the road.

And there it was, Joy thought with alarm and starstruck disbelief – a fierce creature standing up for itself against an all-powerful foe. Her hands went to her heart, witnessing the bravest gesture of defiance she'd ever witnessed in her life.

A tiny, fragile life form standing up against a machine that must have appeared like some mammoth predator stalking it for prey. What hope did it have to win against this unnatural beast?

In the spirit of a true-blue Aussie Anzac during the battle at Gallipoli, this noble possum did not back down. It hissed and postured, angry and defiant making a last stand, demonstrating an awesomeness of pure heroism in what could easily become a life and death situation.

Col kept his foot on the brake and revved the engine a couple times in a mock display of brute force, going along with the game.

Joy watched in fascination. In the face of inevitable defeat, with all the odds stacked against it, the little guy stood to its full height, demanded to be respected, an opponent worthy of being treated with dignity, and not just some insignificant dumb creature.

***

Back at home in the comfort of her own bed, before falling fast asleep, Joy's heart filled with awe and respect as she reflected on the little possum. Inspired by such a remarkable display of courage and heroism, she vowed, this was how she would face her own challenges ahead.

Chapter Sixty

Another quarterly Occupational Health & Safety Committee meeting was in session, as boring as usual. The only difference being Leland was not acting as the Chair this time and therefore proceedings were dragging on. In fact, Leland was a last-minute apology for the meeting, the cunning bastard. Why hadn't she thought to do that?

Fiona tapped a folder placed in front of the conference table. It was stuffed with regional reports from the mid north area under her control. Attempting one of Leland's tricks, looking calm, controlled, and interested, inwardly she willed the speaker holding the floor to finish her whinge. How much could a person say about the edges of anti-slip matting outside a few health facilities' sticking up and being tripping hazards. *Hadn't she heard of duct tape?*

Fiona must have drifted off because the next words to enter into her awareness were from the Chair thanking Derrick for his agenda item concerning a Worksafe Directive. It was her job to talk to it.

"Fiona, could you enlighten our meeting with a brief description of its substance?" The Chair turned with officious concern to stare at her.

"Thank you," she nodded with authority. "The directive Derrick is referring to originated from the Workers Compensation Tribunal in point of fact. It came to their attention, insurers and in-house workers compensation officers were booking in medical examinations as after hours appointments. This had become standard practice given the shortage of medical specialists available on Eden Isle. Our health system depends on visiting specialists from interstate and their schedules are heavily booked." Fiona paused to allow this justification to sink in before continuing. "The tribunal received a complaint from one employee but deemed it sufficient to send a memo to all providers covering new guidelines on the matter."

The Chair looked concerned. "What are the implications in terms of procedures and budgets?"

Playing to the audience, she rolled her eyes. "It's going to cost more and take up more of our officers' time arranging medical appointments." *Simple as that*, she thought. "This will also cause procedural delays in handling compensation matters, resulting in frustration for workers wanting their cases sorted quickly."

Committee members started mumbling to each other. Derrick piped up. "As a representative of the union, we are concerned about more delays in processing claims and the impact this will have on employees already suffering from stress."

Fiona had no sympathy. What did he expect her to do about it? It was a tribunal decision and out of her control.

The Chair took a pragmatic position. "More stress equates to higher payout figures," he stated rather bluntly. Again, murmurs travelled around the conference table.

"I've begun liaising with our workers compensation team and will work with them to find ways to alleviate the difficulties posed by the new directive. With cuts to our budgets already, it will not be feasible to package out employees with excessive payouts. I will instruct Personnel to use all their available resources to scrutinise the veracity of claimants' entitlements and act in the best interests of our department and state government."

Members nodded. This was what they wanted to hear. Fiona's reassurances imbued them with renewed loyalty to their role within the cause. Fiona smiled. Leland would be proud.

After the meeting, Leland wanted to catch up with her. Fiona's head was full of statistics and pie charts, and duct tape. All she wanted was to be left in peace with a strong coffee for ten minutes before having to think again. But no such luck.

Entering his office, Leland motioned her towards the seats around the table in the corner, a signal she was there for another long haul.

"How'd the meeting go?" he asked, perfunctorily, not really interested.

"The usual," Fiona said without elaborating.

"I've heard through official channels, there will be an election in March," Leland confided, as if divulging a serious piece of top-secret information.

Fiona shrugged. "Everyone expected this would be the case."

He frowned. "The review into the Isle's health service was submitted to Cabinet yesterday. It was disastrous. Looks bad for the Minister. Most likely scenario is our CEO will be sacked."

"Bearing the weight of blame," Fiona nodded pragmatically. "It will hit The Meridian news tonight. Anyone tipped for the job?" she asked, studying Leland carefully. Were his ambitions about to be realised?

He didn't take the bait. "We need to finalise Joy O'Connell's workers comp matter before it draws more attention with the press. We can't afford for the Minister to be put further in an embarrassing situation over the incident."

Fiona wanted to blurt that it would take as long as it needed to take to achieve the outcome in the best interests of the department. Better sense prevailed. This was about politics, not internal efficiencies.

"Dr Evans completed his psychiatric examination. He hasn't let us down." She handed across a copy of the report. "Marcus Hammond, her current psychologist, is proving useful. He submitted a report helpful to Evans' assessment. He mentioned it was Joy that complained to the tribunal about after hours appointments causing all the fuss and resulting in that memo being issued."

"That woman is nothing but trouble," Leland mumbled as he skim read pages, flipping to the end and spending more time on the concluding statements, his main concern. "The sooner we shut her down..." He stopped with an intense interest in the report findings suddenly.

"Good. He's rated her WPI at seven percent. That's bloody brilliant. A Whole Person Impairment rated less than ten percent is below the section 71 threshold required for a psychological injury claim. Over twenty percent and we'd be looking at a case for negligence. That's where the real money kicks in." He grinned from ear to ear. "Talk to the insurer. See if they can stop her fortnightly payments altogether now."

Fiona knew it wasn't going to be this easy. Usually, a diagnosis of PTSD warranted a rating of at least ten percent. Dr Evans' report was brutal. It effectively denied Joy's legal entitlement to a lump sum payment in compensation for an injury sustained at work through a negligent manager. "Her lawyer will counter with a second opinion, using his own, more sympathetic psychiatrist. In good conscience, we can't make any drastic moves until we receive it." Feeling a momentary pang of guilt at the idea of stopping Joy's payments that she lived on, she added, "Evans agrees with the PTSD diagnosis and says Joy will probably never work again." *Again, never working again should have been ten percent in its own right.*

He frowned, not happy with Fiona arguing. "There's nothing stopping us offering her a nominal payout to quit. Try twenty thousand, saying it's based on Evans' not finding any significant impairment. Make it a "once and for all" basis for all her entitlements with no chance to make a future claim for injury. You never know your luck – she might get spooked enough to accept." Leland gazed at the painting of black and orange blotches, lost in thought.

Fiona knew that look. His mind was formulating a winning strategy.

"If that doesn't work, you know the routine," he stated matter-of-factly.

She grimaced. He referred to a strategy known as *weaponising the victim*. This involved a type of character assassination: inferring Joy was a liar, faking her symptoms, attempting to scam the system, and ultimately leading to a motion to dismiss her claim at the tribunal. It was all too easy to do with employees on workers compensation particularly those on stress-related claims. It didn't take long to push them to the edge, forcing them to quit long before it reached the tribunal.

In fact, Dr Evans' report was the first step in their weaponising strategy.

Chapter Sixty One

Joy fidgeted in the chair next to Dr Vitkay's desk. He concentrated on opening her medical file on a personal computer while at the same time asking the routine *how are you* question. She didn't want to answer by going off onto a predictable tangent, rattling off her symptoms and summarising how she was coping with PTSD. Yesterday's telephone call from John Emerson was on her mind. She wanted some answers.

John had advised that Dr Evans' assessment of her whole person impairment had come through with a rating of seven percent. This was hard to believe. The strangling had upended her life to such a degree she didn't know who she was, and some arbitrary rating system decided ninety-three percent of her old self was left intact. Well, it felt like eighty percent of her life had diminished. It was a set up. They were rating the wrong things!

Guilt at letting her lawyer down chewed up her gut. She'd talked too much during the psychiatric examination, mistakenly believing if Dr Evans knew her life story, he would see her as a human being and not simply an insurance claimant. As a result of her naivety, her fortnightly payments were in jeopardy, along with any hope of a lump sum compensation payout for the injury Poppy had caused. What was she going to live on for the next nine years before she could access a pension?

Why did they bother pretending a medical examination was objective and ethical when it was basically an interrogation designed for failure? To *erode the evidence*, John had warned. She'd never work again and yet according to *Dr Evil* this equated to only seven percent of her life. She wondered, if Dr Evil was in the same position, never being able to practise psychiatry again, would he rate himself with such a low score when his identity and sense of self-worth had been choked off so carelessly?

Of course, John had cut her off mid-whinge, not interested in her *feelings*. There was no time for Joy to debrief about the unfairness of the system. She had to focus on the business at hand. John was unconcerned about the rating. It was anticipated and part of the department's strategy in a protracted negotiation process just getting started. He'd seek a second opinion on Joy's WPI from a more sympathetic psychiatrist. An appointment would be made sometime in the new year.

In the meantime, she was to sit.tight and let him do his job. In other words, *trust him*. There would probably be a letter arriving in the post offering a minimal payout in accordance with the seven percent WPI assessment couched as an "Once and Final Offer." Joy was to ignore it. Her only job was to secure another medical certificate from the GP.

And here she was.

Dr Vitkay smiled in that kind, but tired way busy doctors all seem to convey. Joy's sessions were intense and always took more time than the standard fifteen minutes. At least at this appointment, Michelle was a no show. She'd texted her cancellation while Joy was in the waiting room. In some ways, this was a relief. There wouldn't be a need for Dr Vitkay to justify his decisions to the insurer, this time at least.

Impatience getting the better of her, Joy confronted her GP. "Have you received Dr Evans' psychiatric assessment of me?" she asked, more bluntly than intended. Receiving a sympathetic nod, she demanded, "What does it say?"

Clicking a mouse, Dr Vitkay opened a document and began to scan its contents. Talking to the screen, he said, "Dr Evans agrees with my diagnosis of Post Traumatic Stress Disorder." Quoting from the report, he selected a relevant passage and read out, *'Ms O'Connell described sufficient symptoms to meet the diagnostic criteria for PTSD'*. He looked up with an expression of professional vindication and kindness.

From internet sources, Joy understood a diagnosis of PSTD generally scored at least ten percent on WPI assessments. Dr Evil showed his true bias, the traitor.

"What does it say about my returning to work?" she asked anxiously.

He scrolled through the document, snatching phrases to read out: *'prospects of her returning to paid employment are poor... resistant to changing her attitude that the workplace is unsafe... if not for her post traumatic bitterness she could have recovered enough by now to return to employment in some capacity... it seems unlikely that any action taken by the employer could allay her concerns.'*

He scrolled through more pages but didn't add anything more.

Joy contemplated the statements, on one hand reassured she wouldn't be forced to return to work but disturbed on the other hand at how her comment to Dr Evil about the system inflicting moral injury on top of her PTSD was warped and twisted into a statement about her *bitterness* preventing this return to work.

"He makes it sound like I'm the one to blame. There was a lot the department could have done to make me feel safe. If they'd taken my word over my boss's and acted as if she was the crazy one instead of me that would have been a good start. Instead they've chosen to gaslight me, re-defining reality, trying their hardest to convince me that strangling a person is somehow a joke."

"This was wrong of them," Dr Vitkay agreed, but then added, "Dr Evans believed it was unlikely you were in imminent danger. He states there was no malicious intent on the part of Mrs Bryant."

Joy shook her head in resignation. "What I can't understand is how all these other people claim to know what she intended to do. Isn't it strange how all these people formed opinions based on secondhand comments after the fact and yet, won't believe my firsthand account of the event despite the fact I was the only other person actually there! And I had no reason to lie about what happened."

Dr Vitkay concentrated on skimming through the report. Holding up a finger, he began to read: '*even though Ms O'Connell believed her life was at risk during the incident, from an objective view, the trauma described does not clearly qualify for an index trauma, that is, a situation in which an individual fears death or serious injury*'.

"What's this trauma index he's referring to?" Joy's voice quaked from angry disbelief.

Dr Vitkay shook his head. "I've never heard of it."

"Then tell me, how can a psychiatrist – with medical training – state strangulation is not life threatening? This is the sort of stuff that messes with my mind. He's implying my traumatic response was an overreaction. What would be a normal reaction to being strangled?"

He grunted an acknowledgement but continued to scan the report.

Joy continued an emotional rant. "I mean, if I started strangling you right this minute, how would you react? Would it make any difference if I laughed afterwards? I'm sure everyone would call me the looney, not get to work trying to convince you to believe a different version of reality!"

Dr Vitkay was concentrating and therefore not willing to engage in a discussion. After a long pause, he pointed to the screen. "Here it is. '*The approach to treatment described by Mr Marcus Harmond appears to be reasonable. Given Ms O'Connell's progress to date, at least a further ten to fifteen sessions of psychotherapy over the next six to twelve months – along with antidepressant treatment and possible alternative medications – is recommended. Exposure based therapy is the gold standard in the treatment of PTSD.*' That's what I wanted to tell you." He gave Joy a satisfied smile.

Joy picked up on one phrase with alarm. "Alternative medications?"

"Ignore that," he said, quick to dismiss it. With a frown, he explained the report suggested she be referred to a consulting psychiatrist for the management of her PTSD because to date, she'd responded to therapies and pharmacological treatment with partial success. Dr Evans believed she'd benefit from a trial of alternative antidepressants and antipsychotic drugs to see which ones would be the most effective and best tolerated.

"I'm not depressed," Joy interjected. "And I'm not going to put any more drugs into my system that mess with my brain."

He shook his head and offered reassurance. "To me, Dr Evans' advice seems rather extreme... and unnecessary. There is a lot in this report... that is written for the insurer." Pulling out a form, he began to fill in another medical certificate, signalling her time was up. As he scratched a signature, he said, "What I'd like is for you to continue seeing Marcus on a fortnightly basis. This will help and it is all you need in my professional judgement."

Joy thought Dr Vitkay placed more faith in Marcus than was warranted. However, she wasn't going to be openly disagreeable when her doctor was clearly showing his support and not blindly siding with the specialist. She could tolerate Marcus as a counsellor. At any rate, there wasn't anyone else she could have a good and proper whinge with. However, being the person she was – who couldn't quite let go once a point needed to be made –

she had one last stab about strangulation, forcing Dr Vitkay to express his personal opinion.

"Do you agree with Dr Evans that my being strangled was not a life-threatening incident?"

Dr Vitkay faced her with solemn regard. "Dr Evans is wrong to say this in his report. He is misinformed. Maybe it would be therapeutic for you to correct this misunderstanding?"

Taken aback at Dr Vitkay's honesty, Joy winced. "My lawyer says I don't have a right of reply."

"What stops you writing a letter? You feel strongly about it. This is good."

This was the first time her GP had hinted his disapproval at her treatment under the workers compensation system. He was backing her. For the first time in many months, her feet felt on solid ground, as if honesty, goodness and the truth existed in a few decent people. And she was being supported to make a stand. She wasn't so crazy after all.

"Could I have a copy of the report?" she asked, thinking it would be useful when responding to Dr Evil's ill-conceived opinions.

Dr Vitkay's momentary hesitation told Joy enough. He was willing to defy the system only so far. There were things in the report she was not meant to see.

"I'm thinking about sending him a response," she prompted.

"Okay, sure," he said at last, punching the print button.

Joy held her breath and waited as twenty pages pumped out of his desktop Brother printer. Only when the pages were in her hands, and she was sitting safely in her car did she breathe deeply again.

Chapter Sixty Two

Joy returned home from the doctor's anxious to study Dr Evan's assessment determined to remain analytical and intellectual while prepared for the worst. Dr Vitkay had taken a risk handing over a copy of the report. She wanted to prove he'd done the right thing. His blessing of encouragement would act as a talisman, keeping her focused on what was important.

She kicked off her shoes and dumped her handbag in the hallway and wandered into the master bedroom. Curling up on the scarlet oriental quilt on her bed and puffing up two pillows to use as a backrest, she flicked through the report, scanning its bold black headings getting a feel for its structure. Cool headed, she began to concentrate on reading its content.

First impressions were not too damning. A lot of Dr Evans' commentary on her family relationships and work history followed what she'd told him almost verbatim. Although describing her as *'an overweight fifty six year old woman with a purple rinse'*... well, maybe it was factual... Was size fourteen overweight? The wording was unfortunate. He made her seem like an old frump. She swallowed the insult along with her pride, refusing to be baited.

His comment '*Ms O'Connell was over inclusive at times and required redirecting*' – well, that was just mean spirited when he'd asked general, open-ended questions that made it hard to be specific. Joy desperately hoped John Emerson wouldn't react too badly reading that she'd ignored his advice about being circumspect.

After a few minutes, she reached for a pen in the top drawer of the bedside table and began underlying controversial sentences and errors in the facts, as well as scribbling notes in the margins of the report.

The first shock came when she saw the list of documentation supplied by her employer that Dr Evans had referenced in preparation for the examination. Everything starting from the original workers compensation claim and first medical certificate, her incident report and grievance, through to psychological reports from Bev, Return to Work Plans from Michelle, and a surprise report from Jane Manners describing a performance review when Joy had mentioned breast cancer (when had they talked about that? Joy had no recollection), all Dr Vitkay's medical certificates with details of medical treatments and therapies, and a letter from Dr Sasha giving her two cents worth of professional opinion about Joy. What could that woman possibly contribute towards the assessment?

Probably the biggest surprise was seeing Marcus listed as supplying a psychological report a week before the examination. Interesting how he'd failed to mention that small detail to her during their previous session.

Quickly turning pages, she found the paragraph describing the contents of Marcus' psych report. He stated that she'd made minimal progress since he'd become involved in her treatment. He planned to provide at least eight sessions of therapy to desensitise her memory and improve her emotional resilience and confidence. This included CBT, exposure-based therapy and EMDR. Joy had shown reluctance to cooperate with the proposed treatment plan, insisting on unproven techniques: Ecotherapy, mindfulness and regular exercise, believing these would better address her needs. Her beliefs and her symptoms consistent with a PTSD diagnosis remained entrenched.

So, this was how *Mr Please Trust Me* paid her back for refusing EMDR therapy. How could his opinion even count as he'd only seen her a couple of times so far? Joy decided to have a few words with him at their next meeting.

Likewise, Dr Sasha had seen her only once for all of twenty minutes, most of which was Joy having a hysterical panic attack, and yet she saw fit to write a damning assessment stating Joy was uncooperative. She wasn't even her usual GP. Her short, abrupt letter was obviously written out of spite.

In disbelief, Joy read out loud: *'an attempt was made to discuss a gradual return to work plan with Ms O'Connell. She reacted with profound reluctance to follow such a plan. Therefore, it became difficult to manage her case appropriately'.*

"What a liar!" Joy gasped, into her empty bedroom.

The enormity of the massive betrayal from all these people she'd trusted during a period when she wasn't coping with life and needed help in figuring out what had happened to her – they'd all colluded behind her back, siding with her employer. Her counsellors, rehabilitation coordinator, medical practitioners – It was too much to process. She stared at the papers with cold disbelief.

Throughout all the counselling sessions and medical appointments, when Joy had poured out her mixed up, messed up feelings, bared her vulnerabilities, confided heartfelt confessions, she was fooled into relying on professional confidentiality. They'd lead her to believe she was safe and could trust them; that they cared and supported her journey to recovery.

Each one had covered up the real agenda concerning their 'support'. It had never been completely about rehabilitating her. Their ethical and professional role was compromised by a primary function to gather information to report back to her employer. Not in a factually correct and objective way either, but in a professional code that skewed Joy's half-baked thoughts and haphazard words to suit a purpose – to collude in a deception that enabled it to be used against her. *To erode the evidence* in order to limit her employer's liability.

Compounding the betrayal was the realisation that throughout the whole process, from the very beginning, not one of them had explained directly and up front that their sessions were not private and confidential. No one told her that reports would be written without her permission.

No one explained how the rules had changed because it was workers compensation. No one gave her the courtesy of mentioning their discussions were the property of her employer.

And this ownership allowed the material to be passed on to third parties – expert witnesses, their lawyer, her lawyer, the insurer, the tribunal... Who knows how many others were allowed to read these reports about her personal life and her mental health issues without her permission. The scope of the invasion of her privacy was overwhelming.

To Joy it seemed that these therapeutic sessions were treated with the flippancy of gossip. She'd been like some naïve teenager confiding in her friends and gleefully they'd passed on all her private thoughts behind her back.

She should have known better. They'd played her like a fool.

Pulling herself together, she struggled to race through the remaining pages of the report, although her vision blurred, and her heart thumped in synchronised accord.

Dr Vitkay had been careful in paraphrasing the final recommendations. What Dr Evans had said was: '*Given Ms O'Connell's limited response to the SSRI, fluoxetine, a conventional antidepressant, it would be appropriate to refer her to a consultant psychiatrist for management. There are a number of alternative antidepressants, atypical antipsychotics and anticonvulsants that may be of benefit in managing PTSD. A degree of trial and error is likely to be required to establish a medication regimen that is effective.*'

The shock of his actual words caused Joy to sit up ramrod straight, with her feet firmly on the floor. *Anticonvulsants?*

"Oh my god," Joy cried out. If she didn't improve, the mad doctor wanted to experiment on her with a cocktail of different antipsychotic drugs. It was a thinly veiled threat embedded in medical-speak, warning her of their power over her life. She must remain quiet and compliant. Or he could turn her into a numb and dumb zombie with a stroke of a signature on a prescription pad. He held the strings that decided whether to section her to an institution. All on behalf of her employer as part of workers compensation.

She was caught within a powerful system able to control a narrative through denial, trivialisation, and the redefining of reality. They had the ability to turn violence into a joke – as if by magic. Wave a wand and turn her into crazy. By the stroke of a pen, drug her and commit her to an institution.

Joy was struck with a realisation: throughout this process, she hadn't been a person. She'd been something less: a claimant, a victim of the system. Silenced. Dehumanised. Someone who's story must not be told.

And in her naivety, unknowingly, she'd been recalcitrant, waving her arms around drawing attention, speaking out as if she had rights and was an equal in the process. How stupid could a person be? She was a threat, a problem, and needed to be shut up. And shut away.

The truth was that she was disempowered and devoid of basic rights – apart from those conferred by the all-powerful department. What the department could give, it could take away. At this time, her life was not her own.

Her department was not any employer; it was the Department of *Health*. The sole arbitrator of her mental state.

Now that was ironic.

This understanding was terrifying. Joy sat up on the edge of the bed and sucked in air as if she was choking. Refusing to cry, she resolved to reject their threats and intimidation.

PTSD did not make her less than any other person.

Recovering was now the lesser of her worries. The fight had changed; it was not about healing from trauma. It was a fight for survival of her autonomy, a basic human right.

The need for vindication overpowered all other needs.

Joy tossed the report on the bed, scattering its pages across the quilt like blood splatter. Her head pounded with a restless build up of energy needing to vent. There was so much Dr Evans needed to hear, but her mind was in turmoil. In order to think clearly, she had to move, to run, to escape the confines of the house.

Twisting too quickly, her elbow knocked a book off the bedside table. Dr Fellowes' book on mindfulness had fallen askew onto the carpet.

Staring at the book as if it were a sign, Joy took in deep breaths desperate to invoke inner peace.

Since Honor had been away on her Japanese holiday, Joy had neglected to go for a walk or practice mindfulness. Her sister's voice in lecture mode arose from her subconscious. *The best therapy is going for a walk.*

This was something she could do in the here and now. Walk off her distress and find a quiet spot by the brook to attune with nature. Picking up Honor's book, she smoothed its dog-eared pages and decided to take it with her as a talisman of sanity and protection.

Chapter Sixty Three

At the doctor's surgery, waiting for an appointment with Marcus, Joy flicked through a Christmas edition of Better Homes and Garden magazine, not caring it was last year's but hoping for inspiration. Christmas was next week, and she wasn't prepared. Her heroic sister had offered to host a Christmas barbeque lunch at her place, despite her and Col arriving back from Japan a few days ago. Apparently Honor never suffered from jetlag.

Gemma insisted they all bring something to share and nominated her mum as the hors d'oeuvres queen thinking she was doing a favour. Joy hated fiddling and fussing with miniature smoked salmon blinis and cocktail meatballs. *Just bring a cheese platter*, Gemma had insisted. Joy wanted her contribution to be a bit more upmarket than that.

Turning a page to a full colour spread of pre-dinner delicacies, a table centrepiece caught her attention. It was a wreath made out of red cocktail onions, fresh green basil, creamy white baby bocconcini balls and sliced salami, with a tea light candle glowing in the middle. Excited, she began to read the recipe instructions. In the background, her name was being called softly at first – which she ignored – then with more volume.

Sighing, she resisted an urge to tear out the page and pocket it. Instead, she tossed the magazine onto a pile in the corner and followed Marcus down the corridor to the consulting room. His summer fashion statement varied slightly from his winter look, being a short sleeve business shirt, a tie, and a lightweight knitted vest over matching, saggy trousers. He waited at the door, beckoning her in like a true gentleman. For some reason, this raised her feminist hackles. The man couldn't do anything right.

"How are you, Joy? Are you looking forward to Christmas?" He'd seen her with the magazine.

Joy wasn't in the mood to pass pleasantries. She'd come prepared with a list of dot points. "I'm not too good at all," she announced with a glare of defiance, pleased to see Marcus' surprise. "As you know, a few weeks ago I saw Dr Evans for a medical assessment--"

Marcus cut in. "Right, how did that go?" He leaned forward in a paternal manner.

As if he cared. "Well, I found out that you provided a report on my progress without my permission. I was under the impression our counselling sessions were private and confidential. Why didn't you tell me?"

Marcus smiled. "Here, let me read out what I wrote. I don't want there to be any secrets between us." He turned to his laptop, opened a document and with a flourish of largesse selected a few paragraphs to read to Joy.

"I know how to write medico-legal reports using their language," he bragged, taking her into his confidence. "For example, when I wrote '*it is my personal belief you will be able to return to work*' this is a subjective comment that doesn't hold much weight. Using a phrase like '*objectively your symptoms are consistent with a diagnosis of PTSD*' means it is based more on medical science and will be taken more seriously. Anything like 'in my opinion', 'it is my belief', phrases like that are report fillers to make it appear as if I've written something substantial."

"But why did you tell them I could eventually return to work when we agreed from the start that you would not send me back?" Joy's voice came out as a high-pitched squeak.

He returned a puzzled expression, as if surprised at her lack of admiration. "Well, most of the report lists all your PTSD symptoms and how various therapies haven't worked so far which wasn't good news. And let's face it, Joy, you're not the easiest client to deal with. I had to say something positive."

That was his justification for selling her out. *He had to write something positive.* Joy had no response. Shaking from nerves, she moved on to the next dot point on the list.

"Dr Evans wrote *'from an objective point of view'* my being strangled was not a life-threatening incident. As a doctor, how can he say something so blatantly untrue?"

Marcus nodded in understanding. "Yeah, well, he's playing the game. It will be up to your lawyer to find another expert to dispute the facts of the matter. One expert's word against another's when it goes to the tribunal for a decision. The rules of evidence in tribunal matters are not as rigorous as in courts of law." He smiled kindly.

Joy wanted to burst into tears. It was all a game to them.

"It's how the system works. It's the same for everyone. Don't take it personally," he said gently.

His words of wisdom offered little comfort. Maybe it wasn't a big deal to him, and every other person on workers comp was a victim of the system the same as she was – to Marcus that might explain things, but it didn't make it right to treat people like this.

Joy was in a fighting mood. "It's not *personal*? It's all some sort of game! As if that makes it easier to take – or morally right," she spluttered with contempt. "As if that is even a true statement. Of course, it's personal. People, not computers or machines, are writing up reports, making decisions supposedly based on their *personal* expertise. I'm more frightened of my medical team and the authority they possess to inflict damage than I am of Poppy, and that is saying something.

"It's *not personal* is your way of justifying their lack of empathy and compassion, as if I'm the one screwed up and not these people devoid of humanity. I do not know how to reach them to convince them of my pain and agony over what happened. It's an evil thing to do to a person, treating me like a big nothing. *It's not personal to them* because they are soulless."

Catching her breath for a moment, she shook her head warning Marcus not to stop her rant. "You sit there and tell me I am not a person in this process. That indicates it is dehumanising. And I'm supposed to simply accept it. *Don't take your dehumanising personally.* Nice one. As if."

Marcus looked perplexed at her lack of acceptance. This was the way things were. "Joy, if your viewpoints are not helping you get better then let's explore what needs to change in your thinking."

He made it sound like a perfectly rational suggestion. As if Joy was in fact in control of her life and actually had choices instead of being caught in a system that persisted in negating reality.

"How do you suggest I work that delusionary magic trick to transform a psycho boss into a jolly, benign larrikin and an unsafe workplace into neutral ground? What crafty counselling rabbit can you pull out of the hat, Marcus, to make that disappear?

"Why not be honest instead of pretending I'm in therapy when in truth, I'm in a mind controlling, brainwashing, gaslighting *game*. One where they hold all the winning cards because they've neglected to tell me the rules;

I've been kept in the dark, isolated, silenced, nothing I say matters, I'm not sure who I can trust--"

"--Joy, don't you trust me?" Marcus sounded hurt.

"--because it's their agenda, their politics. They won't hear anything outside of this. I can't appeal to their better nature, their hearts, or even their knowledge of right or wrong, truth versus lies, morality or basic human decency," Joy continued, "because these don't fit into their agenda. These concepts are not relevant – that is the nature of evil. It is frightening. I can't even say I'm at their mercy because mercy is a human quality and the game is impersonal. I'm the only one in this *game* that has everything to lose."

"Like?" Marcus prompted in his best counselling tone.

Joy stared at him. As if it wasn't obvious what was at stake. "Like my mental health, who I am as a person, my financial future! They could force me into early retirement and poverty."

By this time, her emotions were running out of control. "I'm starting to hate all this! All these people who treat me as a big nothing! You know what? I totally get why there are mass shootings, if people have these experiences and are broken by the system. Life begins to seem pointless, and no one gives a shit about you or anyone else. Why should I give a shit about anyone else either? It becomes easy to see everyone as the enemy; they are either deliberately and actively against you, or simply some anonymous participant in a system that crushes you; people who go along with the cruelty, colluding in it... it's the same logic as a mass shooter – it's not meant to be personal! That's their message." Joy slumped, out of steam and defeated.

Marcus waited a brief moment before asking, "Are you telling me you're planning a mass shooting?" He laughed at the jest. "Do you need a hug? I want to give you a hug," he said.

The inappropriateness of the comment stirred up Joy again. "And that's another thing. Before hugging me, my grandson always asks *do you want a hug?*. He's only nine years old and he understands it is unacceptable to physically impose himself on another person without their permission. If he knows this, how could a mature sixty two year old manager not possess as much self-control?" Joy dared Marcus to interrupt with an inane comment. He remained silent.

"If for the sake of argument, Poppy felt the need for a stress release and she wanted to get physical with me in order to feel better, how hard would it have been for her to ask my permission?"

Marcus replied, "Not very hard."

"Right. All she had to say was *do you want a strangling, Joy?* I would have told her '*No, but thanks for asking.*' She would have left my office to go off and ask someone else. See how easy that was; she only needed to ask."

Marcus burst out laughing. More seriously, he speculated. "I wonder, had a man strangled you would your employer have handled the situation differently?"

"Like it's only funny if it's a woman on woman act of violence," Joy mocked.

Marcus winced, aware of the political incorrectness of his comment.

Joy frowned, deadly serious. "I'm going to prove to Dr Evans that strangling is not a joke, it is life threatening, it was a crime and what he said was professionally unethical and medically incorrect. He needs to be disbarred, or de-registered or whatever they do to doctors."

Marcus held his hands out as if stopping a charging bull. "That sounds like a plan," he said. "I applaud your drive. How are you going about it?"

"I'm going to do some research and then I'll set it out in a letter." Before Marcus could agree or disagree, Joy added, "I know you're going to say: this is not a smart move and I should leave it to the experts. But I've decided not to play by the rules. I don't care anymore."

Marcus shook his head. "I'm not arguing with you, Joy. If you feel this is something you need to do--"

"--It's just that the guy freaked me out. In his report he recommended they experiment on me with a cocktail of antipsychotic and anticonvulsant drugs using the excuse a psychiatrist needed to *manage* me. How intimidating is that – threatening to drug me to a point where they turn me into a submissive, drooling zombie!" Marcus chuckled in the background. Joy ignored him. "He also recommended exposure-based therapy, saying it was a *gold standard* in treating PTSD. But he doesn't know what he's talking about – this is completely the wrong treatment for me."

"How so?" Marcus asked, having recommended the very same in his treatment plan.

"I liken it to forcing an abused wife to keep seeing her ex-husband, trying to convince her that the more she's exposed to him, the more she'll see him like everyone else does. *He's a really nice guy with a great sense of humour. As if!*" she scoffed.

Marcus looked puzzled momentarily. "Oh, I see what you mean," he said eventually.

Joy referred to her notes. "Apparently, unless I shift my cognitive schemas there's no chance I'll improve. What is a cognitive schema and which ones do I have to change in order to get better?"

Marcus was on safer ground. "He's talking about the way you have framed your situation to make the department and the people trying to support you through your traumatic experience as the enemy out to get you. Your lack of faith in the system is a cognitive schema."

Joy nodded, thinking about this. "That's one thing he's got right. I'm happy with my cognitive schemas being the way they are. Don't even consider trying to change them," she said, smiling at Marcus for the first time during their session.

"You don't make things easy for me, Joy," Marcus quipped. "What am I going to do with you?"

Joy became thoughtful. "Sometimes I think all I need is empathy from all the people trying to fix me. I don't feel that has happened so far during this process."

Amused, Marcus said, "Naturally, you know better than your counsellors, Joy. Next time we meet, show me the research studies on treating PTSD with empathy so I'll know what to do."

Chapter Sixty Four

J oy balanced a bottle of Rose' under one arm while holding an hors d'oeuvres tray with both hands, shuffling very carefully up the brick pathway to Col and Honor's front door. Christmas carols wafted through the air from the back garden, along with a faint hint of smoke smelling like lighter fluid on charcoal. Jaxon opened the door before she knocked.

"Hurry, Granny. We've been waiting for you. My cousin Ryan is visiting from the A-C-T. Uncle Col's started the barbie," he prattled on with excitement. "What's that? It looks good. I'm starving, can I have some?"

"Let's ask your mum first, Jack-a-roo. Where is everybody?" Joy refused to be pressured. It was hard enough for her to get moving this morning, prepare a Christmas dish, and leave the safety of her home to attend a family crowd scene. As much as she loved her family, they were a noisy mob. She sighed knowing some things had to be endured. Duty called.

Jaxon led her through the family room and out the French doors to a barbeque patio area decorated with strings of gold tinsel and baubles in the shape of stars hanging off the pergola. A long table was set with gold rimmed China plates, sparkling wine glasses, and silver cutlery on a red and green tartan tablecloth. A CD of the Three Tenors sang operatic carols in the background.

Col saw her first and waved tongs in the air as a greeting. Joy smiled at his Father Christmas apron and red elf hat with a fluffy pom pom, tacky as. Honor jumped out of a patio chair with a shriek of joy, elegantly dressed in white capri pants and a soft flowing scarlet silk blouse.

Joy's flashing candy cane earrings, India-inspired, green tiered skirt and red t-shirt fit somewhere in between Honor and Col's style continuum. On a bench in a corner of the garden, Kodi, her brother Ryan, and Gemma were locked in conversation, casual in jeans, Christmas t-shirts and sandals.

Joy stopped and waited to be shown where to place her food and drink offerings. Honor rushed to grab the tray and position it in the centre of the table.

"This looks beautiful," she cooed.

Joy was relieved. It was the right decision to make the edible wreath she'd seen in that magazine from memory. She'd decided to replace a tea light candle with a pot of balsamic dressing as a dipping sauce in the middle, with the skewers of salami, tomatoes, bocconcini and basil artfully arranged in a circle around it.

"You must be stoked with Ryan visiting," she said.

Honor beamed. "It was such a nice surprise. Kodi arranged it. Let me get you a glass of wine and then we can start in on the nibbles. Col's only just fired up the barbeque." Honor was fussing about as a hostess. "I want to show you our pics from Japan."

Taking a seat at the table, Joy pulled back plastic wrap from the tray and grabbed a skewer to sample it. Jaxon had been hovering around waiting for this moment. With a sleight of hand, he grabbed two skewers and disappeared to hide next to Col. Honor handed over a flute of red and sat opposite Joy, and with a sigh of contentment took a sip from her own wine glass.

Opening up her iPhone, Honor began scrolling through photos until she came to the ones from their recent holiday. "This is Minaroo and his wife Akiko, the family hosting us in Okinawa," she said, beginning full-fledged descriptions of the food, customs and shopping expeditions that made up their short trip.

"Akiko and I found we had something in common. She was a ceramics artist working in a style similar to my mosaics. She allowed me to inspect her amazing studio and we swapped ideas on methods and artistic influences. It was wonderful," Honor said, pointing to a pic of a long, whitewashed table set up with pottery vessels and bamboo handled paint brushes of various sizes. In the background, a wall of shelves hosted handmade pots and porcelain dishes pieced together with veins of gold and silver.

"This is an ancient technique for repairing cracked vases using sap from a particular Japanese plant and mixing it with powdered gold and silver. It binds pieces together in the most amazing random patterns." She enlarged a pic and held it up to Joy. "Do you like them?"

Honor was a good storyteller and Joy found it easy to listen and look at the colourful photographs, and live vicariously through them. She knew PTSD would prevent her ever again travelling overseas to exotic locations. There was a touch of envy at how easy everything came to Honor, but at the same time, she was happy for her sister.

The stories came to an end after lots of oohs and aahs. Sensitive to monopolising the show, Honor asked, "Enough about me and my travels far and wide. What have you been doing? Are the mindfulness exercises coming along?"

Joy gave a rueful smile. "I was going really great practising mindfulness. Then all the workers comp stuff reared up again. I was forced into being examined by a psychiatrist. I call him Dr Evil. His job was to discredit my truth. Not very ethical but totally legal. This set me back again. I hate it when that happens."

"I'd hoped the exercises would help you to be more resilient to it all," Honor said sympathetically.

"Dr Fellowes says some people are more resilient than others. I've been thinking about this notion of resilience lately and I'm not sure I agree with him," Joy said.

Honor chuckled. "This is so typical of you, Joy. Tell me, why don't you agree with the expert?"

Joy refused to be chastened. Instead, she held out an arm and swept it in an arc pointing to perfect, healthy flower beds, a result of her sister's green thumb. "You love gardening and all your plants are thriving because you know where the right spots are for each of them. If you left a shrub in a small pot on your patio, in the shade, and you didn't water it, it would eventually wilt and look pretty sad."

Joy waited for Honor to agree before continuing. "This would have nothing to do with how resilient it was. It would be really unfair to compare it to a similar shrub that was thriving, one planted in the right spot in the garden, in rich soil with plenty of sun, water and fertiliser."

Once again, Honor nodded.

"If you watered the potted shrub, maybe it would bounce back; maybe it wouldn't, but it would be wrong to blame the shrub if it didn't."

Honor nodded, following the analogy. She said, "You're saying people are the same. No one lives in isolation from the environment. Like plants, each of us needs certain supportive inputs to be present in order to be healthy and happy."

"Exactly. Context matters. What I'm beginning to see is that I haven't been allowed to bounce back because the environment of workers compensation is not conducive to healing. In fact, it is an added stress in my environment that has been damaging and constantly setting back my mental equilibrium."

"You'd have been better left to your own devices, in peace at home," Honor pondered, taking a sip of wine.

"Possibly," Joy said, reaching for another skewer of salami and bocconcini. A delicious scent of roast lamb, garlic and rosemary wafted across the courtyard.

Kodi and Gemma joined them at the table. Kodi studied the platter, deciding on which skewer to take. Gemma topped up their glasses of wine.

"Mum, it's Christmas. You're not supposed to bore Auntie Honor with your workers comp crap again," Gemma exclaimed. She, too, grabbed a skewer and delicately picked off a piece of salami.

"It's okay," Honor started to say.

The two glasses of wine Gemma finished earlier had gone to her head, making her chatty. "Did you know she's researching strangling so she can write a letter to Dr Evil?"

"No, she hadn't mentioned--"

"--Do you know how many ways there are to strangle a person? Mum found out on martial arts websites you can do it one handed, two handed, from the front, from behind, the side," Gemma leaned over and spoke slowly, "an elbow in a voice box, a knee on the back of the neck when holding a person down. Strangling isn't the same as choking. You don't have to cut off breathing. Any method that presses on the veins and arteries in the neck will block oxygen to the brain. You can even talk – beg for your life – while being asphyxiated at the same time."

Too late, the others understood Gemma was talking from personal experience. Honor glanced across at Col signalling for him to intervene.

Ryan and Jaxon were paying attention to Gemma's monologue with great interest.

"Mum says they teach this stuff in advanced martial art classes. You don't want to get it wrong because it only takes seconds to give a person brain damage or even kill them," Gemma explained. She lifted a glass with a shaky hand and gulped more wine.

Ryan took the opportunity to show off. "I was playing Trivial Pursuit last weekend with friends and one of the questions that came up was *the cause of all deaths*. Guess what the answer is?" He didn't wait. "Most people would say it's your heart stopping. Wrong! It's *lack of oxygen to the brain*." Glancing around the table, he grinned.

Gemma nodded soberly. "Cut off someone's oxygen to the brain for ten seconds and it's like giving them a concussion on the footy field. Every second after that increases the chance of permanent brain damage. After twenty seconds they can go unconscious and be dead within a few minutes."

Joy put her arm around Gemma's shoulder, offering comfort. Her daughter was dredging up memories of the abuse she endured at the hands of Jaxon's father. With guilty hindsight, she realised it had been ill advised to discuss her research results with Gemma in preparation for a draft letter to Dr Evans. In a bubble of self-centred, intellectual absorption, she'd neglected to consider how upsetting these reminders of physical violence would be to Gemma. Clearly, it had been building up in her daughter's system for some time.

Her mother's comforting hug did not stop Gemma's ramblings straight away. "Next time you watch James Bond, count the seconds from the start of a strangling scene," she lectured. "Even in pretend fights, the actors are careful to never go past ten seconds. The fight scenes may go a lot longer but the strangling doesn't. Count it if you don't believe me."

"Is that true?" Col asked. "That's interesting."

Jaxon was excited. "Awesome, mum. I'm counting next time."

Suddenly, Gemma was crying into her mother's shoulder. "I can't listen to any more of your workers comp stuff, mum. It upsets me too much."

"I know, darling. I'm so sorry," Joy whispered in her daughter's springy red hair. "It won't happen again, I promise. I can sort it out by myself. You're not to worry." She looked up apologetically at the other family members. They were stricken mute with sympathy, unsure what to say or do to offer condolence. Prior to this, references to Gemma's relationship with her ex had been a taboo subject, one she refused to speak about. They all thought she'd been so strong and brave.

Honor broke the awkward silence first. "The lamb tenderloin must be done by now. Col, would you check it, please?"

Obediently, Col poked his tongs at the boneless lamb roast, studied the juices oozing from the flesh, and decided it was sufficiently medium rare to come off the hot plate and onto a carving board. He carried it to the table with pride. Honor jumped up, announcing she'd fetch the roast veggies from the kitchen oven. Kodi followed saying she'd help.

Gemma sniffled a bit more before sitting up flushed in the face but composed.

Sensing a lull in the festivities, Jaxon ran over and started tugging at his mother's t-shirt, jumping up and down with excitement. "Is it time yet?" he asked his mother, breathlessly.

Nervously, Gemma glanced at Joy before giving Jaxon a nod. With a 'whoopee' he disappeared into the garden. Turning to her mother, in a conciliatory manner she began to deliberate. "Remember how much you loved Bonnie? She was like a member of our family. It's been three years since she died. Auntie Honor, Kodi and I have been talking."

Joy's face fell. "Tell me you haven't!"

Gemma rushed on. "We figured this past year has been so difficult for you. We wanted to do something nice to help get things back to normal. We thought this might be a way to introduce a routine and stability into your life."

Her voice started to sound pleading rather than pacifying.

Jaxon stumbled towards them carrying a wriggling, black bundle of fur with a Christmas ribbon tied in a bow around its neck. A purple lead dragged on the ground; it was a match to the purple streak in Joy's fringe. The smile on his face was brighter than a Christmas star.

"Now, mum, don't panic." Gemma smiled warily at Jaxon. "If you don't want him, we can take him back to the RSPCA."

"No, Granny! They'll put him to sleep if you give him back!" Jaxon cried out. The bundle of fur wriggled free and dashed off, doing a runner. Jaxon ran after him, yelling, "Come back, Buddy!"

With a shake of her head, Gemma resumed the argument in favour of a pet. "He's house trained and desexed. He has his shots."

By this time, Honor and Kodi arrived with bowls of roast vegetables and warm bread rolls. In the background, keeping quiet, Col began to carve the roast into thick slices.

Carefully positioning the dishes on the table, Honor picked up on the conversation. "We joined in to buy a bed and blanket."

"And a food bowl with a plastic mat," Kodi added enthusiastically.

"He comes complete with a bag of Roo Crunch and two tins of wallaby mince," Gemma coaxed. "Come on, mum, you love dogs."

All Joy could think was whether she was capable of looking after a dog, training it, remembering to feed it every day. Some days, she could hardly care for herself.

"We thought a dog would get you out of the house every day. You'd take him for walks and get fresh air and exercise..." Honor was saying.

"You can play with him, Granny. Look, he loves go fetch." Jaxon tossed a tennis ball and let go of Buddy's lead. The dog ran off. Joy was not convinced he'd return with the ball. He'd already lost his Christmas bow somewhere in the bushes.

Kodi joined Jaxon in hunting for the little guy. She reappeared with Buddy snuggled into her neck. "He's so gorgeous and cuddly," she enthused. "How great to sit and snuggle with him while you watch TV, Auntie Joy."

Gemma put in the convincing shot. "He would be something else to care about so you're not in your head thinking about stuff so much."

"A therapy dog," Kodi whispered, cuddling Buddy like a baby and giving an impression she'd be reluctant to give him up.

Gemma couldn't act as a sounding board anymore. She was offering a replacement; something else to offer comfort and solace on Joy's worst days. Their logic was sound. The family wanted what was best for her.

Whether *this was it* was debatable.

Casting a critical eye over the dog, she tried to work out what mix of breeds he was. He had a coat of soft curls like a poodle, with stubby legs like a Westie. He'd probably be smart, but would have a lot of energy. Joy exhaled with resignation.

Maybe it would work if she kept Buddy as an outdoor dog, sleeping inside at night. *Not on the bed.* He was adorable. It would be terrible if she gave him back and the RSPCA put him down. Gemma assured he was house trained. Joy only hoped to be a good owner for the little chap; he deserved that at the very least.

Kodi handed him over. "Here, Auntie Joy. Give him a cuddle. You'll fall in love." Buddy wriggled and scratched before succumbing to Joy's embrace. His pink tongue licked her fingers before he closed his eyes to sleep, a warm bundle next to her heart.

This clinched the deal.

Soon, the table was filled with a Christmas feast including platters of carved meat, bowls of roasted vegetables, minted peas, bread rolls, and gravy. Kodi placed Christmas crackers alongside each place setting much to everyone's delight. A clatter of dishes being passed around and plates being loaded up soon drown out any remaining residual awkwardness about dog ownership. A sleepy Buddy was deposited in his bed and covered with a blanket. His lead was unclipped and pushed to the side.

After the mains, to the cheers of the crowd, Honor proudly carried out the prize: their traditional family Christmas dessert, a giant pavlova filled with whipped cream and covered with peaches and assorted berries, drizzled with raspberry coulis.

"Awesome, Auntie Honor," Jaxon gushed.

"I knew I married you for a good reason," Col complimented.

"Dad, you say the same joke every year," Ryan moaned.

By the time the remaining smears of cream were licked from the bowl and she had finished a second cup of tea, Joy was feeling the last bit of energy drain from her reserves. If she waited and toughed it out, an ugly panic attack would be on the cards. It was time to collect Buddy and go home. She hated leaving before helping with the cleaning but the others were relaxed, lounging and patting their full tummies, in no hurry to start washing up.

Jaxon offered to carry Buddy's bed and blanket. Gemma grabbed a bag with the dog food and feed bowls to take to the car.

Joy clipped on Buddy's lead and started to walk the drowsy dog. Refusing to cooperate, he stubbornly remained in place. As she pulled, he walked a few steps then stopped. Frustrated, Joy pulled some more and tried to move off, coaxing him with an order to 'come'. Buddy defied instruction and instead chased his tail in frantic circles, coiling the lead around her ankles until she was tied up, unable to move without tripping.

Not a good start. Joy was too tired to begin a lesson in walking. Untangling the lead, she picked up the nervous puppy and carried him to the car, avoiding eye contact with family members. She suspected they were placing bets on how long Buddy would last.

Chapter Sixty Five

Another Monday morning passed with Joy's head down conducting research. Papers fanned across the kitchen table, in no particular order. Articles, reports and random blogs downloaded from the local library's community computer were covered in highlighting pen in neon yellow and orange, colour coded for later, as well as handwritten notes scrawled in exercise books. It had cost Joy a small fortune printing all the pages but was worth it if they helped prove her points to Dr Evans concerning the latest scientific medical research about non-lethal strangulation.

Buddy was happy to lay on a doggie pillow curled up at her feet. When it was time for a comfort break, he'd sit up and stare expectantly, waiting for Joy to notice and push him out the door. After doing his business, he'd yelp twice to be let back inside. Occasionally, he wandered over to his handmade, designer ceramic dog bowl – Kodi's Christmas present – and noisily lapped water.

Joy kept a stash of chew sticks nearby. If Buddy appeared restless, she'd take him through a routine of *'sit, stay, shake, drop, roll over'* and then offered a lot of praise while handing over a pork oinker. This would keep him busy crunching for a good twenty minutes, after which he'd nap. Buddy was turning out to be no trouble and, admittedly, good company. When she came across an interesting fact or statistic in one of the papers, Buddy was a good listener.

The most exciting discovery in all the downloads was a long, detailed submission to the New Zealand government from their Law Reform Commission. It made a case for strangulation as a new offence warranting mandatory sentencing. Much to Joy's surprise, strangulation was a hot topic of law reform around the world in regard to domestic violence. A few states in Australia had begun changing their laws around it. Eden Isle was the exception, *being twenty years behind the times* – as every mainlander remarked within the first three months of making a tree change to the place. This report provided all the justification needed.

With obsessive intensity, she began to highlight sentences, then whole paragraphs and eventually whole pages to later formulate into a comprehensive argument.

Suddenly, Buddy yelped and ran out the room. A knock on the front door broke her concentration. *Not now.* Joy continued highlighting, ignoring the interruption. Buddy barked and scratched at the door in a frenzy. A few more knocks, this time more insistent, were accompanied by a voice yelling, '*It's me Joy*'.

Sighing loudly, she padded over to the hallway and addressed Buddy. "Hey, what do you think Honor wants? Is she checking up on us?" He continued barking and leaping in the air, hitting the door. "Just a second, I need to put Buddy on a lead," she yelled through the heavy wood panel.

As Honor entered, she bent down to give Buddy a warm hello and a scratch behind the ears. Excited at the new visitor, he disgraced himself by lunging over and over again trying to impart doggie kisses. His sleek tail whacked Joy's legs, wagging like a propeller.

Holding him down with outstretched arms and laughing at the antics, Honor asked, "How's he settled in?" meaning *how are you coping*.

"He's been a little champion. No trouble. Although there are a couple bad habits we need to train out of him," she answered, pulling the lead and the dog away from Honor to allow her to stand up. "Sorry. Come in, I'll make us a cup of tea." Uneremoniously, Buddy was pushed out the door. He was meant to be an outdoor dog.

Honor pulled out a chair at the kitchen table and strung the straps of a shoulder bag across the back. Hesitating, she cast a look over the scattered papers, noted the topics, and gently stacked a pile to clear a space. "This is impressive. Looks like you've found a heap of information. What do you plan to say to Dr Evans?"

Over the boiling of the kettle, Joy said, "Lots. It's been a real eye opener." Returning to the table, she leaned on a chair and began to expound on what she'd learned. "Did you know that until recently in law a person's hands were not considered lethal weapons and that was why strangling was not seen as dangerous?"

Honor snorted. "That's ridiculous." After a short pause, she added, "It's like going through airport security when they confiscated my nail file. Col and I joked that some women's nails are like talons and much more dangerous than a flimsy nail file. They didn't laugh."

Joy chuckled. More seriously, she continued. "The whole notion of what they refer to as *non-lethal* strangulation has been little understood and largely ignored in law for a long time. Mostly because it's more a women's issue relating to domestic violence."

"That would be right." Curious, Honor sifted through a few papers, skim reading the contents.

"I was reading a report that equated strangulation to waterboarding," Joy said, rifling through her notes until finding an exercise book with newly drafted points to go into a letter. Reciting from the text, she said, "...both leave few marks... both can cause loss of consciousness... both create intense fear and can result in death." She stressed the last sentence as if written in bold capital letters. "And both demonstrate the abuser is in a position of authority and control over another's life... It is a form of intimidation and coercion..." she read.

"An assault that is more like torture maybe than an attack of violence," Honor nodded deep in thought. "Even if there isn't an intention to kill you, the abuser is making that statement: I am capable of killing. That's frightening."

"Exactly. It's a death demonstration."

"A practice run."

"That's what messed with my head with the court case. This notion of proving intent, as if it mattered whether Poppy intended to kill me or not. How was I supposed to know at the time?

"Until she stopped strangling you, and you were still alive, there was no way of knowing her intentions. You were in no position to resist; you could only wait and pray." Honor agreed. "That must have been terrifying for you, Joy."

The kettle whistled and Joy dropped the exercise book to see to their teas. She returned with mugs and Tim Tams. Honor cleared space for them.

Joy resumed the conversation. "I plan to write it all up in a letter to Dr Evans."

Honor pointedly surveyed the mounds of paper. "It looks like it could be a very long letter. Do you believe all this trouble is going to be worth it in the end? I'll bet your lawyer wouldn't recommend stirring the pot when you're about to be offered a package." She sipped tea, peering over the rim of the pottery mug.

Joy wondered how two sisters from the same mother could have such different views of the world. "It's not about the money. It's about vindication. Can you understand that? If they repeat a lie often enough, it becomes accepted as the truth. Being strangled was not a joke. Dr Evans is a person of high standing, a medical expert, who is perpetuating the myth that strangulation poses no risk of death nor serious injury to a woman. This is simply not true." She paused to catch a breath and gulp down tea.

Honor looked unimpressed. "All I'm trying to say is don't go charging in like a bull in a China shop. Be more cautious when money is at stake."

Joy tried once more to gain her sister's understanding. "It's my mental health that's at stake! They're telling me I'm crazy when they are the ones wrong."

"You've got a lawyer. Let him do the hard work. He knows what he's doing. Trust him."

Joy knew, as good as John Emerson was, his interests were a monetary outcome. And not financial restitution for a wrong; not for justice or some moral principles that were at stake. He was too pragmatic for that. It was purely a transactional business outcome.

"I don't want to argue. Go ahead and try to change the world, Joy. That's your thing," Honor huffed, as if she were the injured party. "How's that been working out for you," she mumbled under her breath. "Anyway, I can't stay long. Mainly, I came over because Kodi's been pestering me to check on Buddy."

Faintly disappointed in the abrupt end to a robust discussion but understanding this was Honor's typical way of dealing with unpleasant topics, she accepted it was time to change the subject. Joy leapt out of the chair. "I'll go get him. I've been teaching him tricks."

She returned, dragging a reluctant Buddy on a lead. Digging into a pocket, a few dog treats were produced. Sensing they were about to play a game, Buddy sat to attention.

"Good boy," Joy cooed. "Shake," she commanded. Buddy complied and received a reward. His tail wagged like a power blender. The next command was drop and then roll over and play dead. Like a real trooper, Buddy followed orders to the letter with his tiny feet sticking up in the air. Joy breathed a sigh of relief. At least, she could demonstrate one area of her life that would achieve approval from her sister.

As hoped, Honor clapped in delight. "You taught him to roll over and play dead! How adorable," she exclaimed. And then ruined the shiny moment by patting Buddy's tummy and commenting in a silly voice, "Maybe you could teach that trick to your owner."

Joy returned a rueful smile. "In America, they call it '*playing possum*'; Archer used to tell me I needed to learn to play possum. I guess I never have. It's not in my nature."

Honor chuckled. "I know the problem. You're an Aussie possum, Joy. In Australia, our possums don't play dead; they are fiercely wild creatures that stand in the middle of the road and fight back."

They both laughed, sharing the memory of an encounter with a True-Blue Aussie Anzac possum on the track from Gemma's place last month. This lightened the mood and ended Honor's visit on a happy note. Sisterly affection and family solidarity were restored, as only recalling the symbol of a fierce, brave possum can do.

Chapter Sixty Six

An exercise book with the handwritten letter to Dr Evans lay open on the table. Joy's elbows scrunched a mess of papers on either side of it. This must have been the tenth time she'd re-read the letter. She couldn't think of anything else to add, although a vestigial corporate brain cautioned that the wording was emotive in places. Not dramatic or overly exaggerated, she argued with herself, just... angry.

This was her truth. There was no other way to write it. Strangulation was terrifying and abusive behaviour and authorities such as Dr Evil continued the abuse by effectively silencing victims when they spoke out wanting justice and understanding. It was time for this to change.

On second thought, before posting it, she'd better show it to Kodi for a second opinion. With her creative writing skills any advice on wordsmithing would be welcome. The goal was to present a convincing argument to Dr Evil, not get him offside.

When the weekend finished, she'd type it up at the Community Online Centre and post it.

A loud pounding on the front door startled her out of a deep trance. Buddy, asleep under the table, dashed out of the room with high pitched yelping that pierced straight through Joy's chest. She flinched. The front door was getting scratched from his protective thrusts as he attempted to dig his way through the wood to the visitors.

Viewing the mess on the table, a dirty coffee mug and plate littered with toast crumbs from breakfast sitting atop a pile of dog-eared reports amongst mounds of photocopied articles and exercise books filled with notes, Joy debated whether to rescue the door or tidy up. Grabbing the dishes, she dumped them in the kitchen sink with a clatter. Returning, with a sweep of her arm tried to scoop papers across the table into one big pile. The pounding on the door became more insistent and Buddy's barking more snarling.

Abandoning the cleanup plan, she ran to the door and grabbed Buddy by the collar. Smiling faces greeted her at the front doorsteps. Buddy whined wanting to run free; his tail wagged and walloped her legs in excitement.

"We're here, Granny," Jaxon shouted with glee. "I was knocking but you didn't answer."

"What a surprise. Come in," Joy stepped aside to allow Jaxon, Gemma and Kodi into the hallway. All three bent down to pat Buddy. He rolled onto his back revelling in the attention but causing a log jam. "I get it. You're here to visit Buddy, not me," she joked. Kodi replied by cooing *'you're sooo cute'* to Buddy, while scratching his tummy vigorously.

Gemma screwed up her face. "Yes and no. Jaxon and Kodi couldn't wait any longer to check up on Buddy. But I wanted to say I'm sorry for my tipsy speech at Christmas. I didn't mean it." She reached over and gave Joy a sideways hug amongst all the chaos. "I'm here for you, mum. Anything you need."

"No, no, honey. You never have to apologise to me." Joy hugged back and then said, "Come on through. It must be time for a cuppa." She glanced at her watch. "Or lunch. Is that the time already?"

"Can I take Buddy for a walk, Granny?" Jaxon pleaded. Joy gave Gemma the look and got a nod in return.

"Off you go then," she said, handing him the lead. He was off like a shot.

Gemma yelled after him, "Stay on the sidewalk and be back in twenty minutes for lunch." In her head, Joy took bets he hadn't heard one word.

Standing around the kitchen table, anxiety took hold. Joy began to stack papers and transfer them to a coffee table in the lounge room with frenetic obsessiveness.

Observing the mess and aware of her mother's impulse to clean up, Gemma offered assurances. "Leave it, mum. I can see you're busy."

"We'll make lunch. You can relax," Kodi said. She rifled through some loose pages, peering at articles. Curiosity got the better of her. "Is this research for that letter you're writing? Mum was moaning to dad about it. According to her, you are going to tell an expert that he doesn't know what he's talking about." Kodi grinned. "Awesome. You are my hero."

Joy blushed. "It's important for experts involved in workers comp cases to apprise themselves of recent medical research before making statements which are out of date and grossly misrepresent the facts," she said, primly quoting from the letter.

Gemma frowned. "Sorry, mum, if we are interrupting your work we can go."

Joy noted her daughter's reluctance to discuss the case, despite the earlier apology. "In fact, I've just finished writing the letter. I was hoping one of you could proofread it before I type it up." She picked up an exercise book and opened it to the right page, flicking pages to indicate it wasn't very long. "It might be a tad more emotional than I usually write."

Kodi snatched it before Gemma could say a word. "Cool," she said, pulling out a chair and dropping down to sit, all the time concentrating on reading the letter. Joy watched for telltale signs of approval and disapproval. Gemma disappeared into the kitchen and began rummaging through the fridge for sandwich fillings, keeping out of the discussion.

It seemed like an eternity before Kodi nodded and looked at Joy. "Is it true you couldn't find any other reported cases of a boss strangling a subordinate on the whole internet? That's incredible."

"There was one where an angry employee tried to strangle his boss, from the front, one handed. But that was all I found," Joy said.

"Awesome. You're a first," Kodi gushed, as if that was something deserving of a medal.

"Not surprising, I didn't find any jokes that involved strangling either. It seems, apart from Poppy and the Magistrate, no one else in the wide world – not even comedians – think strangling is funny. Oh, except for a sarcastic meme obviously about domestic violence: *You say neck hugs; I say strangulation*'.

Kodi snorted. "That meme was written for you. Disgusting as it sounds, my guess is that Poppy was deriving pleasurable feelings out of strangling you. That's why your psych's keep saying you weren't in danger because she wasn't displaying any negative emotions such as anger. No one thinks something like an act of sick pleasure seeking is in fact life threatening violence.

And why I feel violated as if I've been sexually abused, thought Joy feeling too ashamed to voice this aloud. Her niece could be too perceptive at times.

Returning to the exercise book, Kodi said, "I like the bit where you draw attention to strangulation in relation to domestic violence and discuss the misperceptions about what constitutes violence against women." She read out *There is a fine line between fatal and non-fatal strangulation. Abuse victims who have been strangled have seven times the risk to go on to be killed by their abuser'.*

"Now that's scary!" She continued reading out loud *'...there is no doubt that until recently strangulation has been underestimated. It constitutes criminal behaviour... Although this particular form of attack is not limited to family violence... it's been established as a new crime in a number of countries'* and I like where you write *'to my mind, violence is violence, whether in the private or public domain'.* "Well said, Auntie Joy." She looked up with admiration.

Joy basked in her approval. "If anything, occupational violence violates even more laws and social contracts between the abuser and the victim," she stated officiously, quoting again from the draft letter to Dr Evans.

Kodi gazed out the window deep in thought. "My boss at the Shire Council is really smart when it comes to dealing with men. She says guys feel compelled to help women when asked; they can't stop themselves. I suggest you add a paragraph at the end of your letter asking Dr Evans to take some kind of action on your behalf. If he's a real man, he won't be able to resist helping you."

Gemma came in carrying a plate piled with ham and cheese sandwiches. Overhearing their conversation, she said, "Good on you, mum, for calling out that jerk on his bullshit! But as Kodi says, what do you hope to achieve by sending the letter? You need to say that in the final paragraphs."

Joy thought about this. "I want him to revise the incorrect and ill-advised statements made in his psychiatric assessment of me."

"To better reflect this new world-wide understanding of the medical facts and the trend towards a higher social conscience towards violence against women," Kodi added.

"Whether in the domestic or occupational domain," Gemma contributed.

"I like it," Joy said. "Write that down before I forget."

Kodi wasn't finished. "I reckon you should also appeal to his authority, as a man who has an opportunity to demonstrate leadership on the forefront of the issue of non-lethal strangulation, to raise its significance as a crime and pioneer change in attitudes within Eden Isle's health system." She smiled conspiratorially.

Joy glanced at Gemma for permission.

Gemma shrugged. "What have you got to lose? If you don't ask, you don't get."

A scurrying of paws in the hallway and the slamming of the front door announced Jaxon and Buddy's return, just in time for lunch. They both had an uncanny sense of timing... or sense of smell. Joy smiled to herself.

"After we eat, let's add in all that extra stuff. We can read it one more time before I type and post it," Joy suggested.

"I can type it for you at work tomorrow," Kodi offered. "Come by at lunchtime and we can go to the Village Spice Café. You too, Gemma."

"Sounds like a plan," Joy and Gemma agreed in unison.

Chapter Sixty Seven

Gil didn't like to admit he was having reservations about his wife. From the kitchen window, he sipped morning coffee and watched Poppy play magic knot games with Riff in the backyard. In this instance, using thick ropes, she demonstrated how to tie a noose and then pretended to hang a stuffed teddy bear from the roof of the pergola, yanking a cord and loosening the knot at the last minute, letting it fall onto the paving stones and laughing at the joke.

That was a bit over the top, even for her. Next, they moved on to the knotted handcuffs trick. This time, Riff extracted himself with ease, rubbing his torso against Poppy's and running a hand through her hand and up her arm, and twisting his body in intimate physical contact in order to untie their knots. Poppy showed her delight at his success by whipping his bottom with the end of the rope. She laughed like a teenage girl.

Gil and Poppy had discussed the foster care of Riff over dinner a few nights ago. She had been accepting extra, longer placements for him on top of the regular fortnightly visits, despite constantly complaining of a heavy workload. Gil questioned whether she was becoming too attached to the lad. He'd noticed her touchy feely approach with Riff and wondered if this was appropriate, especially as twelve-year-old boys starting puberty have all the confusion of testosterone running through their systems. Poppy huffed that she was a nurse and from her professional observations, Riff was a troubled kid, starved for affection and stability. She'd decided to provide a predictable routine, playing games and giving him extra cuddles and pats on the bum as a sign of warmth and care. *What was Gil's problem?*

Peering closer at the games being played outside, Gil frowned. This time it appeared like Poppy was teaching Riff to enjoy bondage. Running around the garden she was attempting to lasso him as if he were a rodeo steer. When caught, she jerked the rope, temporarily tightening it around his shoulders before the constrictor slip knot came loose. Riff grinned as if enjoying the prank.

Gil's instincts warned there was something wrong about the whole business. Riff's eyes reflected a deadness behind that grin, as if he waited for the right moment to return the gag. The kid came from a screwed-up home. It wasn't smart of Poppy to encourage malicious tendencies, even if she thought it was funny.

Maybe Gil was jealous. This was unlike him. Ever since Poppy confided about the circumstances surrounding Harold Gray's passing, he'd felt a malingering sense of misgivings that he couldn't pin down.

True, Poppy expressed a lot of remorse at what happened, giving the geezer a massage as usual and not expecting his frailty would lead to a heart attack when it hadn't all the instances before. Despite the old pervert's dementia and unnatural inclinations, she'd been his nurse for a while and had developed affection towards him. Apparently, they had an 'understanding' whatever that meant. It wasn't exactly in the rule book for community nursing duties Gil had surmised. Whatever she meant by it, Poppy didn't elaborate and frankly Gil didn't want to know. However, he suspected there was more to the story.

True, her kind heartedness meant she'd tried to resuscitate Harold but couldn't revive him despite working on him for quite a while. That must have been gross. And certainly, it was a tragedy. But she was quick to reassure him the department didn't care about the incident provided her report stuck to official departmental explanations. There was no risk of getting into trouble.

Their conversation left Gil with a sense of déjà vu. Poppy's inclination towards giving spontaneous neck massages to clients and staff (and her foster child) was getting out of control. The fact she kept getting away with it gave her an attitude of invincibility, as if her employer had given tacit permission in some nonjudgmental state of largess, rather than simply turned a blind eye to these incidents. She was protected by the system and therefore free to continue her impulsive, pleasure workouts believing she could do no wrong.

Regardless of all this, Gil wasn't so much concerned about her work life as he was their personal love life. After Gray's funeral, it was as if another thin barrier of inhibition had been removed from Poppy's psyche. When it came to their bedroom play acting, she'd ramped up her passionate indulgences with more uncensored pleasure.

As much as he loved his wife, she was beginning to scare him. Her choke holds were maintained for a few seconds too long, causing him to black out after coming. His thrashing about in suffocating terror excited Poppy more than ever. And this posed a dilemma: it was becoming less fun for him because he genuinely feared for his life. Afterwards, he was left with migraine headaches.

When complaining he was losing his memory and turning into one of her dementia clients, she laughed mercilessly, dismissing his fears and labelling him a selfish chicken shit. If she needed longer to get off, it was his fault and therefore, he should indulge her.

There was something terrifyingly attractive about his wife's aggressive demands to slavishly satisfy her sexual desires. Her overpowering dominance in the bedroom used to arouse lust in him like nothing else.

Maybe he was getting too old for it. His survival instincts were overtaking his desire for an out of this world orgasm.

Gil finished the last dregs of coffee from his mug. He shook his head to clear the stupidity. He must be working too hard if this was his latest preoccupation. Let her have fun with the foster kid and get some of her insatiable appetite out of her system. Watching Riff play with her in the garden convinced him the kid wasn't discouraging her ministrations.

This brought to mind Poppy's announcement. Riff had asked her to be his partner in his school's end of term "Show Case". It was like a talent show where students could nominate a special ability relating to what they'd learned over the term and show it off on stage. He wanted to demonstrate the magic rope tricks he'd been learning to show off to his parents. It was a big deal, the first time the kid had achieved something worthy of pride. Surprising her with this shy request made Poppy feel special, almost motherly. No wonder she was putting so much time and effort into practising with the lad.

Gil had to try to be more supportive of Poppy's efforts, rather than hypercritical. Sometimes, Poppy was right calling him a selfish chicken shit.

Chapter Sixty Eight

The Crown Solicitor's office accommodation at Whalers Cove wasn't regal and polished mahogany panelling in the style of an old English courtroom Fiona expected when visiting private lawyer chambers. It was functional in a grey filing cabinet sort of way looking like many government offices that hadn't been updated since the seventies. It didn't prompt an image of professional confidence and success. No wonder Leland wanted to take this meeting in person.

He'd insisted they drive to the meeting, leaving at the crack of dawn. Fiona couldn't stomach breakfast at such an early hour; now her tummy growled in protest. On the way, the radio had played Radio National news, announcing the latest controversies concerning various candidates competing in the state election. The same old, same old. She'd struggled to stay awake.

Leland hadn't helped. He'd been unusually quiet, probably considering his chances at winning the department's vacant CEO position, particularly now with Joy O'Connell's letter to Dr Evans circulating around the workers compensation team. If it leaked to the press, the department would be hit with a red hot shockwave – a disaster less like witnessing a fireworks display and more on scale of a raw and indiscriminate explosion of dynamite, she mused without humour.

Let's wait and see what the Crown Solicitor advises, Leland had curtly ordered, effectively stopping her grumbling and further conversation on the trip over.

Fiona suppressed a yawn as they waited in a stark, functional conference room, its saving grace a line of windows overlooking the harbour. The view slightly obscured by vertical venetian blinds open and twisted in places. A cruise liner was docked with its gangplank down waiting for passengers to disembark and begin their frenzy of shopping at the shoreline markets. Shopkeepers and café owners went about their business with practised efficiency, drawing up security shutters and setting out tables on the wide sidewalk. The peaceful scene did not relax Fiona.

Leland wandered over to a kitchenette set up in the far corner of the room. He oozed calm like a soft whip ice cream dispenser. The man was a composed and calculating machine ready to play the battle strategist. He lived for this type of crisis. Fiona wished he'd shared his thoughts in the car before they met with the Assistant Crown Solicitor responsible for the case. She hated walking into these situations unprepared for the role she was meant to execute. Leland seemed to derive mean pleasure keeping her in the dark, testing her resourcefulness and flexibility under pressure.

Messing about opening drawers and cupboards, Leland returned with two white mugs of coffee. Taking a sip, Fiona tried not to wince. The tepid coffee was generic, government contract instant.

Leland said it for her. "God, that's disgusting. After this meeting, we'll get a decent double shot at the Cove Trattoria."

The conference room door opened and a young woman, dressed in a black suit jacket and trousers, breezed in announcing "Good, you've got yourselves coffees". Fiona thought she looked to have come straight out of university. After dumping a thin file, yellow pad and ball point pen on the table, she reached across to shake hands. "I'm Rebecca Howard. Leland, Fiona, nice to meet you."

Leland opened a briefcase and pulled out Joy's original letter clipped to its fat attachment, the New Zealand Law Reform Report on a New Crime of Strangulation. He slid it across to Rebecca. In bold letters across the top Joy had typed the words PRIVATE & CONFIDENTIAL. Clearly, this meant nothing to Dr Evans when he decided to post it on for them to deal with.

Rebecca picked it up and skim read the letter, nodding. Placing it back to the middle of the table, she commented, "It's well written for an administrative assistant. She makes a compelling argument. Within Eden Isle's law reform circles, it's well-known that strangulation is coming to the attention of legal jurisdictions across the world, and within some states on the mainland, with the view it should be made a criminal offence with mandatory prison sentencing. We've been watching New Zealand's sentiments with interest."

"She most likely had help writing it," Fiona replied. "Although I don't believe her lawyer has seen it yet. John Emerson does things by the book. He's predictable in that way."

Impatient, Leland interrupted. "Is this going to pose a problem going forward with Ms O'Connell's case before the Workers Compensation Tribunal? And if so, how do we cordon the impact?"

Clearing her throat, Rebecca began to lecture on what they already knew. "The tribunal consists of a panel of medical practitioners and non-medical members of the community. They will make a decision based on reports, assessments and the plaintiff's statement as to whether compensation is to be awarded. This is calculated on the percentage of whole person impairment directly attributed to the workplace injury. Their decision is final and non-appealable.

"As I said, Ms O'Connell's statement is articulate, logical, factually correct and persuasive. The panel will find it hard to ignore."

"And therefore, we cannot allow it to be presented to the tribunal," Leland finished for her. He began drumming fingers on the table.

"If it goes to the tribunal, everything submitted will be on public record," Rebecca reminded him.

"It's political suicide. The woman is a stone in my shoe," he grumbled.

Rebecca waited patiently for instructions.

Thinking out loud, Fiona said, "She doesn't know when to let go; she latches on to an idea like one of those obnoxious terriers and keeps shaking your leg with this righteous attitude as if all that matters is the truth and nothing but the truth."

Leland gave her a look to shut it. Fiona blushed recognising the blunder. Trying to amend the mistake, she added, "So far she's countered every one of our tried and true moves to control the narrative, keep her quiet and out of the picture. Anyone else would have given up a long time ago. Instead, it seems every move we made spurred her on to protest louder."

"She must be one of those feminist whistleblower types," Leland blurted, darting a look at Rebecca, hoping he didn't give offence. "I mean, she thinks she can hold the department to ransom for what happened. It always boils down to greed."

Fiona chose to ignore Leland's ill-advised comment about assertive women and instead looked to Rebecca for advice. "How much risk to a final payout figure does Joy's statement pose?"

Rebecca responded by opening the file and extracting several pages. "I've just received from John Emerson a second psychiatric assessment on Ms O'Connell. You know Dr Evans scored her at seven percent whole person impairment. Emerson's psychiatrist gave her a score of nineteen percent. The good news is that it is below twenty percent, meaning under Eden Isle law Ms O'Connell is not able to sue the department under common law for negligence. The bad news is that the gap between seven and nineteen percent is too great to be statistically valid, thus effectively raising doubts concerning either score." She waited for the import of this to sink in.

Leland shook his head with concern. "The panel would be perfectly justified in ignoring both reports and making up their own minds on the day."

"Based on compelling arguments," Rebecca agreed with a wan look of sympathy. "It's reasonable to speculate a WPI score somewhere between the two, say ten to fifteen percent."

Leland rummaged through his briefcase and pulled out a calculator. Mumbling under his breath, *'part time salary times years until retirement times ten percent WPI formula'* he scrawled notes on a pad of paper and crunched numbers on the calculator, doing the maths. He held up the final result in Fiona's face. She gasped.

Recovering, Fiona managed to say, "We have to get her to agree to a lesser settlement before it goes to the tribunal."

"Or risk the wrath of the Minister," Leland warned. Fiona knew his prospects of becoming the department's CEO rested on managing the matter without it going public, especially with the election only six weeks away, and without an excessive payout. It was a tough balancing act, and rather unfair timing for him, she thought.

Leland began to fulminate. "She needs to be silenced, more permanently this time around." He turned to Fiona. "Can you talk to Dr Vitkay and convince him to prescribe that cocktail of alternative antipsychotic meds that Dr Evans recommended? That should do the trick. We'll make her too *out of it* to think straight, let alone talk back."

Shocked at the blatant callousness, but not wanting to be overtly disagreeable, Fiona fumbled her response. "I don't think... Dr Vitkay is ethically obliged to follow his own... he's not been the most malleable...," she coughed and tried again. "We've found Dr Vitkay resists outside interference." Stopping mid stuff up, before Leland turned nasty, she glanced at Rebecca entreating her for a save.

Rebecca cleared her throat to gain Leland's attention. "We are in agreement that it would not be in the best interests of your department, nor the state government at this time, for Ms O'Connell's matter to continue on to the tribunal. Fortunately, with this letter to Dr Evans, she showed her cards early, giving us an advantage in terms of damage control. We have some tactics to employ within a broader legal strategy. The first is to seek a dismissal of her claim altogether through a motion to discredit."

Intrigued, Leland leaned forward with hands folded under this chin while Rebecca outlined the next steps. Hurriedly, Fiona captured the plan in note form. She avoided asking where the money for this would be found in their tight budget. To prevent Joy getting any money, a lot of money had to be spent. Rebecca's tactics had better work.

At the end, Leland was captivated by Rebecca's shrewd game plan. His obvious admiration for the young lawyer was nauseatingly flirtatious.

Fiona understood that Rebecca's strategy was sound. It returned them to a position of control, handling perceptions within the narrative of Joy's case for compensation.

It was just that parts of it sat like rocks in her gut. She told herself, it was all legal and allowed. But it seemed to carry a dirty taint of foul play. She couldn't allow herself to become spineless at this point. She had to do what was required. This was her job after all.

When the meeting closed, Leland was shaking Rebecca's hand and grinning broadly. "We'll keep you informed of the progress we make over the next several weeks," he assured her.

Chapter Sixty Nine

One minute, Buddy was dozing at her feet, a dopey bundle of cute, and the next he was growling deep and throaty as if agitated. Suddenly, a demon beast burst forth from his blanket bed, charged across the lounge room to the French windows, and began furiously yapping at something outside. He jumped in the air and flung himself at the glass panes attempting to get at whatever was out there.

Joy snapped shut Fellowes' book she'd been reading and threw it on the coffee table unable to concentrate. This barking was becoming a pattern. It had been going on for the past couple weeks – sometimes from the crack of dawn – and no matter what Joy tried to do to calm Buddy and shush him, the barking would continue until she got so mad, he was flung outside. He'd started out so well at Christmas and had been an angel for weeks. Then suddenly, an alien had taken over his personality.

She tried not to feel like a failure but her good intentions and training tricks simply did not work. Buddy was meant to be an outdoor dog, she justified. It didn't solve the problem, however. He would continue barking, whether inside or outside. Double glazed windows and a solid wood door muffled the noise. A yapping dog and PTSD was a bad combination.

Her nerves were stretched to breaking point. Home was no longer her sanctuary. Buddy was causing an aversion to it.

This morning, his barking coincided with Joy's mobile going off and John Emerson's name coming up on the display. With a choice of pushing Buddy out the door or answering the call, she ignored the dog and took the call. It had been weeks since she'd heard from John and she needed reassurances on the second psychiatric examination. Dr Sanjay hadn't seemed all that different to Dr Evans, however, this time she'd been more restrained in her responses and the interrogation was over in half the time. She hoped John would approve.

She answered the phone with one hand covering an ear, and increased the volume to maximum, marching into the master bedroom and shutting out Buddy.

John Emerson wasted no time in getting down to business. She found it difficult to hear with Buddy carrying on in the background but didn't dare ask John to repeat a word of his monologue.

She gleaned he'd been happy with the new WPI results. Dr Sanjay scored her at nineteen percent. He'd send the report to her. He'd rejected the first and final offer sent before Christmas. He was waiting on a new offer. Negotiations were progressing with the department. The tribunal required these negotiations before agreeing to a hearing.

He'd disconnected before Joy could say she didn't care what they offered. She wanted to go all the way to a tribunal decision. It wasn't about the money; it was about vindication and having it all on public record.

She stared at a dead phone. It didn't matter at the moment. Her plan was to keep rejecting offers to force the department to defend their position on strangulation in front of a panel of their peers.

Buddy's yelping increased in intensity. Joy peered out the window trying to see what was causing the carry on. Nothing. As usual, the dog had turned psycho for no reason. Exactly what she didn't need right now, while the workers comp matter was ramping up and she needed all her wits about.

Joy collected Buddy and held him close in a cuddle, stroking his head. Calming somewhat, he continued deep, low growls that reverberated against her chest. As she opened the back door, he began to squirm. Joy found him hard to hold; he was stronger than he looked. With a shrill yelp, he twisted from her arms and ran off towards the fence, barking at an imaginary enemy.

Probably a possum, Joy decided. Closing the door, her heart was racing. A nervous, yappy dog was not something she could cope with, especially at this point in her workers compensation case. It upended her equilibrium; the opposite outcome Honor and Gemma had wanted. No wonder he'd been given to the RSPCA in the first place. She should have known better than to rehome a dog with issues. Was it too late to give him back? She'd ask Gemma.

***

That afternoon at Gemma's, Joy sank into a lounge chair luxuriating in peace and quiet. No barking dog. Even Gemma's instant coffee didn't leave its usual bitter aftertaste and the ultra-rich raspberry blondies weren't upsetting her tummy. Her anxiety was lessening, and she felt safe and calm. They discussed Doc Martin's phone call briefly but there wasn't much to say. It was all happening behind the scenes and didn't directly involve Joy. Her lawyer was in control, and she had to trust him.

When the topic of Buddy's bad behaviour came up, Gemma begged her to reconsider. "I've heard of a natural remedy to calm dogs," she said. "Tryptophan is what he needs, along with B vitamins. Give him a chance, mum."

Joy exhaled a long breath of doubt. "Chill pills for Buddy? I'm the one who needs to take them." They laughed.

After a few minutes of quiet communion, sipping coffee and basking in the warm rays of summer sun shining through the lounge room windows, Gemma shivered inexplicably. "What is it?" Joy asked, worried.

"Weird, but I feel like someone is watching the house." Gemma tiptoed to the lounge room windows and stealthily pulled back a net curtain to peer outside.

"See anything?" Joy asked, wondering where this paranoia was coming from all of a sudden. Several years ago, Gemma's ex-partner had stalked her and that had nearly sent her over the edge of mental health. "After all this time, you don't think it's…"

"I can't see anyone. It wouldn't be him. A friend told me his Facebook status shows he's married with a baby now." Nonetheless, Gemma continued to observe for several minutes.

Becoming unsettled, Joy asked, "Are you worried for your safety and Jaxon's?"

Gemma let go of the curtain and returned to the sofa. "No, it's okay. Don't start worrying, mum. It was a passing feeling. There was nothing out there. My sixth sense is obviously on the blink." She laughed, but Gemma's maternal instincts heard a different message.

"I can stay the night, if you need me to be here," Joy offered.

Gemma considered and then shook her head. "You can't, mum. What about Buddy?"

Any charitable feelings towards Buddy and her responsibilities as a pet owner had dissipated after a week of non-stop barking. Gemma was a mother and granny first. "He'll be alright staying outside for one night. It's summer and he's got a blanket. He was supposed to be an outdoor dog," Joy argued.

"Mum, don't fuss. We'll be fine," Gemma was saying before another shiver passed through her. "Jaxon will be home from school soon. Why don't you stay for dinner?"

Joy could tell her daughter didn't want her to leave. She'd hang about until after dinner just in case. It didn't get dark until after nine this time of year. Driving home shouldn't be too stressful. "Of course. I'd love to," she assured Gemma.

***

By the time Joy returned home, the night was pitch black causing massive anxiety. She expected Buddy to announce her arrival with shrill barks. The only sounds in the garden were frogs croaking. "Buddy," she called.

Silence.

Locking the car, she walked across the driveway to the front gate. The latch was undone, the gate ajar. She was sure it had been closed properly when she left for Gemma's in the afternoon. "Buddy?" she called out again.

Would someone in the neighbourhood be so mean as to let him out?

Or did someone snatch him? Rumours were circulating around the Shire of dogs being snatched from the streets and sold overseas to the clothing trade for their pelts.

Fear, guilt and heartache overwhelmed Joy. Lamely, she commanded, "Come, Buddy." No response. Was he lying dead on the side of the road, a little ball of black curls, hit by a passing car? It was too terrible to contemplate.

Dashing into the cottage, Joy searched for a flashlight. Starting with the streetscape, she ran through the neighbourhood and flashed a high beam along the gutters, up the curb and sidewalks, calling his name. After thirty minutes, tears were streaming down her cheeks. Buddy was gone. She'd been a bad owner; he'd deserved better. What would she say to Jaxon?

Defeated, she climbed the front steps. One last time, her flashlight crisscrossed the front garden in vain hope. "Come, Buddy," she whispered through salty tears.

A muffled whimper came from around the side of the cottage. Joy scrambled to a hedge row of camellias, crouched low and scanned through branches and leaves with the flashlight. "Buddy?" she whispered, not wanting to spook him. A black shape emerged from the bushes. "I've got you. I've got you," she kept repeating, hugging a shivering doggie to her chest.

After carrying a scared Buddy into the house, Joy swaddled him in a blanket and rocked him like a baby. For once, he didn't squirm and fuss. Something had spooked him badly.

It was only when Joy was preparing to go to bed, a terrible thought crossed her mind. This incident was too bizarre to be a coincidence. She had to warn Gemma, just in case.

Chapter Seventy

A few days later, mid-morning, Joy perched on a garden bench in her backyard basking in the warmth of a perfect summer day. She'd chosen a shady spot under an old oak tree, where a light breeze rustled its leaves and caused a dappled light effect. Buddy was keeping her company and behaving better than usual. Instead of running up and down the fence line yapping, he'd stayed at her feet, not yet over the scare from the other night.

Pen in hand, Joy blinked from glare reflecting off a pad of paper positioned on her knees. She pushed sunglasses higher on her nose. Although there were no further updates from John Emerson, she decided to take the opportunity during a lull in proceedings to draft her statement to the tribunal. It was essential to get it right and she had a lot to say.

So far, she'd managed to write down some dot points:

PTSD – trauma injury not mental illness

No cure. Have for rest of my life

New 'normal' – note: list changes to everyday life. Social life before and after.

Life pared down to bare basics.

Can't tell by looking at me I've suffered trauma.

Therapy dog – drives me crazy.

She crossed off that last point. She was too ashamed to mention her failure with Buddy. During last night's late phone call, Gemma had taken the news of nearly losing Buddy and someone tampering with the front gate with concern but also an element of calm composure. She was glad Buddy hadn't run off, saying it showed he clearly loved his grouchy owner. When it came to Joy's suspicions about her ex-partner, Gemma dismissed this with a tight laugh. *'Mum, your PTSD is causing your imagination to run wild. You most likely forgot to secure the latch'.*

Joy trusted Gemma's common sense. Nonetheless, the incident weighed uneasily in her gut. Glancing at her watch, thankfully it was morning tea time. A cuppa would be the cure for these first glimmers of growing anxiety. She dropped the pen and pad, and set off to the kitchen. As soon as she stepped inside, Buddy began to carry on, running up and down the garden barking furiously. She shook her head in exasperation. So much for thinking he'd changed after the scare.

Lost in thought, picturing Christmas and Jaxon's delight at presenting Buddy and wondering how she could possibly give up Buddy even if he drove her crazy, she poured steaming water into a mug and dangled a tea bag up and down. Several hard, aggressive knocks on the front door startled her out of these pleasant musings.

Panicking, her first reaction was to run into the master bedroom to hide. Feeling childish, she began taking deep breaths trying to be sensible and composed. When sufficiently 'mindful', she lightly padded to the front door and put an ear to the solid huon pine slab, listening for any clues as to who might be there. There were several more pounding knocks, heavy and demanding, which caused her to jump back. And then a gruff curse, boots on pavement, and a gate opening and slamming shut. Buddy was going psycho in the back garden, shrill, high-pitched yelping that gave an impression of being murdered.

She waited a few minutes before opening the door a crack to ensure he was gone – whoever that was! Her heart pounded through her chest up to her throat in terror.

She really needed that cup of tea.

Returning to the garden bench, mug in hand, Joy tried to calm and shush Buddy. Having nothing to do with that, he continued to bark and snarl in a righteous frenzy of doggie bellicosity. This time at least, he was being a guard dog, Joy sighed stoically. Although this signified nothing to her frazzled nerves.

As she took a sip of soothing tea, a man's head poked over the back fence, saw her and dropped back down. She flinched with shock, not sure if she should run back inside. Too late, he appeared in her garden, a large man with a beer gut, balding, dressed in jeans and a loose t-shirt emblazoned with a heart shaped logo that stated *I love Eden Isle.*

"Shut your goddamn dog up! Or I'll do it for you," he started yelling. "What kind of person are you to let a dog yap all day long!" The stranger shook a fist at her. "I'll report you to the council and have it put down," he threatened.

It wasn't Gemma's ex. This thought and the disconnect between the cheerful logo on his shirt and his flushed face contorted in fury threw Joy off centre. Who was this stranger and what was he doing standing there?

Thankfully, he didn't come any closer but stood his ground in no rush to leave. Joy froze to the spot, unable to move, much less speak, with a heart fluttering like a bird caught in a net.

Her silence enraged him even more. He continued to rant and rave about staying at a B&B across the road for the week and needing peace and quiet, all the time swearing and calling her disgusting names. Joy managed to grab

Buddy, as much to use him as a shield from the guy as to protect Buddy. The little beast fidgeted and whined, wanting to get to the man. Despite getting scratched, Joy held tight.

She made an attempt to de-escalate the situation, spluttering, "This is my home; I live here. You have no right to trespass onto my property without permission…" and then she tried to gain his empathy imploring, "I've got PTSD. It's hard for me, I can't take any anger or aggression. Please leave…" But the man ignored her entreaties and continued to intensify his intimidation.

The final straw came when spittle streaked out of his mouth as he screamed, "If your dog doesn't stop barking, I'll kill it!"

This threat spurred her into action. How dare this arrogant mainlander decide that just because he'd booked a holiday, he could invade the privacy of her home and scream about his rights to peace and quiet. As if by purchasing a bed and breakfast for the week, this somehow gave him an entitlement to impose demands on the neighbours. Well, this was her home and not a tourist experience. Sorry, but it was not included in the B&B deal! The jerk.

She didn't have to stay and listen or accommodate his demands. There was a limit to being polite and hospitable to a trespasser.

If he'd been capable of a civil conversation, she would have sympathised with his position. Buddy was driving her crazy too. She'd wanted the dog to shut up for the past few weeks. She was trying chill pills but they would take another few days to work. Peace and quiet were her priorities too. But threatening and screaming wasn't the solution to the problem.

Running to the door lugging Buddy into the safety of the house, she shouted through the screen, "I'm calling the police. Leave now or they'll make you."

Shaking his head as if to clear it, the man stalked off, stopped and returned, shook his fists and shouted a few more expletives, before eventually disappearing out of the yard.

Joy pulled the door shut and locked it. Buddy squirmed and ran off in the direction of the front door, barking like a rabid animal.

Joy slumped in a chair with her head in her hands. Every time she started to feel 'normal' and was making progress towards equilibrium, this kind of shit happened, sending her spiralling into a black abyss of anxiety. Congratulations, Honor! Her sister was right once again. Joy drew trouble as if she were an iron lodestone. Not knowing what to do, a flood of numbness washed through her.

Home was not a sanctuary now. Her last place of safe refuge had been swamped by fear. This invasion to her security and Buddy's incessant barking built up like debris of mud and stone carried in by a flood of anguish. An aversion to her cottage and her pet surged through her heart. She had to fight it before it overwhelmed. A restless grief rose to the surface, pressuring for decisions.

A debate went on in her head about whether to call the police. The guy had threatened to kill her dog. Could she take any more drama and confrontation?

In the end, she packed Buddy in the car and drove to Gemma's.

***

The timing could not have been worse. Joy arrived at her daughter's the same time Jaxon skipped off the school bus. In no mood for cuddles and playfulness, she jerked Buddy out of the car and marched up the stone path to the porch.

A surprised Gemma greeted them at the door. Frowning and grumpy, Joy walked in, yanking the lead attached to a reluctant dog. A cowering Buddy slipped and slid alongside his owner without tangling the lead around her legs, for once. Jaxon saw Buddy and ran shrieking in excitement, puzzled as to why Granny was ignoring him.

On the way over, she'd spent the trip ruminating about the past few weeks of disruption to her life and how the neighbours would be offside now. She blamed Gemma... and Honor and Kodi. Everyone thought they knew what was best for her. But this idea of a therapy dog wasn't one.

The dog had to go. It was all too much pressure. She wasn't coping. He wasn't worth the hassles.

"I'm over it," Joy announced in a shrill voice laced with stress. Her daughter stopped as if she'd pressed an imaginary pause button waiting for the volcanic eruption her mother's words predicated. Pushing past, Joy ended up in the family room pacing up and down with Buddy.

"Mum?" Gemma asked, carefully.

"It's gotten to be too much," Joy groaned. "Buddy has to go back to the RSPCA before he drives me crazy."

"No, Granny! They'll put him to sleep," Jaxon screamed. Buddy dug his heels into the carpet and refused to move, stopping Joy's pacing and giving Jaxon a chance to pick him up in a protective hug. "It's not fair," he yelled. Joy let go of the lead and burst into tears.

"Sit, Mum. I'll get you a cup of tea and you can tell me all about it," Gemma said soothingly. Jaxon ran off to his bedroom carting Buddy like a rag doll.

Over a cuppa, Joy let loose with a tirade on a scale her daughter hadn't witnessed since the early days of PTSD. Guilt accentuated the tremendous stress caused by a looming tribunal hearing where all her hope hinged on one last determination. Their verdict would be the irrevocable, conclusive factor that decided the quality of her life in retirement, and more importantly, a last judgement on the merits of her story. It was a final chance at vindication. To make her case, she needed a clear head and sound intellect. With cognitive impairment arising from PTSD this was hard enough – *'and now an angry lunatic came out of the blue and invaded her one last sanctuary leaving her with no place that felt safe. Jaxon was right. It wasn't fair... to Buddy. He deserved a better owner'.*

"But you love him, mum. He's bonded to you," Gemma entreated. "Don't punish him for his natural instincts to protect you."

"Is that what he's doing?" Joy smiled ruefully, finally winding down enough to feel despicable at losing it and upsetting Jaxon.

"Give him time for the chill pills to work," Gemma said. "If they don't work in a few days, we can look at other options. Your veterinarian may have some ideas about what to do. Just don't make any rash decisions in the heat of the moment."

Gemma's words made good sense. Joy began to calm down. "I know it's not really Buddy that's the problem. It's the workers comp crap getting to me. I want it over already." She slumped and let out a long sigh of frustration deflating residual tension. In a more even tone, she explained, "I haven't been sleeping again. The crux of the problem is they're forcing me to retire and I don't really want to. I see myself as a working woman."

"Oh, Mum. I'm so sorry."

"What am I going to do with myself? There's nothing to look forward to."

Gemma frowned with concern. "The timing for Buddy was wrong. We should have got him after you retired." They sat in silence for a few minutes, wondering where to go from here.

"The good news, I guess, is that the horrible guy wasn't your ex stalking you," Joy said.

"Yeah, I have to admit I keep getting a feeling I'm being watched. Talk about not sleeping lately, that's me, too," Gemma admitted. "I'm so exhausted."

Joy studied the dark circles under her daughter's eyes with worry. Even Gemma's freckles appeared faded from washed out fatigue. Barking erupted in the vicinity of Jaxon's room. Next, they heard Buddy was doing his usual thing, leaping at the front door, scratching with his paws, all the time emitting piercing shrieks.

"See what I mean," Joy rolled her eyes in resignation.

Gemma frowned. "There's someone out there. I can feel it." She tiptoed to the window, parted the net curtains and peaked out. "I can see a car parked outside, Mum. Have a look." Her voice was shrill with panic.

Joy glanced out the window, not convinced but wanting to de-escalate her daughter's melt down. In a monotone, she said, "Do you mean the black sedan? It's probably someone taking a wrong turn and re-setting their GPS."

"Probably," Gemma said with a quavering voice, not convinced.

"Buddy needs to work off all that energy. Do you want to come for a walk with us?" Joy suggested.

"Sure. If that car's still out there, why don't we go over and ask what he's doing parked outside my house? Set our minds at ease," Gemma said.

But in the short few minutes it took for Jaxon to tie his shoelaces, attach a lead to Buddy, and step out onto the front porch, the sedan silently disappeared down the road.

Buddy, of course, sensing his days could be numbered, walked to heel next to Jaxon like the perfect pet, wagging his tail in pleasure. Every so often he'd cranked his head towards Joy, displaying little white pointy teeth, as if smiling for her approval.

When they arrived back home, Jaxon locked Buddy away in his bedroom to continue playing. Joy could hear a toy being thrown accompanied by laughter and cheers of encouragement.

"It would break Jaxon's heart if you gave Buddy away," Gemma said.

Joy glanced in the direction of Jaxon's bedroom. Could she be so selfish and do that to her grandson? It was her sanity at stake after all.

Seeing her mother's indecision, she said, "Why don't you leave him with us until the palaver with the tribunal is over? I'm not saying we'll keep him forever, just for a little while."

"I could use a quiet interlude to get my head right," Joy agreed. It was a temporary circuit break, not a permanent solution, but she'd take the opportunity when it was offered.

"Maybe I can train that horrible barking out of him in the meantime."

Gemma, it seemed, still believed in miracles.

"Sweetheart, if he keeps up the barking, Jaxon needs to understand. I'm going to have to return him even if that means..." Joy couldn't say it.

"I know, Mum."

Chapter Seventy One

Two weeks of reprieve from a yappy dog allowed Joy the luxury of worrying about her workers compensation matter without the additional hullabaloo. John Emerson had yet to contact her about a new settlement offer but his phone call was expected soon. It would be the next step in a long-protracted negotiation process prior to going to the tribunal. The legal process was happening in the background and was out of her hands. She trusted John had everything under control.

This was a chance to practise Honor's advice and 'let it go'. With firm resolve, she settled into the cushions on the sofa and opened Fellowes' book. Starting a new chapter, she tried to read his philosophy of *living in the here and now.*

It didn't work. Fifteen minutes later and stirrings of the wrongness of his judgmental messages erupted into a full blown attack of self-righteousness. It didn't fit her experience. In fact, it was just the opposite.

He lectured about opening one's heart to nature and ceasing the distractions and constant chatter in one's head. This is what caused disequilibrium and negativity, he accused, followed by instructions for an exercise on how to stop the tendency of escaping to elsewhere in the mind.

When Joy attempted this *mindfulness to induce flow*, it didn't work. When she sought to quiet the mind, all she could see was an angry tourist invading her garden with a face screwed up in vitriolic aggression. It would not be possible to sit in relaxed openness amongst nature in her garden despite the beautiful summer weather after what happened. Try as she might, his presence lingered as a ghost in the shadows, lurking behind the fence like a ghoul waiting to jump out and terrify.

Unless Honor came over to insist on their weekly walks, Joy remained hidden in the cottage watching DVDs, back to her old couch potato ways. Even going to the grocery store caused such apprehension, it was left to the final minute when the last dregs of milk were gone and she couldn't stomach black coffee no matter how desperate for a caffeine fix.

The horrible tourist had left a niggling sentiment she couldn't name and couldn't shake. Gemma's superstitious imaginings about being watched had infected her as well. Spending days escaping to elsewhere viewing DVDs about fantasy lands, fairy godmothers and magic wands granting sparkling wishes was a thousand times preferable than living in the here and now. Fellowes was wrong – reality was too ugly to cope with sometimes.

When she read about the habit of busyness causing psychological discord, once again, she took exception to Fellowes' preaching. Clearly, the doctor had never experienced PTSD personally. Thinking about her daily employment routine at the centre, one of constant activity and social interaction *BTS* compared to the tedium of her current lonely, bored existence stuck at home without anything to do, it was a no brainer as to which one she'd choose. If given a choice.

Each morning she awoke to a cavernous gap of nothingness – no plans, no work, no social life, no purpose and motivation. This caused her disturbing PTS disorder, not busyness.

Restless and annoyed with experts reinforcing the message that it was all her fault for not managing her mind better, Joy dumped the book on the coffee table. Standing up and stretching the kinks from tight shoulders, she padded across to the French windows to check the garden for intruders. Nothing out of the ordinary. Except that niggling feeling back again.

On a mission to continue finding fault with Fellowes' philosophy, she returned to the sofa and persevered with finishing the chapter.

He lived up to his reputation. Fellowes lectured about the spiritual significance of developing what he labelled 'patient endurance'. It meant a quality of open expectation, waiting for the storm to end, the seas to calm, the floodwaters to reside...

And for the dilemma she was caught up in to resolve (for good or ill).

She needed her wits about her, not to settle into a state of *waiting* in a kind of compliant, disempowered acceptance. Having to endure the workers compensation process didn't mean she had to do it in a state of blissful resignation. If she was in the game, this required a fighting spirit. Ultimately, vindication would provide the peace she sought.

Fortuitously, John Emerson called the next day to advise that an offer to settle from the department had been received. Insulting – it was a repeat of the previous low figure. His secretary would post a letter explaining the offer and the options open to her, along with attachments of two reports of interest. His letter would include an explanation of consequences against each option. She must think carefully before responding.

In a worst case scenario, if she rejected the latest offer, the employer could terminate weekly compensation payments pending a tribunal decision. Emerson thought this was unlikely. The matter was listed for a hearing and the department's reputation would suffer if they played hardball too overtly.

Whatever her decision, her instructions would be final. He required an answer within the next week.

Joy wanted to declare in no uncertain terms she would never accept an offer because she wanted her moment in front of the tribunal. However, Emerson barely gave her a chance to grunt an acknowledgement before he moved on to another matter of legal procedure.

He explained, the respondent had challenged the claim. A motion to discredit for exaggerating her injury had been tabled by the employer, largely based on Dr Evans testimony. Emerson assured *It was nonsense.* There was nothing to worry about. He'd argued the merits of Joy's case, citing Dr Sanjay's assessment and his objection succeeded. The tribunal dismissed the motion.

Despite not understanding what the legal jargon meant, it was obvious from the self-congratulatory note in Emerson's voice, he'd earnt his money. Joy managed to murmur a meek *thank you* before a dead phone indicated he'd ended their conversation.

Now it was just a matter of waiting for his letter to arrive.

Chapter Seventy Two

Two days later, John Emerson's letter arrived in the post box.

Joy sat on the edge of her quilt in a patch of sunlight knifing through the windowpane, quickly skimming over John's blunt legal logic, paging through to the reports attached. Her heart sank. Forgetting Buddy was at Gemma's, she called out his name, needing the comfort of his alert, smiley face. Needing to hug a warm, alive creature to remind herself of affection and the reality of a more natural world. She was met with silent emptiness.

John's one page letter stated she had three options left open: accept the offer, reject the offer and put in a counter offer, or reject the offer and go to the tribunal for a final decision.

John pointed out if she lost at the tribunal, the department could ask for their legal costs and expenses to be awarded.

As if this added pressure of losing and having to pay the department's legal bill wasn't bad enough.

The attached reports were worse. All she had to do was look at the reports where her employer had preferred to pay a lot of money to other people with the sole aim of discrediting her, rather than pay her fair and just entitlements as set out under current legislation, to understand how the odds stacked up.

At first glance, the offer could be mistaken for a large sum of money, like a winning lottery ticket. Until the calculations were made.

The department was offering to retire Joy on what equated to living on unemployment benefits for the next eight years until eligible for the aged pension. It didn't come close to what she'd get by staying on workers compensation. It was massively less than *Before the Strangling* with a salary accruing long service leave and superannuation until she decided to retire. There was nothing in the settlement offer compensating for the workplace injury, nor an admission of liability. It was their *get out of jail free* card.

It was a white glove slapped in her face. They were demonstrating their powerful position and challenging her – live in poverty or take your chances at the tribunal – and lose everything anyway. This was war and she was the enemy that had to lose.

Since her marriage to Pete, the one thing she feared most was being forced into poverty and unable to work her way out of it. After their divorce, she'd put a financial plan in place based on retiring at sixty five. She'd worked hard, put money aside and budgeted frugally to ensure a comfortable lifestyle in old age. But there hadn't been enough time for this plan to amount to any significant sum.

Ironic how the best laid plans can fail, when one was a trouble magnet.

She stared at John's typical, coldly objective legalistic letter. And the two attached reports that changed everything, sinking into depths of despair.

Dr Evans' second report was the most disappointing because her letter appealing to his better nature had clearly been ignored, if ever read. There was an element of humiliation in realising this. The report's lack of ethical and scientific scruples raised gasps of angry indignation. She was not afforded a right of reply. His views stood on their merit and his reputation, unlike Joy who was not deemed worthy to comment on her own behaviour.

As Marcus had explained, unlike courts of law, the tribunal did not require factual, medical rigour under its rules of evidence. Dr Evans could rely on his credibility as an expert witness; his opinions would not be held up to scientific scrutiny or justification.

Fortunately, John had been successful in a dismissal of the motion to discredit. But the damage to Joy's humanity was done nonetheless, and this was the department's intention. Pure and simple intimidation. There had never been an even playing field. She'd been naïve to believe she had a chance. They'd boxed her into a corner.

A numb acceptance of inevitable defeat kept her from breaking down. She had to apply a strategic brain to this final piece of negotiation before making a decision. In her heart, she wanted to continue to pursue the matter to a tribunal decision – out of sheer bloody mindedness. It wasn't about the money; it was always about vindication, truth and reality. But at what cost?

Before making a decision, it was more important to alert members of her family as to what had been going on. It affected them as well. She hated this more than anything else.

Gemma would take it badly given the history with her ex-partner.

Chapter Seventy Three

The next afternoon, Gemma, Honor and Kodi sat around Joy's kitchen table, held mugs of hot tea and waited patiently, accommodating her whim in holding this urgent family meeting. *Something to do with her compensation claim*, she'd cryptically mentioned. A bored Jaxon went off with Buddy taking him for a walk.

Too agitated to sit still, Joy paced between the kitchen and the table, first grabbing a sugar bowl, then returning for a jug of milk, and finally settling Oreo cookies on a plate in the centre between them. Her heart wouldn't stop racing and her stomach was nauseous from apprehension. There was no way she'd be eating any cookies but it was a way of avoiding the issue for a few minutes longer.

Standing in front of them, all eyes on her, she bowed her head as if praying. "There's something important I need to tell you," Joy stammered. Her head was woozy making it difficult to focus. "I'm not sure how to say it. But firstly, I'm so sorry about it. I feel totally devastated."

Kodi snorted, unimpressed with the drama. "Spill it, Auntie Joy. We'll cope."

"My lawyer advised me that the department attempted to dismiss my claim for compensation arguing I've been exaggerating my PTSD injury." Joy's voice cracked holding back an urge to weep. There were gasps of outrage and she held up a hand to quiet their protests. It was hard enough getting it out without interruptions. "I was put under surveillance. There's been someone staked outside my house for weeks, spying from seven in the morning to early evening. And worse, he's followed me whenever I've left the house, when visiting you and meeting you for lunch. You, too, have been on spy cam tapes as part of my surveillance. They've listed your addresses and car licence plate numbers. My lawyer sent me the surveillance report."

Gemma went pale and slumped in the chair. "Is it still going on?" she asked in a tight, stressed voice.

Shocked because this hadn't occurred to Joy, she didn't know how to answer. Darting a look out the window proved a useless gesture. The surveillance guy had never been spotted before. "I feel like I'm being watched and followed all the time now. When I step outside the house, I start to hyperventilate and weep."

Gemma hugged her chest and nodded with understanding.

Honor cut in, pleading disbelief. "Can the government do that without permission? Is that even legal? I mean, they were spying on you out of working hours and on your day off as well. How is that fair for an employee?"

Joy nodded. "I looked it up and it's hard to believe but apparently as long as they don't record voices, it's legal. I wanted you to know as soon as possible because it's horrible you've been caught up in my legal battle unknowingly."

Kodi shrugged. "I've got nothing to hide," she announced boldly.

"It feels like I've been violated, it's such an invasion of my privacy," Gemma whispered, looking as if she was going to faint. "I knew we were being watched. I felt it in my bones." She lifted a jug and tried to tip milk into her tea but both hands shook so much, blobs of milk spilled on the table.

Struck with guilt, Joy said, "I'm so sorry. The surveillance guy was good. I had no idea he followed me around, videotaping my movements – grocery shopping for heaven's sake. He waited outside my old meditation classes thinking I was still going." She laughed in disbelief. "How did he know to go there? He knew all this personal stuff about me. How intrusive is that! It never crossed my mind that the department would go to such extremes to win. It scares me sick."

Honor was disgusted. "Joy, you are the most honest, truthful person I know. It's so unfair they're besmirching your good reputation by implying you are a liar and a cheat!"

"They're the cheats," Kodi said, thumping the table.

Joy winced. "It's not the way I wanted to end my career, in a blaze of humiliating accusations rather than pride and glory." She shook her head in confusion. "What doesn't make sense is that my doctor's the one writing medical certificates saying I'm totally incapacitated for work. He's the one telling me I've got PTSD. I'm not diagnosing myself. Like I didn't even know what PTSD was until I was diagnosed with it."

"Yeah, if the department was questioning his diagnosis, why not get a second or third opinion?" Kodi said. "What's a video of you grocery shopping going to prove?"

"It's not as if you can diagnose someone's state of mind looking at a video!" she agreed.

"Can I have a look at the report?" Kodi asked. Joy handed across the surveillance report along with Dr Evans' clinical assessment based on it.

Around the table, they went quiet, trying to make sense of feelings about being spied on by an agency of the government. They lived in rural Eden Isle, not a totalitarian regime like China. These things didn't happen to people in sleepy Lower Teasel. The plate of cookies emptied as they waited for Kodi to finish skim reading the report.

Eventually she put it down. "This makes me laugh, Auntie Joy. In Dr Evans professional opinion, you had too many groceries in your trolley. How is that even relevant? I'd like to see his PhD thesis on the correlation between the number of grocery items in a shopping cart and elevated anxiety levels for women with PTSD! As if. What an idiot." Smirking, she leafed through the pages and pointed to a paragraph. "Apparently, individuals prone to panic attacks only do small shops and use the self-checkout at Woolies. Did you know that was a medical fact? You must have been faking your symptoms because you went through a staffed check out with a full cart!" she said, mocking.

Honor snorted. "Is that the best he could come up with? Only a psychiatrist from the mainland could make that statement! As if there are any self-checkouts in Lower Teasel!"

"Or that I'd have a panic attack at Woolies. Grocery shopping relaxes me, and I've never found teenage check out operators that scary," Joy said. "Mind you, I probably do over-shop."

"The guy is talking out his ass," Kodi stated. "How can he watch a video and say your approach to grocery shopping proves you don't suffer from symptoms of PTSD or that because you are smiling at the checkout operator this means you're not anxious or depressed? It's so blatantly unethical."

"My counsellor tells me Dr Evil is held in high esteem amongst psychologists," Joy said with a smirk.

"Makes you question the whole business of psychology and counselling in my opinion," Honor quipped.

Gemma remained quiet throughout this dialogue. Finally, she spoke up. "You said your lawyer and Dr Evans have viewed the surveillance tapes. I wonder how many other people have? It creeps me out thinking about being spied on in my home and personal private space – and then as well, all these people looking at us on tape without permission."

"It's such a disturbing invasion of our privacy," Honor agreed.

Joy thought about the answer. "I imagine, the workers compensation team plus department managers would have seen the tapes. The Crown Prosecutor. My lawyer sent it to Dr Sanjay for his opinion. And the tribunal panel members would have seen it when the motion to discredit was put forward."

"That's a lot of people," Gemma whispered, looking troubled.

"I didn't even know about the tapes and wasn't given an opportunity to comment on them before they were submitted as evidence to the tribunal," Joy said in her defence. "Like in the report you are referred to as my *'friends'* – not my family – implying I have this vast social life. And I'm not allowed to correct the assumptions for the record.

"That sucks," Kodi said.

"Mum, I wonder if Buddy's barking is related to the surveillance?"

"It makes sense. His behaviour changed right about that time."

Gemma became animated. "What about that aggro man who entered your garden? Maybe he wasn't a tourist. Maybe he was the surveillance guy angry at Buddy's barking, giving his stake out away?"

"Wait," Kodi shouted. "There's something in the report... here it is. '*Spot check on subject's residence, no activity noted. Agent RTG makes a pretext call to see if at home*'. I wondered what a pretext call meant. I think that Gemma's right."

"The knock on the door, entering your property and yelling at you – it was all a set up for their spy cam to tape," Gemma said with horrified amazement. "What the...!"

The enormity of the extremes the department had gone through to trap and trip her sent palpitations of dread ripping through Joy's body. The power of their amorality defied all she knew about honesty and justice.

"I was about to have my beautiful little dog put down over it." She began to weep in anguish. "Jaxon would never have forgiven me. And I love Buddy. It would have broken my heart."

"They're evil. I can't stand it, Mum," Gemma joined in, weeping too. "When's it all going to end?"

Chapter Seventy Four

The next morning after a restless, sleepless night, Joy crawled out of bed to answer a call on her mobile. Honor's name displayed in bold caps. Her sister rarely called, preferring to text rather than converse. Sensing something wasn't right, Joy answered in a fluster.

Her sister opened the conversation by saying, "Now, I don't want you to get upset, so before I say anything, I want you to know Gemma is fine."

Naturally, Joy's heart started thumping like the bass in a heavy metal band. "What happened?"

"Yesterday, on the way home from your place we were about to drop Gemma and Jaxon off but Gemma started having trouble breathing; her chest got tight and she began to suffer from agonising heart pain. It was quite scary."

"She was having a heart attack!" Joy gasped about to have one of her own.

"It's okay; she's fine. There's no need to panic. We decided to take her to Emergency without delay," Honor explained.

"Why didn't you phone me straight away?" Upset and furious, Joy's voice raised in volume. "Where is she? I need to go to her."

Honor was contrite. "Gemma insisted not to contact you until we knew what was going on. After all the horribleness about being spied upon, she didn't want to upset you any more than necessary."

"I don't care about all that when my family is in trouble," Joy cried.

"I know. We tried to talk her out of it but your daughter can be stubborn. The doctors hooked her up to an ECG machine, took her bloods, and then gave her some tablets. Within the hour, she was fine. Believe me, Joy. It wasn't a heart attack."

"What was it then?"

"Stress. An intense attack of anxiety. They kept her in overnight to monitor her heart to be safe and they let her out first thing this morning. She's home resting."

"Oh, god. All the surveillance shit got to her. I knew she wasn't coping before that, but I never imagined she was that bad. I should have kept quiet and not burdened her. Was it wrong to tell her about the stalking and the video cam?" Joy was overcome with maternal guilt and worry.

Honor was soothing. "It's not your fault, Joy. You weren't to know. They dosed her up on Murelax and ordered her to bed for the week. A good rest will be the best thing."

"What about--"

Honor read her mind. "We're looking after Jaxon, so don't worry; he's fine."

After their conversation, Joy dressed quickly in order to rush over to Gemma's. On the way, a cold fury built up in her system. The department had overstepped the boundaries of decency when they interfered with the sanctity of her home and the privacy of members of her family. The question was *what was she going to do about it?*

At the last minute, she decided to stop at the local florist for a bunch of colourful gerberas to brighten Gemma's mood. The florist rang up the purchase, took her EFTPOS card and then politely told her it had been declined. *Did she want to try again?*

After another go with the same result, Joy realised her fortnightly compensation pay had not gone into her bank account. There wasn't enough money in savings to cover an eighteen-dollar bunch of flowers. Returning the flowers with a red face, she started to dial Michelle to find out what was going on, but when it went to message bank she remembered it was the Saturday of a long weekend. She'd have to wait three more days to sort out the problem with the Workers Compensation Pay Officer.

Another reminder, the department could play hard ball with her life.

Chapter Seventy Five

Joy was overcome with shock and guilt at seeing her usually vivacious daughter lying in bed as limp as seaweed. It was so unfair she'd been caught up in Joy's workers compensation battle, stalked and spied upon by strangers. No wonder this had triggered a massive stress reaction. It would take several days of rest and reassurance before Gemma's heart settled into a more peaceful rhythm and she began to feel safe again. If this was possible while the tribunal hearing hung over them like the Sword of Damocles.

Returning home, the embers of Joy's guilt flamed into a wildfire of anger. The government should not be allowed to get away with this, treating her like some kind of terrorist on a watch list. There must be an authority overseeing this type of over-reach on the part of government departments where she could register a complaint.

Nothing came to mind. Perhaps Jim at the Compo Hotline could offer a suggestion.

Joy waited for the receptionist to call up her file on the Compo Hotline's in-house computer system. It was taking longer than expected. The on-hold music piped in from a local country radio station was giving her a headache.

"Thank you for waiting, Ms O'Connell," a chirpy voice came back online. "I've been told Jim has taken three months long service leave, so we will allocate another consultant to speak with you. I'll need to take some details."

This news confounded Joy. Why couldn't just one person involved in her workers compensation matter last the distance?

"Can I have your date of birth and the name of your employer?" the girl asked in a rote business tone.

"That will be on my file when I spoke to Jim before," Joy answered, rather annoyed at the receptionist's ineptness.

"I'm sorry but we don't seem to have a record open on our files. When did you last speak to Jim?" The receptionist was polite but puzzled.

"Not that long ago." Joy tried to remember. "Back in... I'll have to check my diary. But I've asked Jim for advice on at least two other occasions over the past few months. He was very helpful. One of my concerns was put in a report to the tribunal." She decided to be firm with the receptionist, who obviously was too lazy to look up the details.

The line went dead and then Joy heard the sound of faint but rapid keystrokes at the other end. "Umm, no. I'm checking his closed files as well. Nothing. Would you like us to start a clean file on your matter?"

The question hung in the air. A *clean* file. A blank slate, white, empty, wiped clean. No history of her version of events.

The message was clear.

Joy ended the call without further argument. So much for the spiel about the hotline's independence. The power of the government to erase its tracks was frightening.

One research scientist defined PTSD as *entrenched fear*. Looking back over the past year, Joy decided this was as good a definition as any.

She had feared Poppy. She had feared her employer pressuring a return to a workplace with Poppy in it. She had feared her doctor's power to withdraw a medical certificate during each fortnightly medical review. She had feared each and every person on her workers compensation team – counsellors, the return to work coordinator, psychologists, psychiatrists, lawyers – with their duplicitous pretence of supporting her when their jobs depended on maintaining the status quo of the system. There had been no one she could trust in this process.

Until this experience, she never fully grasped what it felt like to be a victim. It was confronting to admit to her intelligent, assertive feminist self – that once rebelled at any threat to self-determination – she'd been forced into compliance and disempowered against her will. *She'd fought back but had been powerless to defend against their persistent assault.* She didn't recognise this person she'd become.

In the wake of trauma, an intractable conclusion slowly took hold of her limbic brain: the world was a fearsome place of impersonal evil and random acts of cruelty. Where she believed once in concepts such as security, benevolence, justice and rightness, now such notions mocked her. They'd become dead markers of what was once meaningful from a time when the world made sense. She was left angry at the betrayal of colleagues and cynical about the goodness of strangers.

She recalled Marcus spouting an old maxim at her in an attempt to sound like the sage counsellor during one of their earliest sessions. '*Trauma changes you*', he'd pronounced.

As if knowing this helped at all.

He was wrong as usual. Joy knew, trauma doesn't change as much as destroy. It leaves a pitiful, vulnerable shell of a person, where a vibrant Joy once thrived.

Her GP diagnosed depression and decided she could be cured with pills. But he was wrong, too. Joy wasn't depressed, she was lost. She could not find her *Self*. This was the problem.

Dr Fellowes was also wrong. Mindfulness was not a cure. PTSD was an overabundance of conscious awareness. PTSD forced Joy to sit in a discomfort of emptiness, lost and alone in a place of not knowing – a hellish version of mindfulness.

Joy envied all those unaware people with their rose-coloured filters that screened the glare from their world and coloured life as predictable, safe, nice. She missed optimism and faith. She no longer belonged to this once familiar world.

She hated being this way, a victim of the system. She hated them for doing this to her.

Trauma had thrust her out of time. She was tuned to an alien wavelength, out of sync with friends and family. Hypervigilant to an ever-present danger only she could sense as real. Left with a hypervigilant anxiety that rejected all life's soft nuances and gentle aesthetics, knowing these could not be trusted. She expected jagged edges and sharp falls in her future.

She told herself, living with PTSD meant accepting some things could not be recovered. The strangling wiped clean the previous person she had been, leaving a blank file. It forced starting fresh, letting go of all the old, moving on to find a new normal, accepting this new non-self – a white canvas waiting to be redrawn.

Chapter Seventy Six

Marcus was being his usual, annoying self, not showing the least surprise at her horror and outrage at being spied upon by her employer – *the government* – but instead acted in his best 'counsellor' mode, calm and slightly superior in the face of her emotional outburst. It would be like him to say something like *she looked cute when angry*; if he did, she'd punch the guy.

Soon after visiting Gemma, Joy had booked this emergency appointment with him. Seeing her pallid daughter out of hospital, lying in bed weak from chest pain, knowing it was her fault, was the straw that broke an ironclad resolve.

Guilt, outrage and a mother's instinct to protect her family combined with an accumulation of anger at all the useless, do-gooder counselling interventions – over twelve months of professionals telling her what to think and feel, her employer and magistrates re-writing reality to suit their purposes, no one being honest about the true purpose of any of it – all this formed into a *fuck it all* fighting spirit.

If surveillance was simply another part of the workers comp *game*, it had become a game of war and her opponent was powerful, well-resourced and treacherous. One she could never win against.

Joy needed to vent failure and debrief inevitable defeat as part of *'the show'*. She would use Marcus. Anyway, he deserved to be a sounding board to her loss and despair. That was his job.

This game plan was not about winning. Assessing the opposition in light of recent events, she understood success had never been an option. This next move was simply to put her in a better bargaining position when accepting the extent of the losses; to go out on her terms, not intimidated into agreeing to theirs.

After visiting Gemma on her sick bed, a defiant Joy decided to quell emotional knee jerk decisions and get smart. It was not just about her PTSD anymore. It was about protecting her family. She could resurrect the negotiating skills that came naturally after years of working as a management consultant. After a SWOT analysis of the current problem, taking into account the current political climate leading to an election, Joy plotted a path. One she could live with, despite its blow to the ego (whatever was left of that part of her 'self'). It came down to a choice of values. What was truly important at the end of the day?

It was a calculated risk but what was there to lose? For the sake of securing a better outcome, she must employ strategy.

It was never about the money.

The greatest losses had already been taken away: her daughter's health and peace of mind. This was unforgivable. And, just as unforgivable, Joy's last place of sanctuary, home, a property where she felt safe in an unsafe world.

No monetary value could be placed on these losses.

Marcus knew what these had meant to Joy. And yet, he'd been instrumental in facilitating the losses, aware of how devastating this would be to her.

He must have known she'd remember participating in his word association game about home as sanctuary. At the time, she never fathomed this simple therapy technique, shared in trust, could have shattering ramifications.

He'd proved his character by this betrayal. He was another player in the game, a spy in her midst, reporting back these snippets of insights craftily pulled from her psyche for the department to use against her.

That did not mean she had to opt out of the game without one final engagement. She could be a poker player with one final bluff. Knowing Marcus's perfidy, having taken his measure and understanding his complicity, he would be the last hand she played.

"I almost had my dog put down," she shouted into the counselling room, avoiding eye contact with Marcus and continuing a well-rehearsed rant. *The implication she was out to cheat the system like a common criminal instead of a decent, albeit injured, employee offended on so many levels. As if stalking outside her home, trying to catch her out and driving her dog crazy in the process, achieved anything except entrenching her PTSD symptoms worse than ever,* she carried on like a fishwife.

In a coup de grace, she screamed, "My daughter ended up in hospital with a suspected heart attack over this! How dare they intrude into the privacy of my home and family. They had no right."

Marcus was unmoved. Smiling in a smug, superior sort of way, he said matter of fact, "Of course, they had to check out if you were faking. There's a lot of money at stake." Demonstrating a total lack of empathy, he dismissed Joy's sense of violation with a wave of his hand.

His indifference stirred her wrath like a witch's cauldron. After all, this was an emergency appointment set up because she was not coping.

"How can Dr Evil argue that I'm faking my symptoms just because surveillance shows I'm making an effort to get out of the house more often, go for walks, visit loved ones? These are all the things my GP recommended as part of my treatment towards recovery. It's like saying that because I take prescribed meds and they are working, this means I don't suffer from anxiety and therefore I'm a cheat." She looked to Marcus for acknowledgement, but he remained unmoved. It wasn't like she had been the one telling people she had PTSD; countless doctors and psychologists had been making the diagnosis and telling her this was her problem. She didn't even know what that diagnosis meant in the beginning, let alone knew how to fake it.

She continued to over explain. "Meds aren't a cure; they mask symptoms. Just because I may not look like I'm suffering from PTSD doesn't mean Poppy didn't damage me! It's like Dr Evil's punishing me for following doctor's orders. How does that work? It's crazy logic."

Before Marcus could respond, Joy carried on, not particularly interested in his CBT response. "The health department gives new meaning to the notion of rehabilitation. Arguing I'm faking mental distress while all the time testing the limits to my sanity.

"*Let's see how far we can go before we drive her crazy,*" Joy mimicked. "How's intruding into my home and agitating my sanctuary, and violating my rights to privacy and the enjoyment of my personal space, supposed to assist my recovery? They've deliberately intimidated me to cause a breaking point," Joy declared. "They are pure evil. They've made the world a scary place."

As she caught her breath, Marcus seized the opportunity to offer advice. "Joy, there's nothing good or bad, but thinking makes it so. Not everyone and everything is bad. I believe there are good people in the world," he said with an air of wise counsel.

"Yeah, they're the ones with targets on their backs," she responded flippantly. The last thing she needed was to have Hamlet quoted at her.

Marcus chuckled, as if she was delightful rather than cynical and paranoid.

Joy didn't want to be good – or nice. That woman was long gone. A new Joy, ferocious and pragmatic, had replaced her.

"They want to intimidate and harass me into taking the money and running, not go to the tribunal where everything goes on public record. If I take a payout, the department has no case to be answered; no admission of liability; no apology given for the wrongness of what was done to me."

"But afterwards, you could move on with your life, rather than keep circling around this crusade you're on to prove you're right and they are wrong," Marcus cajoled. "Most people's workers compensation experience is similar to you; you're not the first or only one. I've heard it all before. You're not that different. Would it be so bad to let this go, Joy? You're one small person caught in a monolithic system trying to change the way things have always been."

Joy gazed at the wall behind Marcus's head, a doctor's consulting room with ghoulish anatomical posters and advertisements from pharmaceutical companies offering solutions to intimate health problems. This was the moment of tactical truth. She had to sound convincing. "What you're asking is *does it really matter if I deserve to be treated as a human being with rights?* Does my voice deserve to be heard, acknowledged and validated? Should I stand up for what I believe in – my right to sovereignty, privacy, reality? Or do I cave in because that's the easy option?"

Marcus looked chagrined. His role was to convince her to take a payout and she was stubborn, as predicted. "If I were you, I'd accept the inevitable, cut my losses and stop fighting shadows. If you ever want to achieve health and happiness, you have to learn to be more flexible in your views."

Joy smiled at the lame attempt to dissuade her from persevering until the bitter end. "Let me quote Henry David Thoreau: *The cost of something is what I like to call life that has to be exchanged for it.*"

"Meaning?" Marcus asked.

To Joy it seemed so obvious. "It's about my values, Marcus. It's never been about the money or the easy way out. What's most important is vindication.

"They've squeezed the life out of me, choking my spirit, demonstrating they've got me in a stranglehold. I want to breathe again.

"The only way to do this is to see it through. Like a soldier on the shores of Gallipoli, I have to know if I can run the distance despite guns blazing on all sides. I want to go all the way to the tribunal to prove the truth still matters."

Seeing his face pinched with exasperation spurred Joy on to rub in the final tactical points.

Faking intense sincerity, she told him, "It's not about politics. I want the tribunal panel to respect me as an individual, not be convinced I'm some cheat out to defraud the system before I'm able to defend myself. I want to read my statement out loud to the panel, explaining that what I've lost cannot be measured or costed on a WPI scorecard. I want to have my story on public record."

In fact, it wasn't difficult acting out the part of a righteous individual seeking justice. Inside her heart, she felt exactly this way. If her daughter hadn't been so affected by the government's surveillance, she would have bulldozed down the legal path regardless of the potential of financial and mental destruction. Money be damned. There were principles at stake.

However, everything changed when the department intruded into her family's privacy. The priority was to end the drama and its traumatic consequences as quickly as possible, with the best outcome she could negotiate. Now her head overruled her heart. But no one needed to know this. As a player in the game, the ultimate bluff was required.

The threat about going on public record was also a bluff, but Marcus didn't know that. In her fragile state, the last thing she needed was more scrutiny under the public's spotlight. But tactically, it was an election year and she knew the government would shy away from any hint of a scandal. She had to convince her snitch of a counsellor that she was a zealot out for truth and justice, regardless of the consequences, beyond reason and common sense.

It seemed to work. Marcus smirked at her naivety. "You're a public servant working for the government. You've taken an oath of confidentiality regarding your employment. How much do you think they'll allow you to say on public record?"

Joy looked him in the eyes with grim determination. "Let's put that theory to the test, shall we."

She hoped he'd taken the bait and would report these sentiments back to the department as per his usual ingratiating style.

Chapter Seventy Seven

The school hall echoed with the hum of a hundred tiny, excited voices. It was Show Case time.

Immediately upon arrival, they split up. Gil claimed a rickety chair in the middle of the room with a good view of the stage. Poppy went off with Riff to mentally prepare him for the rope trick routine he would be showcasing and to wait behind the stage curtains for their act. The cramped room was overheated and stuffy, with siblings, parents, and grandparents all squashed elbow to elbow among rows of fold-down seats. In organised chaos, miscellaneous teachers directed traffic while teacher's aides and school administration staff lined up against the walls waving to kids, screwing up their faces with cheesy grins beaming encouragement.

Up front a roped off area segregated the grades. The first row of prep students sat straight and obedient, waiting for their teacher's command to file up the stairs and onto the stage. The second row occupied by first graders fidgeted and pushed against their neighbours' shoulders revealing a show of nerves and eliciting stern frowns from their teacher. The other rows were yet to fill with starring pupils.

Stifling a yawn, Gil studied the program. Riff's magic show was scheduled towards the end in between his year six classmates demonstrating their special talents. Noting what came before on the program, he gritted his teeth. An hour or more of squeaking singers dressed as superheroes, and out of tune musical instruments playing versions of *Waltzing Matilda*, a poetry recital of Banjo Patterson for *god's sake*, and a fashion show of cardboard and crepe hats were some of the remarkable acts listed.

Sitting through the whole event was going to be a mark of his capacity to endure torture. He hoped his wife appreciated the effort being made. This gala meant so much to the kid. Poppy was determined nothing would go wrong. Gil couldn't understand Riff's burning desire to show off to his parents, no hopers that they were. However, he was chuffed that Poppy had spent so much time teaching and preparing Riff for this moment of glory. She was a champion agreeing to be part of the act.

In a self-congratulatory mood, Gil deserved some points for taking time off work to attend. This must count towards something in her good books. Lately, some of her behaviours with Riff were bordering on disturbing and he had been considering the best approach on how to open a discussion about his concerns without appearing to be a jealous husband. Poppy's feelings required delicate management. She never took criticism well and had ways of performing acts of subtle punishment when offended. His increasingly debilitating headaches were a case in point. When it came to confronting his wife, she was right – he was a *chicken shit*.

The lights dimmed, followed by the crowd noise fading. A microphone was tapped, emitted piercing feedback, and the Principal opened proceedings with a welcome and some quick, no nonsense remarks about the purpose of the event, finishing with wishing the participants good luck. Much to Gil's relief, she was in a hurry to get the show on the road, and over and done. He crossed his legs and leaned back, prepared to nap through most of it, if he could get away with it. He drifted off to the shrill notes of a recorder playing *Twinkle Twinkle Little Star*.

The echoing sounds of a CD playing the country song, *Old Town Road*, aroused Gil from a light bit of shuteye. Focusing on the stage, he was in time to witness Riff dressed in a cowboy hat, jeans and a check shirt with a kerchief around his neck, riding a stick pony and swinging a lasso hoop above his head.

Riding up to a hitching post prop, he proceeded to tie a rope into a highwayman's knot and anchored it around the post. Theatrically waving a cap gun and blasting off a couple of noisy shots, he yanked the knot and it slipped free with a flourish. Making a getaway, he rode the pony to centre stage and took a short bow to encourage applause. Placing the stick pony to one side, with an outstretched arm he signalled Poppy on stage like a born showman.

She was dressed in a matching outfit, complete with a cowboy hat emblazoned with a sheriff's badge, a kerchief tied around her neck, and a rope of her own. Her part of the act was to tie handcuffs around them both so Riff could demonstrate breaking free. Riff was a true actor. He held up their arms, pulled and twisted the ropes to demonstrate the strength of the knots, all the time screwing up his face with frustration and puzzlement. When he had the crowd enthralled, he pirouetted in a magical dance that untangled the knots and allowed him to break free. While he was giving a curt bow to enthusiastic clapping, Poppy acted the part of a Keystone cop, shaking the ends of her rope as if surprised.

Riff waved his rope in the air in challenge and ran off in a silly stride. Poppy chased after him in circles shouting 'stop thief', shooting a cap gun, and wildly flinging arms in the air before falling flat on her face and sending her hat flying. All part of the act. The audience laughed at their antics. Gil clapped the loudest.

Riff disappeared to the sideline for a brief moment to exchange ropes in order to perform the piece de resistance. It was their final knot trick. Gil had seen them practise it many times in their backyard.

While Poppy ran around the stage circling a lasso in the air, Riff tied a slip knot and formed his own lasso.

The idea was to toss it across Poppy's shoulders and pull tight as if he'd roped a steer, making a joke out of turning the tables on the 'sheriff' by being the one doing the catching. Poppy would wiggle and pretend to struggle to get free, making the knot tighten more and more. When all looked hopeless, Riff would yank one end of the rope and the knot (and Poppy) would slide free as if by magic. Ending the show with laughter and applause.

It should have been foolproof.

At first, Gil was laughing and clapping with the rest of the audience. Riff had lassoed Poppy and she began squirming and struggling flamboyantly. The way Gil saw it, his wife was being a ham, milking the act for all it was worth and stealing the show in her usual, over the top way. Riff was pulling the rope tighter and tighter, a determined look on his face. Within half a minute, Gil sensed something had gone wrong.

Poppy fell to her knees, grabbing the rope and spluttering. The audience roared louder, believing this was all part of the act. But Gil could see the lasso when pulled had slipped above her shoulders and settled around her neck. It was beginning to choke her.

Riff was caught up in getting the performance right, so he kept jerking on the rope with intense concentration, in effect tightening the knot and making the situation more dire.

A realisation slowly dawned on Gil. The slip knot had caught – probably where Poppy's kerchief was tied – and rather than slip free, it was wedged tight.

This should not have happened. With all their rehearsals, they neglected to practise dressed in their cowboy outfits.

Gil watched frozen in fascination. Another minute passed; he remained seated like everyone else, simply one more person in the crowd expecting the situation to right itself.

A voice at the back of his mind niggled to stand up and put a stop to what was happening on stage. His wife was being publicly strangled while the audience cheered on, unaware of her fight for breath. This niggle of conscience warred with a stronger force: an abiding fear of her mixed with a jealous streak of cruelty. It taunted, saying the kid was giving Poppy a dose of her own medicine. Let her suffer a bit longer.

An almost ecstatic expression crossed Poppy's face before it turned purple and her body pitched forward. Gil shifted, surreptitiously loosening his jeans that constricted an unbidden hard-on. A male teacher in the wings began to register that this was no longer part of the act and ran on stage in a flustered panic. The man tried to wrestle the rope out of Riff's hands, but Riff was so focused on succeeding with the performance he hung on and refused to let go and instead jerked it a few more times. More precious seconds passed. Poppy's body went limp, her arms and legs splayed like an upturned bowl of spaghetti.

Titters from the hall continued, some believing it was all part of the act albeit a sick joke. But the majority of parents and grandparents began to comprehend that things had gone terribly wrong. They began to place hands over their little kids' eyes to shield them from the unfolding calamity.

Glued to his seat, Gil valiantly struggled to suppress a building eruption of hysterical laughter. It was horrifying and dreadful, he kept telling himself. But at the same time, he pictured his wife's favourite way of getting off in their bedroom – now Riff had forced her into doing this so publicly in front of a room full of primary school students. You had to admit the irony made one want to burst into a good belly laugh. Watching Riff's steely resolve to hold on and not let go, even after seeing Poppy turning blue, made Gil wonder if the kid had done it on purpose as some sort of retribution. Maybe he hadn't welcomed Poppy's overly friendly touching as much as she believed. Grudging, Gil had to admire the lad's ability to plan a good pay back.

Eventually someone had the presence of mind to close the curtains. They came together at a snail's pace. Gill watched as a teacher gave up a last attempt at loosening the knot and instead decided to slide her unconscious body off stage with Riff 'helping' by continuing to pull the rope – tighter. Gil saw the principal on a mobile phone, looking harassed. Probably dialling triple zero for an ambulance.

A commotion erupted across the aisle. A man dressed in a flannel shirt and track pants with a woman in a tank top and leopard spotted leggings pushed through the crowd, shoving their way backstage. Gil suspected they were Riff's no hoper parents, going to prep him about not speaking to the police without a lawyer.

Nothing would happen to a twelve-year-old. No worries there. Riff was safe from prosecution, even if they could prove that it wasn't an accident.

Gil woke up to the fact he needed to make a move and check on his unconscious wife, otherwise people would start talking. By all calculations, she'd probably been choked without oxygen for a good five minutes. It wouldn't be good.

Chapter Seventy Eight

Fiona Blackwell held her chin high while waiting to report to her boss, the new Divisional Head, careful to keep a neutral expression of compliant subservience. The guy kept his head down, reading some file on the polished executive desk, as if too busy and important to acknowledge her presence. As if Fiona didn't see through this classic bureaucratic display of asserting dominance and right to rule. It was pitiful if he thought she was a threat. All the fight had gone out of her. It was just a job.

Inside she was seething with self-recrimination. Brendan DeSassenay had been Area Coordinator for the south, her equivalent and recent rival for the position vacated by Leland. Two weeks after the election, Leland's appointment to Chief Executive Officer, Department of Community Health was announced by the re-elected government, leaving her to Act as Divisional Head until interviews were held. Leland had always hinted his position would be hers, if she played by his rules.

He must have played this game with each of his Area Coordinators. She wasn't special after all.

True to form, demonstrating his prowess as a political player, Leland survived the O'Connell fiasco without any tarnish sticking to his titanium-coated hide. The re-elected Minister of Health was his good mate again. Leland got the credit for saving the government embarrassment over the potential grenade that was the Joy O'Connell matter. Fiona bore the brunt of recriminations for its mishandling. She'd anticipated some fall out, being placed in the role of Leland's fall guy from the start. Her mistake was to misjudge Leland's cunning about looking after his own career rather than hers when the election result was announced.

It was supposed to play out differently, with a reward for acting the part of Leland's obedient subordinate, the good public servant following orders and doing her job. Instead, once the government was re-elected, taking away the imperative to suppress a potential threat to the government's image, all Leland's previous promises were off the table. And the smarmy, blemish-free guy from the south won the job.

In her view, the O'Connell case ended better than hoped and she deserved some credit. No sane person could have believed the department would escape without some settlement paid out. For heaven's sake, the woman had been strangled by one of their managers, no matter how much reality was re-written, words twisted, or truth denied. It could have gone a lot worse had the case made it all the way to the tribunal hearing. The medical members of the panel could have been trusted to look after the interests of their health system and department, but the ones representing the general public were the unpredictable side of the risk equation. Any number of them could have had an attack of conscience and awarded Joy the top end of her entitlements.

Leland argued to take their chances at the tribunal, which had all been posturing for the sake of his image as a strong leader. In effect, it was a delaying tactic; the hearing would have been scheduled well after the votes were counted and the Liberals returned or not. Had the outcome been different, it would have been anyone's guess as to who was appointed CEO of Health.

Fiona had missed the political cues and argued for a more pragmatic solution, one that benefitted the department's bottom line during a time of tightening budgets. Cut their losses, end it quickly, bury it before it found its way to the press.

In her feedback session after the interview, Leland had explained – all chummy and patronising – that there was nothing wrong in her approach, except it wasn't *ballsy*. He questioned whether she had the balls to make the tough calls. She hadn't proved this to him, hence his recommendation to appoint Brendan to the job.

Fiona's cynical reflections were interrupted by a wave of Brendan's hand as he signed a document with a flourish, shut the file with a thud and tossed it to a chrome out tray.

"Fiona, how are you?" Brendan asked with fake charm. "What have you got that grabs my attention in your handover report?" he smiled, all teeth and boss-like slick.

With the O'Connell case closed, there were no pressing issues requiring immediate attention. Fiona's report was as mundane as the job required. She led with a matter of procedure on a long list of boring routine matters.

"The Acting Manager at Quamby Bluff Community Health Centre is on extended sick leave due to an accident on her day off. I believe she's sustained a brain injury. With the extent of cognitive impairment, there's little possibility of returning to the job and she'll eventually be pensioned off. It's quite a tragedy and staff are unsettled as a consequence. I recommend we advertise and fill the vacancy as soon as practicable."

"Done. Next item," Brendan commanded.

At least the new boss was decisive. Fiona could live with that.

Chapter Seventy Nine

Amberlie waited in the doorway of the Shamrock Room blocking seniors from entering and causing a logjam in the corridor. Honor had enough to do without having to deal with whatever the young admin thought was so important it had to happen right this minute. Grunting from the effort of lifting another chair from a stack of five piled against the back wall, Honor yelled across, "Some help would be appreciated." Amberlie looked from side to side, as if to hail another carer to assist. *Bone lazy* was the thought flitting past Honor's mind.

A petulant Mr Blundell rammed his walker into the back of Amberlie's black and white poke-a-dot leggings and pushed past, causing a yelp. At last, she moved inside allowing a steady stream of clients to shuffle through. Making a point, Honor frowned at Amberlie to stress how much her timing was ill conceived.

Missing the cue, Amberlie skipped over and held a large manila envelope under Honor's chin. "I'm collecting for a 'get well' present for Poppy," she said, shaking the envelope and rattling its contents of coins. "There's a card inside for you to sign."

Distracted by Mr Blundell making his way to the kitchenette where a recently boiled kettle jetted scorching steam into the air, Honor mumbled, "Leave it over there. I'll do it later." Anything to do with Poppy was her last priority.

Not to be brushed off, Amberlie stood in the way. "That's what everyone's been saying. I don't have time to keep coming back. This isn't part of my job description, you know. I'll wait." She crossed her arms and wouldn't budge. Seniors bumped her in passing, anxious to find their seats and peeved about their goal being obstructed.

"Yeah, okay," Honor said, twisting around the slim young woman. Marching over to Mr Blundell, she caught up with him lifting the hot kettle with a quivering hand about to pour water into an empty mug, an OH&S incident in the making.

Steadying the kettle with a firm hand, and with a loud, slow voice, she said, "We'll get you a cup of tea very soon, Gerry. Let's get you to your seat for now." He was turned around and guided to his usual place at a corner table. Honor took a couple deep breaths and surveyed the room.

Satisfied order was restored, she reluctantly turned to Amberlie. "Right, you were saying Poppy's not well?"

"Haven't you heard?" Amberlie asked. "She's in hospital. Something happened on the weekend when she was attending a function at her foster kid's school. I think she had a stroke or something. No one's saying much."

"I know the drill. It's all personal and confidential," Honor nodded.

"Exactly." Amberlie looked relieved at not having to explain again for the tenth time this morning.

Honor pulled a purse out of her handbag and opened the coin section. "How much are people contributing?" As much as she was loath to donate anything towards the joking strangler, it was important to be seen being part of the team. That didn't mean she had to be overly generous.

"Not much, unfortunately. They've all been complaining it's off a pay week, so they haven't any money to spare. At this rate, all she's going to get is a card and a balloon." Amberlie pulled a face as Honor dropped a couple gold coins into the envelope. "But it's not my problem."

Chapter Eighty

J oy stood at her wardrobe studying a row of blouses. She bunched them together and wrenched them off their hangers, tossing them in a heap onto her queen size bed. Picking up a floral top with soft flowing sleeves, she held it up against the light streaming in from the cedar framed windows of the Federation cottage. She'd loved wearing this top to work; it made her feel pretty and young.

It was stuffed into a green garbage bag destined for the Salvos. The same bag marked for all her work clothes. At the back of her mind, she heard Gemma's lecture about the burdens of old stuff and the Zen concept of decluttering and simplifying one's life. She'd related a Buddhist parable about a student asking his lama for advice and a glass overflowing. The student was unable to take in any wisdom because his glass was already full, presumably filled with unnecessary clutter.

'It's all about freeing yourself so you can move on without past baggage. Life is change, mum. That's a rule of the universe'. Start new – new beginnings, new dreams.

Joy winced at Gemma's glib commentary, as if change was so simple and easy. When she was young, she supposed it was easy to pack up and move, seeking new horizons, full of plans for a better future. Now inertia consumed her. She remained unconvinced that she had a better future; past experience proved otherwise. Her financial outlook indicated otherwise.

Joy felt too old and defeated to conjure energy around her daughter's well-meant platitude.

There was some comfort surrounded by all the paraphernalia that projected a reminder of all the selves she'd been throughout different periods in her life. Images of Joy when she liked herself, recognised herself, identified as that self. When she knew who she was.

She'd lost this surety after the assault.

Returning to the task at hand, she assessed a sturdy antique oak chest at the foot of her bed. It stored clothes too good to throw out, all mixed sizes. Over the years she'd lived in hope a future diet would restore her figure to a past ideal. Joy sniffed back tears. Who was she kidding? This was a futile wish long past its use by date. *Just throw it away* was her daughter's recent mantra. The contents of the chest would all have to go. At least this decision was easy.

It was a half hearted act of defiance. They'd forced her to retire. She'd never earn a wage again. Her old work clothes represented a life choice taken from her.

'You'll be happier in the end, mum, lightening the load'. She'd tried her best to be supportive. It wasn't her fault it sounded lame.

Marcus told her that trauma changes you. But growing old did too. And life experiences, good and bad, both changed a person. How many times had she changed throughout her life? Many, if her wardrobe was a true reflection.

Why was this time so different?

Perhaps because before this, she'd been the one deciding who she wanted to be, weighing up her choices, consciously and deliberately making a change: to have a child and become a mother; go to university to study; risk a second marriage; get divorced and become a single, working woman; leave a stressful albeit successful career for a job in administration. All variations on the theme of Joy's self-image, a person she deliberately constructed as *the self of Joy*.

And this time, part of the impact of trauma was that the changes to her 'self' had not been by choice. They'd been inflicted on her.

When ordering new spectacles the day before, the optometrist had asked conversationally *what do you do?* She'd paused a few seconds frozen in shame, unsure how to formulate a response. It was two months since she'd signed the paperwork and accepted a settlement package and even so, she continued to identify as a working woman. Except she wasn't. She didn't know who she was anymore, let alone what she was going to do with her life.

PTSD had emptied her, left her bereft of most secure absolutes in life. Including who she believed herself to be – i.e. a working woman.

I don't do anything was her first knee jerk reaction, followed by *I have PTSD* as an explanation, but she didn't voice either of these thoughts. She managed to mumble, *I'm retired*, as if that was a good thing.

Gemma was right. It was better for Joy to accept this new reality. It was time to figure out what parts of Joy were there to keep and hold on to; what bits needed to be discarded, no matter how well loved and seemingly too good to throw out, the ones that didn't fit anymore.

Trying to choose which items to keep and to discard served as a reminder, she did not belong to her belongings. Surrounded by all these chunks of familiar old memories, once a composite landscape of a former, undiminished Joy, they'd dismembered into pieces of a puzzle, icebergs scattered in a frozen ocean, no longer attached to land. They no longer defined the Joy standing in this room.

Who was she? Perhaps within the emptiness, over time, the shattered puzzle pieces would coalesce into a formed picture of a newborn self, rather than remain broken like humpty dumpty.

In a spontaneous act of frustration, Joy wrenched the scarlet quilt cover off her bed and stuffed it into a garbage bag. It mocked her. It symbolised a *Joy-before-the-assault* when her heartbeat with passion born from a zest for life – not one that raced from anxiety.

Later, she would replace it with a bleached seersucker comforter, removing her previous personality to match a new interior design.

***

That night, a vivid dream woke Joy from a deep slumber. Turning towards the clock, it read three a.m. No surprise. Four hours of sleep as usual. Half awake, images from the dream world emerged in a lazy stream of consciousness before dissipating before her sleep encrusted eyes.

Leaning across to the bedside table, she pulled out a journal buried beneath Dr Fellowes' book deciding to capture snatches of the dream memory. She wrote:

...thrown into another dimension unexpectedly, unable to find bearings. Concerned people grab hold and try pulling me back through the dark fog of the void. They are stretching me thin. To return is death but they don't understand.

I shout 'stop' but my voice is not heard. It is garbled, nonsensical, a foreign language. They say this is a symptom of my illness.

Confused, I resist being tugged in both directions.

....I need a guide to help navigate this new alien world I'm entering and ask my helpers to do this. They refuse. This feels like... a betrayal of trust. They insist I return. There is no going back, only forward into the blank unknown.

I begin to fight. They pull me back – I pull away. Their good intentions are damaging.

...those who have chosen this path stand on the other side and speak of peace and healing... a spiritual path...

I am caught between worlds. It feels like hell.

Not a nightmare. A consolidation of experience. A message about a journey ahead through the Dark Night of the Soul to find this new Joy, a person she could accept. And love.

Dr Vitkay proved true. He was the one person in the workers compensation process whose professional judgement she could trust. She was suffering from a crisis of the spirit after all.

Chapter Eighty One

"Do you question whether you made the right decision?" Honor asked as they completed a second circuit around the Quamby Brook Common. "Given the timing with Poppy being pensioned out on sick leave, maybe you could have gone back to your job at the centre?"

During the course of their walk, Joy had been explaining to her sister that the settlement money was at last in the bank, finalising the end of the workers compensation matter. This meant, except for cashing out superannuation into her bank account in a few weeks, it was over. She was free at last.

The question was so typical of Honor. She had a way of poking a sore point and casting doubt about Joy's choices, even after the fact. It was hard to know where to begin an explanation. As if the answer was ever simple.

Joy power walked on, aware of gravel crunching underfoot and the beat of her heart in rhythm with her steps, strong and steady. She was pleased at her fitness level and how easy it was to keep up with the other Johnnie Walkers as they continued a third circuit. This, at least, was something she could do despite PTSD.

It was a perfect summer day on Eden Isle, with a touch of cool breeze offsetting the intensity of the direct rays of the sun on the back of their necks. Joy breathed deeply, inhaling the freshness of freedom and the wholesome reality of nature. For the first time in fifteen months, she understood this was what normal should feel like.

"Family was more important than the money. Knowing there was an election coming up and the department would avoid any hint at going public, I was able to negotiate the best settlement I was going to get from them. I gave them the 'win' and came away with a calculated amount I could live on until the pension." Joy wasn't proud of the decision but she knew it was the right one. "At least, I did it on my terms, not theirs."

"I guess that's true," her sister replied, although an air of scepticism lingered.

After all Joy had shared with her sister about what she'd been through, Honor still couldn't grasp the full extent of the damage the strangling incident caused to her psyche. She'd been naively unprepared for the workers compensation process, learning the hard way how the system organised itself around the power to wound further, to isolate and marginalise her, to define her as sick, broken, unworthy; to push her out of a community of belonging to a place of shame.

Their process was worse than Poppy's original assault.

She never stood a chance. They always controlled the outcome. Their final act of skullduggery with surveillance proved the lengths they would go to for the sake of winning. Triggering Gemma's heart attack scare was the final low blow.

And the worst ache was trying to explain her decision to those she loved – her sister, Kodi, Gemma, Jaxon – who believed she'd given up, given in, let them win. The hardest decision she'd ever had to make.

It was something about not becoming like the people she was battling. Remembering what was of more value. *"The cost of something which I call life that has to be exchanged for it"*. The stakes were high.

Vindication would have felt good, appealing to her ego. But not so good, continuing would have pushed her to the edge of her reserves and sanity.

It was about who she was, when all was stripped away. Was it that important to know what the tribunal experts would have decided? They were final referees in the game. But it was always their game, their rules. Joy knew the truth, reality, what mattered. It was enough to believe in herself.

All these thoughts ran through Joy's mind and could not be vocalised to her sister waiting patiently, expecting simple, straight forward answers to the mystery that was Joy. Honor wanted her to agree to the notion she should have fought on, got more money.

Gazing up to the deep blue sky splotched with cotton puffs of clouds, a perfect Eden Isle summer's day, Joy's survival instincts whispered white was the colour of angels and heaven; the white light of healing; and of pure and unstained new beginnings.

Her journey towards recovery could at last begin, unthwarted by the hell she'd been subjected to under workers compensation.

This thought about healing caused her to emit a sharp, short laugh. Hope proved harder to destroy than her sanity. That was something at least.

"What's funny?" Honor asked, sounding puzzled.

Joy shook her head.

In character, Honor proceeded to lecture with an air of judgmental common sense. "The extra money would have set you up for retirement. Instead, you gave up, so suddenly, just like that. I always imagined you would stand up for your rights to the bitter end, stubborn person that you are. Usually you never let go of an issue." With sudden inspiration, she added with sincerity, "Like that fierce possum we saw on the road that night."

Joy smiled at her sister's about face on *letting it go*. "I am that possum, Honor. In fact, that little guy's act of courage profoundly influenced my decision at the end. In the face of inevitable defeat, with all the odds stacked against it, the possum stood to its full height, demanded to be respected, an opponent worthy of being treated with dignity, and not as some insignificant, dumb creature.

"That was me, too."

"I was also in a contest against an all-powerful, heartless machine. And like our possum, I stood up for my entitlements against a monster that followed me along the whole length of my journey, shone headlights on my every move, and insisted I comply with its superior authority."

"I was caught up in a dark wilderness, too – of bureaucratic processes, pitted against unseen, nameless combatants just doing their jobs, who played by secret rules that skewed the outcome in their favour – it was a game to them but seemed like life and death to me."

"And there I was being all noble, a mighty possum, standing my ground, hissing in the face of danger, a courageous creature demanding to be treated with dignity and respect, insisting I was worthy and not insignificant."

"Good – so far."

"But this was the first part of the story, and not where it ends. There's another half to this noble story of courage and heroism, one our brave Aussie possum demonstrated. And which helped me live with my decision."

"Bravery in the face of danger is a risky business. The finale in the story was that after our possum stood its ground on that dark night of the soul, faced an all-powerful foe, proved its courage, *it wasn't an idiot*. It didn't wait to be run over. It ran off into the scrub."

"It ran off into the scrub, Honor." Joy repeated the sentiment and waited for this to register. "That's nature's lesson." Honor looked sceptical.

"The little guy taught me: Bravery is a noble and heroic gesture, something we should acknowledge and respect. But sometimes in situations where you cannot win, the price of standing up for your principles to the bitter end is not worth the risk of being flattened to a pulpy mess. Sometimes it is more sensible to fiercely look your enemy in the eyes and then *get off the damn road*."

Honor stopped in her tracks and gazed at Joy with an unreadable expression. Then she burst out laughing.

"When we finish here, come over to my place for lunch. I have something I made for you inspired by my trip to Japan. I've been waiting for the right occasion," she said.

*****

Joy gazed at Honor's gift positioned on a rosewood stand on the dressing table in her bedroom. She thought back to the surprise after unwrapping it and her sister's nervous explanation about wanting to do something special with the bag of fluoxetine pills Gemma had dropped off after the clean out. She wanted it to be a tribute to Joy's experience.

Joy had been awestruck. And immediately burst into tears. Her sister was a true artist at heart.

Honor had created a mosaic portrait of a woman pieced together using chips of glazed ceramic and tiny oval pills dipped in dazzling colours of acrylic paint. In parts, chips were bound together with a gold adhesive. Honor proudly explained this was an experimental technique; she was trying out her own version of the Japanese art of Kintsugi.

She'd captured the four elements in the woman's portrait: the eyes blazed with fierce fire; strands of grey hair with a purple streak writhed in the wind like the snakes of Medusa; her body merged into an earthen mountainside reminiscent of Quamby Bluff; with a waterfall of molten veins of precious metal cascading down the side of the bluff like tears. Overall, the effect was a swirling chaos of colour and texture, a picture of a woman standing proud against a backdrop of the natural world. Wild. Defiant.

A portrait of a character with rough, sharp edges being battered and shaped by mysterious currents, proudly standing her ground within the terror and wonder of universal forces.

Honor named it "Self Worth" *because of all the people she knew, Joy had the strongest sense of her own self-worth and she admired this so much.*

Joy held her hands to her heart and rocked back and forth as if bowing to the merit of the piece. Any words of praise would be unworthy.

Pleased at her sister's response, Honor had gone on to explain Kintsugi translated as *golden joinery.* Some artists called it the 'art of precious scars', where mending puzzle pieces from a shattered object and re-forming it into something of value also highlighted the unique beauty of each fracture and flaw.

The portrait was positioned so it would be the first thing she would see upon waking each morning. Joy wondered if Honor understood the deep significance of her creation – or if it was simply a demonstration of her talent showing off a new technique. It didn't matter. She loved her for it.

And then she burst out laughing. As much as its artistic cleverness evoked a sense of awe, it also never failed to elicit a sense of mirth as well.

All those pills had a use after all.

About the Author

I grew up breathing Los Angeles smog. Mum moved us to the clean blue skies of Adelaide and married an Aussie, resulting in my dual citizenship. I spent my feminist career days as a recalcitrant within Canberra bureaucracy. After 9/11 I escaped to the wilds of Tasmania to write and raise chickens.

Circumstances now allow me to write full time, living the dream! Women's literature is my preferred genre (e.g. Ellie O'Neil, Josephine Moon, Katie Fforde).

My writing qualifications include a Bachelor Degree from the University of South Australia and I hold memberships with the Tasmanian Writers Centre, the Devonport Writers Group, Deloraine House Writers Group, and formerly with the Meander Valley U3A Memoir Writing Class.

I self-published a feminist cartoon book called Good Vibrations in 1997, co-authored with Wendy Newton and illustrated by Mark Godfrey [National Library ISBN 09587168 0 3].

If I could draw I would be a cartoonist. My humour is the sense of the ridiculous.

Acknowledgments

The author acknowledges the Traditional Custodians of country throughout Australia and their connections to land, sea, the sky, and community. She pays her respect to all Aboriginal and Torres Strait Islander peoples today along with her gratitude living in rural Tasmania on Tyerrernotepanner, Panninher and Leterramairrener country.

A huge thanks to Lisa Bolton, proofreader and editor of my many books.

Also, thanks to The Rural Publishing Company for their excellent work taking on this big job with such professionalism.